REVELATIONS:

BOOK ONE OF THE *LALASSU*

Published by Past the Mirror Publishing.

ISBN: 978-0-9940121-1-1

REVELATIONS:

BOOK ONE OF THE LALASSU

Jennifer Carole Lewis

To my real life superheroes:
my two boys and my friends.

Without you, I wouldn't have dared to fly.

Thank you

Lalassu: Akkadian noun meaning specter or hidden.

WEDNESDAY

Chapter One

Wherever there is prey, there are hunters. Jungle, ocean, city—the location doesn't matter. Predators will always find the vulnerable.

People spilled across the Lost Eden's dance floor, a constant tide of glittering men and women ebbing to and from the bar. Dim lights flattered the desperate and popular alike, hiding the first glimpses of age-drawn wrinkles.

Past experience had taught Dani Harris that she could choose whomever she wanted from the crowd to go home with. The small army of free drinks lining the bar behind her only reinforced the lesson. But she'd come here with a specific purpose in mind, dressed in her guaranteed-to-attract-attention, curve-hugging red silk dress, her black hair artfully tousled to evoke sweat-dampened pillows and her eyes painted with smoldering charcoal for a classic bedroom look. All she needed was a suitable candidate.

Toying with the straw in her drink and scanning the crowd, she made note of the few potential candidates. Her fingers clenched the straw, crushing it with her growing unease. Since she'd sat down, the sexual tension had ratcheted up, becoming as tangible as the dry ice fog. Guilt gnawed at her, but she'd already pushed her luck further than she should have. She didn't have the time to indulge in her conscience. Time to choose and hope she didn't end up too badly scarred.

The thickly muscled black man with the shaved head in the corner kept fondling the waitresses and the customers, using his size to intimidate any potential protests. The blond in the custom-tailored leather jacket up on the VIP platform, whose companions avoided eye contact as he carried on an energetic monologue, ignoring the buxom redhead cuddled up to his side. A pair of massive bodyguards stood guard at the entrance. And finally, the guy with the purple hair, piercings in his nose, lip, and tongue. He was harassing the female DJ, trying to climb into the booth. They were the best she could hope for tonight.

Brilliant light strobed the crowd in time with frenetic bass and drums. Dani scanned the club again, shaking her head lightly. The crowd was beginning to turn ugly, shoving matches breaking out on the dance floor. The oaky taste of her whiskey went sour on her tongue. She should leave and try her luck elsewhere.

"You can't leave just yet." A deep male voice cut across the ambient noise.

Perhaps she had a winner after all. "Why the hell not?"

"Because then I wouldn't get a chance to talk to you." It was the blond from the platform. "And you should know that I personally find it inexcusable."

"What would that be?" She didn't offer him a seat but wasn't surprised when he took it anyway. Up close, his looks were even better: easily over six feet with broad shoulders and a well-used gym membership.

"Whoever left you waiting. He should have his head examined. Let me buy you a drink." He lifted his hand in the bartender's direction. Immediately, the young Latino man behind the bar abandoned the thirsty crowd to bring Dani's new acquaintance a glass of scotch.

His glib smugness struck sparks of irritation in her, but long practice helped her to keep her feelings masked under a seductive smile. *Time for a test.* "You know what they say. No matter how hot you are, someone is tired of your shit." Dani looked deliberately at the VIP platform. "For example, I think Miss Copper Top over there is getting tired of yours."

The buxom redhead in question glared down at them with a ridiculously childish, sulky pout. The blond glanced over his shoulder and waved his hand in a universal gesture of dismissal. Immediately, one of the bulky bodyguards approached the redhead and said something to her. She shouted something inaudible through the music and actually stamped her foot. The gentleman insisted and began escorting her off the platform.

"She won't be a problem anymore." The blond turned back to Dani, clearly pleased with himself. For the first time, his smile reached his eyes. He'd enjoyed the public spectacle and humiliation. "I'm Josh Hinton, and my family owns this club."

Dani watched as the woman was summarily hustled out the front door. She forced herself to relax her grip on the smooth glass tumbler

10

before she shattered it.

"Breakup via bodyguard. A new low mark for the record books. Somewhere between text and Post-it note." Dani shook her head and started to get up again.

Josh immediately grabbed her arm and held her down in her seat, looming over her. "You didn't tell me your name."

Dani searched the room, considering her options. The bartenders were studiously ignoring her companion. The people who had been sitting beside her at the bar were long gone, pushed aside by Josh's evident ego. A wild recklessness burned inside her, urging her to lash out and escape. But common sense warned her: no one wanted to get involved, and no one would stand up to help—and even if they did, she would still be trapped by her own demons.

Her mouth dried as a scrap of memory flickered briefly despite years of suppression. He must have seen the fear in her eyes. Predators always sensed fear no matter how deeply it was hidden. She'd learned that lesson the hard way.

"I think you're starting to understand." He let his hand trail up her arm, his thumb casually brushing against her breast on the way past. "I always get what I want."

The bodyguards had descended and now stood on either side of Josh like unmovable monoliths, an unbreakable prison wall. Dani swallowed hard. It was as if the three men sucked up all the air around her. "You could have any other girl here. Why not pick someone more interested?"

"I like the challenge. Come with me to my apartment. You'd love the view." He ran his hand freely up and down her side, a chill slither like the rasp of a reptile's skin.

A human predator doesn't take victims in public. A second location will be chosen in advance for the attack. Once a victim reaches the second location, chances of survival drop to nearly zero. Never go quietly to the second location. The words whispered inside her head, distantly remembered from the urgent plea of a police officer who'd spoken at her school.

"Don't freeze up, and don't pretend it isn't what you came here for in your little red dress." He slid his hand up her thigh, inching up the hemline. "Everyone comes here to have a good time."

Dani studied the looming bodyguards. Not a blink or even a grimace of disapproval. The time for second thoughts was over. She wasn't going to do better tonight. This was her punishment and the sooner she accepted it, the sooner it would be over. "Is that what you came for?"

"Business mostly. This tourist trap has a lot of things to recommend it." He took a healthy swig from his drink.

It certainly had. The town of Perdition had a reputation as the "New York experience without the expense," according to the tourist board. Between conventions and other events, the majority of the population changed on a weekly basis. It was one of the reasons her family had chosen to live here.

She put down her drink. No amount of whiskey would make this easier. She got to her feet but the bodyguards quickly blocked her exit. Adrenaline surged and her legs tensed to run, but instead she forced herself to keep her wits. Blindly fleeing never helped. She couldn't resist a flash of strength, glaring down at Josh, still perched on his stool. "Does this intimidation approach ever actually work for you?"

He grinned. "I like you. You're interesting. Most people don't have the balls to call me on anything." He stood up. "Let's get out of here. Come on, I'll show you I can be a nice guy with the right motivation."

Dani kept her face impassive. Maybe this wouldn't be as bad as she feared. Josh moved in for the kill.

"Trust me. I'm worth it. I guarantee it'll be a night you'll always remember."

Or one you'll always pray to forget.

Chapter Two

"Why did I let you talk me into this again? We could have drunk beer and listened to crappy, distorted music at home," Michael Brooks protested as he and his friend, Joe Cabrera, stepped out of the cab in front of Lost Eden.

"True. But with way fewer gorgeous ladies to look at." Joe grinned. "Come on, man. This is a celebration. Your tip helped us nab the creep peeping in windows and helping himself to women's underwear."

Michael hid his smile. Joe wasn't even paying attention to him anymore. His focus was on the line of young women dressed in an eye-catching rainbow of colors. As a veteran, yet single, cop, Joe quite enjoyed using his reputation as an emergency flirtation device.

Some of the women eyed Michael as well, but their stares left him more worried than intrigued. Previous girlfriends had told him that he was the image of a modern poet with his shoulder-length light-brown hair. They described his eyes as soulful and compared his face to models and statues. But every single one of them had fled quickly enough. He'd learned to carry himself with an aloof confidence to avoid encouraging intimacies that could only lead to mutual disappointment.

Instead, he focused on the unique dangers the club could hold for him. He pulled on the thin leather gloves he always carried. Without them… he shuddered to think of the information overload he would have to process. Crowds were always more difficult than individuals.

For everyone else, touch was something casual. It could at times become sensual or intimate, but no one else had to fear it. Every time Michael's skin touched someone or something else, he became privy to their inner thoughts, their darkest secrets, fears, and hopes. In an emotionally charged atmosphere like the club, sometimes he didn't even have to touch someone. He simply absorbed it, as if by osmosis. But it wasn't the worst that could happen.

Every so often, he would touch someone or something and receive a coercive flash, as though something downloaded instructions into his brain and forced him to follow them. *Go to this location. Tell this person about what you saw.* Trying to stop himself brought on a massive headache, as if giant arrows were being physically shoved into his head. He'd never tried to hold out for more than half an hour and he'd been nearly blinded by the pain.

Four years ago, one of those flashes had taken him to the police station, to Joe's desk. It led him to the one detective in Perdition's police force willing to listen without dismissing him as a crazy crackpot. Another prompted him to sign up for training in working with developmentally delayed children, starting a career where his gifts were uniquely helpful. Each flash took him places he would never have gone otherwise and they were always important or helpful, but they also left his life in chaos. He wished he could speak to the great cosmic design engineer and arrange for a slightly less disruptive and painful method of suggestion.

A limo drew his attention, pulling up to the curb behind him. Coming around to open the passenger doors, the driver gestured irritably at him to move out of the way. Michael obeyed, coughing on the stench of exhaust as he found a place beside Joe.

The club doors opened and a couple came out, flanked by bodyguards who must have been genetically selected for their lack of neck. Something about the man raised Michael's hackles, despite his charming exterior. Maybe it was the tight grip on his date's elbow or the smug satisfaction on the blond's face, but he screamed "predator" to Michael's instincts. Michael was about to propose to Joe that they stop them from leaving when he got a good look at the woman.

Beautiful, with flawless olive skin and dark smoldering eyes, she seemed entirely unconscious of any possible danger from her companion. She glided confidently down the short stretch of sidewalk as if she were immune to peril. Peeks of red flashed from underneath her half-open dark coat and Michael was irresistibly reminded of brightly colored poisonous snakes displaying to warn off predators or lure in prey.

Their eyes met and her full lips parted in a brief but chilling smile before she vanished into the depths of the car.

"Damn. That girl is a man-eater. I doubt he's getting out alive

14

tonight," Joe commented.

Michael stared after the limo as it pulled away, wishing he'd stopped them but not sure which one he would have warned. A slight tugging pulled at his mind, nowhere near the power of one of his flashes but still a warning.

He started to walk after the car but Joe grabbed his arm. "Come on, man. Don't go into the woo-woo shit right now. We got some partying to do." Even through the fabric, Joe's eagerness and impatience seeped into him. Secondhand emotions always felt strange, like having a colored filter put over his eyes or hearing a second radio station bleed into another. He would never mistake them for his own feelings, but it could be distracting and disorienting.

The two men entered the club, and the emotional atmosphere hit Michael like a bat to the head. It seethed and roiled, barely contained by the flesh-baring bodies inside. Anger and sexual desire twined in and around him, crushing his breath in his throat. "This isn't a good idea," he managed to force the words out.

"I'll get you a drink." Joe waved away Michael's words, his attention clearly focused on the available young women.

Michael took a deep breath to center himself. He could only imagine how much worse it would be if he hadn't worn his long-sleeved coat and gloves to protect him. But he knew better than to try and explain it to Joe. From the very beginning, the rules had been clear: *I don't want to know if you saw it in a vision, got a note from your Magic 8 Ball, or were sung to by gnomes and werewolves. Just tell me what I need to know, and I will take it from there. Don't drag all the weird freaky crap into it. I'll trust you like any other source until you give me a reason not to.* Joe lived up to his word, acting on whatever Michael brought him. And Michael kept his share of the bargain, leaving his methods in the shadows, no matter how isolated it left him.

Joe tried to get the bartender's attention, but the young man was staring at a couple exchanging frenzied kisses against the bar. The man's shirt had been ripped open and the woman's skirt pushed up to her waist. Their kisses resembled an animal attack more than a natural result of mutual attraction.

"Damn, dude, get a room," Joe joked.

The man twisted away from the woman, his face flushed dark. He was about the same height as the detective but easily outweighed him, clearly a weight-lifting enthusiast. He growled, "What did you say?"

"I said get a room." Joe straightened, facing the other man head on, showing no sign of being intimidated.

"And who do you think you are?"

Michael kept himself in the background, searching for other trouble before it could be stirred up and focused against them. The rest of the patrons were busy with their own pursuits, but it wouldn't take much to strike a spark in this powder keg of emotion. He spotted the woman disappearing into a back room with another man and braced himself.

"Detective Joe Cabrera, Perdition Police." He pulled his ID and badge out of his pocket and held it up. "Now I came in here to get a drink, have a laugh with some ladies, and enjoy a good time. If you want to hook up, no skin off my nose. But take it someplace private or I'll have to arrest you for public lewdness, and that's going to annoy both of us."

The shiny badge took some of the wind out of the other man's sails, but when he noticed his hook-up had disappeared, he swung back to the detective. Joe signaled the bartender for drinks, suggesting he felt the situation had been resolved. Michael hoped his friend was right as he stripped off his glove and casually moved between the two men. He brushed lightly against the other man's bare hand, using the tips of his fingers as if accidentally touching in the crowd.

Sharp stabs of sexual frustration and roiling, irrational spurts of rage. Not good.

Michael's arm and fingers wanted to curl into a preparatory fist, echoing the other man's oncoming attack. Michael braced before he could launch.

The man threw his punch, aiming at the back of Joe's head. But Michael grabbed the man's wrist and pulled, shifting him off-balance as he came past.

The man stumbled and fell. Icy humiliation swirled into the emotional mix. He hauled himself up, glaring at Joe and Michael.

"What the—?" Joe began, but the man launched another assault, charging at them.

16

With precise timing, Michael took a half step to the side and swiveled, letting his attacker lurch past him. *Please let that be enough.* He didn't want to have to hurt someone over drunken frustration.

The man fell into a barstool. The thick pole supporting it had been bolted into the floor and the impact rang loudly enough to be heard over the music. Michael winced in sympathy.

Slowly, the man got to his feet, rubbing his head. The violent rage vanished from his face, and he seemed more bewildered than angry.

"Are we going to have a problem?" Joe asked, standing beside his adversary, his fingers lightly resting on the gleaming handcuffs dangling from his belt.

The man stared blankly at the cuffs. "I... I'm sorry. I don't know what happened."

"I think you had a little too much to drink. Why don't we get you in a cab to go home?" Joe took charge, waving off the bartender and spectators.

Keeping to the background, Michael helped the other man straighten up. With luck, no one would remember this as anything other than a somewhat one-sided bar fight. He made sure to touch the other man's skin, confirming the fight had truly gone out of him. Confusion and embarrassment poured over him, as if the other man were waking up from a vivid but bizarre dream—nothing like a normal drunken misunderstanding. Something wasn't right here.

He looked out over the crowd. Nothing was visually different from before. People were still dancing close to each other, entranced by the pulsing music and lights. But the emotional sense of it had changed, more consistent with flirting than tear-their-clothes-off sex. Everything had lightened, and people were intent on having fun again. What could have caused such a dark atmosphere? He took a breath, enjoying the relief from the terrible pressure, but he couldn't quite calm the alertness that had him scanning the club again and again, searching for what could have agitated the entire group.

No helpful compulsion alerted him to the source of the danger, but Michael didn't have to be psychic to be uneasy. A faint tugging pulled at his subconscious, warning him he might not have much choice in finding out the answers. Something dangerous was out there, something going bump in the night. And if he didn't find it, it might find him.

Chapter Three

"It is a lovely view," Dani agreed, looking out at the lights of the city spread across the darkness. The thick, plush carpeting in the hotel suite cushioned any potential footsteps. The expensive yet generic furnishings provided anonymous luxury for the right price. She'd seen dozens of them, and they'd long since ceased to impress her.

"Not half as pretty as you." Josh smirked.

"Careful. You're almost charming. Your reputation will be ruined." She left the window to sit on the sinfully soft leather couch, tucking her legs under her. "You mind if I ask you a question?"

Josh shrugged, taking a hefty slug of scotch.

"What's with the Neanderthal act?" she asked. "There have to be easier ways to get a date than intimidation." Now that she'd surrendered to her course, her mental processes were clear enough to indulge a little curiosity.

"It saves time." He settled next to her on the couch, smugness evident in every sinew.

"Saves time," Dani repeated flatly, surprised.

"Yeah. You can waste a lot of time pretending to give a shit about her boring job or bullshit dreams, and then she still won't sleep with you. Telling her what I want right up front saves me time."

Dani shook her head, trying not to show her contempt. "That is fucked up."

"Got you here, didn't it?" Josh began to drag his fingers along her bare arm. "Or are you still going to pretend this isn't what you were looking for?"

"You got me. I was searching for someone like you," Dani admitted. No point in keeping up a pretense now. She stood, making sure he got a good eyeful of her generously curved figure. Tossing a condom on the glass coffee table, she slowly pulled down the side zipper of her dress, letting the red silk fall in a puddle at her feet.

"Now that's what I'm talking about." Josh eagerly ogled her

19

crimson bra and thong.

"I went to three other bars before I hit your club. I almost gave up before you came over." Dani slowly straddled him. She only had to keep his attention a little longer and then this would all be over.

He wasted no time and began pawing at her breasts while she talked.

"You had those two thugs-for-hire, your entourage, and Miss Copper Top. I could tell right away that you were a man who got what he wanted and didn't worry about anything else."

"That's me." He pinched her nipples through her bra. She hated it when guys did that. Some of the anticipatory guilt faded.

"The staff were afraid of you. I could smell it, see it in the way they avoided meeting your eyes and in how quickly they tried to leave. Miss Copper Top reeked of fear, too—fear and desperation. You have something over her, don't you?" she guessed.

"She likes my lifestyle and my money. But she got boring."

Dani began to unbutton his shirt. "So you ditched her. Picked up something shiny and new."

He kneaded her buttocks, pushing his crotch against her. Dani forced herself to keep a smile on her face. This was about what was necessary. She had to keep her head in the game no matter how much she loathed letting him touch her. *Soon. It'll be over soon.*

He ripped at her thong, tearing the fragile fabric. The sharp sound sparked buried memories. Dani closed her eyes, fighting the surging darkness inside. *This isn't the time. Not yet.* Her stomach churned, knowing what was next.

While she battled her inner demons, a determined and oblivious Josh shoved down his pants and hauled out an impressively mediocre erection.

"Do you know why I was looking for you?" Dani whispered, leaning in to roll the condom over his meager assets. She barely got it on before he began to thrust up into her.

"This works better if you don't talk," Josh grunted, pumping frantically.

She needed skin-to-skin contact. She spread her hand over Josh's pale chest, sweat making it cool and sticky against her palm.

Concentrating, gathering her personal self—what she thought of as her soul—Dani reached deep into her psyche.

And touched a monster. The Huntress: terrifying, insatiable hunger; ancient rage howling for blood. Linked to the Goddess of her ancestors, it was part of her family's bloodlines, a genetic curse worse than any cancer or disease.

Her eyes burned as if on fire when she opened them. A brilliant crimson circle would be glowing around the outer edge of each iris to declare the Huntress's presence linked with her own.

"What the fuck?" Josh whimpered, staring at her gleaming eyes, the sharp bite of fear overwhelming the musky scent of his expensive cologne.

"Time to wake up." The Huntress boiled up, surging through her and into Josh as he jerked and twitched in orgasm. Dani bit her lip as it left, rasping like harsh sandpaper against the inside of her skull. No matter how many times she did this, it was agony—even if the alternative was worse.

A familiar glaze washed over Josh's eyes as he stared at something distant and invisible. A weak, strangled whimper passed through his thinned lips, a primal cry for help. Dani held still, all too aware of the secondhand sensation of the Huntress sinking her psychic fangs into him and wrapping him in her coils. She grew heavier and heavier as the monster pulled Josh's soul deeper into the planes beyond the physical. All that remained was the tenuous link between Dani and the Huntress— the trail the Huntress would use to return. Emotions echoed down the connection, forcing Dani to be a passive observer of their struggle.

He was fighting hard against the attack, but no one won against the monster she carried. Once in the Huntress's world, he couldn't hide or lie to himself. Josh would be forced to confront the frightened coward behind his pompous bullying. He would be exposed as a spoiled, pathetic excuse for a human being. He'd have to feel the contempt and fear he'd inspired in others, experience the pain he'd caused. Once the Huntress had stripped him bare of all his illusions, it would spit him back out into his body. And then it would be sated, leaving Dani free of its demands for a while, at least.

She didn't know why it needed to Hunt as often as it did or why it fed on self-delusion. She didn't want to. Through the monster inside her, she caught glimpses of what the victims endured, which was more than enough. Maybe there was a time when her mother might have been able to explain, but it had passed, hidden along with their crumbling altar and buried in oppressive silence. Dani had been forced to rely on family legends and old journals, which painted the Huntress and its priestesses as conduits to the divine. The priestesses brought their lovers face to face with the gods, showing them what they truly were without the comfort of masks, intentions, or plausible lies. Of course, none of the legends talked about how painful it was or how humiliating it could feel. As far as she knew, no one had ever denied and managed the Huntress the way she did. Certainly none of the stories warned about the dangers of not satisfying the Huntress's urges. Dani had been left to struggle with all of that on her own.

All she knew for certain was that the men she slept with would freeze with glazed eyes at the moment of orgasm. Faint echoes of their moment of clarity resonated through the Huntress and back to her. After a few seconds, their souls returned and the Huntress slithered back inside her, content and quiescent once again. And she would have a few weeks of relative peace and normality.

Five weeks since her last Hunt had left the Huntress restless and dangerous. It became contagious, leaching out of her like a psychic toxic spill. She'd seen the damage at the various bars and clubs she'd visited tonight. People who'd gone out for a good time had ended up in thrall, pursuing the Huntress's twin lusts: sex and violence. She'd left the Hunt far too long this time. She'd hated the idea of once again allowing some random jerk inside her, but she'd hated being a source of destruction even more. She'd seen rapes and murders happen under the Huntress's influence, and the responsibility scarred her already-battered heart. Trapped in the never-ending cycle, torn between the two demands, she could only try to scrape out some room for herself in the middle.

She Hunted carefully these days, searching for those who saw themselves as predators. After a night with her, the men would be catatonic for two or three days before coming back to themselves. Or at least mostly back. She'd seen previous lovers from time to time, and they were clearly shaken. Most went through mental and spiritual changes similar to someone who'd been through a near-death experience. Some simply ran as soon as they recognized her. They'd all recovered at least, all except…. She refused to dwell on it.

The Huntress slid back into her mind, rasping past her consciousness to bury itself deep in the darkness beyond. Dani accepted it with reluctant resignation.

Josh shook and drew in a ragged breath. Dani got off him, leaving him to curl up in a fetal position on the couch while she went to clean herself up. She hated this part of her life, but she'd learned to do what was necessary. The Huntress demanded regular feedings, and she chose to Hunt the predators: the jerks and assholes who made life miserable for everyone around them. It didn't make a difference to the Huntress, but it kept the shreds of Dani's conscience somewhat intact.

Josh wasn't as bad as some of the men she'd Hunted. Selfish, arrogant, and entitled, but not evil. With luck, he'd come out of this a better person. She pulled his wallet out of his pants and eased out a twenty, enough to buy a new set of panties to replace the pair he'd ruined.

Now for the difficult part: making sure no one came looking for her.

Out of her purse she pulled a little vial of custom-made ecstasy pills with an added ingredient that would explain Josh's symptoms. She'd never asked her supplier for details. She was burdened with far too much knowledge as it was. Tossing one underneath the couch and another on the low coffee table, she studied the scene to make sure her work was done. Tucking the vial back in her purse, she screamed as loudly as she could.

The bodyguards burst into the room. She crouched in the corner, well away from where Josh trembled and whimpered.

"What happened?" one of them demanded.

"We were… and he… oh God!" Dani hid her face in her hands, pretending to cry, eager to put this entire night behind her. One of the bodyguards picked up a phone to call 911 while the other noticed the pill on the table. That was a relief. She hated having to point the damn things out. She avoided looking where Josh lay twitching.

She had planned to slip away in the chaos of emergency services arriving, but to her surprise, the bodyguards hustled her into her clothes and out the door, pressing a wad of cash into her hand. As they shoved her into the private elevator, they warned her: "You were never here." *Suits me fine.* She hailed a cab to return to her car and counted up the money. More than four hundred dollars. Even with expenses, not bad for the night.

Her sleek, black GT convertible was parked exactly where she'd left it, tucked into a seldom-traveled side street near Perdition's main nightlife strip. A fast car for a fast life. Dani couldn't help but smile as she climbed inside, letting her fingers trail along the smooth, polished steel and slick paint. She loved racing invisibly through the night, thrilling to the intoxicating combination of wind and throbbing horsepower. She inhaled the clean scent of wax and leather seats. *Home.*

Her phone rang before she could pull into traffic. The number wasn't familiar, but something warned her to answer anyway. "Hello?"

"Dani, we're in trouble."

"Eric?"

Her brother's voice was practically unrecognizable. Fear roughened his voice, cracking his usual deep, rolling bass. It wasn't rare for her brothers to call for help—mostly for bail money—but this was different. He sounded desperate. "You have to come get us."

"What's going on?" Adrenaline sharpened her senses, allowing her to pick out individual threads of different scents floating in the air.

"The bodyguard job… it was a trap. Vincent's been shot."

Dani's heart stopped, and the Huntress hissed beneath her subconscious. "I'm coming. Where are you?"

"A place called Rick's Gas and Go. Route NY 13."

It was close—ten minutes south of the city. Dani floored the accelerator, cutting across the sparse late-night traffic with reckless disregard for public safety. The engine throbbed through her seat, enhancing the fury vibrating through her veins. "Vincent… how bad?" She couldn't make herself ask if she was racing for nothing.

"It's in the leg. He's bleeding a lot, but he'll be okay." She'd never heard her confident elder sibling so at a loss. "I've been carrying him. You have to warn Mom and Dad—"

"I'm getting you first," she snarled as if denial and willpower could hold off the worst. A chill crept up but she smashed it down along with the accelerator, dismissing such inconsequential matters as speed limits.

Eric drew in a sharp breath. "They're coming. I see lights."

"Hide! Find somewhere and hide. I'm almost there," Dani ordered, but the line clicked dead. She threw the phone on the seat and clenched her hands on the steering wheel. Anger and fear vied for supremacy, coiling through her tightened muscles. *Just a few more minutes.*

Chapter Four

"Report!" André Dalhard snapped at his aide while he signed documents, his large hand swallowing the slim designer pen. Karan Samil allowed himself a strictly internal moment of amusement. After close to fifteen years of working together, his boss still barked orders as if the reports had not been prepared before he stepped into the expansive penthouse office. A solid glass wall gave a spectacular view of Berlin's lights below, but Dalhard wasted neither time nor attention on it. The heavy granite-topped desk faced away from the windows, its smooth surface uncluttered by papers, mementos, or pictures. All business, all the time, everything precisely in place, from Dalhard's slicked-back dark hair to the lines of his bespoke suits. Karan appreciated precision—so rare in life.

Karan calmly began to read the highlights of the company's daily report from his tablet. "The new team of geneticists believes they have an appropriate carrier virus for transmission. All they need is a source of suitable DNA. I have sent out messages to our agents to find potential candidates."

"What about the French military contract?" Dalhard interrupted.

"*Député* Chenier is no longer in a position to object to us being awarded the contract. Tina has encouraged him into some quite risky endeavors. He is sufficiently upset by his actions that she does not believe formal blackmail will be required. He is likely to voluntarily resign by the end of the week." His own lack of compassion did not trouble Karan—he had no patience for the weak and foolish. "The National Assembly will vote on the experimental protocols next month."

"Send her a bonus," Dalhard ordered, putting down the pen.

Already done. "Of course, sir." Karan pretended to make a note.

"This time will be different." Dalhard straightened, placing his hands on the massive desk as if about to pronounce sentence. The desk dominated the minimalist décor, all designed to intimidate onlookers. It matched Dalhard perfectly—he managed both his legitimate corporations and underground organizations with merciless efficiency. Over six foot six with a competitive wrestler's frame and uncompromising Gallic features, Dalhard often used his size and presence to dominate those around him.

"This time we will not be thwarted on the threshold of success. I want every precaution taken." Dalhard thumped his fist on the desk and rose.

Karan held very still. He knew he was indispensable to his employer and had a certain immunity to the man's erratic temperament. But he knew better than anyone what Dalhard was truly capable of. The end not only justified the means, it was the only point of consideration.

The ping of an incoming alert provided a convenient distraction. Karan watched the brief video clip from an American agent, his eyes widening as it played out.

"Sir, I believe you will want to see this." A few taps on his tablet transferred the video to the large flatscreen on the wall.

A young man with a strong build and dark curly hair effortlessly picked up a gurney and flung it through the air at three men wearing the navy blue and gray Dalhard uniform. The fourth man was unluckily missed, and the young man grabbed him and lifted him as if he were made of paper. "Who is he?" Dalhard demanded.

"A recruit for our testing program. He claimed to be a discharged soldier with combat experience in Afghanistan," Karan read in the attached file.

"Claimed?"

"Given this footage, it is unlikely he has any military experience—his secret would have been discovered. He gave us a false name, although with enough substantiation to make it through our initial checks." Karan despised people too lazy to do their jobs properly.

"Sloppy work. Find out who is responsible. I want them gone." Dalhard examined the cuff of his jacket for any loose or frayed threads.

On screen, one of the uniforms staggered up and drew his gun. He was tackled from behind by another young man, with thick dark hair and a scraggly beard. He grabbed the guard's hand and even without sound, it was clear he had crushed the bones. The guard collapsed screaming, and the two fled. Another guard fired after them before racing off screen.

27

"A second one," Dalhard whispered. "How?"

Karan skimmed the report. "Preliminary testing suggests they are brothers, although we did not realize this initially. Their DNA is being shipped to the lab for comparison. It may be the keystone we've been searching for."

"Strong and fast. Any sign of enhanced senses?" Dalhard's eyes gleamed as he eagerly leaned toward the screen to watch the end of the clip. "What happened after this?"

"The subjects broke through two secure doors and escaped onto the street. They made it to the gas station on 13 but were recaptured before they could contact anyone. One was shot in the leg during the escape but should make a full recovery."

"Not the ideal way to discover what we wanted. I want them alive and cooperating," Dalhard murmured to himself, staring intently at the screen as the scene replayed. "I want us there as soon as possible."

Alarms began to stir beneath Karan's calm. The men in the video were an unacceptable level of risk, uncontrollable and unpredictable. "All we need is their DNA for the testing protocols."

"Turning housecats into lions, but these are the lions themselves." Dalhard flicked a miniscule fleck off his sleeve. "If they are brothers, their modifications must breed true. Tell the facility I will be there myself to assist in persuading them. They should be kept sedated. I don't want them damaged further."

"Yes, sir." Karan made careful notes on his tablet. "The jet will be standing by."

"Good. I'll deal with our other acquisition at the same time."

Another potentially disastrous choice. "The parent has resisted but has limited resources. If necessary, an allegation of abuse should force—"

"Force is unnecessary when persuasion will do. But prepare the allegations—I don't want to waste any time if these brothers are what I believe them to be."

Karan bowed, irritation threatening to crack his carefully crafted demeanor as he left the office.

André barely acknowledged his aide's departure, absorbed in watching the video play out, noting the numerous small details: the elder

28

one so protective of the younger—potential leverage. The ease with which the two of them moved. He'd been right to compare them to lions.

Karan had never seen true physical supernaturals in the course of their work. All of the current acquisitions were more along the line of psychic abilities. But André had never forgotten the first time he'd seen one. He'd only been a teenager at the time, joining his father to learn the darker side of the family business, but seeing a man lift a tractor over his head to hurl it at a set of test dummies stayed with him. The potential of such strength, harnessed to the correct bidder, would be incalculable. Dozens of countries and regimes would pay handsomely for their very own super-soldiers. And he would control the source.

Karan would see the value soon enough. His aide might well be the most valuable discovery André had ever made outside the supernatural community. He'd first come to André's attention after one of Karan's fellow soldiers suffered massive third-degree burns from a caustic chemical hidden in his locker. The investigators couldn't definitively tie anything to Karan, but the wounded soldier had publicly threatened him earlier.

Posing as a counselor, André had interviewed Karan. It didn't take long to uncover the cold and practical mind of a true sociopath pulsing under the mask of normality. Add in a fierce intelligence and the patience of an ambush predator, and André knew he'd struck gold. He'd immediately offered Karan a job as the head of his shadow organization, managing the borderline and outright-illegal aspects of his work. The young man took to the job like a shark to water, slipping effortlessly into the perfect balance of patience and ruthlessness.

The stars were aligning for André. He could feel it. Not one, but two ferals, gifted with enhanced strength and speed. Both healthy and in condition to serve as the blueprints for his project. If he'd been a different man, André might have thanked God. Instead, he simply enjoyed the glow of self-satisfaction.

Competitors called him crazy to his face, relegating him to the tinfoil-hat crowd because of his belief there were people with supernatural powers. He devoted a substantial portion of his time and fortune to finding them and using them to his advantage.

A young psychic from Thailand had been his first confirmed acquisition. Only twelve at the time, she could see into the future with uncanny accuracy. It allowed her to survive the tsunami that wiped out the rest of her family. A handful of forged documents liberated her from the local orphanage and brought her under his care. Now she concentrated on predicting stock trends, tripling his portfolio's value every few years.

Next had been a young man from Russia who was literally indestructible. Claiming to be a great-grandson of Rasputin, his skin had been immune to bullets, electricity, flames, and blades. His loyalty bought with a cheap suit and a lot of vodka, he served as the first test subject for DNA profiling. Unfortunately, his immunity had not extended to disease. He developed acute pneumonia and staff had been unable to use the usual intravenous antibiotics and fluids. It was impossible to penetrate his skin to even begin an IV, so he'd died. To add further insult, his DNA proved incompatible with the program, killing the donor recipients.

There had been a few others: a thief who could alter her skin color to blend into the shadows and a circus performer who could see things happening miles away. He'd spent millions of dollars researching hundreds of people claiming extraordinary gifts and discovered that most of them were frauds. But he'd continued to find the occasional nugget among the dross. Year by year, his paranormal stable of talents grew, giving him an edge against his business competitors.

Patience had been his byword. But this video made it hard to remember. He was so close... so very close.

30

Chapter Five

Rick's Gas and Go was a blemish of light squatting in rural darkness. The GT convertible screamed into the empty lot, laying down rubber as Dani spun to a halt. Jumping out, she shouted. "Eric? Vincent?"

No answer. Only faint whispers of the wind moving across empty fields. The station was long closed for the night with no one to question or ask for help. Her mouth and lips were dry as she scanned the area, and her hands kept tightening into fists. She pushed aside the fear threatening to lock her in place and began to search.

To Dani's eyes, the deep shadows of night were easy to pierce—a world washed in blue and indigo. Blocking out the harsh lights of the station, she studied the sparse weeds struggling to survive in the thin soil, nothing higher than her ankle. No ditches.

"Vincent! Eric!" she shouted again.

Nothing stirred.

Dammit. Spinning back, the light from the station blinded her. *The phone.* It was just outside the deserted convenience store, a relic from the days before cellphones. The heavy receiver swung from its silver cord. Squatting down beside it, she inhaled deeply, running the air through her nose and across her tongue. Beneath the stench of oil and gasoline, she caught the coppery tang of fresh blood.

Fuckshitcrap. Despair hammered at her. She and her brothers had always stuck together, taking care of each other when no one else bothered. In a flurry of constant relocating and hiding, her brothers were the only ones she could rely on. Their parents had certainly been too preoccupied with their own challenges to notice what their children were going through. She'd come as fast as she could when they'd called. But it hadn't been enough—another failure.

Moving slowly over the ground, disturbing the air as little as possible, she swung her head back and forth, trying to track where the

31

blood scent came from. Her artfully disheveled coiffure and two-inch heels were a nuisance now, so she kicked off her shoes and whipped her hair back into a practical ponytail as she skimmed back and forth close to the ground, inhaling deeply like a bloodhound. *There.* Off to the side and partially in shadow, a pile of old pumps and fragments of broken machinery was the only cover available near the cold bright lights. With Vincent hurt, they would have hidden rather than fight.

Studying the jumbled bits of metal, Dani noticed something that didn't belong. Fresh flakes of rust and scratches dotting the concrete in a six-foot swath in front of the pile. Picking up a cracked alternator, she found fresh marks in the metal. The pile had been disturbed and then put back to avoid leaving obvious signs of a struggle. She shoved the junk aside and revealed something she'd hoped not to find.

Fresh blood smeared on the ground.

Dipping her fingers, she brought it close to her nose. At this range, there could be no doubt. It was Vincent's: an unmistakable blend of liquor, old smoke, and leather. After years of living in the next room, she knew his scent better than her own. Fury blazed, tightening her arms, back, and teeth. The alternator clenched in her fist groaned as her fingers dented the pitted metal.

Rising, she was about to stalk back to the car when she noticed a stray cat staring at her from the edge of the weedy field. Its eyes were glowing green and its fur was a patchwork of colors. Above it, a slim crescent of moon rose over the fields.

Chill curled over her skin as she remembered seeing this exact scene before—almost a month ago, with her sister.

Gwen had been drawing by candlelight, curled in the corner of her room, looking more like a little girl than the young woman she was. Dani set the basin full of warm water down on the irregular flagstone floor and knelt beside her. The stale odor of old sweat couldn't completely hide the delicate hints of lily-of-the-valley. It was her sister's smell and couldn't be completely smothered, no matter what—just like Gwen.

Part of her hated these visits, hated how Gwen was locked up in their family's farm house, unable to step outside for even a few minutes. But the larger part of Dani treasured them: brief moments of lucidity, hints of the little sister who might have been. Dani always stood between

32

her sister and the dangers of the world, standing over her bed when they were little and beating up anyone who dared to hint that her baby sister wasn't normal.

But Gwen wasn't normal, and it couldn't be hidden any more, no matter how much she'd wanted to deny it and believe it wasn't true. So Dani hid her frustration and came home to help her parents take care of her as often as possible.

"It's important," Gwen insisted, not looking up.

"I'm sure it is. I brought the stuff for a bath. Maybe we could do your hair tonight." Dani touched her sister's stiffened, close-cropped strands. The darkness of her hair only emphasized the chalky pallor of Gwen's skin. Blue veins traced a net, as if trapping her determined spirit inside her fragile body.

"Not many pleasant images. Always remember the dark times best. Want to show me witches burning or battlefields. Sometimes it's like I'm drowning in blood." Gwen's voice choked at the end and her bony fingers closed around her throat.

Dani caught her sister's hand in her own, hoping to distract her from the visions and voices that tormented her. "Not today. Not here."

"No. Not here." A small mercy, given the amount of effort they'd put into creating this one safe haven. Gwen stared at the closed door, her huge eyes even wider in fear. "Out there, they scream and beg. All of them lining up and shoving to get inside—"

"They can't get in, Gwen. Not in here. I brought some food, too. Mom says you're not eating." She showed Gwen the plate of fruit and gently steaming muffins.

Gwen's face lit up in a childlike, beaming smile, brightening her bruised eyes. "For me?"

"Come on, wash your hands and I'll do your hair while you eat."

Gwen spread her thin fingers decorated with charcoal smudges. "Sometimes I can't tell if it's dirt or shadow. Is it still winter?"

"It's spring now. The birds are building nests and there are flowers by the side of the road." Dani dipped a cloth in water and began to wipe down Gwen's fingers. "Soon it'll be summer, and the sun will blaze hot in the sky, and the kids will play in their swimming pools. The ice cream truck will drive through the streets."

33

"Ice cream. I'd forgotten about ice cream. Do you think you can bring me some?"

"Absolutely. But for now, these are still nice and warm." Dani broke off a piece of muffin and put it in her sister's cool hand. It was always chill and clammy in here, no matter how they tried to heat it.

"It's so easy to lose track of time." Gwen bit down on the soft pastry. "I forget so many things. That's why I have to tell you. When the patchwork cat stares at Diana's moon, you have to find the shadow that doesn't belong. It's important. I put it down for you."

Dani froze in the middle of pouring warm water into a bowl, breathing harshly. Gwen's mind was constantly distracted and scattered. For this one message to stick long enough to be communicated meant that it was important to her. But that didn't mean Dani was going to be in any position to do anything about it. She finished pouring the water and brought the bowl to her sister's side.

"Cat. Moon. Shadow. Got it. Now eat." Dani took a sponge and began to work water through her sister's grimy hair.

Gwen continued to pick at the muffin on the plate. "There are so many stars. We don't even know all their names. We don't notice when one goes missing." She stared up at the uneven stone ceiling as Dani carefully washed her hair. "The storm is coming, blotting them out one by one. But we can't see because we don't know their names. The darkness will swallow us all, because we've abandoned the gods. Crumbling clay swept up in the trash."

Gwen's ramblings were filled with more cryptic hints over the last year. No one was sure if she was developing a true predictive gift or simply repeating what she'd been told. This latest exhortation sparked shame and defiance in Dani. If she'd followed family tradition and sacrificed herself to the Huntress, Dani would have become a conduit to the gods, receiving proper divine warnings for the entire *lalassu* people. But none of those warnings had done a bit of good in the past. They hadn't saved Gwen or her father.

Dani took a deep breath, pushing her anger down. Gwen wasn't taking sides, only repeating garbled and confused messages. She knew about Dani's struggles for freedom, the hard-won balance with the Huntress. She knew about the guilt gnawing at Dani's core, the twin fears competing for dominance: that she would someday fail to contain the Huntress and that she would disappear into the alien predator. Gwen had only been seven when she encouraged Dani to flee, telling her it wasn't time and that if she stayed and completed the ritual, the Huntress would swallow them all.

Dani cupped her sister's face with her hand, bringing Gwen's focus back to the present, although it was a visible struggle.

"You don't have to be afraid of the dark," Dani whispered, the refrain familiar from their childhood.

"Because you're nastier than anything else out there." Gwen smiled, twisting around.

"Damn fucking right." Dani smoothed her sister's wet hair against her skull, smiling back.

"But this is bigger than you. Old wounds come back to bleed again. I can hear his footsteps echoing all around us, walking over our hiding hole. Too close to chase away. If you hunt alone, you'll fall," Gwen insisted.

"I don't do partners." The thought of being responsible for someone else turned her stomach. She was failing enough people as it was.

Gwen looked up with stricken eyes, muffin crumbs tumbling from her chin. Dani immediately relented. She couldn't bear seeing her sister hurt.

"I'll be careful," she promised. Gwen's gift gave her access to the past and present with ease, along with occasional glimpses of the future. But she couldn't always tell one from the other. The visions had driven her mad long ago. Sometimes her advice was right on target and other times she begged Dani to stop atrocities from hundreds of years ago.

"If you hunt alone, you'll fall." Gwen's bony fingers cut into Dani's wrist, surprisingly strong. "Find the invisible man who sees the hidden truths. Find him, Dani." Gwen's eyelids sagged, her spate of prescience exhausting her.

Dani finished washing and rinsing her hair, combing it out and drying it with a towel. The plate of food lay forgotten on the floor. She helped her sister into bed—a thick, feather-stuffed mattress on a sturdy wooden frame. Plenty of heavy quilts and duvets were heaped on top to

35

keep Gwen warm. Her drawing materials were scattered all over the uneven stone floor.

Tidying the room, she'd gotten a better look at the sketch pad. A weedy field with a cat sitting at the edge and a crescent moon rising above.

Exactly what she saw now in the gas station's parking lot.

"Damn. I hate it when she's right," Dani whispered to the sky. Just when she thought this day couldn't get any worse.

Find the shadow. Gwen's final warning echoed through her head. Spinning on her heels, she went back to the rubbish heap. She dug through the trash, searching.

Beneath a rusted-out muffler was a patch of shadow slightly darker than those around it. When she touched it, instead of cool concrete, she found smooth plasticized fabric. Pulling it out, she discovered it was a torn fragment from a lightweight jacket, dark blue nylon. The shadow was found. Now she supposed she'd have to track down this invisible man. She sniffed at the nylon, catching a hint of gun oil and cheap deodorant. Was the jacket his? Or another path of investigation?

"You could have been a little clearer, Gwen," Dani muttered at the sky, tucking the fabric away in her pocket. She'd hang on to it and search for this invisible man. But meanwhile, she would check into other leads.

Whoever took her brothers had made a serious mistake. Danielle Harris did not fuck around with anyone who threatened her family.

The Hunt was on.

36

THURSDAY

Chapter Six

The shrill buzz of Michael's cell phone cut through his vague and disturbing dreams. Groggy, he thumbed it on and noted the time. Six a.m. "Hello?"

"Michael? I'm so sorry, but I need help." Heavy crashes punctuated the woman's plea.

The sleep-fog vanished from his brain as he recognized a client's voice, and he sat up. "What's happening, Martha?"

"Can you come over, please? Quickly?"

"I'm on my way."

A muffled grunt of pain and a click ended the conversation.

Michael's brain kept cycling with worry as he got dressed. Martha wouldn't have called if the situation hadn't been desperate. He'd given her his private number years ago and she'd only ever used it three times before today. Every single one of them had been because of an overwhelming disaster.

He barely remembered to lock his apartment as he ran out the door. As he drove, he found his mind pulled back to the club last night despite his worry for Martha. What he'd felt had haunted his dreams, and he knew he must be missing some crucial piece of information. Perdition might have a reputation as a sort of East Coast Vegas, but the dark mix of lust and violence wasn't part of the regular club scene here. Most of the people just wanted to have a good time.

If he was honest, it wasn't just the club that he was obsessed with—it was the woman he'd seen. Something about her tugged at him, made him reluctant to dismiss her as a man-eater. He wished he'd gone after her, stopped her from leaving with the blond man. Joe would have helped. But she triggered an uncomfortable wariness, a subliminal warning shivering and shredding the edges of his interest.

He forced himself to put aside the previous night as he pulled up to the visitor parking of Martha's modest apartment complex. He took the stairs up to the second floor and knocked on the door. Heavy insulation did not completely shield the shrieks and thuds from inside.

Martha opened the door and let him in. Her pale eyes were rimmed in red and he could see fresh bruises and scrapes on her skin. Her years hung heavily on her, making her appear much older than her mid-thirties.

"What happened?" he asked.

"I don't know. Last night, she wouldn't sleep. She started tearing everything apart and hasn't stopped. I tried to give her the sedative but she won't let me near." Martha gestured helplessly at the fragments of toys and furniture strewn around the apartment, rubbing at her mottled arms and tugging at the wisps of brown hair escaping her ponytail. "It's been all I could do to keep her in the apartment."

Now that he was here, he could feel her exhaustion and fear buzzing and scraping in his mind. She wanted to help her daughter, but at the same time, she was desperate for the screaming and attacks to end. Martha was such a font of patience, but she had clearly reached her limits for the time being. Her emotions were almost insubstantial; she simply didn't have the reserves for anything stronger right now.

Ready for anything, Michael slipped across the living room to peer into the bedroom. A preteen girl crouched in the middle of the floor, rocking back and forth, grunting to herself. Sandy-brown hair tangled around her head and debris scattered the floor around her. The brightly painted room was strewn with chunks of compact fluff, fragments of rubber, scraps of fabric, and irregular planks of wood—yesterday, it had been a sturdy bed with a rubberized mattress.

"Bernie?" he called out cautiously—then ducked as a chunk of wood the size of his head slammed into the wall nearby. Her terror slammed into him with equal impact, literally knocking his breath out of his lungs. As he struggled to inhale again, Bernie screamed as if she had been stabbed and began flailing wildly enough that he risked serious injury getting close to her. She looked like every demonic little girl in a horror film. Michael pulled back into the hall to regroup.

Beside him, Martha shoved the heel of her uninjured hand across her eyes, angrily wiping away tears. Michael studied the little girl rampaging like a Tasmanian Devil. This wasn't her first fit of destructive mania, which was why there were only a few pieces of cheap pressboard furniture scattered around the apartment and heavy protective plastic shields bolted to the walls. Bernie had been diagnosed as a delusional schizophrenic five years ago, at the age of six. Michael had been her therapist since then, trying to help her recognize the difference between the real world and the one full of animals and people who tried to get her to do things.

Michael took a deep breath and made a plan. Bernie could be incredibly strong during her manic fits. She was completely unaware of her own pain or of hurting anyone else, and she threw her entire body weight behind every blow. They needed to get her calmed down long enough to take her medication.

"I tried to hold off calling as long as I could," Martha said. "I haven't seen her like this in years." She bit her lip hard enough to dent it. The skin under her eyes was gray with exhaustion, and her hands were shaking. Michael had watched her sacrifice everything—career, savings, marriage—for any chance to help her beloved daughter. But the constant stress and chaos took its toll. "I don't want to have to take her to the hospital again."

Bernie quieted for a moment, her eyes flicking back and forth as she watched things invisible to everyone else.

"You made the right choice, Martha. I told you: you can call me any time, day or night. Can you think of anything that might have upset her?" If they could understand what had triggered the incident, they would have a better chance of bringing Bernie out of it and, more importantly, avoid a repetition.

Martha shook her head.

"Okay. I'll see if I can get her calmed down enough to tell us." Taking a deep breath, Michael stepped inside.

Bernie spun to face him, her face twisted. She launched herself at him, tiny hands curled into claws. Michael caught her and folded himself around her in a protective hold, using his wiry frame to keep her still. He'd trained in various martial arts for years and instead of using those skills to hurt, he'd found a way to use them to help heal. Bracing himself, he wrapped his wide hands around hers and opened his mind.

Immediately he was swallowed in chaos, plunged into Bernie's hallucinations. Shadowy people were shouting at him, but it was as if he were listening to a badly tuned television. They sounded like the teacher from Charlie Brown, distortion turning the words into random squawks. They hovered all around him, shouting as if volume alone could convey

41

meaning.

She struggled and screamed loudly enough to set his ears ringing but couldn't get enough leverage to get away.

"I'm getting the medication." Martha said, her fingers white from gripping the doorframe.

"Give me a minute here," Michael grunted, adjusting his long legs to pin down Bernie's flailing limbs. She was unbelievably strong, throwing all her weight against him. Sometimes holding her was enough to break the cycle and allow her to regain control. He didn't want to force-feed her a sedative if they didn't have to. Bernie's terror was beginning to subside, despite her thrashing. Michael shifted slightly, moving from restraint to protection. He wrapped around her, placing himself between her and the shadowy hallucinations that surrounded them, clamoring for attention. She gripped him tightly, her eyes squeezed shut.

"It's okay. I've got you," he whispered into her sweat-tangled hair as he cradled her. Through their connection, he sensed she hadn't been indulging in random destruction. She'd been searching for something. He could sense her desperation as if it were his own. But he had to pull her away from it to break the mania and bring her back.

"Bernie, it's Michael. Ignore everyone else. Listen to my voice. It's Michael." He kept his voice low and calm, practically speaking into her ear as her fingers dug painfully into his skin. He began to sing softly, a silly little song to the tune of *Old MacDonald*.

> *"Bernie always likes this song, E-I-E-I-O.*
> *But Michael always sings it wrong, E-I-E-I-O.*
> *With a quack-moo here and a baa-neigh there.*
> *Got it wrong, always wrong, every time I sing the song.*
> *Bernie always likes this song, E-I-E-I-O."*

He kept singing, making up the verses as he went along. As Bernie calmed, Martha's anxiety began pricking at him from the doorway. The shadows' bellowing faded as if on a radio being set to a different station. Slowly he built up the protections in his mind again, leaving just enough room for Bernie's emotions to seep through. Eventually, he felt it was safe to let her go.

She blinked up at him, her eyes and cheeks swollen from crying, but she didn't launch into a new assault. Michael wearily counted it as a success, smoothing the sweat-lank hair away from her face.

"Thank God," her mother sighed. "Bernie, honey, are you okay?"

"Tired. And my hands hurt." Bernie held out her fingers—the nails were split past the quick and were bleeding sluggishly.

"I'll get the bandages, sweetie."

Michael watched Bernie carefully as her mother scurried away. This could be the end of the manic episode or it could only be a temporary lull. He wished he knew how to help her more. After five years, sometimes he felt as if he were fighting a losing battle. Martha had tried medication, intensive therapy, even hospitalization, but nothing seemed to help for long.

"I got lost," the little girl announced.

"I know. But you found your way back."

"Because you helped. But you won't be able to help in the new place."

"What new place?" Suspicion threatened to sharpen his voice, but Michael forced himself to maintain a pose of nonchalance. He didn't want to risk setting her off again.

"The new place I'm going to live. Chuck says it's scary and that they'll hurt me." Tears glistened in Bernie's hazel eyes.

Chuck was one of Bernie's hallucinations: an eight-year-old boy who prompted her to do horrific things like lighting furniture on fire or hitting other children. Michael forced himself to release the breath he was holding. Chuck was rarely a good sign. "Chuck doesn't always tell you the truth."

"He's mad a lot. His mom and dad forgot him and left him behind. Just like my mom will forget me."

"Your mom would never forget you, Bernie-pie."

"You won't forget me, will you? You have to help me. Promise me." Bernie's tiny hands wrapped around his, crushing his fingers with the strength of her grip. Terror and desperation roared through the physical contact. Whatever was going on, it was more than a passing childish fear.

He held her gaze, hoping she could see his conviction and

43

determination. "I promise. I'll do everything I can."

Chapter Seven

Michael's hands clenched into fists as Bernie relaxed. Her mother returned with wet cloths, antibiotic ointment, and bandages, preventing him from finding out more. Bernie was silent while they cleaned and bandaged her hands. Together, Michael and Martha inflated an old camping mattress and set it up in the living room with blankets and pillows.

Bernie crawled into the nest, clearly exhausted. "Please find it for me," she whispered, clutching Michael's hand. The fractured image of a brochure swam into his mind, jumping around too much to see clearly.

"I will," he promised, tucking her in.

Bernie closed her eyes and was asleep before they left the room.

The clock showed five minutes to ten—barely halfway through the morning and Michael was weary enough to collapse, himself. Luckily Bernie had been his first client scheduled for the morning, and his afternoon client was away on holiday. Martha silently offered him a coffee. He gratefully accepted.

"Thank you so much. I don't know what I would have done if you hadn't been here." She rubbed at her eyes with the back of her hand.

"It was a rough one. Get some sleep yourself while she's quiet."

"There's so much to do. I have to order a new mattress and clean up the mess…"

"It'll wait," he said firmly. "You should rest. I'll let Celina know to cancel Bernie's session with Anne this afternoon so you both have time to recover."

"I hate to lose a day…" Martha began.

"This is a marathon, not a sprint." He'd told her the same thing many times over the years. "Pushing both of you when you're exhausted won't help anyone."

Martha's smile didn't reach her eyes. She seemed empty, beaten, and battered down. Michael's heart ached with wishing he knew some way to

45

help her that they hadn't already tried. "What else is on today?"

"I have another meeting with Expanding Horizons this afternoon."

"Expanding Horizons?" He frowned. "Who are they?"

"They've been calling me for weeks. They have clinics in California for children with severe psychological issues. They've opened one here and they approached me about Bernie."

"Sounds expensive." Michael kept his face neutral, but internal alarm bells were starting to ring.

Martha pulled a brochure out of her purse, still glossy despite crumpling. Michael eyed it as if it were a snake about strike, recognizing it as the one Bernie had been searching for.

"It's a live-in facility, state of the art with a multidisciplinary medical team." Martha smoothed the brochure. "They've offered us free treatment. They said Bernie is a fascinating case since there are so few children with schizophrenia. I hate the idea of her living with strangers, and I've told them so. I suggested an outpatient program, but they said they couldn't accommodate it. I keep wondering if maybe they can help her and I'm being selfish to hold her back." He could feel her indecision teetering back and forth. She wanted to hope but had been burned before by fancy establishments that promised all the answers.

"Ah." He couldn't quite figure out what to say. Bernie was terrified of the brochure and what it represented, but he had no way of convincing Martha without more information. Staring at the glossy pictures, he decided to do something he almost never did. He opened his gift wide enough to let him pick up emotional impressions from objects as well as people.

Martha frowned. "I'm surprised you don't know. They said Celina recommended us to them." Her anxiety scraped against him like a rasp against wood.

"Maybe she forgot to tell me. Mind if I take a look?" He picked up the pamphlet and nearly dropped it as it bit him.

It wasn't a literal bite, but his fingers ached as if it were, while needles of agony and despair stung his brain. The bright, shiny photos of attractive young women helping developmentally disabled children took on a sinister cast. Snippets of children crying and dry voices reciting medical terms assaulted him. He slammed the walls of his gift shut. *Chuck*

46

was right. This is a bad place.

But how could he convince Martha? Even people who claimed to believe in psychics quickly became unnerved at what he saw. If he told her about his visions, at best she'd cut him off. At worst, he might find himself under investigation. It was difficult enough being a man working with children in these paranoid times. Any suspicion would end his career in a heartbeat.

He loved working with the kids no one else could connect with. His psychometric gift allowed him to see into their minds through physical contact. Using that knowledge, he could help them in ways no other therapist could.

"You should trust your instincts," Michael said slowly. "Bernie's been making progress with us. There's no rush to change things."

"But free treatment." Martha rubbed at her bloodshot eyes. "Why aren't these decisions ever easy?"

"You're exhausted. You can't make a decision in this state. Get some rest before you talk to them. Let me keep this, and I'll do some research, find out what I can." He held his breath. She looked so defeated that he suspected it wouldn't take much persuasion from Expanding Horizons to convince her to sign up. He wished he had some more direct help for her. Maybe he could talk to Celina. She knew about a lot of different grant programs.

"Thanks, Michael. You've been a godsend with her. No one else managed to get so much done with her." Martha squeezed his hand and her exhaustion and determination sapped what was left of his energy. "You've been a good friend to us."

"I'll see what I can find out about this place." The rising sun logo across the front burned into his eyes. *Expanding Horizons: Making a difference one step at a time.*

"It would help ease my mind about sending her. Thanks again." Martha yawned.

After making her promise again to sleep, Michael headed to Different Ways, the treatment center he worked for. *Celina wouldn't have recommended a new program without speaking to me. Maybe I'm wrong about what I sensed. Maybe I sensed what Bernie was thinking when she held the brochure.* His attempts to convince himself rang hollow, and an urgent feeling grew in his mind. Not quite a coercive flash, but not something he could ignore, either. The insight from the brochure was trying to bring something to his attention. Whether it was God or the Universe didn't matter. Even without it, he wouldn't abandon Bernie.

He pulled in to the lot and, as always, the sight of the center cheered him up. It had been a regular family home, but when Different Ways moved in, they'd painted the exterior in bright primary colors and planted a wide variety of flowers and trees. A fenced-in playground held brilliant swings, slides, and jungle gyms. Everything about the place shouted welcome and proclaimed that the kids came first. His shoulders unknotted, and he relaxed for the first time since Joe had suggested they go out to celebrate. Leaving his car, he took the back door into the administrator's office, the nerve center of the entire operation. "Hi, Celina. I've just come from Bernie's. She's had a rough night, and they need to cancel their sessions."

"Poor thing. How is she?" Celina flicked her attention back and forth between several computer screens, her blond ponytail bouncing in accompaniment as her fingers flew over the keyboard. Sometimes Michael wondered if she wouldn't have been happier as a cyborg. Of course, she wouldn't have been able to wear the latest fashions anymore, so maybe she was better off as a human.

"We got her calmed down without having to sedate her. Listen, have you heard of a residential treatment program called Expanding Horizons?"

Celina frowned, tapping her finger against her teeth as she thought. She shook her head. "No. Why?"

Michael frowned. One lie caught: Celina hadn't recommended them. "Bernie's mom has an offer of gratis treatment from them. I wanted to check it out, make sure it's a good program. Billy's family is away right now, so I'm just working with Bernie. Instead of subbing at the center, could I have a few days to check into them?" He hated having to ask for favors, but something told him this would take more than a day to figure out.

"That's fine for today, but tomorrow I need you at the center for the lunch shift. We're already short-staffed. Sorry." She smiled at him, patting him on the hand.

48

Long practice kept him from pulling away, but with the morning's exhaustion, his defenses weren't up to keeping her out. Her mind buzzed on multiple levels simultaneously like a cocktail party with a half dozen people trying to speak to him at once.

"What's wrong? You don't look so good." Genuine concern silenced at least half of her levels.

"Late night. And a rough morning." He straightened, discreetly removing his hand from her range. It would have been easy to lie and claim to be ill, but after years of discovering people's secrets, he hated even the slightest hint of an untruth. He might be forced to look beneath their masks, but he didn't want to have to wear one himself.

She rattled on for a few minutes, giving him time to recover. "Did you at least enjoy the show last weekend? Brad and I tried to go but couldn't get a sitter." The show had been a special presentation called Page-Bound Heroes, featuring original art by artists from Marvel and DC Comics.

"It was great. I got some signed cover art." She rambled on, but Michael extracted himself as soon as it was polite to do so. He felt guilty for cutting her off as he thanked her and left the center. Their mutual love of animated stories had come out during his first job interview. They'd talked for hours, debating Marvel vs. DC and sharing their favorite lines. Somehow, he'd still gotten the job. Knowing he had a kindred spirit in the office made coming to work easier.

He walked slowly back to his car, remembering the bad old days when he was younger and couldn't keep other people's thoughts and emotions at bay. Comics provided the ultimate escape. Inside the pages, people who were different became heroes, not freaks. He liked to imagine himself as one of the heroes, using his secret abilities to help others while maintaining a mild-mannered persona as part of his disguise. He stared down at his gloved hands. It wasn't really a disguise, but he was doing what he'd dreamed of. He couldn't live with himself if he didn't find a way to help Bernie. This might not be a comic book, but he had a promise to keep and a little girl to save.

Chapter Eight

The smoky, rundown bar called Last Down barely clung to the edge of the Perdition city limits. It was the home of the desperate and the parasites who fed off them and would have required extensive renovations to qualify as a dive, except for the bank of state-of-the-art televisions mounted on the walls. They showed everything from dog races to an ESPN feed—no bet too small or too large.

Bracing herself, she sauntered into the bar as if she owned it. It had been six years since Dani last set foot inside the wretched bar and inhaled its ingrained stench of cheap liquor, stale cigarette smoke, and toner ink. Not long enough, in her opinion, but this was where her brothers' journey had begun. The jacket fragment and the invisible man would both wait until she'd searched the more traditional routes.

A few patrons blinked in surprise before hastily turning back to their private machines. The mix of ex-jocks, strung-out gambling addicts, and slovenly couch-coaches all added a cloying layer of grasping desperation to the fetid air. In her fitted leather jacket and tight pants, she did not fit the typical clientele. Unusual people tended to be potentially inconvenient at best or dangerous at worst. The patrons here knew that it paid not to pay attention.

"Hey there, Chomp. Long time." Dani sat down next to a paunchy man in a bright Hawaiian shirt. He'd been nursing a beer and eagerly avoiding making eye contact with her, but her brothers had come to him, and now it was her turn. It took effort for Dani to remain relaxed and not grit her teeth.

"They're not here, Dani." Chomp might have been attempting to play cool, but his pale skin and the biting scent of his terror gave him away. "They haven't been here in weeks."

Disgust tugged Dani's lip downward. *Vincent and his fucking "system" to make easy money.* She'd refused to have anything more to do with bailing him out or asking for extensions from people who used body parts as loan collateral. Her disgust deepened as Chomp sneaked glances at her breasts despite the high-necked T-shirt she'd worn precisely to avoid this particular situation.

The Huntress uncoiled inside, aware of nearby prey. Dani fought it down, relieved when it settled without the usual struggle, still sated from the previous night. "I'm not happy, Chomp. Can you guess why?" Frustration made her tone sharper than she'd initially intended, and her quarry's eyes leapt back to her face. Those closest to them gathered their things and scuttled away to more remote areas of the bar.

"I'm sure we can work this out." He licked his lips. "Your brothers are good men—"

"Not in the mood," she growled through clenched teeth. "What did you tell my brothers?"

Chomp raised his hands in the universal symbol of surrender. "Look, I haven't done anything—"

"First lie." Dani's hand shot out, clamping on Chomp's neck. Her fingers dug deep into his oily skin to get a good grip. She needed him alive and conscious and talking.

Bam! The cheap wood veneer on the bar splintered as she slammed his head down.

"Ahh! Not the head! Not the head!" Chomp wailed, pressing meaty palms to the blood oozing from his forehead. The doors slammed repeatedly as the bar emptied. No one wanted to be collateral damage.

"Want to go for lie number two? What did you tell them?" Dani's fingers curled around his neck. She would need to scrub for a week to get his dingy oil out of her skin. The knowledge did not improve her temper.

"You need to be more specific—" Chomp squealed in pain as Dani's foot smashed into his knee.

"I am not in the fucking mood to play games, Chomp!" she threatened. *He set my brothers up...*

"Then maybe you should leave." A massive hand clamped on her shoulder and pulled her away.

Dani looked up. And up at the massive hulk of man-flesh glaring down at the two of them.

"What the hell am I paying you for? She hit me! Twice!" Chomp whined. His piggish eyes darted back and forth between the two of them. The stench of fear still stung her nose, but gleeful pride started to swell up. He was proud of his little giant of a bodyguard. He thought it would

51

keep him safe.

Men. Always thinking size matters.

"It's time for you to leave. Now," Hulk informed her.

Chomp smelled eager, and he'd settled in tight to watch his goon attack.

"All right, big guy. I wasn't looking for trouble." Dani smiled, flashing her dimples. Immediately, Hulk's grip loosened on her coat. *Good. If he'd ripped it, I'd have to kill him.*

She spread her arms, incidentally giving both men a good eyeful of her tight T-shirt. "How about a little bet? A coin toss. I lose, I'll go right now. I win, I get to ask my questions and you buy me a drink. Deal?"

Chomp's rapid exhalation sent a sharp spike of anxiety up her nose, but from the male interest suddenly rising from Hulk, she'd gotten his attention with her proposal. Despite having seen her attack Chomp not five minutes earlier, he was dismissing her as no threat and seeing a potential conquest instead. *I hate doing this.* She could practically watch his brain cells reach their final conclusion. He was going to try to be charming.

Some vestige of self-protection remained. "I toss the coin."

"No trouble at all." She winked. "I'll even let you call it."

He let go of her to dig a coin out of his pocket, grinning as if he already had a mental strip reel going. He jerked his hand up and the coin glittered as it flipped in the air. "Heads."

"Any way you want it." Dani watched as his eyes tracked the coin, her knees bent and hands loose. She might only get one shot at this.

The coin spun and bounced on the bar before settling. Hulk bent over to see what it was and Dani struck. Her foot lashed up and her heel smashed solidly into his temple with a meaty crack. He jerked back, losing his balance, eyes wide in surprise.

Chomp let out an odd mix of a wail and groan, scrambling away from his would-be protection.

"You did say heads, right?" Dani grinned, punching straight from the shoulder and snapping Hulk's head back hard enough that his teeth clicked together. She could do this all day, especially with the Huntress seeping encouragement into her veins. For once, she and her demon were in perfect agreement. This idiot needed a lesson, and she needed to release some of her frustrations in a good old-fashioned, completely justified ass kicking.

Hulk struggled to stand, the arousal she'd scented earlier replaced with rage, suggesting that visions of murder had replaced his mental pornography. She'd humiliated him in front of others, shown that his massive size alone didn't make him a fighter. He didn't want to dominate her now. He wanted to kill her.

Stand in line, asswit. It was delightfully simple. She channeled all of her frustration and fear about her brothers into teaching this steroid-enthusiast the error of judging a fighter by her appearance.

His first blow was a haymaker that could have rung her ears if she hadn't seen it coming a mile away. She dodged with ease, clucking contemptuously from the side as he overbalanced and wavered.

He charged again. *If this is the best you have...* Boredom replaced any sense of satisfaction from the fight. This was more like dealing with a toddler's tantrum than a battle of equals.

The patrons had long since scattered like rats. Hulk tried to smash her into the floor with his fists. As she rolled out of the way and back onto her feet, movement attracted her attention: Chomp disappearing into the back. *Crapfuck! Like a damn cockroach.* No more time for games.

"This time, I'd fucking stay down if I were you." She swept Hulk's legs out from under him, sending him flat on his ass again with a resounding thud. A solid punch to his skull left him limp on the floor. Spinning, she sprinted after Chomp, catching him as he fumbled with the back door.

"Why are you doing this to me? I sell information! It's how I earn my beer money! You don't have to hit me!" he babbled, the stench of terror almost covering the first hints of urine.

"What did you tell Vincent and Eric, Chomp?" Dani growled, hoisting the rotund man off his feet. "Where did you send them?"

"I didn't tell them anything! I swear! I don't know what you're talking about."

"You got them a job. Three weeks ago." She tightened her grip on his collar.

"What? Oh, yeah. They brought it to me. Bodyguard work. It was legit, they wanted some help with the background checks," he

53

whimpered. There was no scent of deceit, only terror with faint whiffs of irritation.

"Guess again. It was a trap." Fresh fury ignited in her, setting her hands trembling with the urge to strike. The idiot hadn't even known he was setting her brothers up.

"Oh God, oh God." Chomp swallowed hard as if about to vomit. He didn't know all her family's secrets, but he knew enough to recognize danger. "Forgive and forget" was not in their vocabulary. "I didn't know. It looked legit, I swear. The company wanted military veterans, so I hooked your brothers up with papers."

Chomp's little network of connections and criminals had provided everything. She wished her brothers had worked with her family's usual forgers instead, but Eric hadn't wanted their parents to know. "Give me copies of what you gave them."

"I don't have them here. They're at home. Please, I'll get them and bring them to you. No charge."

Her sharp ears caught the sound of sirens pulsing shrilly, drawing closer. Time to wind up and slip back under the radar. There was no trace of deception and the stench of cringing fear was overpowering. Chomp would do what she needed.

He slid down the wall as she let him go, unable to support his own weight. Disgusted, Dani stepped away. *A legitimate job*—the one thing they had all been told would never be possible. A forbidden dream she and Eric shared. She'd found one and her brother had obviously tried the same. *It's supposed to be fucking simple. Everyone else in the world manages it. Why not us?*

"You know, I liked it a lot better when you used to flash your tits at me," Chomp muttered under his breath as he straightened his clothes. He probably believed she was too far away to hear him.

Bad guess. She didn't even realize she'd hit him until the ache in her knuckles penetrated her rage. Chomp must have dropped after the first blow, but she'd kept on punching the wall, leaving a web of cracks in the cinderblock. Dust clung to her swollen hands. Chomp lay on the floor at her feet, not moving, blood staining his thinning hair. *Oh shit. I better not have killed him.* His pulse thumped regularly under her fingers. *Unconscious. Damn, means I have to wait for him to wake up.*

"Freeze! Stay where you are."

Dani held still. Maybe she could take them out before they shot her, but unlike Hulk, police had schedules, partners, and check-ins—too much attention. Besides, without the Huntress's influence she didn't much enjoy hurting people for no good reason. Drawing a deep breath, she prepared herself. No matter how far she tried to run from her past, it always pulled her down.

"Turn around. Slowly."

She turned, slowly, smiling widely enough to flash her dimples. "What seems to be the trouble, officer?"

Chapter Nine

"I don't know what you expect me to do, Michael." Joe Cabrera sighed, fiddling with his shield and identification.

"There has to be something. A restraining order or an injunction. They said we sent them, but Celina's never heard of them."

Michael had come directly to the police station after hitting a brick wall as he tried to find out anything about the treatment center. There were websites for the centers in California, and people answered the phones politely enough when he called. They were more than happy to share the results of their special blend of treatments. They were sending him information packets. Referral websites loved them, parents raved. He couldn't find any trace of what he had seen was happening there. He'd hoped Joe could advise him on a legal way to prevent Bernie from being taken there. The busy squad room was full of cops doing paperwork, talking to minor offenders. Michael retreated to a corner to avoid emotional contamination, keeping his gloves on.

"Based on what? The testimony of a mentally disturbed child who suffers from hallucinations and has never actually been to the place in question?" Joe spread his hands. "Even if they lied to the mom about who sent them, my hands are tied. There's no evidence I can use. Unless you think the mom is unfit...?"

Michael shook his head. Even if it had been true, it would only put Bernie in foster care, which would be even worse. He ground his teeth. He'd hoped Joe would have some solution he hadn't seen, some way to keep Bernie home without tipping his hand.

"I'm sorry, man, but all I can do is file a report about your concerns. Then it's on record, at least. I don't like it any more than you do. I trust you, but I can't go to a judge and say my friend touched a brochure and now he knows this treatment place is hurting kids." Joe threw the brochure down on his desk. Michael knew his friend's frustration was at not being able to help, not his request.

"No. I get it." Michael pushed his hair back from his face,

wondering if he should cut it before shoving the thought aside. *Where can I go from here?*

"Find me something. Anything. Something I can use."

He nodded, his mind already busy searching for alternatives. Maybe he could visit the place himself.

Joe reached out and grabbed his arm. "Hey, be careful. Don't get yourself hurt or dead or anything. I'd hate to have to write up that paperwork." Rough concern, frustration, and the desire to help seeped through the contact.

Michael smiled. Joe might not want to know all his friend's secrets, but he would crawl through fire to help if he could. "I'll do my best."

"Damn straight. Look, why don't we go out tonight? We can talk things out, maybe figure out some shit."

Michael was about to agree when he noticed a growing group at the front of the station. "What's going on?"

"Dispatch said they were bringing in some people from a fight at Last Down. Two guys went to the hospital and the team brought in the only suspect who didn't scuttle back into the shadows." Joe gestured toward the door with a handful of files. "They must be taking her statement."

Michael spotted her and forgot what he was going to say.

The woman emerging from the ring of uniformed cops was indescribably unique and impossibly familiar: the woman from the club. He couldn't believe she was actually there in front of him. Even with her hands pinned behind her in handcuffs, she looked as if she were in control. Long dark hair tumbled over her shoulders, and big dark eyes laughed and flirted with those around her. The smile lurking in the corners of her lips suggested a certain jaded amusement, as though nothing could shock or discourage her. She was tall, and her tight jeans and T-shirt flaunted her statuesque figure. She carried herself with grace and ease, as if the cuffs were only fringe jewelry and her escort a matter of honor rather than detention.

"Earth to Michael. Wipe the drool off your chin," Joe teased, thwacking him lightly with a file to get his attention. "Not that I'm blaming you."

Details of the conversation slowly swam back into his brain. *Bar.*

Hospital. Suspect. Assault. They led him to an uncomfortable conclusion. He was unable to look away as one of the officers removed the cuffs and escorted her to a desk. "You think she did it?"

Joe paused, riffling the file in his hand while he thought. "Hard to believe. From what I heard, those guys looked like a truck hit them. No one hits that hard. Besides, she came along easy enough. Not like she tried to hide."

The woman ran her hand down the officer's arm, smiling at him.

"You want to go over and ask her name?" Joe was grinning.

"Wouldn't that be an ethical violation?" Michael couldn't get his mouth to stop spouting whatever went through his dazed brain.

"If *I* asked her, it would be a cop-suspect thing. But you're a free civilian, entitled to pick up women in any situation you like, no matter how weird. Be a hell of a story to tell your grandkids." Joe shifted his voice to imitate a piping five-year-old. "Tell us how you met Grandma." Then, lower again, "Well, son, it was like this. She was arrested for assault and—"

"Actually I don't think she's being arrested," Michael interrupted, keeping his attention on his mystery woman. She was standing up, collecting her bag and leather jacket from the officer. Winking at the man, she sauntered away from the desk, hips rolling with every step, coming closer.

"Guess she's not a suspect after all. Hmm, he still should have gotten a statement," Joe muttered.

Michael's mouth seemed full of glue, making teeth, tongue, and lips a congealed mess incapable of speech. He wanted her to look at him, to talk to him, and yet he also wanted to stay in the background and not come off as a blithering idiot. She was only a few steps away, then one step. Still no notice of him.

She swept past without a glance in their direction. Michael bit his lip as a frustrating mix of relief and disappointment weighed him down. But he still couldn't take his eyes off her… which was how he noticed the tube of lipstick that bounced out of her bag and rolled onto the floor. Michael bent automatically to pick it up and froze as images pounded his brain even through his leather gloves.

Every single one was of her face. Winking, smiling, lips thinned in determination, turning a corner, glancing up. Her features slammed into his brain again and again along with an irresistible magnetic pull.

This way.

I'm supposed to follow her? He'd never gotten a flash so cryptic and so clear at the same time. The perfume of jasmine and oranges lingered in the air.

"Man, you okay?" Joe bent down to help him up. "She wasn't that hot… oh crap, you just got some woo-woo shit off her stuff, didn't you?"

Michael nodded. The woman pushed open the doors to leave, and his head throbbed in time with her every movement. "Sorry, but I think I have to go."

"Far be it from me to stand in the way of creepy weird shit. Good luck and keep me posted."

Sprinting to catch up, Michael spotted her sliding into a cab. A thrill tingled along his nerves and brain. Helping a beautiful, mysterious woman just like a hero in a detective story, exactly the sort of thing he'd always dreamed about doing with his gift. Racing down the steps, he leapt into the next taxi in the queue and uttered a line he never thought he'd get a chance to say.

"Follow that cab!"

Chapter Ten

A smile, a wink, and a twenty convinced the cabby to hurry. Disgusted with the time wasted in the police station, Dani considered simply not showing up for work tonight. Vincent and Eric were still out there somewhere—she refused to allow herself to believe otherwise. The longer the delay, the colder the trail would be. But her earlier impulsive actions left her no choice except cooling her heels. Chomp would still be in the hospital. He might not even have regained consciousness. Either way, he would definitely be the subject of police interest, and she couldn't afford to attract any more.

Frustration threatened to stir the Huntress. She'd not only failed to get the information from Chomp, she'd gotten distracted taking Hulk down and nearly lost her only real lead. It wasn't the first time her impulses had interfered with her goals. She'd lost her temper, forgetting her own strength, and she knew how dangerous it could be. If she wanted to have any chance at rescuing her brothers, she couldn't afford mistakes.

She splayed her fingers, pleased to see the puffy redness gone. Whatever else the Huntress did to her, the quick healing was a welcome side benefit.

Think it through for a change. If she worked, she got her money for the night and avoided attracting any more attention. Besides, her job was the only place she felt balanced and powerful, all sides of herself coming together. She needed that right now, to wipe away the foul taste of failure from her tongue. She reminded herself that she'd made it out of the police station without being put into any official records. That was a minor achievement but hardly a resounding success. Flying under the radar was a Harris family specialty, but it wasn't Dani's style.

Arriving at the club, she couldn't help but smile at the giant, glossy promotional posters picked out in cheap illumination. Let her family whine about the importance of being invisible. She'd earned her place here as one of the starring performers.

Michael couldn't believe this was the right spot. *Here? You really want me here?* More anecdotal proof that the Universe enjoyed a sadistic sense of humor.

"You getting out or what?" his cabby demanded.

His quarry had already vanished into the club. Posters of scantily clad women made it clear what kind of performance to expect. He'd made it this far in his life without having to go into a strip club, and breaking the habit wasn't appealing. The strongest compulsion he'd ever experienced writhed under his skin, itching like cheap wool. There wouldn't be any peace until he did what was necessary, which meant he needed to get this done so he could focus on helping Bernie.

He examined the other businesses on the street. A tattoo parlor, a sex shop, a Goth-oriented boutique, and two parking lots with spotty illumination breaking the twilight gloom. Nothing he really wanted to hang around in, waiting to see when she came back out.

"Getting out." He paid the driver and stepped out, coughing at the grit in the air.

The building might have been a movie theater in the thirties and forties. The marquee proclaimed the Blue Curtain Club was the home of the Jewels of the Night, the city's top burlesque act. The red and white paint was flaking away in patches. The brilliantly lit signs blinked to attract attention, tacked on after the fact like cheap costume jewelry. Swallowing his discomfort, Michael stepped up to the bored bouncer. Relinquishing his ID and a twenty-dollar cover, he pulled back his glove long enough to get a blurred stamp in return and permission to pass through the beaded curtains into the club proper.

The business might not have spent much outside, but inside, the club was decorated in warm sensual reds and golds. Waitresses in tight corsets and heels clicked efficiently through their rounds. The bar stretched across one wall, and a small stage dominated one end of the club. Most of the tables were a mix of businessmen, frat boys, and, to his surprise, women in shiny club attire. Michael claimed a tiny standing bar table and ordered a beer. He took the time to survey the room, searching for his mystery woman. A heavy compulsion weighed him down, pressing his feet into the floor.

Maybe she was in trouble. Or something could be about to happen to her, something he could prevent. Guessing why the compulsion wanted him there seemed futile. He shifted uncomfortably, wishing the universe had picked another time to play with his life. A pair of dancers on stage performed an improbable series of acrobatic maneuvers in lacy body stockings. Funny, in a crude and bawdy kind of way. Anticipation and amusement buoyed the crowd, lightening his spirits despite his attempt to stay focused.

He shook his head as the dancers produced bananas from hidden thigh sheaths and the crowd broke out in laughter and applause. He disapproved of strip clubs in general. Too many women ended up in them, stripped of their choices along with their clothes. People shouldn't prey on other people's desperation. No one should have to accept humiliation for a paycheck.

Of course, this one didn't seem to quite fit the mental image he'd gleaned from various psychic intrusions. It was well lit. There were no booths along the back for private performances. The women on stage might be in provocative costumes, but they weren't just wiggling and jiggling for the crowd. The crowd itself was light and cheerful, enjoying the show but not demanding more.

The compulsion crawled along his nervous system as he sipped the beer he'd ordered. *Why am I here?* Curiosity added its own weight to press him into his seat. He felt as if he were on the cusp of a major change, the end of the world as he knew it.

The acrobats accepted wild applause and cheering as they skipped off stage, waving gleefully at the audience. A hush of anticipation fell over the crowd. Michael glanced at the eager smiles around him. People hurried from the bar to reclaim their seats and the waitresses discreetly withdrew to the edges of the room.

The lights dimmed, drawing his attention to the panels behind the small stage. The silhouette of a woman appeared against the panels, igniting applause. An unsmiling pair of men in tuxes appeared from the wings, glaring at each other.

A familiar song began, and the panels slid aside to reveal a woman with her back to the crowd, her curves sheathed in a glittering black dress. She moved away from Michael, dipping her hand into the man's pocket to pull out a long rhinestone-studded string. She held it up to the light and then tossed it away with a shake of her head.

Michael smiled despite himself. Cute. As the singer turned to face his side of the audience, Michael's jaw dropped as he recognized her. She looked very different with her black hair piled high in curls and wearing elaborate stage makeup. But after his earlier flash, he would have recognized her no matter what disguise she wore. It was his mystery lady.

Chapter Eleven

Oblivious to Michael's shocked realization, the singer continued with *Diamonds Are A Girl's Best Friend*, making the rounds of the men and pulling sparkling ornaments out of their pockets and decorating herself as she moved around stage. Two other women joined the performance, but he kept his attention focused on her. She'd been sexy at the club and the police station but now kicked it up to a new level of indulgent sexuality. Discomfort nagged at him, as if he were trespassing on something private that had accidentally been put on display.

The number came to a close, with all the women glittering in their jewels and the male props banished from the stage. "Ladies and gentlemen," an unseen MC announced, "the Blue Curtain Theatre and Club is proud to present our lovely Jewels of the Night, beginning with the lovely and fiery Ruby!" The strawberry-blond dancer dressed in brilliant crimson sashayed forward, lifting her skirts just enough to reveal high heels covered in shimmering red sequins.

"Our beautiful and exotic Opal!" The statuesque woman with chocolate skin shimmied up, her white dress glittering with an iridescent rainbow of colors.

Michael stayed focused on the third woman, held by both his compulsion and sheer disbelief.

"And of course, the star of our show, the incomparable and always-sexy Onyx!"

The black-haired singer stepped forward, lazy bedroom eyes sweeping the audience as she undulated her spine in her clinging cocktail dress. "Diamonds are good, but sometimes a woman has to be her own best friend," Onyx said. "But this isn't what you came here to see. You came here and plunked down your hard-earned money to see dancing and singing by beautiful women."

The audience clapped and hooted with approval. Uncomfortably, Michael began to wonder if he'd misjudged the entire thing. But why would he have been compelled to come here if not to rescue his mystery woman?

Onyx pressed an open-mouthed kiss onto Opal's scarlet lips and the audience broke out in enthusiastic hollering. Michael looked away. It was more than just discomfort at the voyeuristic display—he could sense an aura of danger around her. Masked by the sensuality, it changed a commonplace act of titilation into something darker, like a cobra swaying to hypnotize a mouse.

"Every lady here is a precious gem, ladies and gentlemen." Onyx's arms spread wide to encompass her fellow dancers. "Every one a stone cut into a beautiful, glittering work of art and illusion. But maybe it's time to strip away the illusion. What do you think?"

Her darkened lips curved in a delighted smile as the crowd shouted. Reaching out, she yanked down the zipper keeping Ruby's dress closed. The strawberry blonde's eyes and bright-red lips went round and she clutched the loose fabric against her. Michael quashed his automatic instinct to intervene. It all had to be part of the show.

Onyx flicked a finger underneath the material as if peeping underneath while Ruby winked approvingly at the audience. "Tonight, you'll look beneath the fantasy." Onyx sauntered over to Opal, slowly unzipping the other dancer's costume. She paused to listen to the audience's encouraging applause before shaking her head, zipping it back up.

The audience erupted in wolf whistles and shouts, and Onyx smiled at them, stripping down the zipper fast enough that Michael would have bet money it would rip. But it had clearly been designed for this kind of hard usage. Her eyes swept the crowd, meeting his for the briefest moment. He sucked in a breath, the air resonating in his chest as if he'd inhaled a chiming bell.

It vanished when the performer's mask was firmly in place once more. "A little fantasy can be a good thing. Because fantasy is just another word for imagination." She sauntered to the back of the stage, glancing over her shoulder at the rapt crowd. Slowly, she began to pull down the zipper of her own dress. "And we can all use more imagination."

Michael couldn't help his body's reaction to the thought of getting a glimpse of what lay beneath the sequined fabric. But he wished he wasn't

65

sharing it with sixty other people. Erotic arousal began to overwhelm the earlier amusement of the crowd.

The drums and lights flared as all three dancers dropped their costumes simultaneously, revealing multi-colored corsets and knee-length fringe. Dancing and rolling to the music, the stage was a frenzy of decadent sexuality. The sense of release from the audience threatened to overwhelm him, but Michael's gaze remained firmly fixed on Onyx. She smiled as she slowly undid the fastenings on her corset then held it closed, winking at the crowd as she flashed one side then the other. She teased them all as if each person were a private lover. *Who is she and why am I here?* The curiosity would drive him crazy if he didn't get answers soon.

Eventually the three dancers were draped in provocative poses, sparkling pasties and G-strings catching the stage lights. The floors shook with stamping feet and the music couldn't be heard over applause and shouting.

Onyx lifted her hands and the audience quieted as if puppets on her strings. "We are a dream come true and like all the best dreams, when the night is over… we're gone."

The stage lights snapped off, leaving the club in absolute darkness. As the house lights slowly brightened, the panels were closed, and a young woman in a bikini twirling hula-hoops on her arms occupied the stage.

Michael took a long swallow from his beer to moisten his dry mouth. *That was what I was supposed to see.* He was grateful it was over but still disappointed at the separation. The feeling of compulsion eased considerably. He still felt pressure to remain but nowhere near what it had been before. Yet he was no closer to knowing what he could possibly do with this newfound information. And more importantly, how long was it going to take before he could turn his attention back to Bernie?

"Good show, Dani," Becca congratulated her, stripping out of her signature "Ruby" jewelry. The backstage area bustled and glittered as performers hurried to get ready for the next act in the cramped and

66

crowded cubicles.

"Thanks." Dani smiled, enjoying her hard-won respite. "Ready for the next round?"

"I hope they have the sound system synched this time. Last night I didn't know whether to shimmy or booty-shake."

The women laughed, hastily swapping out costumes for the next performance, due to start in twenty minutes. All except Tanisha, who played Opal. Frowning, Dani stepped over to where her fellow dancer peered out from the wings. "What's up?"

"He's here again," Tanisha whispered.

"Redneck Whiskey Boy?" He'd shown up every night for the last week with his horrible clothes straining over his paunch and a dark mullet peeking from under a stained baseball cap. Glancing out, Dani spotted him in his usual spot, front and center at the long stage catwalk.

"He was waiting in the parking lot last night. I asked Raoul to smuggle me into a cab out front and drive my car home later." Despite her efforts to hide it, the fear in Tanisha's voice came through loud and clear.

Dani's fingers tightened around the curtain, wishing she could simply pummel the ass and drive him out the door. But with Chomp's bruises fresh in her mind, she suggested a less confrontational approach. "Switch spots with Ruby for the next number. It'll keep you away from his side of the stage," Dani suggested. "There is no way he's native. Eventually the convention will leave or his business will be over and he'll be gone. We only have to wait him out."

"Thanks." Tanisha didn't sound enthusiastic.

"We stick together. Go get ready." As the other woman walked away, Dani lingered in the wings. Redneck Whiskey was loud, obnoxious, and way too free with his hands. Clearly, the idiot believed this was just another strip club. *How did I miss him when I was out there?* Even as the thought echoed, she knew the answer.

The guy in the back, third table, stage left, the one wearing the leather gloves indoors. Audience members tended to blur together after a while, but something about this one caught her eye. Sandy-brown hair framed a face that could have been carved out of marble by one of the old art masters: cheekbones to make any woman sit up and take notice,

67

expressive and mobile lips begged to be explored. She didn't usually like long hair on men, but on this one, it seemed to fit. And his eyes—every time she'd looked, he'd been watching her with a strange expression. None of the mindless lust and smug entitlement most men brought to the club. Instead, his eyes were kind and somehow both innocent and knowing, as if he knew everything about the griminess of the world, but didn't let it touch him.

Dani's fingers curled against the worn velvet curtains as she stared at him. She'd never seen such a beautiful man who was so completely lacking in arrogance or even awareness of his own good looks.

"Earth to Onyx. Showtime. Remember?" Ruby called.

The stage beckoned. And after, she'd see what to do about the sexy professor.

Chapter Twelve

It was almost one in the morning before "Jewels of the Night" surrendered the stage after four different performances. Michael spent most of the evening trying to understand why he was there and figure out his next move. He tested the compulsion, easing toward the exit or the backstage entrance. Each time, a physical tug pulled him back toward his seat. Whatever was guiding him wanted him to wait. The same sensation had dictated his actions when he'd first approached Joe, keeping him at the station until the shift changed to make sure he spoke to the right person.

Onyx was clearly the right person this time, but the more he'd watched, the less he was convinced this was another rescue. Maybe she could help him with Bernie and Expanding Horizons. He couldn't see how, but that didn't mean it was impossible. He fiddled with his beer, still his first. With Joe, he'd initially pretended to be a witness reporting a crime, but he couldn't think of a plausible excuse to talk to her. The dancers probably tried to avoid interacting with the audience outside performances. There would be security set up specifically to deter overeager patrons. He'd like to avoid sounding like some kind of psychotic stalker, so maybe he could follow her and meet her in a neutral location. *Because following her is somehow less stalker-ish?* Nothing presented itself, and the compulsion began to feel as if it was trying to physically drag him across the club's floor.

A young woman circling through the crowd at the bar caught his attention, dressed in jeans and a T-shirt, her dark hair pulled loosely back into a ponytail. Without the elaborate makeup and costume, the patrons didn't seem to connect her with her stage persona, but Michael recognized her instantly. Marveling at the audience's blindness, he took another long swallow of beer to gain time to think. She would be used to men approaching her and probably knew a wide variety of dismissals. He needed a plan.

As she settled at the bar, her dark smoky eyes met his. She held his gaze, making it quite clear that she wasn't simply surveying the room. A smile quirked her full lips and she nodded her head to the empty seat beside her in an unmistakable invitation.

His feet were moving before his brain caught up to the situation. *So much for having a plan first.* He eased himself carefully through the crowd, avoiding physical contact as much as possible before finally dropping into the seat beside her. "That was some fairly impressive dancing up there," he began. If he could manage to keep up a casual conversation, maybe inspiration would strike. Now that he was close, he could sense her lazy sensuality and curiosity. He opened his mind further and caught faint washes of sadness and worry. She wasn't as carefree as she'd like to appear.

She flipped her inky hair back over her shoulder as she looked him up and down. "You would know—you sat through each show. See something you like?"

His mouth went dry again as she smiled an invitation. "Actually, I hoped to speak with you."

"About what?" She turned her seat around and leaned back on the stool, resting her elbows on the bar behind her so her breasts thrust forward. He couldn't resist a quick glance but kept his attention on her face. Any sense of compulsion vanished: this was the moment he'd been sent here for. He had no reason for his certainty, but this woman would lead him to a way to help Bernie. He only had to convince her that he wasn't crazy and that she needed to help him, all without betraying his secret. *How hard could it be?*

"Professor?" she prompted, and he felt the first stings of irritation from her.

"To start, I wanted to return this." He dug into his pocket and handed her the tube of lipstick she'd dropped at the police station. He winced inwardly—this was not moving away from psychotic-stalker territory.

She accepted the tube. "Hell of an excuse, Professor. Is that all you wanted?"

"To be honest, I'm not sure why, but I felt like I needed to meet you, speak with you." His mouth clearly had not gotten the memo about waiting until his brain came up with something reasonable. *Ding, ding.*

Sitting through the whole show, returning the lipstick, lame excuse to talk. I have officially hit the psychotic-stalker trifecta. She's probably preparing to call security right now.

To his surprise, she only laughed. "You want to talk? Don't waste any more time then. Let's get out of here."

Michael blinked, and his lips parted as his jaw dropped. This was both easier and faster than he'd expected.

"Onyx…" the bartender rumbled.

"Relax, Raoul. I'm in my civvies. The fraternizing rules don't apply." She picked up her purse. "You coming, Professor?"

Like a little puppy dog. Well, more like a gorgeous six-foot-two puppy dog. Dani was still riding high from the performance and thrilled by her accurate instincts. He was nervous, but in an endearing, eager-to-please kind of way. Not a threat. The Huntress within stirred, sensing the raw attraction, but Dani easily sealed it back up where it coiled into sated sleep. Outside the back, they stepped into the alley behind the club. The garbage bins stank slightly of old alcohol, but otherwise it was relatively clean… and private.

A faint worry crossed her mind, threatening to spoil her fun: could the Huntress be starting to lure men from a distance? And so soon after a successful Hunt? She couldn't remember dropping the lipstick, but he'd sat through an entire show to give it back to her—not even Canadians were that nice. He could be a plant from whatever group kidnapped Vincent and Eric. The phone call should have disappeared from any call record, thanks to the elite anti-tracking software installed on it. But that didn't mean there weren't other ways to track her down. Just because he was innocent didn't mean he wasn't being used.

She hoped he wasn't part of a trap—he was even more attractive up close. Underneath the baggy sweater and discount jeans was a ripcord body begging for proper display. He kept his eyes on her face rather than darting down to her breasts. And he smelled like apples, vanilla, and cedar smoke—enough to make a girl hungry for pie baked in a wood-burning stove.

"I'm not a professor," he said, stopping a few feet from the club's door.

"Oh?" Dani's smile widened. The temptation to tease him and break his serious expression was more than she intended to resist.

"You called me a professor. I'm not. I've never taught anywhere."

"Then why don't you tell me your name? Or should I make something up?" she drawled.

"Michael Brooks. I'm a childhood developmental therapist." He awkwardly hitched his man-bag back up onto his shoulder. She could see him clearly enough, but the alley would be dark enough to hide her from him. He made no move toward the brighter street, reigniting her suspicions.

"That's one I haven't heard before, Mike." Bankers, lawyers, business people, those she was used to.

"Michael," he corrected. "I'm guessing Onyx isn't your real name."

"As in the one on my birth certificate? Good guess." She took a deep breath, but still couldn't scent any deception from him.

"Are you going to make me ask?" He smiled, his sense of humor peeking out past his nerves. He smelled clean, his eagerness tickling the inside of her nose. From the way he wasn't intimidated by her usual off-putting tactics, he was determined, too.

Points to the Professor. "You can call me Dani."

"No last name?"

"Not like we're looking to register, Mike." She used the nickname to keep him off-balance, hoping to trick him into revealing what he was after. She kept her voice casual but her body tensed for action. "What made you come all the way out here?"

"Obvious I don't belong, huh?"

"You're different from the usual crowd here. They split into two camps: people who get it, and people who think we're just another strip club." She shrugged to hide the seething irritation the latter invoked. Burlesque was more than wiggling around to music and dropping clothes. It was a nuanced art form that demanded a certain respect from the audience.

"Didn't you ever wish you could do something else?" he asked.

"Like what?" She gave him the opening to proposition her. He liked her, she could smell the arousal he was doing his best to hide. If the

72

kidnapping hadn't happened, she would have guessed he was just shy. At another time in her life, it would have been pleasant to spend time with him, especially with the Huntress coiled into silence. She could have enjoyed the illusion of being an all-American girl for a little while. But now she couldn't take anything at face value. She wished she could allow herself the time to indulge in the fantasy.

The Professor was reading from a different playbook, however. "Like a waitress, or a teacher, or, I don't know, something respectable. Where you don't have to feel bad about yourself after."

"Excuse me? Who the fuck said I felt bad about myself?" Her spine stiffened like a bristling cat's tail.

"Don't you? I sensed—" He broke off with a sudden spike of alarm. Dani's suspicions deepened. He seemed honestly bewildered by his blunder, though. His naïveté might have softened the wrath of another woman.

"Listen, Professor." Her fingers curled into fists at her side. "If you're trying to save me, you can take your moral high horse and stuff it next to the stick up your ass. I like my life. I chose it, and I am damned good at it."

"I didn't mean to offend you." He held up his gloved hands. Dani glared at them. *Does he think this whole place is so filthy he needs to protect himself from contamination?*

"No, you assumed I was some poor, broken soul needing rescue. If that's what you want, there's a ten-dollar club down the street. I'm sure some runaway will be thrilled to be your project. I'm not a stripper. I am a burlesque performer. I create a performance that mixes dance, comedy, and sex. I work four nights a week and make more money than any three minimum-wage slaves put together. I am not a victim." She turned away, ghosts of old judgments rising up to point accusing fingers. Cursing herself, she reminded herself that she had her own rescue to do.

"I'm sorry." Heartfelt and sincere, not a hint of condemnation or disgust. "Can we start again? I'm Michael."

She managed a smile. His eager-to-help buzz should have made him seem younger, but instead only made him seem out of place, like a man from the Victorian Age, before the loss of innocence. "Dani. What brings you here, Mike?"

"I was looking for you. I'm not sure why. But I'd like to have the time to figure it out."

Flowers, jewelry, chocolate—none of them could have struck so quickly to the heart of what she wanted but could never have: someone who wanted to see past Onyx, see past all her barriers and find out what was underneath. She reached out and ran her fingers lightly along his chiseled cheekbones. "Honestly, Professor, I'd like that, too. But I don't think it's meant to be."

His hazel eyes widened, and he straightened. "Your brothers—that's why you were at the police station."

Dani grabbed Michael by the collar and yanked him deeper into the alley shadows, out of sight of the street. She kept her voice Southern-sweet. "And what would you know about my brothers?"

"They've been taken. It must be why I was led to you." He sounded excited, and there was no fear in his scent. He was oblivious to her not-so-subtle warning cues.

"Led to me?"

"You probably wouldn't believe me if I told you." He offered an apologetic smile.

Until she hoisted him into the air and growled. "Try me."

Michael's hands jerked up and grabbed at hers as his feet dangled several inches above the ground. Now his fear swelled to cover everything else as she held him effortlessly. This time, she wasn't letting her prey get away.

"*Lalassu*," he managed to blurt out past her grip.

Her fingers loosened from the shock, allowing him a bit more oxygen. That was a word no one spoke, the secret word that identified a fellow member of the loose underground society of gifted individuals—and the Professor was definitely not one of them.

"Where did you hear that word?" Her eyes ached as they burned, blazing with the red rings of the Huntress. Those flaming circles had been the last vision of many would-be attackers over the years.

"You told me," he whispered.

It wasn't a lie. No stench of dishonesty. Not even fear. His face darkened and Dani released her grip, letting him drop to the cracked pavement. He came down surprisingly gracefully, bending at the knees

74

before regaining his posture.

"I've never seen you before," she hissed, fingers flexing. "Tell me where you heard that word and what you know about Vincent and Eric."

"Please, let me explain!" Michael held up his hands in a plea for more time. "I... I never suspected that there were more people like me. I've kept it secret since I was a kid. When I touch people or things, sometimes I learn things. All I know is what you know." He looked at her, open-eyed wonder creeping past his fear. "You lifted me like I was nothing. You're amazingly strong."

"And I have a charming personality but no patience for bullshit." She forced the Huntress back down, and the stinging faded from her eyes. She couldn't afford to be high on aggression right now.

"It's more than a gym workout. It's what that word means. You're strong and fast. When you touched me, the world got sharper, clearer, because that's how you see it." A delighted grin stretched his face. "Superpowers. You have actual superpowers."

"This isn't Comic-Con. I'm not going to give you an autograph." She spat out the words, at the edge of her control.

He nodded as though he'd expected her answer. "There are more of you, aren't there? For a second, I got a sense of a community. I never knew there were more people out there like me. My parents taught me I needed to hide who I was and what I could do, and that no one would understand." He frowned, and his gaze turned inward.

This is not my night for intimidation. His pain called to her, but she needed to focus on the big picture. "Vincent and Eric. What do you know?"

"I think there's a connection between the people who took them and the people who run a facility one of my clients might be sent to. When I touched the brochure, I knew they were going to hurt her. She knew it, too, somehow."

"People, things—this gift of yours must wreak havoc on your social life." Dani crossed her arms on her chest, taking refuge in sarcasm.

"It can make it difficult. But this must have been fate, our coming together like this. We can help each other."

"I don't do partners." She walked away, heels clicking on the pavement.

"Please! You don't understand! All my life I've been told to keep myself hidden and stay out of sight. To find someone else like me, you don't know what it's like," he pleaded.

Find the invisible man who sees the hidden truths. Find him, Dani. Gwen's words echoed, freezing her in place. He had psychometry; he saw hidden truths. He'd been told to keep hidden, invisible.

"Please," Michael continued. "Bernie is only ten. You're the only chance I have to save her."

Dani closed her eyes as if the lids could shut out his words.

"No one believes her. She's emotionally disturbed, unreliable. They're going to hurt her badly." He moved closer to her. "Please, Dani."

"I'll meet you at one tomorrow." The words spilled out before she could censor them. *Why not?* It wasn't going to kill her to listen to him after she took care of her own business.

"Thank you. Here's where I'll be." He scribbled out an address on a piece of paper. *Of course he's fucking prepared.*

Ignoring his soft smile of gratitude, she snatched the paper and stalked off into the night. The Huntress was roused and ready for action. All she needed was a target.

Chapter Thirteen

"I hate traveling. The jet felt like a roller coaster. I pay their ridiculous salaries to make sure I don't have to bounce across the Atlantic. Make sure it doesn't happen on the way back," André instructed Karan as he barreled down the hallway at their test facility.

The other man simply bent his head and made notes on his tablet.

"Did they give you a progress report from the lab?" Anticipation fueled André's steps. So very close to everything he'd hoped for, everything his father had believed.

"There have been some problems with the computer resources required—"

"I don't care. What are the results?" André stabbed at the elevator button, ignoring the scurrying office workers.

"The DNA has been sequenced. The relevant sections have been isolated. They have a collection of volunteers waiting for your approval." The two men rode the gleaming elevator down to the subbasement laboratory.

"Is the carrier bacteria ready for the genetic transfer?" He tugged briefly on his jacket cuffs and adjusted his shirt's cufflinks.

"Already in replication. We're only waiting for you to select the first volunteer."

"Then we shouldn't waste any more time." The doors opened and André strode into the lab. The technicians were all standing beside the state-of-the-art equipment, barely distinguishable from the white walls in their immaculate white lab coats, anonymous, professional, and clean, exactly how he'd specified they should be.

Two men waited in the center of the lab. Both showed signs of having lived on the streets. Despite a thorough washing, traces of dirt clung under their nails. They kept shifting and tugging on uncomfortably new clothing. André spotted irregular tan and weathering lines on their upper arms, wrists, and necks, evidence of long-term outdoor life. Their sallow skin sagged off their bones. He kept his face impassive but couldn't keep his mouth and nose from twitching in disgust at the dark lines of track marks on their inner elbows. A few days of being fed and cleaned couldn't erase months of abuse.

But there was potential. He noted the muscular arms and shoulders that poor food and drugs hadn't completely stolen away. The first, a tall blond man with a wiry build, snapped to attention when he entered the room. An involuntary reflex, evidence the soldier had not been completely replaced by the addict, unlike the other, who was muttering under his breath and slapping at his clothes periodically.

"Blood reports?" He held out his hand and Karan gave him the relevant folder. He'd studied the histories of both of his potential volunteers but he'd found keeping his prodigious memory a secret gave him the advantage. He glanced at the brief biographies and lines of medical jargon in each file. Ronald McBride, the soldier. Henry Rogers, the twitchy one. "All clean now, I see."

"Sir, may I speak freely?" It was the soldier who'd caught his eye earlier, McBride, a veteran of Afghanistan.

"Go ahead, Corporal." André handed the files back to Karan. This one could be trouble. From his file, McBride had a disturbingly high inclination toward public service, but four years of living on the street and drug addiction may have overcome that tendency.

"Your people have taken good care of us. It's the first time I've been clean in years." McBride rubbed at his elbows, thumbs shoving against the track marks as if he could push the thin scars inside and make them disappear. "It's given me room to think clearly."

"And what have you been thinking?" Dalhard moved closer to the corporal. Other than the scabs and bruises on his arms, the man couldn't have been a more perfect image of an all-American hero if he'd been ordered from a catalogue, his corn-fed, Midwestern–farm boy innocence wrapped up in earnestness. He would play nicely in the promotional material.

"Out there, I didn't much care if I lived or died. Figured I'd already outlived my time, that I should have died with my friends." He looked away briefly, visibly struggling with the memory. "But now I'm not so sure."

"And you'd like to withdraw from the trials." André had no

intention of letting him do so, but he wanted to see how deep McBride's reluctance went.

"The money is good but not worth risking my life for, sir." McBride offered his frankness with perfect innocence.

"Money never is." Power, influence, those were worth gambling for—although he was certain they wouldn't appear on McBride's list.

"Thank you for all your help. I'll find a way to pay you back." The corporal held out his hand, which was exactly the opportunity André had been waiting for.

Taking it, André held it firmly for a moment, concentrating. He needed the soldier's facilities intact. Too much pressure might snap the man's mind. He used a subtle touch to keep McBride's mind open to the possibilities. *Community-minded, that's the best approach.* "But what if there were more than money?"

"Beg pardon?" McBride's eyelids drooped: an excellent sign.

"I read the report on the incident. Your friends were killed when a bomb detonated in the compound you were searching. But they weren't killed by the blast. They went in to rescue men trapped in the debris and were killed by snipers." André held McBride's gaze, not even blinking. He had to establish trust and do it quickly.

The veteran swallowed hard. "That's true, sir."

"You attacked two of the gunmen with your bare hands because your gun had been knocked out of reach. You received a commendation of valor." Sensing the corporal's conviction wavering, André continued. "But what if you'd been stronger, faster? Able to leap across the compound and take them all out in the blink of an eye?"

"That doesn't happen except in movies."

"Oh, but it can." André tightened his grip on McBride's hand, strengthening the other man's hope and suppressing his doubts. "I've seen it."

"You're testing something that makes people stronger? Like the Bionic Man?"

"Only without the special effects. Come on, Corporal. Don't you owe it to your friends to try?" André recognized the perfect moment to strike for the kill.

The corporal's eyes glazed and he nodded hesitantly. André released

79

him. His persuasive influence would keep McBride in the program now. *Thank you, Mother.*

"Devil!" The scream echoed off the gleaming white walls.

André barely had time to frown in irritation when Rogers leapt at him, waving a pipette he'd snatched from the trays. André caught his assailant's hand as the man jabbed at him unsteadily with the plastic tool, still twitching uncontrollably. This was beyond what his gifts could handle. He could persuade and if he caught his victim in a moment of vulnerability, he could layer his influence to ensure complete loyalty, but there was nothing left in the man's mind to work with.

If he hadn't had more pressing matters to deal with, André would have enjoyed pitting himself against the man physically. He'd boxed in college but had given it up when he took over the business. Rogers might be scrawny, but his desperation gave him strength. Perhaps he'd sensed what André was doing with McBride.

"Have to kill you! Demon!" the man gasped.

McBride leapt to the rescue, locking his arms around the assailant's neck and arms to drag him away. A terrified scientist jabbed the struggling man with a needle and he soon collapsed into drugged silence.

"My thanks, Corporal. Clearly, that one is too far gone for the trials." André caught Karan's attention and gave him a brief nod as his assailant was dragged away. Karan frowned in puzzlement but nodded in return. André didn't believe in wasting opportunities.

The technicians led McBride away to prepare him for the testing, leaving André and his aide to take the elevator out of the sterile environment. "Make certain Rogers is kept somewhere safe for the time being."

"He attacked you," Karan pointed out.

André smiled patronizingly. "He would be perfect for the Silver protocols."

"Do you think those will be necessary?" Karan asked.

"Loyalty tests are always useful." André's smile faded. He hated having to explain himself. "How did he make it through the tests to begin with?"

"His record was encouraging. Assault, reprimands for excessive force, firing without cause." Karan shrugged.

"McBride should be perfect, assuming he survives the process. Now what about the brothers?"

As they arrived at his opulent penthouse suite, he caught the tiniest hint of a disapproving frown from his aide. Karan evidently still preferred the riskier and more expensive route of genetic manipulation to dealing with actual ferals.

"They've been kept in isolation since their recapture?" He went directly to the bar and poured himself a neat whiskey. André knew his people wouldn't dare disobey his orders, but prudence demanded that he check.

Karan nodded. "They should be ready for you by tomorrow."

"I'm quite optimistic about our chances." Settling into a massive chair, André wondered how much it would take to crack his aide's façade.

"They've shown stubborn loyalty." There it was: the reason he kept Karan untainted by his persuasive influence—he needed someone willing to point out his blind spots.

Of course, that didn't mean André was wrong. "Loyalty to each other. But look at the larger picture. They presented themselves under false documents, clearly having no idea of what I was truly looking for. These men are used to operating outside society's confines. They survive on the outskirts, which requires a certain disregard for the rules. But there's even more to be excited about—if they have a female relative, there could be ova to harvest. Purpose-bred subjects without the dangers of gene-splicing." Savoring the subtle smoky flavor of his drink, André envisioned the promised future where he was in control.

"And if we cannot acquire their loyalty?"

Karan had to ask; ignoring the possibility would only lead to disaster. But Karan's lack of faith annoyed André. He wasn't in the mood to contemplate failure. "Then I will persuade them. It doesn't matter. We have multiple options to pursue now. We'll do what all good businessmen have done since the first market exchanges: explore our options, nurture the possibilities, and then, when we see where success is possible, commit to our winner."

"And the losers?"

"No sense wasting further resources on dead ends. But we will find our winner, Karan. I'm certain of it. Track down their family, friends, and associates." Two supernatural brothers must be connected with others. This could be the opportunity he'd been waiting for.

Karan discretely withdrew, leaving André to enjoy the initial thrill of the chase in solitude. These were the moments he lived for, when he was on the cusp of discovery. It satisfied his internal primal predator. If his suspicions were correct, then Perdition offered more than he could have dreamed.

Gwen curled up against the stone floor, hands pressed to her ears. Useless, futile, and pointless, but she couldn't help it. The voices chattered as loudly as ever, battling each other for her attention.

"—storm is coming—"

"—blood will betray you—"

"—so cold and dark, want my Mommy—"

"—have to listen—"

"—only one can save us—"

Tears leaked out as she fought to concentrate on the chill of the floor, the roughness against her skin. That was real. Not like the other world calling to her.

"—please save her—"

"—save us all—"

FRIDAY

Chapter Fourteen

"Michael?" As soon as Martha opened the door, her despair hit Michael like a physical blow. Her red and swollen eyes and scratchy voice told of a long night of crying.

"What's wrong, Martha?" he asked gently, shoring up his barriers to keep her emotions from battering him. *Had there been another episode?* He couldn't hear anything from Bernie.

"I should have called to cancel the session but…" Fresh tears and exhaustion welled up in Martha's eyes. "I made a horrible mistake. They took her."

"Who? Expanding Horizons? So quickly?" Michael's heart sank. He'd known about the meeting yesterday afternoon but hadn't expected things to move so quickly. It took time to prepare to transfer a patient between legitimate therapists and facilities—time he'd counted on. He and Dani were meeting after his lunch shift today. He'd been so sure he would be able to do anything with a genuine superhero at his side.

"I was so tired and worn out, and then the man from the center came," Martha sobbed. "He told me everything would be okay and they'd help Bernie and I trusted him. It suddenly seemed like the only option. I signed the papers."

"And they took her right away?" Michael couldn't believe what he was hearing. It had to be a mistake. He must have misunderstood.

"They said a clean break was best, and that I was having too much trouble with her. They took her with them, and she was screaming… oh God, I can still hear her in my head. I'm so sorry, baby." Martha broke down, sagging onto her knees with her fists tucked tightly against her belly.

Michael stepped inside and closed the door to give Martha her privacy. He wanted to comfort her and give her a shoulder to cry on, but he didn't dare touch her. Even from a distance, her emotions threatened to bring him to his knees. "What happened next?"

"That night, I knew I'd made a horrible mistake. I called them and said I'd changed my mind. They said I couldn't, that I'd signed away my legal rights," Martha choked out. "I threatened to call the police, and then there was a lawyer at the door with all these papers showing that it wasn't safe for Bernie here. They said they had evidence of abuse and neglect."

"But that can't be true," Michael blurted, horrified. Martha was the most loving parent he'd ever known. She was devoted to her daughter.

"He had police reports and warnings from social services. I've never seen any of them, but he showed them to a judge and got an injunction or something to put Bernie in their care. I'm not even allowed to call her. What can I do?" She looked at him with terrible hope dawning in her eyes.

Her hope made Michael want to curse himself as a fraud. He'd known, but he'd wanted to protect his secret and so he hadn't told her. He'd gambled on having more time, but Bernie was the one who lost. She was trapped with them.

He kept his voice calm and authoritative. Martha needed the security and comfort of someone to lean on, and he had no intention of letting her or her daughter fall. "Martha, they can't do this. It's not legal. You need to call the police. Ask to speak to Detective Joe Cabrera. He's a friend of mine. He'll help you, I promise."

"I don't even know if she's okay." The quiet desperation in her plea broke his heart.

"Listen to me. Detective Joe Cabrera. Talk to him. I'm going to go to Expanding Horizons right now. Maybe they'll let me see her."

"Tell her I miss her and that I'm sorry. I'll do whatever it takes to get her back."

"I know, and she knows it, too. We'll both do whatever it takes." Cold determination gripped his spine, tightening his jaw and shoulders. It couldn't be a coincidence that his flashes had led him to Dani. Her brothers had been taken and now Bernie, too. There must be a connection between both abductions, and he knew where to start looking.

The address on the brochure wasn't far—twenty minutes outside the Perdition limits, between Perdition and New York. But he'd need an excuse to visit.

A quick stop at the local drug store and he bought what he needed: a tiny plush bear. He ripped off the tags and hastily used some dust from the parking lot to dull the newness of the fur. A simple explanation, close to the truth: he was Bernie's therapist, and he wanted her to have her favorite therapy reward—plausible and unlikely to be checked on.

Expanding Horizons gleamed in aristocratic isolation on a broad and carefully manicured lawn. The grounds were precisely dotted with trees and flowerbeds, all according to a prestigious landscaper's vision. It intimidated visitors, like a sour and domineering old lady draped in lace.

Save the girl. It was always so simple in comic books. A costume, courage, and some witty dialogue always opened doors. *Maybe I should have worn a cape.* Michael doubted it would have helped. The center's money showed in subtle touches: tall windows showcasing the grounds, crystal vases of flowers on the low tables, and solid wood furnishings instead of cheap pressboard, all designed to reassure and impress.

Every inch of it was a lie. Whatever they wanted from children like Bernie, it wasn't to make them better. As he tried to persuade the receptionist to let him past the lobby, the coldness and detachment of the place seeped through his skin so strongly that he couldn't believe other people wouldn't notice it.

"I'm sorry, who are you again?" The receptionist asked, her clothes carefully tailored and her black hair trimmed in a precise bob. Her expression clearly said she had more important work to get to.

"My name is Michael Brooks. I've been working with Bernadette as her behavioral therapist since she was five. We've made a lot of strides in her ability to distinguish between her hallucinations and reality." He gave her his most charming smile, hoping it would work.

"I'm sure we have all your reports—" she began, trying to dismiss him.

"Actually, because of how quickly Bernadette transferred, I didn't get a chance to complete my end-of-treatment report. I hoped to speak to the doctors here to explain our process." He tried to appear innocent and eager as he held up the tiny bear. "And I wanted to give her this."

He sensed a slight softening of the receptionist's icy attitude, but the battle wasn't over. "She's with our doctors right now. I can't disturb a therapy session."

So much for his vague plan of smuggling Bernie out or at least passing on her mother's message. But if he could get inside, maybe he could find another way. "It was her favorite. Could I leave it in her room, maybe with a note?" *Come on. Be a human being.*

She bit her lip, uncertain. Maybe his mental urging tipped the scales, but he could sense the decision coming as her inner conflict settled. "I'm not supposed to... but I don't see how leaving a note could hurt. I'll have to escort you, though."

He agreed without further negotiation and took a moment to scribble a quick note on a sheet of paper. He wished he could tell her that he was going to rescue her, but with no idea of who else would see it, he had to keep it vague. *Hang in there, Bernie. EIEIO —Michael.*

Using a keycard, the receptionist unlocked the doors to the main facility. The reassuring touches of home vanished on the far side. The hallways were stark white, gleaming with a plastic sheen. Large whiteboards with chart information hung beside each door. No art sullied the purity of the walls. No toys littered the floor. No laughter.

No sound of any kind, in fact. Michael's fingers tightened around the bear. Everything outside was muffled, as if it had vanished, trapping everyone inside. He gulped for breath before forcing himself to present a calm façade. This was his only chance to gather information directly from the source.

"This is Bernadette's room." The receptionist indicated the dull gray door to her right. Michael's grateful smile to her was not returned. Instead she glared angrily, clearly regretting her brief lapse of resolve.

Pushing open the door, he tried not to show his dismay. It looked like a prison cell: a narrow cot in one corner with a thin mattress and dull gray blanket and pillow, a toilet and sink barely obscured behind a privacy curtain. Bernadette's favorite doll, Molly, perched on the bed, her bright blue yarn hair and red grin a stark contrast to the muted colors around her.

Lowering his defenses, Michael put the bear beside Molly, letting his fingers brush against the blanket. Immediately an image of Bernie flashed into his mind, knees drawn up and rocking back and forth, eyes wide with terror. Blurry-faced men in white coats were speaking near her. He tried to listen, but the words blurred together. One approached her with a syringe filled with pink fluid. It burned as it went into her arm.

Blinking to clear his head, he composed his features into a pleasant mask. "Thanks." He tried to smile, but his cheeks were weighed down by what he'd found. It was one thing to suspect they were torturing the children in their care. It was another to feel it being done to a child he knew and cared for.

"I'll walk you out." It was not an offer.

Before leaving, he let his fingers trail along the markers lying in the whiteboard tray. He got a sense of excitement and triumph but no images. But it was enough: whatever they thought they might get out of Bernie, they wanted it badly. And they believed they were going to get it. *Hold on Bernie. I'll get you out. I promise.*

Chapter Fifteen

Grumbling at the morning sun poking above the horizon, Dani knocked on a nondescript door in an industrially decorated apartment building. There was absolutely nothing to distinguish it from any other apartment in the city. Only a few *lalassu* knew about it, although they had all heard about the legend who lived there, a man whose talents were whispered around the world.

Inside her bag was sheaf of paper, lightly speckled with blood. Chomp had not been entirely forthcoming when she'd cornered him in his apartment—a situation that suited her mood just fine. The papers held the original ad asking for military veterans, as well as the false service records that Chomp had created for her brothers. She'd gotten the information she needed, and he would be sitting on an extra-soft cushion for a few days, preferably while he thought hard about concepts like respect and keeping his damn observations about her body to himself.

The door opened, revealing a giant of a man with a shaved head decorated with tribal tattoos. "Dani. Come in."

"Vapor," she said, nodding in greeting. He wasn't someone to surprise in a dark alley. Tall, powerfully built with multiple piercings in his lips, nose, and ears, he practically screamed "thug-for-hire." Yet Dani had never seen him hurt or even threaten anyone. His passion was his machines. He'd worked with her family for over four decades but still appeared to be in his twenties. She didn't know how old he actually was, but perpetual youth wasn't his only gift. He found patterns in data and remembered everything he saw, heard, or read. He smelled of dry sand and desiccated wood.

Once the door closed, Vapor got down to business. "You need more of the bad ecstasy crap? The guy I hooked you up with had plenty."

"No, that's not it. We've got a problem." She explained about Vincent and Eric, Vapor's expression darkening as she talked. The Huntress coiled defensively in Dani's gut, rattling a warning.

"Why didn't you come to me right away? Why didn't they?" Vapor demanded, looming.

"They didn't want Mom and Dad to find out. And I thought I could handle it on my own." Dani braced herself for the inevitable lecture. She'd spent years listening to Vapor's exhortations to do the ritual and surrender to the Huntress. He didn't believe it was as bad as she claimed.

Instead, he held his hand out silently for the papers she'd gotten from Chomp. She handed them over with the scrap of fabric from the gas station. Without a word, he sat down at a massive bank of computer equipment and began to type, the clicking of the keys rattling like automatic gunfire.

Dani kept her breath shallow and quiet, knowing she wouldn't disturb him but not wanting to take the chance. The tiny apartment was neat as a pin despite the stereotype of hackers and hygiene being only nodding acquaintances. Of course, there wasn't much space for any kind of mess, as the room was stuffed with racks of computers blinking, whirring and putting out enough heat to make the radiator unnecessary during even the worst winters. Six monitors were bolted to the wall over Vapor's desk. Several were flashing various images from newsfeeds and security cameras; others displayed line after line of code.

He pulled out a heavy, illuminated magnifying glass and studied the cloth, muttering to himself. "Plasticized fabric, mass-produced in China. Stitching done by a corporate clothing manufacturer in Taiwan. Good."

"Good?" Dani asked, knowing how Vapor hated interruptions but unable to keep silent.

He ignored her, continuing to read off the preliminary information. "Right-Hand Man, the company from the ad your brothers answered, orders from them. On the surface, it looks like a real business—lots of different references on various sites for professional bodyguard services. An office here in Perdition, probably for tax purposes. Employees trained and sent to main branches in New York and Los Angeles. Small company, good reputation." He frowned. "And surprisingly effective computer security."

"Is it a problem?" Dani asked.

"Not *that* effective," Vapor said with a tight-lipped grin. His dry scent swelled, revealing satisfaction. "But not simple. It will take time. And it won't be cheap."

"I don't care about the money. Just get it done." She had plenty of cash reserves—part of being ready to run at a moment's notice.

Vapor stopped typing to raise an eyebrow at her.

"Please," she finished. For a guy who could star in his own mug book, he was surprisingly strict about manners.

He nodded. "Anything else?"

"Papers. For the whole family. In case we have to run. I need them fast." The words stank of defeat, but she'd been drilled too long and too early not to have contingency plans ready.

Vapor lifted a metal-studded eyebrow. "These people scare you?"

"They took Vincent and Eric down fast and without showing obvious signs of a struggle. Even with Vincent wounded, Eric should have been able to keep them off long enough for me to get there." Dani hated admitting it, but one didn't stretch the truth with Vapor. He could detect a lie as surely as if he could smell it.

"Good." Vapor nodded, his satisfaction even stronger. "These are dangerous people. You don't want to underestimate them. Come back this afternoon. I'll have the new papers ready."

She thanked him, not wanting to antagonize him, but he'd already turned back to his machines and was tapping away.

Dani left, knowing she was struggling against a ticking clock. *One task done.* Now for the more unpleasant one: telling her family what was going on. It would take more time than she could really afford, but this wasn't the sort of conversation it was safe to have over a phone.

She pointed her car out of the city and drove as fast as she dared. She despised feeling trapped. A seductive smile and great tits wouldn't get her out of a ticket if the cops caught her doing over a hundred on the freeway.

It took over an hour to make her way to the overgrown and pothole-studded lane that led to the entrance to her family home. It was disguised by carefully trimmed long-leaved bushes placed just wide enough to allow a car to pass through. She'd only lived here for a few years in high school but she kept returning, no matter how much she wished she could follow her brothers' example and stay away. Long practice let her make the turn without hesitation, emerging onto a smooth stretch of pavement twisting half a mile into the upstate countryside.

The small farmhouse had an irregular addition of mortared river stones squatting beside it. No windows broke the rough surface. Dani didn't let her eyes linger on it for long despite the fear and guilt tugging at her heart. Squaring her shoulders, she prepared to talk to her family.

If I'm quiet enough, maybe I can talk to Dad instead of Mom. She crept past the creaking boards left to warn of surprise intruders. Taking a deep breath to counteract her instinct to retreat, she eased open the side door into the bright, cheerful kitchen.

"It's a little early for you, Dani," her mother said, her fingers scanning through a braille magazine. Her long dark hair was bound in a wrist-thick braid, and she wore a comfortable peasant blouse and skirt in bright gypsy colors. Her telephone headset rested on the counter nearby, suggesting she was taking a break from her job at a 1-900 psychic hotline. The timer dinged. "Cookies are ready."

Dani hated the way her mother's cloudy eyes stared directly at her, even though she knew her mother could only make out vague shadows. The sight always brought back terrible memories of the night they never spoke about. Now Virginia Harris used her limited clairvoyant powers to navigate the world. She could only "see" about five feet away and a few minutes into the future, but it was enough to warn her to pop cookies in the oven for her prodigal daughter's visit.

Her mother reached out a hand toward Dani and frowned. "You're buzzing. When was the last time you had sex?"

Thus the litany of parental criticism begins. Dani hated it, but would rather listen to a list of her sins than begin to explain why she was here. She pulled open the ancient fridge to search for a drink. "Two nights ago. Don't worry, I'm feeding regularly."

"Did he have problems? I've told you about picking up drunks in bars—"

"It was fine. Rocked his world. Opened his eyes." Popping open a can of a soda, Dani cut off her mother's tirade.

"Fizzy sugar isn't good for you."

"Then why do you even have it in the house?"

"Your father likes it and I don't want to deprive him of all his little pleasures." Virginia shrugged, her opaque eyes narrowing. "What's wrong? There's something you're not telling me."

So much for family banter. Dani took a deep breath, wishing the moment could have been delayed a little longer, or that her mother's powers had the range necessary to pick up the kidnapping on her own. Maybe she could have gotten there in time, with a little more warning. "It's Vincent and Eric. They're in trouble."

"More than trashing a hotel room." *Again* lingered, even if unsaid. Virginia stared blankly at the wall, her milky eyes flickering back and forth. "They were taken."

"Whoever did it was organized. I'm looking into it." Dani turned away. She hated when her mother played up the mystical side of her gifts. *All theater for plucking pigeons.*

"But you went to Vapor and asked him for new identities anyway." Now that Dani was in the room, her mother could probe to see her immediate past and future. Dani wondered if the Professor would stand out in the visions.

"Yeah. I did."

"Have you thought of what this will do to your sister?" Agitation sharpened her mother's voice. "She's finally safe-"

"Trapped. Not safe," Dani growled. She hated how her mother implied she would unnecessarily put Gwen at risk. "I guess I was thinking more of what being a fucking lab rat would do to her."

"Language," her mother snapped automatically, as if Dani were still ten and needed discipline.

"That ship has fucking sailed, Mom."

"What's going on here?" Dani's father rolled his wheelchair into the kitchen as Dani's temper prepared to haul out the heavy verbal artillery. From her mother's expression, she was getting ready to do the same. Walter Harris studied his wife and daughter, his dark eyes snapping up every detail.

"Vincent and Eric have been taken. Whoever did it laid a trap and was prepared for their abilities. It means they were hunting *lalassu*," Dani told her father.

He considered that for a moment, his fingers tapping on the arm of his wheelchair. Despite having been confined to it for almost two decades, her father still conveyed an impression of strength with his barrel-like chest. At times like this, Dani half expected her father to get up and pace, his long legs devouring the ground the way they used to when she'd chased him as a child.

"You think they might come after Gwen. Or us." He reached out for Virginia's hand. "I can't protect us like I used to."

"We can ask for help. The other *lalassu* have to be warned anyway. You know the only way Gwen can leave is if she's tranquilized." Her mother turned her blank gaze to Dani. "This is the kind of threat that needs proper guidance in order to resolve it."

It always comes back to the ritual. How they'd been left without a divine conduit for almost twenty years. Her mother cared more about the stupid statue crumbling in her closet than her daughter. Dani stopped the tirade before it could begin, folding her arms over her chest. "Then step up with my blessing."

"That's not tradition—" her mother began.

"Then fuck tradition," Dani spat.

"Dani, enough." Walter raised his hand, silencing both women.

"Dani?" The plaintive call echoed from the other room.

The tension abruptly dissolved as priorities shifted, leaving Dani emotionally off-balance.

"Go see your sister. We'll talk more later," her father said.

Ignoring her mother's loaded expression, Dani pushed past the heavy wooden door into the candlelit stone room behind, careful to step over the thick ridge of glued salt outlining the threshold. Her sister was curled up in the corner, wrapped in a quilt, with her sketch pad against her knees. Immediately, Dani caught a faint coppery tang of dry blood. She'd hurt herself again, probably a scrape. *There had to be a better option.*

"Ravens fly and croak above the battlefield. Don't distinguish between the living and the dead," Gwen whispered, her charcoal skipping across the page. "People hear the croak and are afraid but the battle has already happened."

Dani ignored the ramblings, kneeling beside her. She spotted the scrapes on her sister's elbows and made a mental note to check them for infection. "Gwen, sweetie. Some bad things may be happening."

"Bad things always happen. Lots of bad things. Lots of good things, too. But bad things are more interesting so that's what they tell me."

Gwen's dark eyes were wide, tracing invisible lines while her hand worked independently.

"People are hunting us." She wondered how much Gwen would understand if Dani tried to explain it to her.

"I know. I knew a long time ago. Tried to tell, but you didn't listen. Thought I was crazy." A little bubble of laughter burst free from Gwen's cracked lips.

"You're not crazy," Dani snapped.

"I think I am. How could I not be? It's never quiet. They never stop talking. Not once. Not for a single second. I could be okay if I could just have a few minutes to think. Just a few minutes." Her bony fingers plucked at her ears.

"Easy, Gwen." Dani captured her sister's hands in her own.

"Be careful, Dani." Gwen rolled her head back around to look at her sister. "You bump in the night but this darkness can swallow you whole—keep you tucked in its belly like a baby. Need someone to keep you safe."

"Hey, I keep everyone safe. Remember? Me against the darkness. All by myself." Dani said the words with breezy confidence, but knowing Vincent and Eric were in danger kept them from feeling true.

"But this time you can't. It'll take you, swallow you and spit you back out as part of itself. And the darkness will swallow the earth." Gwen traced the lines of her drawing. "You need him. He has the light."

Dani looked down and saw Michael's face staring back up at her. He was smiling, his long hair raked back from his temples. She couldn't help brushing her fingers along the edge of the drawing. Only a little while until she met him again and had to face the mess of conflicting emotions churning in her heart. "What do you know about him?"

"Me? Absolutely nothing. Except that you need him. Otherwise the darkness swallows everything." Gwen tore the page out of her book and thrust it at her.

"He's cute, a real-life white knight. Wants me to save the girl, be a hero." Dani rolled her eyes. "As if that ever works out."

"Put it all in little frames with little words. Keep it safe on the page. You have to believe me, Dani. I could be clearer, but then I wouldn't be able to see."

"I know." Tender concern for her sister's feelings swallowed her irritation. Everyone wanted her to be something she couldn't be. Her parents wanted a priestess; Michael wanted a hero. All she wanted was a chance to be herself. *Is that too much to ask?*

Gwen's outburst had exhausted her. She curled up, the charcoal and pad thudding softly on the floor. Dani tucked her into bed and blew out the majority of the candles. Picking up the torn page, she smoothed the rough edges with her fingers. *You need him,* Gwen had insisted. The Huntress coiled at the base of her spine, tongue flickering with hunger. Its evident interest in Michael left Dani chilled. Maybe she needed him. But would he survive long enough to regret meeting her?

Chapter Sixteen

Standing in the parking lot, Dani stared at the brightly painted building and felt more naked than she'd ever been on stage. Children were scattered across the fenced-in yard, playing with toys or climbing on equipment, each with an adult in tow. Everything about the center had been carefully crafted to create and enhance a celebration of innocence. Even the name, "Different Ways," seemed to embody joyful inclusion.

Did I ever have that? She resisted the urge to tug up her neckline, as if cleavage could somehow contaminate this tiny pocket of childhood.

"Nice one, Jason!" Michael's voice rang out, drawing her attention to the odd silence of the group. Dani frowned. She could have sworn children were noisier than this. Ghosting toward the fence, she spotted him coaxing an unsteady five-year-old up the steps of a plastic slide. The boy stared fixedly ahead as he placed each sneaker deliberately on the rungs with a care most mountaineers didn't invest in their footing.

Michael simply steadied him, long fingers spread wide as he prepared to catch the boy if he fell. Raked back behind his ears, his hair was still long enough to catch the little bursts of wind circling between buildings. Dani found herself watching his hands. Strong and capable, with slender, supple fingers like a musician's, they seemed equally capable of tenderness and protection.

You need him. Her sister's warnings were rarely so direct. Maybe she did need him, but the eager thrum of anticipation surging from the Huntress gave her all the reason she needed to be careful. This wasn't some alpha-jerk needing a wake-up call. He was a good man who deserved to get through the next week with all his higher brain functions intact.

"All right, come on now," he coaxed as Jason squirmed into position, carefully aligning his stubby legs with the slide. But just as the boy started to launch, Michael put his hand on Jason's belly.

If looks were bullets, Jason shot enough lead to qualify for manslaughter.

"I know. You want to go." Michael paused, moving his head into the boy's line of sight. "Say go."

Jason glared at him. Dani drifted forward, studying them to figure out why Michael was holding the child back. She wasn't close enough to scent his emotions.

"Go." Michael exaggerated the shape of the word.

Mouth moving but eyes still suspicious, Jason managed a grunt with a vague "g" sound included.

Immediately, Michael lifted his hand and the boy slid down the slide.

He doesn't talk. Dani realized in wonder. She looked around at the other children and the unusual quiet was explained. None of them were speaking. Most were ignoring the adults with them, although the adults were doing their best to gain each child's attention.

Not all the adults. Two young women, a blonde and brunette, stood together chatting beside the sandbox. One little girl dug holes in the sand, but the other child, another little boy, stood. He slowly shuffled forward, keeping his body rigid and barely moving his feet. The boy never glanced back to see if his minder was paying attention, his eyes locked onto the gate latch. Dani moved to the side of the gate in the chain link fence.

After a few feet, he burst into a long-legged run. The chatting blonde squawked a warning, but he was already well out of range. He flipped open the gate latch and eeled through before she could take more than a step or two.

Dani reacted automatically, catching the boy and using his own momentum to lift him up into her arms.

He immediately started to struggle. "No! Put it away!" Despite his wriggling, his voice was almost robotic.

"Not today, bub," she said softly, easily managing his gyrations with her strength.

"George!" the blond woman panted as she reached the gate. "Back inside."

Dani put him down but kept her hand on his shoulder just in case. The woman couldn't seem to make up her mind whether to be suspicious or grateful for the assistance. Dani straightened her spine and lifted her chin, annoyed at the paranoia. *Whatever, lady. Kidnappers don't tend to return the kid at the first opportunity.*

The other adults in the playground focused on their children, though they glanced over from time to time, curious about what had happened. The gossiping brunette blatantly stared at the scene by the gate, completely ignoring the little girl, who continued to methodically fill her sand bucket. Michael seemed to have disappeared, and Dani wondered if he'd changed his mind about working with her until she spotted him shepherding Jason into the building. Dani noticed that he kept stealing glances at her, too.

"Dodge Grand Caravan," George pronounced into the void, turning back toward the parking lot.

"Oh, no, you don't!" The blond woman pulled him inside the gate and latched it, leaving Dani on the other side. With the flimsy barrier between them secured, she recalled her manners. "He loves cars. He's been hoping to touch that van since it got here this morning."

Dani smiled at the boy. "I'm more of a bike girl myself, George."

He ignored her, his eyes flicking along the chain link.

"I'm impressed you were able to hold him," the brunette said, joining them, sniffing out fresh gossip. "He's strong."

Now that the crisis was over, both women indulged in a visual once-over. Their mouths curled in brief frowns as they took in Dani's low-necked shirt and tight jeans. A hint of envy wafted in the air between them. Their obvious judgment left Dani with the perverse desire to play to their expectations.

"How exactly can we help you?" *To leave*, the blonde's tone implied.

"Dani, glad you could make it." Michael waved from the door, dusting off his hands. "I'm almost ready to go."

"You know what they say—if it's good enough, people will wait." She flicked an eyebrow to make sure the Gossip Twins got her message.

She could practically see their brains overloading with the desire to start sharing this particular slice of information right now. Their thumbs actually started twitching as if texting the news.

You really think it's such a big deal that the Professor's meeting a girl? Where have your fucking eyes been? Even in dusty jeans and a plain cotton button-up, his long, lean body couldn't be disguised, and the cheekbones a girl

100

could use to cut bread were on display. He moved with precision, stepping around oblivious children. His slender fingers picked up toys. *If he's got even a little skill… or is willing to learn.* Thoughts of his education sent her internal motor roaring.

"Where did you two meet?" Gossip Twin Number One interrupted the speculative anticipation. A hint of malice underlay the quivering scent of curiosity.

"Burlesque club." Dani loved watching the pair nod for a moment before their brains caught up to what she'd said.

"A… burlesque club. That's different."

"Yeah. He sat through every one of my performances." Dani couldn't resist.

"Ready to go?" Michael came back to fill the stunned silence. His leather gloves were back in place despite the warm day.

"Oh, trust me, darlin', I'm always ready." Dani winked at the stunned Gossip Twins before linking her arm in Michael's. His eyebrows met in confusion, but he didn't resist as Dani led him to her car, making sure to roll her hips provocatively. Glancing back, she saw the two women still staring as she and the Professor got into her convertible.

After a few blocks, Dani couldn't hold back her laughter any more, only pausing when Michael tugged nervously at his gloves. "Oh, come on. You don't think it was funny?" She slapped him lightly on the arm with her fingers.

He winced.

"What? It wasn't that hard." Dani started to pull over, concerned. Sometimes she forgot to hold back on her enhanced strength. Had she hurt him?

"It's not that." He flexed his gloved fingers. "It's my gift."

"You picked stuff up when I touched you? Fuck me. My hand was on your sleeve." She at least knew exactly where she'd hit him.

"Sometimes that's enough, when I've gotten close to the person. Emotionally."

"One night holding your collar in an alley and we're best buds?"

"I've never met anyone like me before. It was a huge deal for me." He sounded as if he were describing a religious experience.

His unwavering honesty began to make her feel small and petty.

Perversely, it also made the desire to tease even stronger. "Damn. If I'd known I was your first, I'd have been gentle."

Part of her hoped he'd smile at the joke, but he still frowned. "You shouldn't have said where we met."

"I could have been more specific about it being the alley behind a burlesque club, but it seemed sordid." Irritation melted away her good humor.

"You don't understand. I could get in trouble."

"From who, the fucking morality police?"

"I work with developmentally challenged children. Parents get spooked easily."

True, and she might have believed him if he'd been willing to look in her eyes. Instead, he focused down and to the side. That told her all she needed to know: he was ashamed. After his little speech the night before, she shouldn't have been surprised, but it still stung.

"It's not what you think," he insisted.

"You're the psychic. It's exactly what I think. You're still on your moral high horse. You don't want anyone to know you were in a burlesque club." Her teeth gritted together and the speedometer rose. "That go for me, too? Embarrassed to be seen with a girl like me? Should I get a big fucking red A to stick on my clothes?"

"There's no need to be dramatic. And this isn't about me. You wanted to shock them." The polite social mask slipped and irritation added a harsh bite to his words.

"Hey, you're the one who came to me, Mike. If I'm too low for you to be seen with, you can hop out at the next fucking corner." She began to pull over. His rejection hurt far more than the Gossip Twins', cutting deep past her defensive barriers.

"This isn't about your job. It's about saving people we care about." He didn't flinch in the face of her anger, going toe-to-toe without backing down.

Despite her hurt, his strength impressed her, even as his reminder of their situation drained her anger, replacing it with edgy anxiety.

"I know you're worried. But we'll figure it out." Michael tried to soothe her. "We just need a little faith."

Faith in what? The gods had long since proven they didn't care about her. Each other? That was a laugh. The Professor thought this was all going to be a grand adventure. He hadn't seen how bad things could end up. *Faith is for suckers.*

He ran his hands through his hair as if shoving the exasperation behind him. "I'm sorry. I shouldn't have snapped at you."

"If it helps, the Gossip Twins back there didn't care that I was a dancer." She pulled back into traffic.

"No, they were more shocked that a beautiful woman was picking me up," he finished. "I think one of them planned to set me up with her uncle."

"Damn. Don't let me stand in the way of those plans," she teased, hoping they were back to even footing.

He smiled and relief uncurled her knotted muscles. Well, maybe not only relief. His mouth was every bit as gorgeous as the rest of him. Inhaling to steady herself, she sucked in his warm scent of apples and vanilla. *Kissing him would probably taste like pie. With orgasms instead of ice cream. Down, girl.*

"Where are we going, anyway?" he asked.

"To see a friend. He's been doing some investigating for me. Hopefully he'll have a lead for us to follow," Dani replied.

With his enthusiasm rekindled, Michael explained the highlights of his trip to Expanding Horizons and the flash-insights from Bernie's room.

Dani's jaw hung open in shock as she realized he was serious. "You went there. By yourself. And gave them your real name?" She tore her eyes off him to re-focus on the road. "These people are fucking dangerous. You could have disappeared in there." The thought hurt more than it should have.

"I thought maybe I could see her or even get her out. But either way, I had to let her know she wasn't forgotten." His chin lifted and for a split second she could practically see the cape streaming in the wind. *Always the hero.*

"This is not something you want to fuck around with, Mike. They aren't going to play by any rules. You could have gotten yourself dead in a hurry if they'd figured it out. You still might." She knew she should stop talking, but the leaden ache in her chest kept squeezing the words out of her.

He glared at her, but his expression suddenly smoothed. "You're worried about me."

"I'm worried about *me*," she shot back.

"No. I'm right. You're worried about me. After all the I-don't-need-a-partner drama." He grinned as if she'd given him the best news in the world.

Sheer stubbornness made her want to deny it. So she was worried. So what? Taking a deep breath, she pulled over and faced him. "Promise me you won't do it again."

"No." He shook his head.

"I don't want you to get hurt." She heard the words and was shocked. *When the hell did I decide to say that?*

"Listen to me, Dani. I don't want to get hurt either. But I won't sit on the sidelines while they hurt Bernie. We're partners. Equal partners. With equal say. We'll decide what we're doing together." His voice and face were completely serious and sincere.

The hope and certainty she could see in him made her feel small and petty. Part of her wanted to unleash withering sarcasm, but something held her back. Maybe it was the memory of her sister holding out the sketch of Michael's face. Maybe it was the intent earnestness in his eyes. But her verbal weapons melted away.

This was the moment of choice. She could crush him, or she could protect him. Clearly, he'd go on to investigate without her, and he'd most definitely get hurt. The only way she could get him through the next few days intact would be to truly join up with him. She faced him and shouldered the responsibility. "Fine. Partners."

Chapter Seventeen

"Who's the narc?" Vapor demanded, dark eyes squinting at Michael from less than an inch away.

"No one says *narc* anymore." Dani rolled her eyes. "He's a friend."

Michael leaned back as the looming giant studied him, tilting his shaved head back and forth like an inquisitive hawk.

Vapor's nostrils flared as if marking his scent for the future. "He's not one of us," the hacker announced.

"He's gifted." Dani's eyes glinted in the light. "You doubt me?"

Michael let loose a sigh of relief as Vapor retreated. He could deal with continuing suspicion, but would rather it happened from across the room.

Vapor cocked an eyebrow at Dani. "Interesting. Your papers are in the envelope."

Michael's curiosity hummed into overdrive. Dani had warned him this man was part of the *lalassu* community, but she hadn't shared what his gifts were. What powers were even possible? He'd definitely stepped into the deep end of his new reality. He wanted to pepper them both with a thousand questions but held his tongue. He had to focus on Bernie and Dani's brothers.

She picked up the plain manila envelope and thumbed through the contents. "And my research?"

Vapor tapped on his keyboard and images appeared on the multiple screens: enlarged driver's photos of young men and women, blueprints for buildings, scans of newspaper clippings. Michael rubbed his chin with his hand, uncertain what to look for in the mass of data.

"What the hell is all this?" Dani demanded.

"Bigger than you could imagine. Bigger and deeper. Your brothers interviewed for Right-Hand Man, which hires and trains bodyguards for a parent company—AD Enterprises. Branches on both coasts and overseas." Vapor rapidly pulled up image after image as he talked. "AD Enterprises is part of a network of companies owned under the umbrella of Dalhard Industries."

Michael stepped forward, studying the information. "It's all shells to keep the parent company clean. Is one called Expanding Horizons?"

Vapor's fingers clicked away, summoning the answer like an ancient magician. "Score one for the groupie. Expanding Horizons, run by Horizon Charitable Foundation, main donor: Dalhard Industries. CEO, André Dalhard. Born in the United States but mostly works out of Europe. Tabloids have spotted him on our side of the ocean."

"Then they have Bernie. But she's not like your brothers. She's only a little girl with schizophrenia." Despair threatened to swallow him. He turned away, not wanting to lose face in front of Dani and Vapor.

"Are you sure about that?" Vapor asked.

Gentle fingers stroked along Michael's arm and determination welled through the contact. "We'll get her back. Her and my brothers." Dani met his surprise with cool certainty. He could feel her compassion but also her ruthlessness of purpose. In that moment, he believed nothing would stop her short of killing her.

"Has she ever shown any unusual symptoms? Things flying through the air? Being afraid before something bad has happened?" Dani asked.

"Talk about it later. For now, let's focus on Dalhard Industries," Vapor interrupted.

These were frightening people with frightening resources. An image formed in Michael's mind of Dani sprawled on the ground, blood pooling below her while empty eyes stared blindly at the sky. His breath stuck in his throat as he reminded himself he didn't see the future. He tried to shove the image away, but it lingered, staining through his thoughts like a watermark. He couldn't bear to see this proud, confident woman humbled by the crushing forces of power and wealth.

He was more determined than ever not to let her or Bernie down. The time for playing a hero was over—now it was time to shut up or step up to the plate. Vapor continued his explanation, and Michael hastily dragged his attention back.

"It's not just your brothers. Dalhard hunted widely. They avoid leaving direct evidence but cannot hide the ripples of their actions. I have found five others who have been taken, and I have strong suspicions of a dozen more."

"Have any of them returned?" Michael asked.

"Only the bodies." Vapor's blunt answer knocked the hope out of Michael.

"A dozen? How could they take so fucking many of us? Someone should have noticed." Dani suddenly froze. "The stars disappear, but we don't see because we don't know their names."

"Poetic but accurate. We are a scattered people, hiding in the cracks of society. With patience and money, anything can be swept from plain sight." Vapor's brows drew together in anger. He glanced at Dani. "Without divine guidance—"

"Don't go there," she snarled.

"You can't deny your responsibilities. The Babylon legacy—"

Dani heaved an exhausted breath. "You know why I can't." Michael felt both fear and weariness from her. He'd only felt something similar once before, when his grandmother had been diagnosed with cancer. The realization of facing an inevitable painful and messy death had provoked the same particular combination of fear and exhaustion. His curiosity sharpened.

"Where are my brothers?" she asked, forcing Vapor back to the subject at hand.

Vapor turned back to the humming bank of computers. "I don't know. Not yet. There are too many possibilities. I hoped the jacket fragment would narrow matters down, but Dalhard ordered identical ones for many of their companies."

"Jacket fragment?" Michael lifted his head, his focus and purpose returning. He spotted the palm-wide scrap sitting on a pile of books and tugged off his gloves.

"Mike, you don't—"

The rest of Dani's sentence was lost as his fingers touched the plasticized fabric.

Anxiety and purpose were the first emotions, carrying images with them: two men in a deserted gas station, one huddled behind the first. The first lunged at him with savage eyes and a defiant roar. Static-distorted orders filling the area as men in combat gear grabbed weapons, trotting in military rows out of a low office-like building... with an address.

107

"I know where it is," he blurted out, jerking back into ordinary consciousness only to lose his train of thought as he became aware of Dani's body pressed against his, holding him upright with ease. He'd collapsed, he realized with dismay. He'd never had that happen during an object reading before.

"Mike?" she whispered, her hand pressing lightly against his forehead and cheek. He caught the edges of the anxiety she ruthlessly suppressed beneath practical concerns, like glimpsing a seashell under roiling waves. *She's afraid. Really afraid. For me.* The revelation was startling.

"I'm okay," he assured her. A little light-headed and his mouth and tongue were dry, but he was okay. Something tugged on his awareness, something he'd missed in the initial flash of information.

She frowned. "You've been out for almost—"

"Twelve seconds. Not exactly a 911 call," Vapor interjected.

Connected by bare skin, Michael felt the sharp jolt of shame stab through Dani. No trace betrayed itself on her face as she stepped back, regaining her cool demeanor. "I've never seen a psychic trance like that. You were just... gone."

"What do you mean, gone?" Whatever happened, it had clearly unnerved her.

"As if your body was empty. Dead." Her voice was rough and barely audible.

Dead. Yeah, he could see how that would freak someone out. Shoving the unsettling thought aside, he tried to ignore the tugging of his subconscious to concentrate on what he did know. "I think I found where they were taken. A large building set behind some low hills. It's out in the middle of nowhere. Perfect place to do secret experiments you don't want anyone else to know about."

"I'm surprised more places don't advertise that feature in the real estate listings," Vapor said.

"There was no name on the building, but I know where it is. It's a small access road off County Road Seven." It wasn't far, probably less than an hour outside Perdition.

"Seven..." Vapor's fingers were flying. "Here."

A large map blinked up onto the screen. County Road Seven was clearly marked, along with a small access road which led to nothing.

"It was there. I saw it," Michael insisted.

"Switching to satellite."

Square by square, the map was replaced by a satellite photograph. Vapor zoomed in on the site, which seemed to show a small loop at the end of the access road and nothing else. Michael couldn't believe the images on screen, his hopes faltering. He'd never gotten false information off a flash before.

"Clever bastards. Think they can hide." Vapor's slim fingers traced the image onscreen. "But not from me."

"Or from me." Dani studied the image intently.

Michael stared, trying to guess what they were looking at when he suddenly saw it—a faint seam in the interlaced green-and-brown vegetation that traced back and around, outlining a substantial building. "Camouflage paint on the roof. But what about winter?"

"White and gray, probably. Unless the satellite did a pass in spring or fall during the transition, they'd be invisible," Dani guessed.

Michael's mind reached toward the image on screen. A logical part of his mind said he should resist, especially if he was going to collapse again. But he didn't stop.

"These men have the money to ensure a spring or fall pass doesn't happen," Vapor added grimly.

"Bernie!" Michael blurted. Dani and Vapor both stared at him. "Bernie is there, too."

"I thought she was at Expanding Horizons." Dani glanced over at Vapor.

"She's been moved. I'm sure of it. She's there. Along with your brothers." Michael thought he'd been worried about her before in that fake hospital. Now he understood real terror. Men with guns, men who killed those they took. And no one would believe any of them.

"I'll check the files at this Expanding Horizons. Confirm he's right," Vapor offered.

"Thanks, Vapor. See what else you can find out about the new place. Blueprints, security, anything." Dani studied the screen. "Anything to help me get in and out."

"Us," Michael reminded her. Dani nodded slowly, her reluctance clear.

"Come back tomorrow. I should have something by then," Vapor told them. The meeting had clearly been adjourned.

Dani's hand was on the doorknob when she paused. "Vapor, one more thing—put the word out. These bastards don't need any more of us."

Michael nodded in approval. The hacker snorted and continued to tap away at his keyboard. "Already done."

Chapter Eighteen

"So what's the next part of the plan? Go to the site?" Michael asked as they got back into Dani's convertible.

"Not yet." Dani's fingers were tight on the wheel. He could sense the churning emotions inside her. She glanced at his bare hands. "You left your gloves."

"We need every edge to save Bernie and your brothers. We have to get them out as quickly as possible." Elation at finding the *lalassu* community and not having to hide his gifts was undercut by his determination not to leave Bernie in hostile hands for a moment longer than necessary.

"Guns blazing? Wouldn't work even if we had guns. We'd just get dead."

Michael sank back. *Of course this wasn't going to be so simple.* "So what do we do?"

"Wait for Vapor to get us the information he promised. Then we figure out how to get in and out. It might take days to find a way in. Meanwhile, I don't want to attract attention by acting differently."

Michael nodded. Lesson one in the difference between real life and stories: in stories, they skimmed over all the preparations. As much as he yearned to charge forward, he recognized the wisdom in Dani's suggestion, but it didn't explain the frustration and trepidation he sensed from her. "What's wrong?"

"I hate waiting," she muttered. "Luckily, I have a shift in a few hours."

"At the club?" Michael asked.

"Yes, the club." Her harsh reply suggested he hadn't been entirely forgiven for his previous assumptions. Guilt swelled. He'd hurt her with his judgment.

Dani continued. "If I have to run, I'll want the money. And meantime, I don't want to drive myself crazy while I wait. Maybe it's not as noble as what you do, but I like it and I'm damn good at it—"

"I'd like to come with you," he interrupted quietly.

She paused. "What?"

"I'd like to come with you," he repeated. "I made a mistake before, judging without really knowing anything about your situation. I'd like to learn more." Her reactions had reminded him of the snaps and snarls of a feral animal. He needed to be the definition of patience to allow her to relearn trust. They'd trained him to deal with clients with similar issues.

A slow smile brightened her face. "That'll definitely give the Gossip Twins something to talk about. All right, Professor, let's go."

He couldn't resist a twitch of a grin at the mental image of Brianna and Kirsten's faces. Tossing his bag into the back seat, he noticed the plain manila envelope Vapor had given her lying there.

"Dani, what's in there?" he asked.

"Something I have to deliver."

Her curt answer didn't encourage further questions, but Michael still pressed on. "Is it part of the Babylon legacy?"

Her fingers tightened on the wheel and he felt a maelstrom of emotion erupt inside her. Guilt, terror, shame, and determination all whirled together in a disorienting mash-up. He started to apologize. "I'm—"

"Just leave it alone. Sit back, relax, and try to enjoy the show." Dani's mask was firmly back in place. Michael settled into his seat, willing to be patient. There had never been a secret he couldn't uncover. And he sensed this was one that had festered in Dani's soul for far too long. Meanwhile, he'd trust his instincts that he was on the quickest path to rescuing Bernie.

"Chuck says it's a star." Bernie's eyes were closed and her head pillowed on her arm as she answered the question.

A woman in a white lab coat made a note on her clipboard before pressing a button on her tablet. She held it carefully to be sure the child couldn't see the screen.

"Please, I just want to go to sleep," Bernie said, her eyes ringed with dark bruises.

The woman ignored her, focused solely on the tablet's screen.

"I don't want to do this anymore."

Silence swallowed her pleas.

"A cup. Chuck says it's a cup."

Observing from an upper window, André watched as the little girl continued to answer question after question. He marveled at her accuracy. "How long has she been doing this?"

Karan consulted his notes. "Eight hours. We moved her from the Expanding Horizons site after one of her therapists came snooping around."

For now, he wanted nothing to distract him from his latest acquisition. He'd deal with the security breach later. "She's the genuine article. Who is this Chuck she keeps mentioning?"

"Unknown. Her records identify the name with a persistent hallucination, a sort of imaginary friend. Perhaps a way to keep from mentally fragmenting while using her powers?"

He shrugged. "In any case, we have confirmation. No sense wearing her out completely. Tell them to wrap it up in the next hour." André waved his hand to dismiss the matter, triumph igniting and uplifting his spirits. "Tomorrow, have them try the sessions at a distance. See what her range is. Are we having any more trouble from the mother?"

"She filed a police report, but we inserted a number of reports from social workers and police questioning her fitness." Karan checked his records.

"I don't want it left as a loose end." He liked that he didn't have to explain it further. But to his surprise, Karan had an objection.

"Eliminating her now could draw unwelcome attention. It should be done at a discreet distance. Perhaps when we have moved the girl overseas?"

André whirled, intending to snap at his aide, but quickly reclaimed his calm. After all, he kept Karan around to warn him of things others might not see. "Discredit her, drug her, kill her. Whatever it takes. Orphans are less messy. What about the other children at the center?"

"None of them show any signs, despite several promising beginnings. They are exactly what they seem, developmentally disturbed individuals." It had been Karan's idea to find supernaturals at the center, among those who would think them crazy.

André crossed to the other side of the observation platform to look down on another pristine white room. Monitoring machines crowded a medical bed in the middle. Ron McBride was strapped down, thrashing against his padded restraints as technicians tried to inject him.

André frowned. "They're risking damaging him."

"The doctors have imposed a chemical coma, but as you can see, the injections and their results are painful enough to overcome it." Karan only showed mild interest: a scientist testing a hypothesis.

"How are the results?"

"Muscle mass has increased by over thirty percent in less than twenty-four hours. His bones are growing, as well. He's almost two inches taller than when we began."

"Interesting. And it's only halfway through the treatment." Excitement intoxicated him. After so many years, the breakthroughs were happening too quickly to savor properly.

"Yes. We can anticipate doubling our current results."

"Excellent. We'll run tests after to see if there has been any cognitive impairment." As long as McBride could stand and pose, and preferably not shoot himself in the foot, they could make it work. He headed toward the elevator.

"The original test subjects have been kept in isolation, as you requested." Karan anticipated André's next request. "Despite the poor food and conditions, they have been healing at an accelerated rate. Their metabolism may make the drug trials unreliable."

"Then we'll try a more direct approach. Bring them to lab seven. We'll run the Silver protocols." André couldn't keep an anticipatory smile from curling his lips.

"I'll have Rogers brought up."

"Good. Any luck in tracking down their true identities?"

"The cell phone was a dead end—too many false trails to follow. But we were able to use facial recognition to find these." Catching up, Karan offered two enlarged pages from a high school yearbook. "Eric and Vincent Harris. Went to a local rural high school with barely two hundred students." Karan handed him a third page.

"What is this?" The picture showed a girl on the cusp of

114

womanhood, with long dark hair and olive skin. Her dark, liquid eyes and full lips hinted at a joke unshared with the rest of the world. He stopped to study the image, and his blood ignited for a different reason.

"Danielle Harris, from the same school."

He couldn't break away from the siren allure of the girl's eyes, even in a slightly fuzzy enlarged photograph.

"No other Harrises attended that particular school. I found their emergency contact information and all three listed the same cell number," Karan finished.

"What number?"

"It is no longer in service. Records indicate it was a prepaid mobile. The address on their enrollment forms also doesn't exist. But they had to be in the area to attend the school."

"Search the area, but quietly. No sense triggering a mass evacuation by their relatives, assuming they've stayed local." Dalhard smoothed his finger over Dani's teenaged image. "And find her."

She was attractive. If she didn't know he held her brothers... he could persuade her to become a willing participant in his plans. A pliant wife would be an asset in his business dealings. Men felt more comfortable dealing with a married man. It implied stability. The ideal situation would be if she were a carrier for her brothers' abilities. He could harvest her ova for any number of subjects.

Even if he couldn't, he was confident he could charm or threaten her into doing what he wanted. He generally didn't use his persuasive gift to its full potential. It had a nasty effect on brain functions, turning people into puppets. Mostly he used it to tip people off the fence onto the side he wanted. His mother had used it to ensnare his father and build the business. She'd taught him how to use manipulation to get people wavering, and then seal the deal with a touch.

Dalhard tore his eyes away from the photo. "Find her. Now."

Sweat trickled along Karan's temple, and he hurried away without another word, leaving Dalhard with the picture. *Who are you, my dear? Are you the piece I've been waiting for?*

"Danielle," he whispered. "Come out, come out, wherever you are."

Chapter Nineteen

Staring at dull concrete walls, Eric seriously considered going insane. There was a family precedent, after all. It would be a definite improvement over staring at blank walls and being alternately ripped up by guilt and fear. He had no sense of time passing—they'd taken his watch, and no natural light filtered into his isolated cell. Only a bare compact fluorescent bulb hung from the ceiling, buzzing quietly and incessantly to itself. He couldn't make out any sounds from the hall or adjoining rooms. No scents reached him other than his own stale sweat.

Meager meals arrived at irregular intervals: stale bread, nauseatingly half-melted cheese, and water. It never varied, and he couldn't anticipate the delivery. The slot in the door would scrape open, and the flimsy cardboard tray would appear.

For a man who always used his enhanced senses to collect more information than those around him, this isolation was doubly disturbing. He'd never felt so alone and helpless... or guilty.

He'd wanted a legitimate job, something with a W-4—something real, not under the table or between the cracks or any of the euphemisms for the unseen and shadowy parts of society. But thanks to his obsession with legitimacy, he was trapped in a cell. He didn't even know if Vincent—his little brother, the pest who followed him everywhere and whom he'd promised to protect—was still alive.

Fresh pain blossomed in his clenched jaw, but it provided a welcome relief from the monotony of his thoughts. Vincent hadn't cared. As long as they had money for parties and to impress women, he didn't worry about where it came from. He'd done well with their gypsy lifestyle as children, always more interested in the adventure on the horizon rather than the pain of ripping up roots with each move. Eric had been the one to convince him to try going straight, painting pictures of themselves as bodyguards to the powerful elite. In the end, Vincent shrugged, agreed, and followed, only to be shot.

The sensory memory sprang up full force: warm blood soaking

through Vincent's trousers after their escape attempt, the coppery scent of his failure. If there had been anything left in his gut, it would have made an abrupt exit. He'd failed at the only important task in the world: protecting his family.

He wondered if they'd gotten Dani, as well. She'd been on her way when they'd been recaptured. If they'd waited, she would have driven right into an ambush. Had they guessed all of them were related? If they knew, the information would lead them to the little farmhouse and Gwen.

"I'm sorry," he whispered the words, knowing Vincent couldn't hear but needing to say them anyway. *Please don't be dead. Please let me have another chance. I'll make this right somehow. I swear it.*

Metal scraped outside, louder than the food slot. Immediately Eric tensed, ready for a fight. *Just let them come close enough, even for an instant.* He would make them pay for locking him up.

Instead, the door swung open. Three men stood in the hall, holding guns pointed at him. Eric stared at them, noting their stance, how their fingers casually rested on the triggers. *Professionals.* He inhaled, breathing in alertness with no trace of fear.

"Come with us, please." The guns never wavered. Most amateurs automatically gestured with their weapons, leaving opportunities to overwhelm them.

Damn.

Eric got to his feet slowly. He didn't have to feign the pain of his cramped muscles. However long he'd been in the room, it had been long enough for everything to knot from inactivity despite his attempts to stay limber. He dragged himself out of the door and limped into the bleak corridor. Gray doors dotted the walls at regular intervals, each with a whiteboard full of cryptic symbols. His guards adjusted their positions, not that he expected any less at this point. All three to his right, which probably meant he should go left.

He obeyed the unspoken command, concentrating on limbering up his muscles. After days in a box, his body wasn't going to move as swiftly or as easily as normal. He needed to find the new limits. *Always watch and be ready for your opportunity.* One of the first lessons his father had taught him. If he could get away, he might be able to find Vincent and get them both out of there.

More guards were waiting beside an open door around the corner. "In here."

The scent of bread and meat wafting in the air drowned his tongue in saliva. Peering suspiciously through the door, he saw a small table with breads and slices of chicken and ham. The promise of food loosened his self-control, and he dashed into the room, nearly falling.

As soon as he cleared the threshold, the door closed behind him with a quiet click. Eric whirled, furious over his error. But the food was still there. Drugged or poisoned, it didn't matter. He needed to eat. Picking up a slice of ham, he forced himself to eat it slowly. Gorging would only sicken him more. As he ate, he took inventory.

A rectangular room, fifteen feet by twelve, he guessed. Ceiling at least twelve feet. Each wall glowed white. The door he'd been shoved through was almost invisible from this side, so no hinges or handle to work with. The table was cheap laminate. It would splinter and collapse if breathed on wrong. Paper plates under the food. No utensils. Nothing he could use as an effective weapon.

Faint vibrations in the floor announced a new arrival. He could make out vehement cursing outside.

The door snapped open barely long enough for the guards to shove someone inside: Vincent. Bruised, thin, and with a bandage around his thigh, but alive. Eric had never seen anything so welcome.

"Asshats!" Vincent pounded on the door to make his point clear. His eyes narrowed when he spotted Eric. "Remind me to never fucking listen to you again."

"There's food." Eric stepped away from the table.

"Oh, well that makes everything just fine. Stick me in a fucking box and poke me, not to mention shooting at me, but spread out a five-dollar snack table and I'm won over," Vincent shouted at the ceiling and walls, his dark curls matted with sweat.

"Eat it while we can," Eric ordered. Dramatics wouldn't help them.

"While we can?" Vincent lifted his shoulders in exaggerated comic surprise. "You mean you have a plan? Count me out. I'm still bleeding from your last plan."

"We have to stick together," Eric said as his brother helped himself to the bread and meat.

"And it's going great so far. Awesome job."

There would be no reasoning with him. Eric let his brother have the last word and focused on restocking calories. The small supply quickly vanished, barely denting their hunger. "What do they want with us?"

"Maybe it's a focus group for testing bullets. Which ones hurt the most going in." Vincent picked up crumbs with a finger.

"Be serious for once."

"I am serious. Deadly fucking serious. Who cares what they want? Does it really matter at this point? We've got nothing to fight them with. And we've already proved we're not bulletproof." His brother glared at him, eye to eye.

"Let me think." *There has to be a way out.*

Sprawling in a corner, Vincent began to hum the theme song to *Jeopardy*.

Despite himself, Eric smiled. "You can be such an asshole."

"Aim to please, big brother." Vincent's smile vanished. "Someone's coming."

Eric frowned. He couldn't feel any vibrations in the floor or hear any steps in the hallway outside. He looked back at Vincent, whose hand was spread wide on the wall beside him. Eric's eyes darted up as the top half of the wall blinked into transparency, revealing a powerfully built man in a suit. *The puppeteer finally revealed.*

Vincent slowly got to his feet, moving to stand behind his brother.

The man nodded at them. "My name is André Dalhard."

"I'd care, but I so fucking don't," Vincent replied.

A hint of a smile touched Dalhard's lips.

"What are you laughing at, fuckwit?"

"I'm glad you haven't been broken. Empty defiance shows you still have hope. Your brother is keeping quiet. He isn't quite so sure."

Eric didn't need to glance back at Vincent to know that his brother got the message. *Stay quiet, learn what we can.*

"It's been a life-long pattern with the two of you, hasn't it? You, the elder, watching out, playing protector. And you, demanding attention, playing the fool so others underestimate you. But there's a missing party to this family dynamic, isn't there?"

Dalhard's amusement was not shared by his audience. Eric refused to answer. He'd heard enough psychics "fish" for information to avoid giving up anything he didn't have to. The phone call might have led them to Dani, but he wouldn't betray Gwen's existence.

"Care to try to guess my age and weight?" Vincent took refuge in sarcasm.

"I care to offer you both a job," Dalhard replied frankly. He signaled briefly to someone out of sight, and a doorway blinked into view beside the window. Dalhard stepped through, and the door immediately resealed behind him. Someone else had to be behind the wall to manage the controls, making the door a less-ideal method of escape.

Dalhard made a show of examining the brothers. "You're doing better with food in your stomachs, but neither of you is in particularly good condition."

Eric took a deep breath to catch Dalhard's scent. Expensive cologne underlaid with the harsh bite of hand sanitizer. *A mask, like the designer clothes.*

"Stupid move, coming in here. What's to stop us from getting a little payback?" Vincent snarled.

"The certain knowledge that you would be killed in seconds. Neither of you have a death wish, and thus I can be certain you will behave as reasonable men. Shall we settle the terms of our agreement?"

"Neither of us has agreed to anything," Eric said. All of his instincts were screaming warnings at him.

"I'm offering two hundred thousand per year, each, plus expenses."

"To do what?" Eric watched Dalhard's face carefully for signs of deceit. He was definitely hiding something, but Eric couldn't put his finger on what.

"Now that is the question. I know you both have certain abilities beyond the norm. I know you've worked hard to keep the fact hidden. You and your sister."

Eric knew the sudden tensing of his neck and hands betrayed him. Even if Dalhard wasn't a skilled observer, this session would undoubtedly be taped and watched by someone who was. He waited, desperate to know what this man had discovered.

"I would ask you to handle certain jobs for me and serve as donors

120

for some scientific experimentation. Nothing too onerous."

Play along. Find out what he knows. Hoping Vincent would follow his lead, Eric took the first step. "I want details."

"And I want out," Vincent announced. "I don't know who you are, freak-ass, but this is not some kind of fucking job interview. It's usually considered bad form to shoot the potential employees."

So much for the hope of Vincent following along. Eric needed a new plan.

"It's also considered bad form to trash a lab and seriously injure nine of your future colleagues. One of them won't walk again. You shattered his lower vertebra with your bare hands." Nothing fazed Dalhard, not Vincent's surliness or Eric's silence. "It was quite a demonstration."

"Take it out of our paycheck," Eric retorted. He needed to convince Dalhard to relax the security measures, and pretending to accept the offer might do it.

"I see we're finally starting to understand each other." Dalhard extended his hand.

The brothers glanced at each other. Vincent looked horrible. He couldn't go much longer trapped in a cage. And neither could Eric.

"I'm traditional," Dalhard thrust his hand forward. "You can learn a lot from a handshake."

Eric took the proffered hand and immediately regretted it. Pressure built in his skull as if someone were driving a heavy wedge deep into his brain. Dalhard's cool green eyes stared at him, overwhelming every other sense. His eyes were like poison seeping into his body, taking up residence like some sort of invasive vine.

The sensation vanished as soon as Dalhard released his hand. Eric forced himself not to reveal how it affected him. True fear began to chill his confidence. Had he made another potentially fatal error in underestimating his opponent?

Vincent took Dalhard's hand before Eric could gather himself enough to warn his brother. Vincent winced at the contact, but Dalhard held on for a few more seconds, staring intently at Vincent's face. Eric gritted his teeth. His brother could spoil everything now with one ill-timed comment.

"Now that we're settled, it's time for a performance test." Dalhard released Vincent and sauntered back to the door.

"What kind of test?" Eric demanded, grabbing Vincent before he could fall to the floor. Vincent shook him off, clinging to the table to keep himself upright.

The door resealed behind Dalhard before the man answered. "I need you to kill a man."

Chapter Twenty

"That's your daughter? How old is she?" Michael asked Ruby, gesturing to a picture of a tiny blond girl grinning at the camera. Dani failed to hide a smile as she flicked through a rack of sequined costumes off to one side. When she'd first rushed him backstage, he hadn't been sure where to look as costumes changed in a flurry of glitter and pasties. Her earlier accusations still stung. He didn't consider himself a prude or judgmental, but preconceptions about exotic dancing had definitely taken root in his mind. His solidly middle-class parents never would have dreamed of venturing into any kind of club, and he'd simply absorbed it as something good people did not do. Now, though, he'd begun to talk to the dancers, seeing past their stage personas to the women beneath.

"Three going on thirteen," the petite blond dancer answered as she painted on her dramatic stage makeup. "My sister watches her while I'm here."

"It must make for rough mornings, being up so late," he guessed.

"She's just so darn adorable when she comes running into my room at five in the morning, chirping, 'Good morning, Mommy,' as if it were the best part of her day. Good thing it gets me going." Ruby laughed.

His preconceptions were slowly smothering under the weight of truth. He wasn't so naïve as to believe it could be like this everywhere. There were reasons people assumed the worst. He'd seen some of the darkness himself, women trapped by drugs or desperation, young girls with no sense of self-worth. That wasn't what he found here, though. Ruby was a single mother who'd found a lucrative way to support herself and her daughter when her ex-boyfriend vanished during the pregnancy. She could be home during the day for her child and earned enough to support them. Opal was putting herself through nursing school. Neither of them had any history of physical, drug, or alcohol abuse, and both had made deliberate choices to work here.

Opal put it bluntly when he asked her. *I could bust my butt for forty hours a week, trying to sell jeans or hamburgers or answering phones somewhere. Or I can make money off guys watching me dance and still have enough time to study.*

He watched as Dani pinned up her dark curls, trying to understand. *So many layers.* He'd seen her protective and gentle side with George and with her fellow dancers. She'd been frantically worried after he'd touched the fabric in Vapor's apartment. But at the same time, she seemed to enjoy shattering preconceptions and shocking people, like Kristen and Brianna at Different Ways. She could be terribly cynical and practical with a core of steel. She accepted the world for how it was, or at least how she believed it was, and she used what she had to get what she wanted. She wasn't anyone he would have imagined being in his life, but now that she was, he had trouble imagining it without her.

Her actions might not be heroic, but she didn't pretend to be a hero. She was gifted, but she didn't feel any obligation to make the world a better place. Her focus was finding and helping her family. Was it really so wrong? He still believed in the classic Spider-Man message, "With great power comes great responsibility," and he'd done his best to live by it. But should everyone have to? The thought unsettled him.

He shifted to one side to let a woman covered in row upon row of inflated balloons pass. His mother taught him to hide in plain sight as a child. *Never let anyone suspect what you can do. Don't draw attention to yourself. Don't give anyone a reason to think twice.* Only invisibility could provide protection.

He'd believed she was wrong until the day he told his father what he could do and found himself on the wrong end of his father's religious beliefs. Only some quick verbal work and months of grounding convinced his father he'd been lying to show off.

But even though he'd cloaked himself in conformity, he'd always thought of it as a disguise, a secret identity. Now he wondered if he'd allowed his talent to dictate too much of his life.

"Earth to Professor. Your brain is about to overheat from thinking so hard," Dani interrupted, moving to stand beside him.

"You've been giving me a lot to think about," he answered honestly. "We were both taught to hide, but you haven't let it define you. You put yourself out there."

"Easiest way to fool someone. People don't ask questions when they already have answers." Dani shrugged and then batted her inch-long

124

fake eyelashes. "No one takes a dancer seriously. Especially not one who takes off her clothes."

"I won't make that mistake again," he promised. Sitting so close, he could catch hints of her emotions. He felt her go quiet, studying the flurry around her. It would have taken Sherlock Holmes to catch the slowing of her pulse, the softening of her features as she allowed her mask to slip. Everyone else probably thought she was teasing him but he picked up the subtle signs of relaxation.

"I half expected you to stammer and blush at the floor when I brought you back here," she admitted quietly. "You impressed me, Professor."

She kissed him. It wasn't a subtle brush of his lips or a shy peck. Her mouth opened, demanding a reaction as her tongue teased his lips.

Part of him knew he should pull away, put up a boundary. They should be focused on Bernie and her brothers. But that part was stomped on and shoved into a closet by the rest of him. Deliberately forgetting all the reasons it wouldn't work, he reached up and cupped her neck, sliding his fingers into the stiffened curls of her hair as he straightened, taking advantage of his greater height. The rest of the dancers, the audience chattering only a few feet away, all of it faded and all he cared about was the heat of her body against his. Her arms and legs were hard with muscles, throwing the soft pliability of her lips and curves into exquisite contrast. He could feel the depth of her fiery lust through the contact, and it sharpened the urgency coursing through his veins and hardening his groin. He deepened the kiss, his masculinity rising to the primal challenge of her femininity.

She answered his bid for dominance, knotting her fists in his shirt and pulling him close. Her internal strength blazed brightly, demanding he be as strong, if not stronger. A jarring thread of dissonance interrupted the perfection of their union. She wasn't sure if he could match her.

He pulled her closer—he wasn't intimidated. Rather than making the kiss into a display of combat, he found a balance, allowing them to overlap like architecture, building and enhancing the other to become more. His mouth and hands shared in her exultation, rejoicing in the sweetness of mutual exploration as partners.

Partners? It wasn't a proper thought, as such, and it wasn't Dani's. It was something cold and alien awakening in her depths.

He became aware of it in a split second, something powerful, hungry, and completely amoral. It coiled in the shadows, preparing to strike. His first instinct was to push Dani behind him so that he could protect her, but he couldn't stand between her and something lurking within her.

Dani jerked away from him, her chest heaving as she struggled to control her breath. Her eyes were wide with fear, and tiny flecks of red glinted at the outer edges of her irises. Something had gone terribly wrong. Michael tensed, unsure what was needed but prepared to do whatever would help her.

"Damn, girlfriend!" Opal hollered, her grin glittering against her mocha skin.

"Never thought I'd see the Stone Maiden fall," Tanisha said.

Most of the performers were grinning and clapping.

Dani's face settled into a mask, hiding the fear. "Ha-ha. Don't you people have work to do?"

Michael settled in to watch the show from backstage. After a lifetime of being shown everyone's most horrible secrets, it was difficult to shock him. Whatever was in Dani came close, though. He might not know what happened, but he was willing to bet Dani did. This time, he wasn't going to let her evade his questions.

Dani was in trouble. Sensual energy crackled through her veins and snapped through her skin. Danger signals flashed all around. The people in the club were more animated, skin flushed and eyes dark. More than one would get lucky tonight in wild, no-holds-barred stranger-sex. Tips were going to be through the roof. It might be good business for the show, but desire and high emotions were not a good mix. Riots started in less tension than what charged this atmosphere. *I have to bleed it off, but where? When?*

She hadn't faced this level of energy since her teens, and everyone here was an adult—there were no virgins to fuzzy up the fantasies playing out. *This could be a bigger fucking disaster than prom.* She'd gone overseas to lie low until the media stories played out.

It shouldn't be happening. She'd just Hunted a few days ago. But the Huntress had awakened and demanded satisfaction. She could feel the psychic poison leaching out of her pores like a tangible mist and half expected to see the contaminating coils circulating through the club from her backstage perch.

She threw a kiss to the crowd, and her lips tingled, remembering the taste of Michael's lips. Kissing him had been an impulse, a spur-of-the-moment decision. His mouth had been so tempting, so close, the scent of apples and clean woodsmoke stirring more than one appetite. It was more than any girl could resist. She'd half convinced herself it would be awkward. Every girl knew a bad first kiss was the best way to end a blossoming crush.

But it hadn't been bad. It had been amazing. A kiss—just a simple, everyday kiss, and her body buzzed like a swarm of bees. She could still taste the tempting, clean sweetness on her lips. Could the rest of him taste that delicious, too? The thought of finding out sent her buzz ratcheting higher.

She glanced at Michael as she went onstage. His brows were furrowed and he'd bitten his lip in concern. *Damn it.* There was nothing "everyday" about what they'd shared, and then the Huntress ruined it by waking up to seek out prey.

Had he felt it, or had she moved away quickly enough? Her hands and body knew the dance routine, performing the steps while her mind chewed through the ramifications of the kiss. If she gave in to the desire flooding her body, the Huntress might devour Michael whole and spit out the pieces. Her hands shook at the thought, fumbling with the fastenings of her corset. If she let the energy level continue to build, next time she might not be able to step away, and the Huntress would still strip away his mind and soul. There were other people to consider, too— no one out in the club had come in asking to get stirred up into a violent frenzy tonight.

The idea of Hunting repulsed her. She didn't want a stranger to paw at her—she wanted Michael's hands on her, Michael's body inside hers. Tanisha was right: the Stone Maiden had fallen and shattered.

Drawing a deep breath, she forced herself to calm down. *Just get through the performance.* Then they could get on with finding her brothers and his girl. Then he would be gone from her life, safe from the monster inside.

"Dani? Are you okay?" Becca asked quietly as they stepped offstage.

"Yeah. Guess I have the jitters." Dani tried to brush off any concerns.

"He's cute."

"Yeah. He is." She nodded as Michael helped one of the part-timers hold her headdress steady while she pinned it in place. Her Professor had come a long way.

"And he likes you a lot." Tanisha joined them.

He won't. The realization sharpened her tongue. "This is starting to sound like fucking high school."

"He's a good man," Tanisha said.

"Which is why he won't be around long." Dani bit hard on her lip to keep from snapping. "We have other things to worry about. Either of you spot Redneck Whiskey tonight?"

"I thought I saw him, but when I looked again he was gone," Tanisha said with evident relief.

"Maybe he finally left town," Becca said, patting Tanisha's shoulder.

"We can only hope." Tanisha's shoulders and jaw were tight. She'd spent too long being afraid to be reassured by a single evening.

"Too bad. I'm in the mood to deliver a spectacular ass kicking right about now," Dani muttered as they took their places for the next performance.

Karan stood in the shadows. No waitress approached to ask if he wanted a drink. No patron tried to muscle past him to get a better view. No one even looked at him. Their eyes slid over his particular patch of the floor without pause.

His talent for invisibility was a large part of why Dalhard hired him. It wasn't a true psychic gift, of course, but rather the innate ability to adjust his demeanor and behavior to remain unnoticed and unremarkable in almost any circumstance. His boss had needed someone inconspicuous who would observe what he could not, go to the places where he did not dare to be seen, someone who could manage the vast reaches of the corporation—both legal and illegal branches—while giving Dalhard plausible deniability. He had never been subjected to Dalhard's persuasive influence. His boss knew it would have triggered a fierce reprisal, and it allowed him to be the one person who could tell the boss when something was a bad idea.

He was beginning to believe he would have to exercise his privilege soon. Dalhard showed signs of obsession with the Harris brothers and their mysterious sister. He was ignoring the progress of the other prospects, not to mention the rest of the business. Karan would ensure Dalhard Industries remained profitable and secure, even if its CEO strayed. Dalhard was useful as a front man. He had patience with the public side of the business, patience Karan would never match. But Karan had spent too long building the company to allow his boss to waste it all on a frivolous obsession.

The club was an example. It had seen better days, likely as a movie theater or vaudeville stage in the thirties, and gone steadily downstream since. The crowd clearly had money, despite the poor location. He made a mental note to examine the business opportunities in these types of performances. Plenty of people and companies could not afford the New York tourist market in the city, but here was a golden opportunity just waiting for someone to shine it up.

The lights dimmed and a new set of performers took the stage. Karan discreetly removed his phone from his pocket, waiting for the right moment.

The women teased the crowd with their feather fans and extravagant accessories, but Karan was not interested in bared flesh or cheap thrills. He studied the woman called Onyx, snapping pictures subtly. He compared the image on screen with the yearbook shot until he was certain. He left the club, rejoining the shadows. Once outside, he sent the text.

She is here.

129

Chapter Twenty-One

"You want us to kill a man." Eric repeated the words flatly.
Dalhard paused to check his phone. "He'll be in shortly."

"Dude, this is the worst joke I've ever heard." Vincent shook his head and turned away.

"I'm quite serious. Think of it as a demonstration. A test of your speed, strength, and ferocity. Properly documented, it should create a great deal of demand." The smoothness of Dalhard's patter slipped. The brothers no longer held his full attention.

Eric studied him, desperate for any information that could help them survive and escape. "What's in it for us?" he demanded.

"Money." Dalhard seemed genuinely surprised by the question, his eyebrows disappearing into his hairline. "Lots of money. I make money, you make money. Mutual benefits. I'm not a villain from a comic book or some overdramatic film. This is all part of a business plan."

The door to the hall opened and a scrawny, filthy man covered in tattered clothes was shoved in. The only thing intact was an old T-shirt with a Superman logo on it. He muttered to himself constantly, wide eyes flickering across the room so quickly it seemed impossible that he could really see anything. The stench of stale urine and booze settled deep in Eric's throat.

Both the brothers frowned and moved away. Vincent covered his nose and made gagging noises.

"This is Mr. Rogers. Kill him," Dalhard instructed quietly.

"No," Eric's answer bounced back reflexively.

"What if I threaten to put a bullet in your brother's head if you refuse?" Dalhard asked, adjusting his cuffs.

"Then you need to rethink your fucking not-a-villain speech," Vincent snapped.

Eric shifted his weight slightly. Whatever the glass was made of, he doubted it would hold against a feral's strength and speed. His mind flickered over the guards' positions in the hall, the brief glimpses of the layout. Could he trust Vincent to follow, after what Dalhard had done to them?

"No! NononoNONONO! Get them off! Get them off!" Rogers began to scream, flailing wildly. Eric and Vincent both moved to the edges of the room, staying well out of his way.

Dalhard nodded to himself. "It's a noble instinct, protecting others. But things are rarely simple, are they?"

"He's crazy. He can't be a threat to you." Eric stepped back, flexing his shoulders.

"Would it make a difference if I told you he was killing pets? Cutting them up for food?" Dalhard offered details as if they were of no consequence, but Eric noted the interested gleam in the man's stone eyes. Eric had to stay focused on their real enemy, not the distraction. Dalhard continued. "Would that make it morally acceptable? What if it were children? What then?"

"I'm not killing someone on your say-so!" Eric yelled.

"Demons!" The crazy man screamed, yanking out a knife and charging at the brothers. *Not just a distraction.*

"What the fuck!" Vincent scrambled out of the way, falling.

Faced with an actual attack, Eric's face hardened, and his movements became fluid and deadly. He had no choice if they were to have any hope. He shifted to avoid a wild knife strike. Stepping behind his attacker, he wrapped thick arms around the man's neck. Leaning in, his mouth moved for a moment before he yanked his hands in opposite directions, using his strength for a painless break.

An audible snap echoed through the room. The man collapsed onto the floor, his neck twisted in a position never intended by nature.

"Worst fucking job interview ever," Vincent breathed from the floor.

Eric slowly straightened and faced Dalhard, his face aching from tension, locked in a dark mask. "You got what you wanted."

"Indeed I did." Dalhard's slow smile of satisfaction chilled Eric. The other man re-entered the room, completely ignoring the body sprawled on the floor. "I'll arrange to have you both taken somewhere more comfortable."

"I take it we have the job." Eric met the man's eyes, but it took every instinct to hold himself steady as Dalhard approached him. His mental resistance to the man's powers might be the only advantage they had right now. He couldn't betray it. Dalhard's perfectly manicured hand fell heavily on Eric's shoulder and once more Eric felt the dizzying impinging of a foreign consciousness. It stroked at his memories, diminishing the horrid crack of snapping bone and suddenly limp flesh. It tugged at the pain of being locked in a box in the darkness and left alone to wonder about his family.

He let the intruder succeed in relaxing him even as he clung to the memories deep inside. *Hold tight. I won't forget what he's done to me.*

"Vincent, are you all right?" Dalhard solicitously helped Vincent to his feet. Vincent's head snapped up.

"Yeah. Yeah, I'm fine." He spoke the words slowly and carefully, as if they might shatter to reveal the lie.

"I'll have more food sent to your suite."

"More food is never a bad idea." His brother's speech rhythms returned. He moved and sounded like the old, carefree Vincent, except Vincent would never have been carefree with a corpse still cooling in the room.

"Follow me, gentlemen. I think you'll like what we have to offer."

Michael's fingers ached from tension as he watched the show from backstage. Superficially it might appear to be the same performance he'd seen last night, but he could see the rigidity and tension in Dani's movements. Something lurked inside her, something dangerous. A smart man probably would walk away, but he refused. She needed his help as much as Bernie did.

He'd be lying to himself if he claimed his motives were all altruistic. The kiss had been amazing. He could still taste a lingering hint of oranges and jasmine on his lips, and he'd resorted to the schoolboy trick of holding a clipboard in front of himself to disguise the aching hardness swelling behind his fly. Part of him wanted to drag her offstage and back to any area with a reasonably comfortable flat surface. The other part of him wanted to forget about the flat surface.

The emotional atmosphere of the crowd tugged his awareness away from his fantasy-fueled discomfort. He scanned faces, surprised to see so many lips curling in contempt and disgust, eyebrows knotting hard over noses. People were talking louder and in shorter sentences than a few minutes ago. Their gestures were sharper and more agitated. The crowd was quickly turning ugly.

What could have set it off? Two nights ago, everyone seemed relaxed and ready to laugh. Now the laughter had a brittle, sarcastic edge. Bells of familiarity started to ring through his consciousness.

The club Joe had taken him to, he realized. That had been like this: anger and desire pumped way out of proportion for an evening out. But it hadn't lasted long.

His mind rapidly put pieces together into a puzzle he wasn't sure he wanted to see. Dani had been at the club. She'd left right as he and Joe were arriving. Something dark and alien rested inside her, something hungry and violent. It had to be influencing people. It sounded like something out of *The Twilight Zone*, but then so did everything else that had happened this week.

The performance finished and the dancers came offstage. Dani avoided his eyes, muttering something about needing a drink. She yanked on a top and jeans with profane energy. He took a step toward her, but she skittered away like a frightened animal, heading for the bar.

"She's definitely got it bad." Opal shook her head, clacking the strings of pearls draped around her.

"She's not the only one." Michael leaned against the wall, raking his hand through his hair.

"Give it some time. You'll both get used to it. I'm going to head home. I've got a paper due this weekend, and I don't like how the crowd is acting tonight." Opal grabbed her clothes to get dressed.

"What about the rest of the show?" Michael asked, surprised.

"Candy will take my spot. She could use the money." Opal nodded at one of the part-timers, a pretty redhead with languorous curls. "And I could use the break."

"Dani mentioned you were having trouble with one of the customers. She called him Redneck Whiskey." Michael couldn't help stealing a look across the agitated club. Dani downed her drink in a single swallow and pressed the glass to her head.

"That's the one. The way he watches, it makes it all feel dirty and sordid." Opal curled her lip. "Usually when I dance, I feel powerful and sexy, like I'm on top of the world."

"But he makes you feel afraid." It wasn't a guess.

"Yeah. Like he's decided to have me gift-wrapped and sent to his hotel." Opal studied the crowded bar. "Listen, do you mind walking me to my car? It's just around the corner."

"It's no trouble at all." Michael smiled. Such a little gesture of chivalry, but now it was familiar turf, an ordinary sort of heroics.

"Thanks. We can slip out back." They walked together out the backdoor exit to the alley. It was hard to believe that only yesterday, he'd followed Dani there. Everything had changed after that moment.

"Raoul's been walking me to my car every night in case Redneck decides to show up. He takes good care of all of us." Opal fidgeted with her car keys. "I hate to bother him when he's so busy."

"You have good instincts," Michael commented as he held the door for her. "People second-guess their instincts too much. They know there's danger, but they don't want to make a bad impression or seem paranoid." *Or are completely overconfident*, his conscience reminded him.

"My instincts have been screaming overtime lately. I don't even notice being afraid any more. I'm too used to it." Opal shrugged.

Michael started to answer, but movement on the street caught his attention. He stopped, trying to resolve the shifting patterns of black against shadow into something that made sense. Opal tensed, and her knuckles paled around the keys.

The shadows became a man dressed in a plaid shirt, blocking the exit from the alley to the street. Opal's eyes widened in fear and she stepped back, shaking her head in instinctive refusal. The door clanged shut behind them, locking them out.

Michael moved to stand between Opal and Redneck. "Step aside."

The man weaved on the spot, swaying back and forth as if too drunk to stand, but no bleariness dimmed his eyes. He barely acknowledged Michael's existence; he only saw Opal. "Pretty, pretty," he crooned as if calling a cat.

Opal clutched Michael's arm, and her terror swamped into him. Her mind and body were frozen, paralyzed by the flood of adrenaline. The moment she'd imagined and feared for weeks was playing out, leaving her trapped.

"Sir, you need to step back," Michael ordered, forcing himself to shut out Opal's panic.

"So pretty." Redneck swayed forward. "Don't want to talk to me."

"That's right. She doesn't want to talk to you." Michael was fairly certain the man wasn't actually drunk, but something had influenced him, pushing aside his inhibitions and judgment. With a sinking feeling, he wondered if it could be whatever lurked inside Dani. He remembered the fight from the nightclub and braced himself. Redneck might be past talking down.

"No one wants to listen to me." The man actually sniffed in self-pity.

Michael eased Opal backward a step. If the other man charged, he needed room to maneuver. He was unsteady enough that they should be able to slip past him if they timed it right.

"This time, she'll listen." Redneck reached into a pocket and pulled out a shiny, snub-nosed gun.

Michael froze. A gun changed the equation. No amount of training let someone dodge bullets.

Redneck charged.

Michael tried to trip him, and the other man tried to dodge. Mostly—the edge of Michael's foot scraped along the outside of his calf, hissing against the fabric and knocking them both off-balance. Michael slammed into the uneven brick wall, scratching his arms and legs raw. Redneck fell forward, his hand catching on Opal's blouse and ripping it wide open.

Opal screamed.

Chapter Twenty-Two

Dani swallowed her drink, ignoring the burn of alcohol on her tongue. Her thoughts were tangled in a Gordian knot and no sword-wielding Greek waited to make it simple. *Do not think about gorgeous men in halters and carrying swords. It's not going to help.* But the usual mental parade of cast members from *300* was oddly flat and unstimulating until one of them began to take on sharper cheekbones and sandy hair flopping boyishly into his eyes.

Not going there! She struggled to regain control. The Huntress snapped in her mind, deprived of its new obsession. It had never been so bad, not even when... her mind shied away from the memory.

Raoul held up the bottle, concern widening his eyes, silently asking if she wanted another drink. Dani shook her head. She didn't dare lose control but couldn't stand the emotional rawness. She waited for the anesthetic blunting of the alcohol to take effect. *What do I do now?*

The Huntress knew. It wanted to sink its fangs deep into Michael and suck his soul out. Sweat trickled around her hairline and down her back as she fought the monster inside.

A scream slashed through her internal battle, uniting both halves at once.

She jumped to her feet, ignoring the startled reactions as she moved far more quickly than any human could have managed. Her body moved before she could consciously pin down where the scream had come from: the back alley.

She burst through the back door, startling her prey. The stench of whiskey identified him even before the plaid shirt. The sight of his victims brought a snarl from both her and the Huntress. Redneck struggled with Michael, who stood between him and a weeping, screaming Opal—*Tanisha*. The dancer's blouse had been ripped open, leaving her plain cotton bra on display.

The bastard threatened people she cared about. Her rage snapped free of any restraint. She surged forward, grabbing Redneck by the shoulder with one hand. His bones creaked in protest under her grip, but she was long past caring. She lifted him up and hurled him against the rough brick wall. Her eyes were burning, and she knew the Huntress's red rings gleamed in the night.

Tanisha's tears barely registered. She knew Michael was helping the girl as the dancer curled against the back wall, obeying primal instincts to find physical security. Leaving her coworker in Michael's capable hands, Dani focused exclusively on her target.

Redneck Whiskey rose heavily to his feet, his face scraped and bleeding. He heaved a booze-soaked breath, ready to launch into denials.

Neither part of her was inclined to listen. Dani backhanded him, all her thwarted lust transmuted into blind fury. Her blow lifted him off his feet and sent him crashing onto the concrete. It felt strangely unsatisfying.

He popped back up, angrier than before. Drugged, oblivious, or driven, something had him fired up enough to keep fighting. His return blow was clumsy. Dani dodged it easily, slamming her fist into his gut.

A sour whoosh of air blasted her as he tried not to throw up. All the fear over her brothers, the frustration of her self-imposed restraint, the simmering pain from every slight and attack in her life, it all coalesced into this pathetic man who bullied people for sexual favors. Dani's vision narrowed into tight focus.

He staggered back, wheezing. "I only wanted to talk."

"He had a gun," Tanisha whispered from where Michael stood protectively over her.

Dani spotted the shiny pistol near her feet. This man deserved to meet the Goddess, but she'd be damned if she'd allow him to lay a finger on her.

Flush from frustration and violence, she bent and picked it up. It filled her hand, comfortably heavy. Fully loaded. Safety off. "So start talking." Dani squeezed off a round, blasting a chip into the pavement beside him. The blast echoed through the alley, drowning out Redneck's whimpers.

She ignored Tanisha's shrieks, concentrating on her prey. He cowered, raising his hands over his head as the tears blubbered out.

"Not so fucking tough now, are you?" Dani sneered, disgusted by his cringing. No one came running. In this neighborhood, it wasn't a surprise.

"What are you going to do?" he whined.

The blazing red circles coalesced around her irises. The Huntress hissed in agreement. *Cull the unworthy.* She lifted the gun and cocked the hammer.

"Dani! Don't!"

Michael's voice—the only one that could have stopped her. Immediately the Huntress shifted focus to its preferred prey.

Dani closed her eyes, slipping her finger off the trigger. "You know what he is."

"He'll be punished. By the cops. By the law." She could hear Michael moving slowly toward her.

Punished? He'll get a slap on the wrist. Everyone knows you can't "assault" an exotic dancer. We're asking for it. Bitterness coated her tongue, drying her mouth. *Better to put an end to him now. I'm finished here anyway.* Rage burned inside her. She'd worked hard to get this job, to find a place of acceptance, and now it was all over because of some petty bully who couldn't accept "not interested" as an answer. *He should pay.*

"Trust me, Dani." Michael kept talking like a damn hostage negotiator. *Couldn't he see what was happening here? Didn't he know better?*

The aggression rushed out of her. Of course he didn't. Despite his extraordinary gifts, despite what they revealed about the world, he still believed. She couldn't be the one to break him. Not like this. Certainly not over a little piece of shit.

She heard sirens in the distance, coming closer.

Redneck still cowered on his knees. Dani squatted, still holding the gun on him. "They better convict you. Because otherwise I'll be coming. And next time, no one will be there to fucking stop me."

Blank terror convinced her that he understood.

"Dani," Michael warned. "They can't find you here."

She'd already been in the police station in the last two days. Dani tossed aside the gun, rising from her haunches. Michael grabbed it and began to rub it with his shirt.

"Get the trigger. Nothing else holds prints."

The haunted pain in his eyes hit her like a slap across the face. After

138

all that, she'd broken his faith with her words just as she would have broken his mind. Unfamiliar shame choked her, and she slipped inside the club as the first cops arrived on scene.

"Thank you for your statement, Miss." Joe finished jotting down notes on his pad while Michael hovered protectively in the background. Instinctively grasping the necessity, Opal hadn't mentioned Dani's name or presence at all. Her stalker had confronted her and Michael, she screamed, and a local Samaritan came to help, disappearing before the cops arrived. Redneck Whiskey wasn't about to admit to anything different. He still alternately clung to the arresting officers and the alley wall, pouring out his confession to anyone who would listen, weeping tears of relief.

Michael didn't quite know how to react. In all his training, he'd never seen someone move so fast or inflict so much damage with so little effort. But it wasn't only the violence. He'd seen Dani's eyes, wild and eager and alight with rings of fire. The Dani he knew and respected hadn't been in control. He suspected the alien presence he'd sensed earlier and wondered if he could have just as easily been the target.

In comics and movies, the violence was always exciting and justified. Good guys hit bad guys, bad guys fell down, and the audience cheered. A simple formula played out in a million variations. But this was different. He couldn't cheer the reality.

"This isn't a place I expected to see you, Michael," Joe interrupted his thoughts. The formal tone told Michael that he wasn't dealing with Joe his friend but rather with Joe the police officer.

"Something different to try." Michael shrugged one shoulder, his fingers playing with the hem on his jacket.

Joe raised a skeptical eyebrow. "You saw what happened."

"I was walking her to her car. He confronted us, pulled out the gun, and grabbed at her. I tried to stop him, but we got tangled up. I got knocked down and that's when the other guy came out. I was focused on Opal. I didn't get a good look." *Mostly true*, he shouted at his conscience.

"This guy has a record of stalking and assault. The girl is lucky this helper showed up."

"She is." Michael glanced at Opal, wishing he could have a chance to talk to her. Her head and arms hung slackly, her eyes haunted and distant. She would need a lot of help to get over this.

"Was it you?"

"What?" Shock dropped his jaw.

"I know you like playing the hero." Joe smiled slyly. "And that's okay, man. But I need to know, is the guy gonna describe you when I ask who hit him?"

"No. It wasn't me. I couldn't do that." Dull thuds of fists and flesh echoed through his mind and revulsion throttled his stomach.

"You've got the training. I've seen you take down guys bigger than this."

"Stopped them. Not hurt them. Not like this."

Joe stared at him, concern furrowing his brow. "What aren't you telling me?"

Michael took a deep breath, forcing the unpleasant memories into the depths of his brain. He had been confident he could handle Dani's invisible monster, but now he wondered if he'd made a major mistake. "I need you to trust me, Joe. Just take care of Opal."

"Tell me what you've gotten yourself into. This isn't a movie, man. You could end up getting yourself killed."

"I won't. I promise." Michael squared his shoulders, meeting Joe's eyes with conviction. "Trust me."

Joe studied him. "Something's changed."

"Did Martha get in touch with you about Bernie?" Michael asked, changing the subject.

The grin disappeared as if dropped. "It's a bad situation. She's got a lot of child protective services reports against her."

Joe's disbelief stung. "They're fake. Martha never hurt Bernie in her life."

"I know you might not want to believe it, but it doesn't look good."

"Joe, I'm telling you the record is wrong. I've worked with this family for the last five years. I would know about any visits or reports," Michael repeated. His mind whirled, settling on a startling realization. He'd met Vapor, who could make records appear and disappear. Expanding Horizons must have someone similar.

Joe raised a skeptical eyebrow, and Michael's hopes sank further. Martha couldn't fight against someone or something who could tip the odds so impossibly against her. The courts wouldn't believe a wild conspiracy theory about manufactured records. His hopes of getting Bernie back through a legal process went from optimistic to being on life support. He looked back at the club's crumbling brick wall to avoid meeting Joe's steady scrutiny. Dani was right to call him naïve. A shadowy, illegal operation might be the only way to help Bernie now.

"Michael, I don't like the look in your eyes. Are you planning to go vigilante on me? We had a deal: you bring me the tips, I arrest the offenders." Joe's hand hovered as if to touch his friend but then fell back.

"If I went vigilante, I'd be pretty stupid to tell you about it in advance. The less you know about this, the better." Michael knew his friend wasn't going to take his advice.

He was right. "Is this about that girl from the bookie bar?" Joe demanded. "Is she the reason you're mixed up in this?"

"The girl in question is ten years old, a delusional schizophrenic being held by doctors who are hurting her. And there's not a damn thing any judge or cop in the city will do about it." Michael held Joe's gaze. The time for playing by the rules was over. Their adversary had already gained a lot of ground by ignoring them.

"Michael, please. I don't want to have to arrest you. Or worse, ID you in the morgue. Come back to the station with me. We'll figure this out."

Michael wanted to. He wanted to believe the two of them could work something out and save the girl—save *both* girls, Bernie and Dani. He studied Redneck again as the medic mopped blood from his broken nose. He watched as Opal gave her statement while shivering under a blanket.

"This isn't something you want to know about," Michael said slowly. "I'm deeper into the freaky stuff than I ever knew existed. I don't know if there's a way back."

"There is always a way back. This could get a lot uglier." Joe's earnestness came from a good place, wanting to protect his friend.

But Michael was past being protected from doing what was right.

He knew the truth, and he had an obligation to act on it since no one else would. "It already has."

The sadness in Michael's voice shot right to Joe's gut. He could see his friend swallowing hard, trying to keep his cop persona intact.

"But I have to see this through," Michael finished.

"Promise to call me if you need help. Any help." It was a final straw to grasp, a slim olive branch to keep their friendship intact.

"I will." But he wasn't sure he would.

Chapter Twenty-Three

Dani watched as the cops gently tucked Tanisha into a squad car to take her home, safely anonymous among the crowd of dancers gawking at the proceedings. She kept well to the back, avoiding any official attention. No one here would betray her, but there was no point risking it. Reckless energy still crackled across her nerve endings, leaving her drunk on her own power. The Huntress coiled around her, far too close to the surface for comfort. Dani should be getting as far away as she could.

But she lingered, watching, unable to stop contrasting old memories of her treatment with Tanisha's. She had expected ridicule and impatience. Instead, the cops were listening with sympathy. They'd put a blanket around Tanisha to ward off shock. Whenever Redneck shifted, the cops shifted, keeping themselves between her and her attacker. Everything was so different from what she'd experienced before. Every gesture the authorities made told her Tanisha would be sheltered. There were no eye rolls, no shrugs, no huffs of irritation.

She swallowed a strange sensation of feeling small and alone. She wanted to go to Michael and go back an hour to when he still looked at her like a hero. She wanted to sit with Tanisha and accept the small comfort the cops offered. But she could never have trusted them, never relaxed in their care. The chill clasp of handcuffs was more familiar than the rasp of mass-issued blankets.

Was it because of Michael? He certainly knew them. He'd been speaking to one of them, a fine Hispanic hunk of manflesh, for at least ten minutes. Could he have convinced them to take Tanisha seriously? Uncertainty only added to her roiling frustration. She couldn't keep her eyes or mind away from Michael for any length of time, and every moment only added to the Huntress's determination.

He was talking to Tanisha again, writing something down, probably a name of someone who would help her. Redneck was gone, hauled away. Everything was wrapping up, coming closer to the moment when she would have to face Michael again. The Huntress hissed in anticipation.

No. I won't let you. It was the first time she'd ever completely denied the inner predator. She'd delayed the Hunt before, turned aside from potential prey, yes. Flat-out shut it down, no.

Inner rage flared, betraying its inhumanity. Colors and noise began to bleed together again as she struggled for dominance with her feral nature. *NOT HIM!*

Then choose another.

Another. Find another man and tempt him into orgasm. Simple, but the thought of letting some jerk paw her was disgusting. The idea of letting some asshole inside of her brought bile rising. *No.*

The Huntress hissed its displeasure, coils clamping around her brain. Dani pulled back, heading blindly back into the club. Maybe another drink would help. Sirens had scattered some of the clients, but not all of them.

Choose my prey, the Huntress urged. It began flicking her gaze around the club, evaluating each male as a potential target.

Dani tried to look away, but her back and neck cramped, holding her in place.

Take one of them. Feed me.

No. She wasn't doing that again. Not now. Her jaw ached from her clenched teeth, as if it might crack under the pressure.

The few remaining clients were snarling at each other, shouting loud, blame-filled accusations. With sickening clarity, Dani knew the rising anger was her fault. With each denial, the Huntress's influence grew stronger. It added to the horror of knowing the Huntress's thwarted influence had tipped Redneck from leering to attack.

I have to get out of here. It became the only clear thought in her mind. Raoul leapt over the bar to separate fighting patrons and send them on their way.

Dani fled, all too aware that she needed to put physical distance between herself and the Huntress's potential targets. Adrenaline flooded her body, narrowing her senses to practical blindness. Thin chipped wood slammed into her fingers. She barely identified the staff bathroom

144

door before she pried it open and collapsed inside. Curling up on the broken tile floor, she buried her hands in her hair and hid her face on her knees. The act of inhaling escaped her as if her lungs had forgotten a lifetime of practice. The Huntress coiled impatiently through her veins, demanding action.

Time ceased to have meaning as she fought her inner nature. Buried memories clawed back to the surface. Crushing weight pinned her down. She had no leverage to throw it off.

Voices floated above. "I'd say she owes us all a little something. She won't remember it anyway. Besides, she said she wanted to have some fun." She couldn't tell if she was hearing it or remembering it.

Why wasn't her body doing what she asked? She should be able to fight them off. Instead, panic clawed at her, shredding the calm she needed to keep her monster contained.

"Dani, honey?" The female voice floated in and out of her awareness, not fitting with the crushing memories.

Dani's fingers dug into her scalp, ripping out long strands of hair. The fresh sting gave momentary contrast with the remembered pain. *It's not real. Not happening.* She told herself over and over again, fighting against the choking memories of terror and agony.

After the cops took Opal and Redneck away, Michael returned to the utterly deserted bar. He guessed most of the clients hadn't wanted to stick around when the flashing lights and sirens arrived. He couldn't see Dani anywhere. Had she left?

Raoul circled the room, collecting discarded drinks and bottles. "Nice work tonight," the bartender said. "Want a beer?"

Michael nodded, automatically reaching for his wallet.

Raoul arched one eyebrow in an expression better suited to Spock than Cheers. "Keep your money. This is on the house."

"Dani is the one who saved her." He couldn't quite repress a wince. No matter how much he tried to tell himself the violence had been necessary, something in him rebelled.

"That's something to keep to yourself," Raoul warned.

"Sorry." He really wasn't any good at the clandestine stuff.

145

"But it wasn't what I meant. You talked to the cops and got them to take care of Opal. But that's not the only reason." Raoul handed him a bottle. "I'm talking about the kiss."

"Oh." Michael looked down, embarrassed.

"I've been here five years, you know?"

"So you know her pretty well?" He wondered if the bartender could help him put what he'd seen into context.

Raoul frowned, toying with an empty bottle. "I wouldn't say I know her at all. Likes to keep herself to herself. But I've never seen her like tonight."

"Me, either." Michael took a long pull on the beer to erase the coppery tang of blood on his tongue.

"You're the first guy I've seen in here who treats her like a person. Every one of these fuckers wants to be in her bed, but you look like you want to talk to her over breakfast," Raoul told him.

"Why are you telling me this?" Michael forced himself to meet the other man's eyes.

"Because I don't want her to get hurt. The Stone Lady does not do emotions well." Raoul's fingers tightened around the glass he was cleaning.

Michael's instincts shrilled a warning, sharpening his senses. "What do you mean?"

Raoul glanced toward the back of the club and shook his head.

"What is it?" Michael demanded, the prospect of Dani being hurt pulling him up out of his seat.

"She's freaked out about what happened. You need to give her some time."

Michael winced at the memory of her pummeling Redneck. "It's hard to imagine. She seemed pretty comfortable."

"She's not invincible. She acts tough but I never met a tough guy who didn't have a scared little kid somewhere inside," Raoul insisted.

Whatever Dani had inside, it was not a scared little kid. Michael couldn't think what to say. He was confused, emotionally exhausted and desperately wanted to return to the blissful ignorance of a few days before. But then he wouldn't ever have met Dani. The price felt indescribably high.

146

"Raoul!" Ruby's shrill shout cut through the theater. She came rushing out from backstage.

"What is it?" Raoul tensed.

Michael followed suit, preparing himself for the next round.

"It's Dani," Ruby babbled. "She's locked herself in the bathroom and won't talk to me. I've never seen her like this."

Michael's long legs devoured the distance across the room faster than Raoul despite having farther to go. He got to the bathroom and heard the sickening thud of flesh against concrete.

"Dani, open the door!" Ruby called out.

Michael slammed into the rough plywood door to force it open. Dani lay curled up against the wall, her eyes blank and empty. Harsh red scratches ripped across her skin. Her fingers were curled tightly in her hair, distorting the skin underneath.

"Oh my God," Raoul breathed.

"Dani, honey, what's wrong?" Ruby asked, joining Michael to kneel beside Dani.

She didn't respond to them. Michael had a sudden taste of what Dani must have experienced when he'd gone into a trance in Vapor's apartment. She was right there, but her body seemed heartbreakingly empty.

"Did that asshole do something to her?" Raoul snarled.

Michael shook his head, his mind whirling. Could the thing inside have taken over?

"Is it drugs? A bad trip?" Ruby glanced at Michael.

"She didn't take anything. Can you give us a minute here?" Michael barely noticed when Raoul pulled Ruby away, giving them privacy. All of his attention stayed with Dani. He had to find out what she was experiencing if he was to have any prayer of helping her.

He reached out and cupped his hand around her ashen cheek, feeling the coolness of her flesh. Immediately he caught jumbled flashes of memory.

A pale young girl with wide dark eyes and dark hair cut close to her scalp, curled up around a teddy bear as she screamed.

Crowded rooms full of teenagers drinking out of plastic cups.

A pin-up girly poster stuck to the ceiling.

147

"Dani, come back to me," he called. "Whatever happened, it's long over. It can't hurt you anymore."

She didn't respond. He held her wrists firmly, pressing his fingers into the pressure points to release her grip. Gently, he disentangled her hands from her hair, almost drowning in the sickening regret that threatened to swallow her.

"Look at me, please," he begged, fighting the first ragged edge of his panic. "Come back. We'll make it okay."

He kept talking, repeating over and over that it was safe, that it would be okay. Sense slowly returned to her dull eyes. She looked at him for the first time since the attack in the alley. He felt her awareness returning, and then a new memory flashed across their bond.

His fist smashed into lax, boozy flesh, and he wanted to crow with the vicious satisfaction of hurting someone who threatened someone else.

Michael snatched his hand back before he could relive any more of the attack. Whatever she regretted, Redneck's beating wasn't it.

Dani slowly closed her eyes. He could still sense her weariness, the effort she'd expended to put the monster back into the bottle.

"How long?" he asked, keeping his voice calm and his movements slow.

"Since I was a teenager," she answered, her voice flat and expressionless.

"Is there a way to get rid of it?" he asked hopefully.

A short bitter laugh barked out between her lips. "No. I could go through the High Priestess ritual. Then it would become me, take over whenever it wanted to."

"Why would anyone do that?" Michael whispered, disgusted by the idea. No good could possibly come from that thing.

"Everyone tells me I shouldn't be afraid of it. But they don't feel it the way I do." A humorless smile twisted her mouth. "Maybe I broke it. Maybe it's the awfulness inside me that made it the monster it is today." He could feel the shame and self-hatred spreading through her heart like a noxious green mold.

"Was that it outside? Did it take you over?" he asked. If it had been the monster, it would mean Dani wasn't responsible.

"Yes. No. Sort of." She shook her head. "We both wanted Redneck

148

to pay for hurting Tanisha. For threatening you."

"And in here?" he asked cautiously.

"No. That was me denying both of us the use of this body. I didn't want it to hurt any more people." Dani winced as she touched the bruise forming on her temple. "If I surrender, it gets to move in full time. I become a sideline act in my own body."

"That's terrible," Michael gasped.

"That's the Babylon legacy. It's what everyone expected me to do. My mother was High Priestess for a time. We moved all the time, staying out of public attention. Most *lalassu* do. Coming home, I'd never know if the trailer would be hitched up to the van and we'd be leaving. Mom used to scare the crap out of me when she was in Goddess mode. We never knew what she was going to say or do. We mostly took care of ourselves and tried to stay out of her way." Her voice might be flat, but Michael caught the tremors.

"But your mother is okay now?" There had to be a solution somewhere.

"Not even close." A bitter laugh escaped her cracked lips. "She spent years barely coming out of the trailer. It wasn't until we moved to Perdition that she started talking to us again and then only to demand that I take up my appointed role. She's relentless."

Michael could feel the echoes of abandonment and horror in Dani. He wanted to hold her, but he forced himself to focus as she continued.

"I think she feels guilty because she burned out her connection to the gods when I was a kid. It blinded her, and that's when she retreated. I had to go through the transition of the Huntress becoming part of me all on my own. I knew what I was supposed to do but the idea of surrendering to that thing… Well, you've felt it." Dani stared at her hands. "Our ancestors were the temple harlot priestesses in ancient Babylon. Our touch could bring a man or woman face to face with the Goddess. That's how it's supposed to work, but that's not what it feels like to me."

He couldn't pull together the words to respond to what she'd revealed. Knowing she had a monster inside her, that it would eventually consume her. What could anyone possibly say to alleviate such knowledge?

149

Her phone trilled, forgotten on the cracked tile floor. Dani picked it up wearily to answer it. "Hi, Mom, what is it?"

Tinny screams and smashing came through the miniature speaker. Dani straightened, energy returning along with purpose.

"Dani, you have to come home. Now!" A woman's voice came through clearly.

Followed by the click of the line going dead.

Chapter Twenty-Four

Michael didn't ask any questions, matching Dani stride for stride as they hurtled out of the club, leaving a shocked Raoul and Ruby in their wake. But he was careful to avoid any accidental contact with her. It hurt, cutting deep into her soul, but she couldn't blame him, not now that he knew what was inside her. If only the pain could slash out the Huntress, slice into its coils to leave it to bleed to death.

Reaching the convertible, Dani barely gave Michael time to slide into the seat before her foot slammed the gas pedal to the floor.

"Do you think they found your family?" Michael struggled with the seatbelt.

Dani's only answer was the tightening of her fingers on the steering wheel and the increasing thrum of the engine. She refused to arrive too late again. This would not be a repetition of Vincent and Eric.

"How long is it going to take to get there?" he asked.

"Not as long as it usually does," she replied grimly.

The trip may have defied the laws of physics on several levels. Dani kept the gas pedal firmly pressed to the car floor, ignoring stop signs, stop lights and all other traffic. Fear threatened to cloud her mind and her focus, so she ruthlessly suppressed it—or so she told herself.

If the people who held Vincent and Eric tracked down the rest of the family, this could be a trap. Chewing at her lip, Dani discarded the possibility. They already held Vincent and Eric, leaving Gwen as the next logical prize. They wouldn't care if she was insane as long as her visions could give accurate information.

Each second ticking by grated on her raw nerves. Knowing she was traveling as fast as humanly possible did nothing to reassure her. *Hold on. Just hold on.* She didn't believe in her family's gods, but she still prayed.

To her right, Michael's knuckles and face blanched in stark contrast to the dark seats. Each glimpse added to the thick stew of guilt and fear. *I did the right thing.* The assertion rang hollow, even to herself. He would never understand.

I should be glad. If he hates me, he'll be out of range. Nothing further to explore. She tried to spin the night into something reassuring, but nothing changed the memory of his face after seeing what she'd done to Redneck.

She'd disillusioned him. Part of her wanted to be angry about her guilt for failing to live up to his white-hat hero expectations. But all she felt was the shame. She'd pulled him into something ugly and nasty, showed him the monsters in the closet and under the bed... and the ones inside her.

Dani risked a glance at him. He leaned against the door, clutching the oh-shit bar and staring out the windshield. As far from her as it was possible to get in the confines of the car. He didn't want to be anywhere near her.

Shoving self-pity and introspection away to reexamine at a time when she wasn't hurtling down narrow country roads at four times the legal limit, she scanned the countryside with a predator's instincts. Any movement, any deviation caught her attention.

The disguised turn-off loomed in the distance. Dani spun the car hard, spraying gravel and ripping away concealing foliage. Forced to slow down to avoid becoming a crash-test on the winding lane, she resented every tap of the brake.

The engine roared as they broke through the protective forest into the family's clearing to find...

Nothing.

No goon squad. No black-ops helicopter. Just slumbering country scenery.

"What the fuck?" Dani swore as she stepped out. The lights burned peacefully in the house windows. No gunplay interrupted the silence of the woods. Granted, her arrival probably scared every woodland animal into shock, but from the call, she'd expected more. Her instincts screamed that she must have missed something.

"Where is everyone?" Michael asked.

Dani stood perfectly still, outlined against the yellow light beaming from the windows. He could see her inhaling deeply. *Testing scents,* Michael realized.

"There's nothing here." She frowned, chewing on her lip.

You mean you nearly turned us into road pizza or tree sculptures for nothing? He'd never been more sure he was about to die than in the last half hour. He wanted to yell, vent the tension drawing his skin down tight, but he kept quiet.

The door of the house opened, and a man in a wheelchair came onto the porch. His broad shoulders and strong arms gave him a strong, commanding presence despite the chair. From the thick dark hair and olive skin, Michael guessed this was Dani's father. "Thank the gods. You're here," the man sighed. "Both of you. Hurry inside, she's waiting."

"What's going on?" Dani asked, hurrying up the ramp.

"We can't be sure. Gwen had an incident—"

"You called me out here because of a tantrum? She has them every fucking day, Dad. She begs me to save people who died in the Civil War!" Dani stopped in her tracks.

Michael blinked, not sure he'd heard correctly. *Who's Gwen?*

"This is different." Walter's quiet assertion allowed no possibility for argument. His dark eyes studied Michael carefully as they stepped into the house. Wheelchair or not, Michael knew Walter would take care of any potential threat personally.

Dani's irritation snapped loud and clear with each clicking footstep as she crossed the kitchen floor. Michael worried that one more stress would permanently break her.

The sound of a soothing lullaby broken by whimpering caught his attention. It was close. He slid around Dani and her father, the two of them still arguing. A short dimly lit hall opened off the kitchen. The sounds were coming from there, from the dark room at the end.

As his eyes adjusted, he could make out an older woman kneeling on a mound of quilts and blankets. Her long hair fell over her face in streaks of gray and black. She stroked something on her lap, something he couldn't quite make out.

At first he thought it must be a child, but then he took in the proportions of the long pasty limbs curled into themselves, the size of the close-shorn head.

Disbelief struggled to quash the revelation. It was a young woman, in her late teens or early twenties. From the stale scent of sweat and the

153

pallid gleam of her skin, one who lived entirely within this room. A room made of inexpertly mortared irregular stones, floor, walls, and ceiling. No window broke the craggy expanses. The only light came from a few scattered candles burning in empty soup tins. A heavy ceramic pot in the corner told him he wasn't mistaken.

"You keep her trapped in here?" Despite a lifetime of maintaining professional composure, anger sharpened his voice and narrowed his features.

The woman raised her head and her milky eyes met Michael's horrified gaze. "Not trapped. Protected."

"She needs to be protected from you." Michael fumbled for his phone, plans of calling the police or protective services running through his mind. She would need a guardian. The state would provide one.

Walter's hand darted out, snagging his wrist, trapping the mobile in his pocket. Michael hadn't heard him or Dani approach, but he absorbed the man's exhaustion and long-held fear. He couldn't help comparing it to Martha, Bernie's mother. Neither of them felt hope for the future any longer, yet kept fighting anyway. But this family had fought a futile battle for much longer.

"You did this to her," he whispered, comprehending. *Not trapped. Protected as well as they could.*

"We had to. She's a medium. A powerful one. Probably the most powerful one in history." Walter let him go. "They wouldn't leave her alone."

"It's why we moved to Perdition. We needed somewhere safe to build a solid structure to keep the dead out. Stone and salt are the only things that work and there can't be any chinks or gaps for them to slip though." Dani took up the narrative, gesturing to the thick line of white crystals around the door. "No electrical wiring to ride in. No plumbing. When we carried her in here, it was the first time she'd ever known silence."

"Until she broke the salt," Dani's mother snapped, still not ready to forgive the trespass and accusations.

"She broke the salt?" Dani paled.

Michael knelt by the doorway. Sure enough, there were a series of thin gaps in the crystals as though someone had clawed them.

154

"She's been agitated all evening. I was trying to calm her down but she ripped right through the salt line. Then she started screaming for you, Danielle." Her mother transferred her blind glare to her other daughter.

Gwen moaned. "Did they come? Tell her she has to come. Both of them."

"I'm here, Gwen." Dani's earlier irritation vanished completely. She knelt by her sister's bed.

Gwen groped blindly, her skeletal fingers clutching at Dani's strong hands. "Did he come? Did you find him? The invisible man?"

"I found him." Dani glanced over her shoulder at Michael.

Me? This was beyond anything he'd expected. He couldn't quite begin to process it.

"He should leave," Dani's mother insisted.

"Virginia—" Walter held up his hand.

Gwen writhed as her body curled with pain. "Won't leave me alone. Won't take no for an answer. Screaming in blood, everything shimmers." She continued muttering nonsense about blood and illusions while the rest of them exchanged helpless shrugs.

"She was so insistent that we call. But then she ripped the phone out of my hand, screaming the shadows would trace it." Virginia cradled her lost daughter. "Whatever has her is strong."

"What did she mean about the invisible man?" Michael asked, keeping his attention focused on Dani.

"Something the dead showed her. I needed to find the invisible man who sees hidden truths, or else the stars would be blotted out one by one." Dani pushed her hands through her hair.

"That's what you meant with Vapor. This person hunting *lalassu*, he's capturing them but no one realized. But how on earth am I supposed to stop him blotting out the stars?" He looked around as if the answer might be written on the walls or floor around him.

"Help me find him and stop him from taking anyone else," Dani replied bluntly.

"Who are you?" Walter's steel-eyed scrutiny eloquently established his mistrust far better than any mere words could have managed.

"My name is Michael Brooks. I'm a behavioral therapist." Even as he said the words, he knew the answers were inadequate.

"He's a psychometrist," Dani explained. "He gets impression through touch."

"I am aware what a psychometrist is." Walter's eyes never left Michael. "I've never heard of him."

"He's not part of the community, but he is one of us."

A frantic scream from Gwen interrupted the interrogation.

"Let me see if I can help her. Please." Michael took a step toward, her but Walter blocked his path.

Gwen screamed louder.

Michael shoved his hair back with both hands, fighting a nearly physical compulsion to help. "Please. This is what I do."

"Let him, Dad. He won't hurt her."

Walter wheeled back reluctantly, his chair teetering on the uneven surface.

Michael ignored him, kneeling beside mother and daughter. Gwen clung tightly to Virginia, her eyes flickering over unseen things, just like Bernie's did. He wanted to take the time to chase down the implications of that thought, but Gwen needed his help now.

"She's lost in the voices." Virginia's voice thickened with tears.

"Then let me see if I can help her find her way home." Michael took a deep breath and reached for Gwen's hand.

Chapter Twenty-Five

The world snapped and fuzzed around him. The stone walls loomed large and shot into the distance in dizzying unpredictability. A low buzz, like a stadium crowd in the distance, filled the air. Michael stared in horror at the thick stone that suddenly seemed like a paper screen separating him from something horrible and determined. The noise grew louder, shattering into distinct voices.

"—see me, know you can—"

"—fight, fight every day—"

"—never told her—"

"—need to have it, just one more—"

"—don't like it here—"

Michael tried to ignore the incessant chatter and the throbbing walls, focusing on the shivering girl. Mindful of the fragile bones beneath the clammy skin, he nonetheless kept a tight grip. "Gwen," he called softly. His voice vanished into the din.

"—scary, Mommy, please—"

"—searching forever—"

"—couldn't hurt me again—"

"—never let go—"

"Gwen, don't listen to them. Listen to me." Michael spoke firmly.

That's what he says.

The thought was so clear that he nearly dropped her hand as well as the link between them in surprise. Gwen's blank stare tightened, flickering back to the present.

"Gwen?"

You have to follow me.

"No, Gwen, you need to come back with me," he urged, not wanting to be drawn deeper into her madness. The voices rose up, snatching at his attention.

NO! The word hit him like hurricane-force winds, a denial negating and flattening everything in its path. Michael winced, his head throbbing from the psychic impact. The voices went silent for a moment, but then began to mutter again.

Gwen stared at him with the shadowed eyes of someone who has been forced to see more than any sane human could ever imagine. *You have to go or else they die.*

"Go where?" Michael choked out.

Here. Gwen's free hand shot out and clamped onto Michael's cheek, the bony fingers digging into his skin. He gasped and stiffened against the assault, but it was too late.

His consciousness flowed out of his body like water. He saw himself fall onto the floor. Gwen's hand lay trapped beneath his head, and for a moment he worried the weight of his skull might break her fingers.

"Don't. I'll be all right."

He looked up, but the Gwen standing in front of him was not the same one lying in the stone-walled room. She was younger, her short dark hair in a pixie-cut and neatly combed. She moved like any other girl, and her eyes were clear and lucid.

Except he could also see her pale and battered body lying beside him, and his own body next to her. "How...?" He couldn't quite get the words past his amazement.

She smiled. "It's a combination of the two of us. I couldn't explain it, but they were sure it would work."

He watched as Dani's mother cradled her daughter while her father stood guard at the door. Dani knelt beside Michael, biting her lip, her hand hovering as if she wanted to touch him, but she didn't want to risk overloading him. Except that he couldn't sense her at all, as if she were an image on television. The realization unsettled him. But he had to focus on Gwen right now. "Who are 'they'?"

"Ghosts. Spirits. Messengers." Gwen shrugged as if the details were unimportant. "They sent a lot of them because it was hard for me to hear the message. You know, because of the crazy."

"You're not crazy. You're a medium. The voices are real." Michael turned back to Gwen, determined to understand what had happened. The walls were still throbbing, but the voices were muted.

"That only makes it worse." Gwen rubbed her toe against the floor.

"Chuck should be here."

"Chuck?" Michael tried to keep his concern out of his voice. Surely she didn't mean Bernie's invisible instigator?

"I had to open the door so he could come in. But don't worry. He's not upset that you didn't think he was real."

"Speak for yourself, doll," a boy's voice drawled with a harsh Brooklyn accent. Spinning, Michael saw a small boy around ten years old standing beside them, as solid as Dani, her parents, or either of the Gwens. The boy wore dull gray trousers and suspenders. His white shirt had the sleeves rolled up and a gray cap perched uncertainly on his head.

"Chuck?" Michael tried to collect his professional dignity and closed his mouth.

"Yeah. That's me."

"Bernie's Chuck?"

"What, you want ID?" The toughened child had no patience for mental processing. "Musta left it in my other pants. You know, when I died."

"What are you doing here?" Michael asked, eager to regain some illusion of control and normality.

"Bernie needs you."

"I know." Guilt weighed him down.

"You was supposed to rescue her! She's scared!" Chuck's pint-sized fury exploded.

"I know." Had life ever been so simple when he was a child? Even then, he'd seen into the secrets people didn't want to share. He'd wanted it to be simple, and that urge had drawn him to comics. Heroes help, villains hurt and in the end, the right side wins.

"I tried to help her. Tried to show her what was wrong." Chuck glared at him.

He remembered Bernie's words. *Chuck says it's scary.* "You were right."

"You mugs never listen to me!" Chuck shouted.

"It's hard for people to listen to me, too," Gwen told him, plucking at her hair.

"Chuck, I'm listening now. But you need to promise something, too." Michael knelt beside the boy, putting them on the same level.

159

"Or what? You won't help?" the boy sneered.

"I've been helping Bernie a long time, and I'm going to get her out of that place." Irritated at the suggestion of abandonment, his voice firmed. He took a breath, reminding himself that Chuck was still a child, no matter how long he had been dead. "But it would help if you would stop telling her to hurt other people or destroy things."

Chuck stared at his feet. "I don't always mean it. I just get mad sometimes."

"I know. But Bernie gets confused. You need to be a good friend to her and help her. One way is to help her know she's not alone. Her mom is fighting real hard to get her back home. And I'm fighting hard, too." He reached out to touch Chuck's arm, uncertain if his hand would pass right through, but instead his fingers settled on warm flesh.

Without any information. It surprised him. He'd never touched someone without picking up flashes of memories or emotional states. It felt strangely empty.

"It's cause I ain't got no body, genius." Chuck shook his head in the universal juvenile disgust at the obtuseness of adults everywhere.

"Can you read my thoughts?" Michael asked.

"Naw. But I know what you can do. And it ain't hard to figure out what you're thinking." He paused, studying Michael. "You really gonna ride in and save Bernie?"

"Maybe not ride in, but I'm going to get her out of there. I won't stop until she's out." As much as it went against his instincts, Dani was right about the futility of a forward assault. This wasn't a comic where everything would work out. They needed a better plan than hoping for the best.

"You have to stay away!" a new voice shrieked.

The wavering figure standing in the corner couldn't seem to decide if it was a skinny man with matted hair or a powerful one bristling with science-fiction weapons. "There's no time!" he shouted. "They're coming!"

"Who are you?" Michael demanded, stepping between the strange apparition and Gwen and Chuck.

"Can't tell you my name. Always want to know my name. That's how they find you, track you down, snatch you while you sleep. Can't

160

give the name. No, no. Not going to get me again." He solidified briefly into the skinny, unkempt version of himself, wearing a T-shirt with a Superman logo. "Have to give the message, get back out there. Need me to fight the war. Can't leave my post."

"He's been shouting so loud, even the stone didn't keep him away." Gwen curled her bony fingers around Michael's arm, crouching in his shadow. "He came right after Chuck."

"Keeps yammering about the message. But the stupid mook won't tell us what it is." Chuck threw his hands in the air in frustration.

"Who told you to give the message?" Michael's training steadied him. No matter how weird the setting and circumstances, this was still a mentally disturbed individual who needed his help.

"Big guy. Told me then killed me. Didn't want to. But they had him. Knew his name."

"What did he say?" Michael kept his voice calm and undemanding.

"Said to find Gwen. Needed to give her the message."

"I'm Gwen." She stepped around Michael.

The skinny man scrubbed his hands through his matted hair. "You are?"

She nodded, her fingers knotting and twisting together.

"What about them? They might be with, you know, *them*."

"I trust them. Please, tell me." Gwen whispered, her weight poised lightly on her feet as if she were prepared to flee at the slightest sign of danger.

"I'm tired. So tired. Running all the time. Trying to keep ahead." He sank down on the ground.

"They can't hurt you anymore. You're safe now," Michael reassured him.

"He said to tell them André is looking for them. He wants power. Tell them to run."

Sharp coppery blood on her tongue warned Dani before her compulsive lip-biting could sever a substantial portion of flesh. Her thighs ached with the effort of supporting herself on her haunches on the uneven floor.

Michael's skin had gone horribly pale against the dark stone floor. He hadn't moved since Gwen grabbed him and they'd fallen together. The clock might only say a few minutes had passed but it felt like hours to Dani. Gwen curled up as if she were simply asleep but Michael's chest barely shifted with each shallow breath. She strained to hear the muted thump of his slowed heart, desperate for any sign of improvement. Only his eyes flickering behind half-closed lids betrayed any sign of life. Even his smell was muted, a pale faded memory of apples and vanilla instead of a mouth-watering inspiration.

Like when he'd vanished at Vapor's. The hacker might not have understood her panic, but it had unnerved her to see everything that made Michael himself vanish out of his body, leaving nothing behind but slack meat. She'd seen enough dead bodies in her lifetime to recognize the difference between the living and the dead, breathing notwithstanding. Her lip slipped between her teeth again as she watched her mother in trance.

"I can't find them." Virginia roused herself, shaking her head sadly. "They've gone somewhere I can't follow." She cradled Gwen's limp body, stroking her arms.

Dani growled at her mother before she could stop herself, her irises burning.

Virginia straightened in surprise, her hands tightening protectively on Gwen. "They're both still alive with spirits intact. For now."

"But you don't know where they are." Dani's voice could have been recorded for demonic possession special effects.

"No. Gwen has always been able to outdistance me on the spectral planes. It's part of her gift. I'm sure she'll be fine," Virginia insisted.

"And what about Michael?" Caught up in her worry, Dani barely realized that she'd called him by his proper name for the first time.

"I don't know," her mother snapped. "All I can do anymore are minor predictions. You want to know if he's going to travel, get a promotion, find an apartment, I can tell you. This is beyond anything I can see since I don't have a direct connection to the divine anymore."

Dani winced at the implication, looking to her father for support. But Walter was quiet, focused on guarding the door to Gwen's room. It always came back to this. If she sacrificed herself, then things would be better. The *lalassu* would be under the direct leadership of the Goddess again. The needs of everyone else came before her apparently selfish preference for survival. The Huntress thrummed eagerly at the thought of the ceremony, pulling and tugging at her psyche. She was tired of fighting it. She hated the memory of disappointment in Michael's eyes. If she threw herself into the Huntress's maw, she wouldn't have to remember it again.

The urge to surrender was compelling. But primal revulsion was equally powerful. Dani shook her head. "I never asked to be part of a line of High Priestesses."

"None of us did. But it hasn't stopped the women of our family from stepping up for over three thousand years. The world needs us." Virginia could have taught a master class in parental guilt.

"Virginia, stop," Walter interrupted gently. "Dani, I know you have your reasons, but you need to think about the bigger picture."

Dani's self-control, already dangerously shredded, dissolved in a tsunami of temper. "The world doesn't need us. We've become con artists and grifters, skulking in shadows and feeding off the world's leavings."

Virginia sniffed disapprovingly. "You can't appreciate the necessity of sacrifice. Your selfish decision could ruin us all. Without the divine, we can't be anything but shades of our true selves. Without a High Priestess, we become vulnerable. If you hadn't been so stubborn, we could have been warned when this man first began to hunt us—"

"Don't! Just don't," Dani snarled. She hated feeling helpless nearly as much as she hated regret. She always charged into the action. She wasn't left on the sidelines. *And I don't do regrets*, she insisted defiantly. Even when part of her wondered if her mother was right. *Please, wake up, Michael. I need you back with me.*

She ignored the parental glances flying over her head. As furious as every arched eyebrow and slow nod made her, none of it mattered right now. More than anything, she wanted a chance to make things right with Michael. She wanted to be a hero for him again.

Gwen's eyes were closed almost as if she were asleep. But Michael wasn't adapting to the trance state. In the silence, she could hear faint rustling, the delicate whisper of shifting cloth—coma-induced micro

163

tremors from psychic synaptic overload.

"Hold them!" Dani shouted, wrapping herself around Michael's prone body as the first seizure hit. Virginia held tight to Gwen.

He thrashed under her, limbs flailing. Dani pinned him, trying to use her weight to prevent him from getting enough leverage to hurt himself. She cursed her strength, enough to crush his bones but not the knowledge of how to keep him intact.

His head bashed against the rock and she released an arm to tuck underneath. But her movement gave him enough room to twist and bounce wildly under her. Dani fought to hold him still. "Michael, please! It's me! Don't fight it!"

His legs bucked in place. *Oh shit. What if it's me? What if I'm downloading memories into him, making it worse?* If she was, it was too late. Virginia kept her hand pressed on top of Gwen's, holding her daughter's fingers to Michael's skin. Breaking the connection meant his spirit might be trapped between worlds forever. A wild blow smashed into her side, hard enough to leave bruises on anyone else.

"Keep him there!" Her mother ordered, trapping his flailing arm. Dani stretched out on top of him, her legs pinning his knees, one arm holding his and the other cradling his head to keep him from cracking his skull against the floor. They were nose to nose, chest to chest, points of contact along every inch, but Dani had never felt so isolated from another person.

His beautiful hazel eyes quivered and swirled under half-open lids, inches from her and yet indefinable distances away. She'd never been so physically close to a man and had him still unaware of her. She didn't like the feeling. It made her want to hit something, smash the barrier between them to pieces. But nothing presented itself to be hit. So she held on.

"Michael, please," she whispered. "Come back. Come back to me."

Chapter Twenty-Six

"She's into you." Gwen rendered her verdict as if it didn't matter in the least.

"So people keep telling me." Michael remembered Raoul's words.

"Because she isn't going to tell you. She's—"

"Scared." Michael crouched beside their unconscious bodies, watching as Dani and her mother argued. The constant din of other voices made it hard to distinguish what they were saying.

Everything from the so called real world felt more distant here. It was eerie, seeing Dani right there but not sensing anything from her. He should be more worried about his body, but somehow he couldn't quite summon up the emotions.

"If you're curious, this is what death is like," Gwen said.

"Am I dying?" He wasn't ready to die. He watched as Dani held herself back from touching him. "Shouldn't there be a bright light? A *This Is Your Life* screening? Reception line of dead relatives?" He wanted Gwen to tell him this wasn't actually the end.

"I've never seen it or talked to anyone who has. People die, and then they step out of their bodies and then no one can talk to them but mediums like me. They try to get their families to see them, but they almost never do. They have to watch as they get relegated to back corners and basements and garages, their lives piled in smelly boxes." Gwen shrugged, more interested in twining her fingers and twisting her arms into poses that would freak out yogic masters.

"Gwen—" he began, the beginnings of panic starting to set in.

She continued, ignoring him. "It's worse when they aren't forgotten. Wouldn't you feel awful knowing your memory was a constant source of pain to someone you cared about? Kids are the worst. Their parents almost never get over it, keeping their rooms as shrines. They don't get it. All they know is that Mommy cries because of them and they want to tell her it's okay. So they scream and yell and pester me to do it."

"I'm sorry," he said automatically, wishing he could help. *If I die, I could try. Therapist for the dead.* He tried to make it a joke but the shouting rising from outside the walls brought home how relentless the dead could be. His heart went out to Gwen, gaining a small glimpse of what she must have to deal with every day.

"I don't think you're going to die. Well, not yet anyway." Abandoning her attempts to twist herself into a pretzel, Gwen crouched down by his body just as Dani threw herself over him. His body started to shake and writhe on the ground. A strange tug began to pull on his mind, like one of his compulsive flashes. It pulled him back toward his body.

"You need to see it," Gwen told him. "It won't make you happy, but you need it."

He couldn't answer as memories overloaded him. He was still separate from his convulsing physical form, but now he couldn't see Gwen's room any more—just the memories from Dani's past.

Did Daddy come home? The question echoed in an immature mind as tiny feet silently climbed down the stairs. An unwitting passenger in her mind, he watched as she tiptoed into the basement. He felt her fear, sharing her knowledge that they had abandoned their trailer, the only home Dani knew, to seek out this safehouse. He knew her father had been gone for weeks, missing her tenth birthday, but the sound of his voice and her mother's pulled her out of sleep. She woke Vincent up and the two of them went to see.

Anticipatory terror seeped into his awareness. He knew the children were walking into a nightmare but couldn't stop the inevitable progression of the past. He wanted to pick up the little girl Dani had been and shelter her from what she was about to see. The images shattered under Dani's fear, leaving him with tiny glimpses. A much younger Virginia, her belly rounded in pregnancy. Walter, lying on the ground, his clothes and skin burned and bloody. Dani's attention was ripped from her parents to focus on a small statue on the altar behind them.

Michael couldn't make out the details clearly, it looked like a woman with a flowing robe behind her. Or was it supposed to be wings? As he tried to figure it out, the dark, rich clay began to fade, the color and strength draining away even as Walter began to roll and twitch on the

166

ground. Virginia looked up in horror, her dark eyes covered with a thick, white film. Michael shared Dani's sense of something unseen and monstrous hovering around her parents, demanding something horrible from them.

The memory vanished into inaudible screams, but another wrapped around him.

A young man, tall, with brown hair. *Justin.* Dani's date to senior prom. He could feel her reckless excitement and had to squash a small spark of jealousy in himself. Only the knowledge that he was revisiting Dani's darkest moments kept it from growing any larger.

Her father had forbidden her to go, but she'd sneaked out of the house, wanting to have a normal teenage moment. Over the last two years, lots of boys from school found excuses to speak with her, joined clubs she joined, offered her rides home. Sometimes their presence seemed to spark something dark inside her but she held it at bay. Her father insisted it was all part of her destiny as High Priestess, that men would always find themselves attracted to her. But Dani was determined to have a normal life. She'd seen how being High Priestess destroyed her mother. Years of trances and never knowing who would be at their home and ever since the night in the basement, Dani's mother barely left her bedroom.

The memory brought traces of remembered fear, but the teenaged Dani put them away with practiced ease. She would be different. It wasn't going to get her the way it had gotten her mother. Michael hoped she was right, that they could find a way to make it work.

At first, the prom was everything Dani hoped for, but things began to go badly. Justin grew sulky and possessive, refusing to let her dance with anyone else, frightening her. Shoving matches began to outnumber dancers on the dance floor. Two boys cornered Lila Svenson and ripped open her dress. The teachers who were supposed to be supervising had vanished into the utility closet.

Michael shared Dani's dawning realization that she was somehow responsible for what happened. His heart was already battered on her behalf, and this was yet another blow. She tried to flee, but Walter appeared at the school as she left. A long lecture on her irresponsibility followed, and the promise of a banishment to her European cousins.

Shame choked the lovely memories from earlier, smothering them.

Another blink. He downloaded more snippets of memory and time had passed.

Dani was older now, more confident. She could use the attraction from her heritage to her advantage—hers and her brothers. Male salespeople routinely gave her discounts and free samples. Her brothers shamelessly traded on the effect, using her to establish contact with Chomp, the local underground connection. Like any young woman, she enjoyed the exercise of her power even if she wasn't always sure about what she was doing. Her mother had finally emerged from her depressed withdrawal, but all of their conversations boiled down to: "Do the ritual. Now!" Dani refused to accept surrender to the alien being she could feel lurking below her conscious mind. The sense of darkness inside was growing, but she was determined to keep it out.

But the monster always lurked beneath the surface. She remained confident, though. If she didn't acknowledge it or call on it, it couldn't hurt her or take over her life. Her naïve bravado hurt so much more when he knew how it all ended.

He still hadn't seen the worst. A darker memory hid beneath the flashes. Michael could almost see it, but Dani's consciousness skittered over it, settling on something more recent.

A tall, blond man in expensive clothes. Michael recognized him from the nightclub, and Dani's memories supplied a name: Josh. The earlier flash of jealousy reignited, and he had trouble concentrating.

Now the Huntress coiled inside, poison dripping from eager fangs—such a difference from a few seconds earlier. He could sense Dani's reluctance. She didn't want to be with this man, didn't want him to touch her. But the Huntress needed to be fed. He wanted to shout at her, to tell her not to do it.

She pulled her prey closer, unwilling to waste time in preliminaries. He tasted her hatred and resentment of the Huntress, a bitter tang on his tongue. She hated the role it forced her into, making her a predator. All she could do was aim at acceptable targets. The Huntress snapped out, slithering across from her body to his through the contact of skin. Ravenous hunger tore into the prey's spirit, seeking something worthy.

But there was nothing. Fear. Paranoia. An inferiority complex

168

masked by bravado.

The Huntress ripped through social masks, revealing this swaggering male as the coward he truly was. It forced Josh to see himself through eyes scrubbed into surgical sanctity, before sending him back into his body. It coiled back inside Dani, sated if not satisfied. Josh curled up on the couch, shaking with shock.

Michael shook his head in denial, struggling to comprehend what had just happened. He shared Dani's knowledge of the inevitable dangers if she didn't Hunt. But to see how the Huntress ripped into Josh and then threw him aside unsettled him.

The memory storm was over. He could see Dani now, struggling to keep him from hurting himself. He winced as he watched his arm flail out and hit her hard. But she ignored it, keeping her hold. He'd seen enough secrets himself not to trust anyone's outer mask, but he couldn't reconcile the violence of her attacks on Redneck and Josh with the tenderness she showed to Gwen.

"It's the Huntress. It's part of Dani's legacy as one of the priestesses of Babylon," Gwen explained. "It comes out through skin contact and orgasm. Through sex, she forges a connection to the divine. But an unworthy partner can't hold up to that kind of shock. Sucks to have to see yourself through omniscient, impartial eyes."

An unworthy partner. A glimmer of an idea started to form in Michael's mind, but he couldn't get past the first part. "She fed him to it."

"She protects you," Gwen pointed out. "She worries about turning you into a vegetable. She knows it hurts them and leaves scars in their minds. Most of her prey never want to see her again. She really wants to see you again."

"Michael, please. Come back. Come back to me." He heard Dani's whisper clearly. If he abandoned her, if he died, he suspected she would never forgive herself.

"It's getting madder. She won't let it out anymore because she doesn't want to hurt you. If she doesn't find the path, I don't know what could happen."

"You don't?" *Didn't Dani say Gwen could predict the future?*

"I see things sometimes, but I don't always know what they mean.

But I only really know what the dead tell me. They're good at figuring stuff out, but it's not a perfect system. They want her to do the ritual and become High Priestess. Mom was High Priestess when Dad got hurt. She was pregnant with me at the time. She did something, made a bargain that changed everything. It took her eyes, scared Dani, and made me crazy. Mom says she's sorry for it a lot when she thinks I can't hear her. It makes me sad."

Michael had more than a little trouble following Gwen's explanation. He struggled with what to ask as she continued.

"It's a test. She has to open her own eyes the same way she opens the eyes of others. She has to face herself, and I don't think she likes herself too much. I like her, but, you know, she's my sister and everything so I kind of have to. She takes care of me and she's nice, mostly. Sometimes she pulls my hair." Gwen rubbed at the side of her head. "And she doesn't always believe me when I tell her things. I can understand why. I get confused sometimes, but she should give me a little credit. It's not easy trying to put stuff into words. It's why I like making pictures."

Michael nodded slowly, brow furrowed as he tried to follow the skips and leaps of Gwen's thought processes.

She smiled, childlike joy beaming out like the sun. "You're nice. I think I'll like having you as a brother. You know, if you don't end up with zucchini-brain."

"I like you, too. Even if you are a little unusual." He smiled back, not wanting to expand on the "brother" part of her comment. They had more important issues to worry about.

Gwen knelt down. "You should get back into your body again. I don't think you're supposed to be that color."

His skin had gone pale and his lips were edged in blue. "How do I get back?"

"I dunno. You have to want to." Gwen crouched by her mother.

Want to. He stared at Dani frantically trying to keep him safe.

"Yes, like that," Gwen whispered.

Chapter Twenty-Seven

Gwen's words blurred and the world fuzzed around Michael. The pain of being slammed back into his body was not something he would have wished on anyone else. A full-body case of pins and needles burning his muscles and skin. Even his eyelids ached.

A weight crushed him down, highlighting every irregular crevice in the floor. Michael coughed and managed to convince his battered eyes to open.

He was staring directly into anxious coffee-colored eyes inches away from his own. Had there been any breath left in his body, it would have been stolen. He felt her panic as if it were his own. A terrible fear of losing something precious, something he hadn't realized was so important.

"Michael?" Dani whispered.

He nodded, perfectly happy to continue without oxygen if it meant he didn't have to spoil this moment. Unfortunately, his survival instincts overrode his romantic ones.

At his first hollow gasp, Dani slid off him, returning to her crouched vigil. He would have cursed his body if any brainpower remained from his body's attempt to reinflate his lungs. He missed the contact of her emotions, feeling diminished without them.

"All right, try to breathe naturally." Walter reached out to Michael, only to find his wrist held in his daughter's iron grip.

"Don't touch him. He doesn't need the overload."

"I'll be okay," Michael wheezed, grateful for the concern. His head felt as if he were trying to squeeze three or four brains' worth of memories into his skull—any more and he might burst.

"Twisted up like a pretzel," Gwen announced from her mother's lap, her eyes flickering over the room as if searching a crowd. "Over and under and round until we came back home. You can put the salt back now."

"Welcome back, love." Virginia cradled her daughter, kissing her

171

sweat-slick hair. Her eyes lifted to find Michael. "Thank you."

"Don't thank me yet." He straightened, wincing. "If Gwen's message was right, you're all in terrible danger." He described the messenger and explained that André was looking for them. "The message was to run. 'André' must be André Dalhard, the CEO of Dalhard Industries. They were behind the company your sons tried to work for. He wants power, and he has his sights set on the *lalassu* as a way to get it."

"We won't leave Eric and Vincent behind. Or Bernie," Dani growled.

"Gwen would be invaluable to them." Walter's hands tightened on his chair.

"Bernie, too." Michael's stomach turned, knowing she was already trapped. "She must be a medium as well." He'd failed her all those years, treating her as delusional when she was struggling with something real and beyond her control.

Gwen yawned from her cocoon of blankets. "You missed a message. For Dani."

"What message?" Dani demanded.

"It's time now. If you don't finish the ritual, the darkness swallows us all," Gwen tossed the words out as if they meant nothing, followed by a yawn. "I'm tired. I want to sleep."

Michael watched Dani's olive skin grow pale and her fingers curl into fists. The second-hand terror swelled through their connection, almost enough to make him want to start screaming on the spot. *There had to be another way besides letting the monster have her.*

"Of course, love." Virginia stood and shooed them from the room.

As they crossed into the kitchen, a thought occurred to Michael. Dani hadn't spoken to him since he'd regained consciousness, not since saying his proper name. She stood by the door, rubbing her arms and tapping her foot, gazing out into the darkness as if she longed to be far away. Part of him screamed with impatience to get on with it. Bernie was trapped with no one but Chuck to help her.

But watching Dani, he could see she was trapped, too. She yanked open the screen door and slipped outside.

Michael didn't wait, didn't pause for polite explanations. He followed her, practically stepping on her heels. "Dani, wait!"

"You should rest." Barely visible against the night, she was an apparition of isolated patches of pale skin floating in darkness.

"We need to talk," he insisted, although his body ached to hold her, give her the comfort she obviously needed. He wanted to forget about the Huntress and his own gifts and take her in his arms. But it wasn't what Dani needed right now. "Please don't shut me out."

"I should have shut you out in the beginning. You'd have been safer if I'd left you sitting in the damn club. You could have died tonight." The faint hitch of suppressed anguish in her voice betrayed her conflicting emotions.

"I'm still here." He stepped behind her, sliding his hand along her bare arm. Fear, bitterness, and self-loathing all coated her like oozing poison. It honestly shocked him to see how deep the festering wounds went. She'd covered it so well with her confident, brash persona. He felt her determination to keep him separate, to protect him. He saw her fear that she would only taint him. How could someone so smart be so wrong? For the first time in his life, he wished he could transmit emotion as well as receive. He wanted her to feel how much he loved her.

Love? Somewhere, admiration and a little hero-worship had transmuted into something deeper, more personal. Once past the initial surprise, it felt natural, as though it would be the easiest thing in the world to say.

But not now. Aside from all the challenges they faced, every trained instinct he had warned him this wasn't the moment to share his feelings. Dani was overwhelmed with hurt and fear. She wouldn't be able to accept it right now.

"I'm still here," he repeated. "And I'm not going anywhere. I've seen the Huntress. Gwen explained that you're protecting me just like you protect her."

"She explained it, did she?" Dani hissed. "Took time out of her busy, crazy day to tell you all about the monster lurking inside her sister? Right before telling me it's time to feed myself to it?"

Dani's eyes opened, revealing the brilliant red rings glowing against the night. Michael drew in a sharp breath. He thought he'd seen them in the alley attack but later convinced himself it had only been a reflection.

She closed her eyes and turned away, her weariness and dejection clear without any need for psychic powers.

"Dani, listen to me, please. I know you believed I'd disappear if I knew about the Huntress. But the truth doesn't frighten me. I've been seeing the worst parts of people ever since I was a toddler. My father told me that my gifts came from the Devil. My mother taught me to hide what I sensed, how to avoid casual touch without being obvious." The bitterness in his voice surprised him. He thought he'd put all this past him long ago, but it still hurt. After over thirty years, a piece of betrayed five-year-old still cowered inside him. "I knew everyone's worst secrets— how the neighbor's wife drank until she passed out every night, how my father's partner stole money for drugs and hookers, I knew about affairs with nannies, addictions, perversions. I drowned in secrets before I even went to grade school. I choked on them." He stared up at the star-speckled sky. "I hate secrets. I hate hiding. I feel like I'm smothered by lies."

That was the key, he realized. The Huntress fed on lies. He couldn't stand not touching her any longer. His fingers sought the smooth line of her cheeks as if drawn by a magnet. She opened her eyes, the red light gone. He felt the quiver of desire waking along her nerves. He pushed back the inky hair falling over her shoulders and savored its silky caress against his knuckles.

"Can the Huntress hear me?" he asked.

Dani stared at him in confusion. "I… it's buried as deep as I can shove it."

"Tell it to listen. I'm not afraid of it. I've never hidden from secrets, about myself or anyone else. There are no lies between you and me." He cupped her cool face in his hand, stroking his thumb along her cheekbone. He felt the first stirrings of hope blooming inside her.

She slid her hand over his chest, pressing her body against him. His groin was afire with hardened anticipation. More than anything, he wanted to lose himself in her and drive away the demons haunting them both. Her ragged breathing made her breasts shiver as they brushed against his chest, and he bent his head, ready to steal her breath with a kiss.

Her fear was rising up strongly, drowning the hope. "I can't control

174

it. I've never been able to control it. And it wants you. It wants you as badly as I do."

"I'm not afraid," he repeated. He pulled her close again. She could have easily broken his grip, but she let him bring her back into full-body contact. His lips brushed against her cheek as he spoke. "We can figure it out together."

"I don't want to hurt you again." Despite her protest, her fingers tangled in his hair and her body pressed tighter against his. Between his lust and hers, it was growing harder and harder to think beyond the moment. He wanted to pull her down on the grass and savor her kissing his neck like she was doing now. He wanted to taste the sweetness of her skin and see if it was all as intoxicating as the softness under his lips. *Please, just a little…*

He sensed it an instant before she did: the coiling predator ready to strike. He readied himself to strike back.

But Dani ripped away as if propelled by electrical current. "Even if you could survive, it would still need to feed. I'd still be the monster it's made me." She shook her head. "I can't risk it, Michael. I couldn't live with myself if it hurts you. I saw your face after I beat up Redneck. I smelled your disgust. I'm not the hero you wanted me to be."

"You are a hero." Michael had a moment of clarity. It wasn't fair to put comic-book expectations on real life. "I won't lie to you. It did bother me. But it was more about me than you. I've cheered the bad guys being beaten up a thousand times, but that time I had to actually see it. It wasn't what I expected. Dani, you can still be a hero. You've got these amazing powers, and you could help a lot of people."

He took her hand in his, wanting to know if he was reaching her. To his relief, the self-disgust was fading, replaced with determination. He pulled her close, confident they would find a way, no matter the odds.

SATURDAY

Chapter Twenty-Eight

"Damn. Whoever they got on the grill knows his work." Vincent happily sawed into his rare steak.

The night before faded like a dream in sunlight when the brothers woke in a luxury suite—like a five-star hotel with plush couches, decadent artwork, and expensive furnishings, but still a prison. No windows broke the silk wallpaper. The only door was locked, and Eric could smell the guards on the other side—for their "protection," no doubt. Breakfast arrived on a room service cart, delivered by anonymous staff who didn't speak or make eye contact.

There had been no further contact by Dalhard. The brothers were left to their own devices, which meant that Vincent indulged in food and drink, and Eric brooded.

Eric ignored his brother, pushing fruit around his plate. The muscles in his arms bunched and twitched as he forced himself to remember the feeling of muscle and bone suddenly snapping under his hands. To see living, breathing flesh become lifeless meat at the flick of a switch. *I did it. I took his life. Not to protect, not to save anyone. Just because Dalhard told me to. I let him think I was a killer for hire.*

It was a mantra he had repeated dozens of times since the interview. He lashed himself with it like a medieval monk, drawing emotional blood over and over. Not because he wanted to be punished but because it was the only way to keep himself sane. His only hope was that the dead man passed on his message to Gwen, giving the family time to run.

The alien presence still squatted in his mind, pumping lulling poisons into his thoughts, trying to anesthetize his memories. It wore on him like water against a stone, grinding away at the pain and shame.

Forcing himself to relive the murder was the only way to keep hold of himself and who he was. He was no longer a good guy. He was a murderer. He deserved the label.

Vincent popped a chunk of meat dripping with juice into his mouth with every sign of satisfaction. Whatever Dalhard had tried to do to Eric, it had worked on his little brother. The weak scent of blood from the rare steak stopped his breath. Eric shoved aside his still-full plate, unable

179

to swallow the food past his disgust.

"Gotta eat, bro," Vincent told him.

"Later." Eric got up, prowling around the spacious suite. He had to find a way to get Vincent out of here. Dalhard had to let them out sometime. "I'm not hungry."

"Your loss." Vincent shrugged. "This is a hell of a lot better than before."

Eric stopped. *Careful. They have to be monitoring us.* "Before?"

"You know. Downstairs."

"The cells," Eric prompted. Maybe Vincent wasn't lost.

"Yeah. This beats that all to hell." Vincent waved the cutlery in wide circles. "I think our luck has changed."

Maybe he doesn't remember. Eric knew the smart thing would be to keep in character, maintaining the illusion Dalhard's powers worked on him, too. But he couldn't quite stop himself. "They made us kill someone." He said the words as quietly as he could.

"Hey, it was him or me, and I'm all kinds of okay with me still being here. Besides, you heard what the guy said—dude was a psychopath. Cutting up kittens for entrees or some shit like that."

Because it would be so impossible for Dalhard to have lied. Eric turned away, unable to watch his brother's carefree demeanor. He did remember, but no heaviness of remorse or guilt marred his scent. Vincent was fine with what had happened.

"Come on, Eric. Don't get all brooding on me. We have a real chance here. This place has money coming out of the fucking walls. We can be a part of that. No hiding who we are. It's what we always wanted."

Eric looked at the silk-covered walls, the elegant furniture, and the sumptuous meal. "It's not what I wanted."

Shitfuckcrap.

The unmarked cop car tailing her had been easy to spot even before the lights began to flash. She wasn't speeding; the taillights were fine. What the hell was this about? Dani pulled over, tempted to pound on the steering wheel in frustration. But breaking her car wouldn't help

180

anything. Her teeth ground together as her day went bad to worse.

First came the almost-sleepless night broken by disturbing dreams. Someone calling to her, someone she was hiding from. She knew deep down in her bones that if she moved, the monster would find her. And it had, no matter how often she'd run or how quiet she tried to be. It tore her to pieces, leaving her trapped and helpless in her own body.

Having Michael just down the hall in the guest bedroom added its own brand of torture: knowing how easy it would have been to ease the sexual frustration seething in her, but no matter how confident he was, she couldn't risk his life and soul. She knew the Huntress and had watched it work. If he was wrong… the possibility had driven her nails deep into her palms and thighs, leaving bloodstains on the sheets in the morning.

She'd made the decision last night while Michael held her. She'd protect Michael from himself and do the ritual. She'd throw herself into the Huntress with the knowledge that she was living up to what he believed she could be, and that he would be safe. Then Gwen wouldn't have to leave her sanctuary on the farm, and the Goddess would help them to rescue the others, offering the sort of detailed tactical plans she'd seen recorded in the Priestess journals. The Goddess had been able to warn the *lalassu* about fleeing on certain ships, such as the *Titanic*. She'd told them the best way to smuggle their people out of Nazi concentration camps. Dani hoped the ritual would reset everything, putting it back to the way it should have been instead of further distorting the conduit. It wasn't like they had anything else to work with. The ritual was their only real chance at success. Michael would want to hold out for another way but every predatory instinct in her body told her there was no more time. Eventually, he would understand.

She'd planned to tell her parents in the morning, but when the time came, her mother hadn't been able to resist pointing out how the ritual was Dani's responsibility and how selfish Dani was to put her own petty pursuits above a divine calling. It was the same old story. Experience told her that even if she tried to explain, her mother wouldn't listen, insisting that everything Dani claimed to experience was a lie, a story she made up to avoid her responsibilities. Even her father insisted she must be mistaken, that the conduit didn't work the way she described. She couldn't listen to one more lecture of parental disappointment and stormed away to her car. Her only regret was that Michael had been busy helping Gwen and she hadn't had the time to tell him what she'd decided. She'd driven into the city to tell Vapor instead. He could help her parents organize a rescue afterward.

Being pulled over by a cop car added a moldy cherry on top of the smoldering pile of crap that was her day. Vapor did not deal well with lateness, but she was not about to do anything so stupid as tipping off the authorities to his existence by calling to tell him what was happening.

Dani caught the scent of gun oil and nerves as soon as she rolled down the window. Officer Stalker waited, his muscled arms crossed over his chest. Cute. Hispanic. *Crap.* Michael's friend, the cop from the attack in the alley behind the club. He held up his badge.

"Danielle Hayden."

That was her alias to get the job at the club. *Damn. Why couldn't this be about a speeding ticket?*

"Come with me." He stared down at her, his eyes hidden behind the blank glare of mirrored sunglasses.

"You've been following me for the last ten minutes to tell me that?" she drawled, hoping he might be enticed.

"I've been searching for you since last night when I recognized your pictures in the employee files. You're under arrest for assault." No humor, only a seething fierceness wafting from under his professional mask. He was looking for an excuse to take her down.

A week ago, she'd have given him a royal brawl. Today, she didn't resist as he ordered her out of her car, snapped cuffs around her wrists, and tucked her into the police car. She wasn't going to hurt anyone else, especially not one of Michael's friends.

At the station, he hurried her into an interrogation room. Bare gray walls dominated by a one-way mirror, metal table, just like dozens of others.

"I'm Detective Joe Cabrera. This is the part where I'm supposed to slap a thick file full of crime scene photos and lab reports on the table and tell you you're in a lot of trouble." He laid a heavy folder on the table between them. "Something tells me it wouldn't impress you. In fact, something tells me that trouble is a comfortable state for you."

"I'm used to it." She briefly displayed the steel cuffs on her wrists, rattling the chain between them on the table.

"My problem is that Michael isn't." Joe bent his head to catch her line of sight again. "I'm worried about him. This guy was taken to the hospital with broken ribs and a concussion." He slapped down a picture of Redneck Whiskey.

"What does it have to do with me?" The pose of nonchalance came easily to her after years of practice. *Never tell them what you know.*

"You were at the club last night. We have surveillance footage. You weren't there when the officers arrived, but we can see you were still there after the attack. There's only one reason for you to have hidden from us. I don't think it's a coincidence that in the last two days, I've had three guys come through here with major injuries after dealing with you." Joe paused, fingering Redneck's picture. "You know what he kept saying in the ambulance? *Tell her I kept up my part.* Someone scared the crap out of him."

"I think a general de-crapping was long overdue. Besides, didn't Michael tell you exactly what happened?" Dani said.

"He lied to me. The same guy who tapes coins to broken parking meters lied to an investigating officer about an assault. So I'm asking you again, what the hell is going on with you two?"

"He's fine. More than fine—enjoying a weekend he'll never forget." She winked at him. She didn't want Michael dragged into this.

"Don't play games with me. You want to pretend he's become infatuated with you, and the two of you are riding each other like ponies? It's bullshit, and if you knew him, you wouldn't even try." Joe crossed his arms over his chest, glaring at her.

"Maybe I'm that good," she suggested but without her usual conviction. The concern coming from this guy strangled her. He cared about his friend and wanted to help him. He saw her as the bad guy, and despite her own insistence that she deserved the title, it stung.

"Lots of men lose their heads over women, but not him. Here's what I know: I know he's a good man who cares about people and wants to help them. I know he's got himself twisted up about that little girl. I know he's desperate to help her. And somehow, he thinks you're going to help him do it."

183

"Sounds like you know a lot." An unusual urge to just tell him the truth threatened to take over.

"I want to know what you have him mixed up in!" Joe bellowed.

Dani opened her mouth to reassure him Michael was safe when she caught the sound of footsteps approaching. This room was at the end of the hall. They could only be coming here. She went silent and waited, her instincts flaring into full alarms.

"This is not the time to play dumb." Joe couldn't hear the approaching footsteps but couldn't ignore the door opening.

"I think that's quite enough, detective. I'd like to speak to my client now," the newcomer interrupted.

Dani studied the man carefully as Joe argued with him. She'd never seen him before. Tall, dark hair slicked back, he carried himself like a man used to getting his way. The detective tried blustering at him but the man ignored him, adjusting his suit cuffs carefully. His designer cologne masked his natural scent. *A deliberate choice? Does he know what I am?*

"My client. Or do you need a refresher in attorney-client privilege?"

Joe reluctantly retreated, leaving Dani alone with a stranger. He wouldn't be able to come back into the room or hear what was said until summoned.

"I didn't ask for an attorney," she simpered, playing the dumb bimbo while all of her senses fired on high alert.

"You should have."

"Maybe I'm not that smart." She shifted on her chair, bringing her breasts forward.

"We both know you have brains. So I won't insult you by lying further." Although it didn't stop him from letting his gaze dip briefly down to her cleavage. "My name is André Dalhard, and I'm here to offer you a job."

Dani froze. Her brothers' captor, here, in the flesh. She hadn't expected to come face to face with him. Face to fist, maybe. The Huntress coiled, reinforcing her own instincts. This man was far more dangerous than he seemed. The harsh bite of cologne stung her nose and she became certain the choice was deliberate.

Dalhard settled himself opposite her as if neither of them had a care in the world. "You could be much more than a stripper in a cheap dive."

"I'm not a stripper. I'm a burlesque performer." The ice in her voice would have deterred most men. Her arms ached with tension as she held herself back from attacking him.

Dalhard chuckled. "Dress it up however you like, my dear; it is far beneath a woman of your talents."

"And what would you know about my talents?" Although she kept her voice indifferent, her mind repeated the question in a panic. Was this an attempt at random collection, or did he know she was connected to Vincent and Eric? Could he know about Gwen?

"I've been told a great deal about them. Vincent has been very forthcoming." Dalhard smirked.

Metal clanged and echoed as she slammed her hands onto the table, abandoning the game. "What the hell have you done with him?"

"I've offered him a job. Eric, too. The same as I'm doing right now with you. Six figure salary, expense account. Everything you could want, Danielle."

"You're keeping them locked up. Prisoners," she snarled.

"I'm not holding anyone captive. They're staying with me because they've accepted my offer."

Strangely, she couldn't smell any trace of deception. Maybe it was being drowned out by the cologne. But the message had been from Eric. "I'll believe that when I fucking see it."

"I can arrange for you to talk to them," Dalhard offered. "Learn the truth for yourself."

"I intend to." Her eyes blazed red, reflecting in the mirror. Thoughts of the ritual nagged at her but she shoved them aside to concentrate on her prey.

"Interesting." Dalhard's smile revealed genuine delight. "I don't often pursue people, Danielle. There are more than enough applicants for any position I care to open. But you would be the crown jewel of my portfolio."

"No one owns me." The seething anger made controlling the Huntress even harder. Both of them wanted to strike out at their rightful prey, but knew not to try in such a public setting. If she could lure him somewhere isolated…

"A partnership, then. I think you'll find I can be quite agreeable and

185

open to negotiation." He took her hand in his.

The Huntress coiled and hissed within. Dani fought the urge to shake her head, to shake off the cloudiness stealing over her mind. It was Dalhard. He was doing this to her. Suddenly, she was a great deal less certain about the outcome of a conflict between them, but she refused to show weakness in front of an enemy.

"I would be a powerful friend to you." Dalhard licked his lips, his eyes dipping briefly down her body.

Alien warmth tried to steal into her muscles from his touch. Dani's jaw ached from grinding her teeth, concentrating on the memory of her brother's blood on the ground. "I'm not for sale," she jerked away from his touch.

"I don't give up easily. Take some time to think and come see us." He pulled a card out of his briefcase and slid it to her. It had an address and four numbers along the bottom. "That's the access code. The time and date are on the card."

The tiny rectangle of fancy paper held her salvation. A way to rescue them without having to go through the ritual. *Or did it?* Surely whatever mental power the man had, it couldn't withstand the Huntress. Dani stood, the monster inside barely contained beneath her human mask. "If you hurt my family, it won't matter how rich you are. Nothing is going to save you."

The steel cuffs bit hard into her wrists before the chain snapped. Blood coated her wrists and hands, splatting against the concrete floor.

"I'll keep it in mind." Dalhard may have kept a cool exterior but his scent betrayed both excitement and fear. He picked up his briefcase and left the room.

Joe waited on the other side of the door, leaving no doubt that he'd watched the entire encounter through the one-way glass. Maybe listened too, although it would have been illegal. He shut the door behind him, staring at Dani's bloody hands. She breathed in his distress and concern.

"I'm not an idiot," he said quietly. "I know this is bigger than my pay grade. But Michael isn't like you. If he gets hurt going toe-to-toe with these people, he's going to get himself dead."

"Over my rotting corpse," Dani swore without thinking. "No one touches him unless I go down first."

186

Joe studied her, evaluating her with instincts honed over years of active police work. After a minute, he came forward and unlocked the remnants of the cuffs from her wrists. "I believe you."

Chapter Twenty-Nine

"Security is tight. They use their own service, patrolling on an irregular schedule," Vapor said. "Cameras everywhere."

Dani felt as if the slim card in her back pocket was expanding, as if she were carrying a highly visible and noticeable brick. *A way in but also an obvious trap.*

"There's something unusual, though." Vapor pulled up a complicated multicolored spreadsheet.

"What am I looking at?" Dani frowned.

"Shift schedules. And every single employee is off tomorrow night." Vapor pointed at various spots on the grid.

Dani decided to take his word for it. Besides, something more important needed to be discussed. "It's part of a trap."

"Duh. But how could they know we'd track them down so quickly? I would have seen any flags in the system—" Vapor stopped as she pulled the card out of her pocket.

"This is the other half." She gave it to him. "He wants me to come see him tomorrow night."

"Except for the part where you're too smart to fall for an obvious trap. Right?"

She wished it were that simple. The last four days since Eric's call dragged on her, sapping her energy. Each of them weighed on her like a massive granite block tethered to her by unbreakable chains.

"Your mom has been rallying the troops," Vapor began. "She's getting volunteers."

"I don't want anyone else to get hurt." She closed her eyes, her thoughts muddled. Last night, she'd believed the only way to stop others from being hurt was to do the ritual. Now, the temptation of the card offered hope of a rescue while her worries about Dalhard's powers warned her away.

"Your Michael isn't going to stay behind," Vapor observed.

"He has to. He's not like us, Vapor. He'll go charging in, thinking the universe will save him because he's some kind of godsdamn hero. But one bullet will take him down forever." Dull pain insisted on her attention, and she realized that she had driven her fingernails into her palms again. It figured—the welts from the handcuffs were nearly gone.

"So you'll go in by yourself to protect him. It's the definition of noble: a grand gesture that makes everyone else miserable and accomplishes nothing." Vapor folded his arms over his chest.

"I don't want him to die! I've already seen it twice when he goes into those damn trances." Icy memories crushed her heart.

"You go in alone, and you'll fail. It's a fucking trap. Dalhard is controlling all the cards, all the ground. You need something he won't expect."

"Michael thinks he can beat the Huntress," Dani looked up at Vapor to see the older man's eyebrows climb in surprise. "That he won't end up like the others."

"Your mother's been riding you about the legacy again," Vapor guessed with the uncanny accuracy that made him so irritating to deal with.

"'Again' would imply she stopped at some point." But being flippant hurt too much. An empty ache left her feeling like a fragile wooden sculpture whose insides had been scooped out. Any more and she'd collapse into herself.

"You gotta take someone's help—Michael, the Goddess, any of us. You can't do this on your own." Vapor didn't have much patience for idiots. Or sympathy. Or emotional complications. Usually these traits were more enjoyable.

"Gwen said I needed him." The words slipped from her lips before she could snatch them back.

"She's right."

Dani closed her eyes, pulling herself back together. Time to end this wallowing. She had work to do, and she would do it without compromising what was necessary. She would protect Michael in spite of himself, even if it meant surrendering to the Huntress. "Thanks for the information," she said, keeping her face carefully blank. "I've got a lot of work to do to prepare."

Vapor couldn't let her go without trying to get the last word. "Don't do anything stupid."

"Hey. It's me." She shrugged, trying to play her normal nonchalance.

"That's exactly what I meant."

Michael spent the morning with Gwen, trying to help her stabilize her grip on reality and trying to distract himself from worrying about why Dani might have left so early in the morning. She'd been gone before he'd had a chance to speak to her. She'd pulled away last night, not quite meeting his eyes when they went back to the house. He'd seen enough of them to know when a secret was in front of his face.

There had to be a way to free Dani from the Huntress without sacrificing the *lalassu* people as a whole. He was sure of it. He just needed to find it. He'd spent the night trying to think about it and trying not to think about how much he wished he was a few doors further up the hall. But he didn't want to push Dani before she was ready. This would be a huge step for her.

He sat down in the kitchen, and Virginia immediately slid over a plate with a mammoth chicken sandwich, fresh red grapes, crisp slices of apple, and gently steaming blueberry muffins. She never once took her hand from her braille computer display or tripped over a syllable while talking on the phone pressed to her ear. Michael picked up an apple slice. Not a hint of brown, which meant she timed his meal to the minute, all before he'd known himself that he was coming out.

The world should be grateful Virginia Harris ended up in a life of seclusion. If she'd wanted to, she could have ruled the world with deceptive ease. All morning she'd been organizing, motivating, and cajoling *lalassu* from around the country.

"It is a marvel. I've learned to mostly hand her things and otherwise stay out of her way," Walter said. "Grab some sodas out of the fridge and come join me on the porch."

Michael followed Walter out, balancing his plate and the chilled cans. Walter parked himself in a corner of the large porch, closing his eyes and enjoying the cool breeze.

"She's certainly well organized." Michael glanced back into the house. "I thought she'd be packing or something. Eric's message to run was clear."

"It was," Walter acknowledged, nodding slowly. "But we can't just go on the run with Gwen. You caught a glimpse of what she can do. Put her in a trailer or a car and she'd be screaming before we could get out of the driveway. Eric hasn't spent much time with his sister since we moved here."

"What are you going to do?" Michael shuddered at the brief glimpse he'd had of Gwen's life. She was having enough trouble with the breaches in the salt already, and those were minimal. Virginia had mentioned bringing someone in who could repair the damage.

"We've spent a lot of time thinking about it. There have been groups interested in the *lalassu* and their abilities throughout history. But pressure really stepped up about twenty years ago." Walter popped open his soda.

Michael got a sturdy emotional sense from Walter, but overlying it was a hunger and anticipation. He was eager to confess his story.

"People in positions of power wanted their own personal action figures." Walter's mouth twisted down in disgust. "We'd been living in secret for almost three thousand years, since the fall of Babylon. But powerful people have ways of finding out secrets."

Michael looked down at his hands but said nothing. *Drowning in secrets.*

"We'll never know exactly when someone betrayed us. Perhaps it wasn't even a betrayal. Maybe someone saw something they shouldn't have and told the wrong person. I didn't know we were being systematically hunted until they caught me."

Michael remembered the flash of Dani seeing her father torn up and bloody. "How did they find you?"

"I worked on the docks, loading and unloading cargo." Walter took a sip of his drink. "Lots of brute force, not too many personal questions. Perfect for a young father and provider trying to stay hidden. One day, I got called into the boss's office and the next thing I knew, someone shot me with a tranquilizer dart."

Walter's grip dented the thin metal can, his dark eyes considering his audience before deciding to continue. "I woke up in a research facility

191

with more needles in me than a voodoo doll. They had me run all kinds of tests, seeing how much I could lift and throw. I heard them talking when they thought I was still sedated and they were planning to use me to make a bunch of copies, like a fucking Xerox machine. But what really scared the crap out of me was when I figured out my kids could be targets."

"I'm sorry," Michael whispered, not wanting to break the flow of the story. He felt Walter's pain and horror, as vivid as ever despite two decades of distance.

Walter closed his eyes briefly, the lines on his face tight. "You're not a father. These days the title seems like more of a punchline than a responsibility, but once it's yours, everything changes. If I'd only been worried about myself, I would have gone down in explosive glory. But I couldn't afford theatrics. I needed to get back to my family and protect them. Which meant making sure those sons of bitches couldn't ever hurt anyone else again, but without going down in a suicidal blaze."

"What did you do?" Michael asked. Maybe they could use the same technique against Dalhard.

"I got out of their restraints, waited until they came to take me for more tests, and then I took them all down. I set fires and used some of the chemicals from their labs to explode their computers." Walter smiled in remembered satisfaction. "I left them with nothing. But I didn't get the boss."

"Who was it?" Michael asked, trepidation knotting his shoulders.

"They called him Dalhard. I don't think it's a coincidence." Walter clenched his fist.

The same man hunting this family across generations. The revelation sickened Michael.

"They know now," Walter said softly, his shoulders hunching in tension. "They know that my children have my gifts, though they may not realize I survived. At first, they wanted me alive. It's probably the only reason I could do as much as I did. When they figured it out, someone gave the kill order. I took four bullets. One in my left shoulder, one in my leg, a graze on my right arm, and the one that buried itself in my spine."

"How...?" Michael wanted to know how Walter could have

192

survived, but stopped before asking, uncertain if he were being rude.

"Luck and generation after generation of pigheaded stubbornness to draw on. Too damn ornery to let them win. I tore myself up, barely made it to a phone and called Virginia. She called in every divine favor she had to keep me alive."

Michael couldn't imagine the kind of adamantine willpower it would have taken to crawl away with a shattered spine. But he could feel the core of determination in Walter, the same core he felt in Walter's daughter. That must be the night from the flash, the one Gwen told him about. It was all connected. "Gwen said her mother had been pregnant, and whatever she did ended up driving Gwen crazy."

"Hard to tell. Gwen was always going to be powerful. Those with great power often lose touch with reality. Frankly, I always thought Superman should be crazier."

Michael smiled at the reference. The two men fell quiet, listening to Virginia issue orders over the telephone through the open window.

"I hope we can do this," Walter said quietly. "I hope it's not already too late."

It couldn't be too late already. Michael frowned. "What do you mean?"

"Dalhard. I never saw him, but he's still hunting us, and those with him haven't given up. We've survived this long by running to new places. We fled Babylon when it fell, heading north to the barbarians on the steppes or across the sea to northern Africa. We were on some of the first ships across the ocean. Lots of people drowned, but a few made it, driven by desperation. But there aren't many places left to hide. Where can we go to escape a multinational corporation with webs across every continent? Everything is documented, numbered and filed. We need a new strategy."

Michael's contentment with the gentle evening soured. They had to stop Dalhard this time.

Walter braced himself as if to deliver something unpleasant. "Without Dani's cooperation, we don't have a chance."

"You're asking her to destroy herself to save you." Steel crept into Michael's voice despite his training. His verbal line made it clear: *go no further.*

193

"We're asking her to become more than she is. To help her people. Dani's always been stubborn. And her mother, bless her soul, has always been more comfortable giving orders than collaborating."

"You think she's putting everyone in jeopardy to rebel against her mother?" Michael struggled to keep his irritation in check. If this was the best fatherly insight Walter could offer, he'd pass.

"No. She ran away to rebel against her mother. Insisted on having a normal life. Or as much as she could, under the circumstances. Virginia wanted to drag her back, but I insisted we let her go. Maybe it was a mistake, but I still think it was the right thing to do. Dani always needed to do things on her own schedule, and I believed she would get bored quickly with having to hide herself and pretending to be less than she was. But somehow, she lost her connection to the community. It's made her hard and cynical. Between you and me, I thought she was gone to us permanently. Until last night."

"Last night?" Michael repeated, suspicious. *Was he watching us?*

"Last night she begged for you to return, she protected you against her own family. She loves Gwen and her brothers and she's always helped them, but she keeps herself at a distance. With you, she's found something she'll fight for without thinking about it, without fearing the consequences. She didn't have that before. But I need to make sure you understand."

"Understand what?" He knew he wasn't going to like where this conversation was going.

Walter turned to face Michael, and he suddenly felt as if he'd come under the gaze of an enormous predator: something that could kill him without breaking its stride. "If you break her heart, it'll destroy her and whatever hopes we have. So I'm asking you now: what are you doing here? Are you enjoying playing in a new world, being a superhero? Or are you willing to sacrifice to join her here?"

It was official. He didn't like it. Michael wished he could escape. "It's a little early to be—"

"It's exactly the right time. I need to know. We don't play by society's rules. We never have. Are you willing to let go of what you've been taught to want?"

Michael's head whirled. His first instinct was to appease and soothe, following his training. But instead he issued a challenge. "That is between Dani and me. Not you."

"Are you sure about that?"

The sense of menace grew until Michael could practically smell rotting flesh in the air as if the breeze had become the breath of a gigantic predator. Walter seemed larger, as if he would leap out of the chair at any moment to attack.

"I won't be part of manipulating her." Michael stood and walked away from the house, ending the interrogation. He expected to hear the chair coming after him but heard only silence. Had it been a test? Had he passed or failed?

His sympathy for Dani increased. His parents had been willing to sacrifice anything to protect their secrets, even their son. Hers were dedicated to this ancient cult. Somehow they'd both broken free.

His parents had never tried to contact him after he'd left for school. It was as if they hadn't wanted to remember they ever had a son. Dani's family was still trying to snare her, sacrificing their daughter on the altar of an ancient religion. There must be another choice.

And if there isn't? His doubts pricked at his resolve. *There are thousands of* lalassu *worldwide, all of them in jeopardy. Families with children. Isn't that worth some sacrifice?*

Every instinct rebelled at the thought. There had to be another way. He just needed to figure it out, fast.

Chapter Thirty

"C'mon, Bernie," Chuck whispered. "You gotta stay strong."

"I miss my mommy," Bernie whimpered. Her fingers hurt from holding on to her bear and doll.

"I know. I made a mistake about her not wanting you. She loves you a whole lot." Chuck twisted his hat in his hands.

"She gave me away." It hurt too much to say the words without choking, but Chuck understood. He always understood what she said even if she didn't say it out loud.

"She didn't. She just made a mistake. You gotta be strong."

"I'm tired. I don't like it here." Bernie cradled the teddy bear in her hands. "Michael said he'd come get me."

"He's coming. Talked to him myself. Told him to hustle."

"Why is it taking so long?" she whimpered. He'd promised to come get her.

"I..." Chuck's confidence abruptly vanished, his face twisting into little boy confusion. "I don't know, Bernie-baby. Wish I did. Let me go talk to Gwen. I'll find out. Stay here."

Where else would I go? Bernie closed her eyes. It was easier now to push Chuck and the others aside, ignore what they were saying. She took refuge in her own mind instead of listening to the dead around her. Michael and her mother and all the doctors told her Chuck was part of her imagination, under her control. But he was real, like the others were real.

She pictured a beautiful cottage, high on a cliff above the sea. No one else there. Only her and Molly and Teddy. She could lie quietly on her bed and watch the blue and white waves crash against the rocks.

Michael will come. He's coming to save me. She repeated the words over and over to herself, holding to them as tightly as she could, trying not to be a little girl abandoned to people who poked at her like an insect. *Michael will come.*

Karan stared at a video feed of the little girl curled on the bed, clutching her toys. Dalhard had overstepped himself in this case. He had gone with the recruitment personnel and used his gift to persuade the mother to give up her child. His impatience for the acquisition threatened everything. The man knew his influence was not permanent in all cases. Strong emotional ties could overwhelm the alien programming. Dalhard should have anticipated the mother would be a problem again. Despite hasty additions to her records, someone in the Perdition police force had taken her claims of kidnapping and coercion seriously. If his boss had only taken the time to set things up properly, they could have whisked the girl away without anyone being the wiser.

Dalhard was completely ignoring the results from the genetic enhancement project. For years, Karan had worked in Dalhard's shadow, increasing the man's financial power and, incidentally, his own. He had always known that a time would come when their interests would no longer converge. Looking at the chaotic mess his boss had caused, he began to wonder if this was that time.

New precautions were in place to deal with the potential problems but he would not breathe easily until they were all back in Europe. If Dalhard insisted on having the sister, he would get her and have the jet on standby. When she walked into the meeting tomorrow night, she would not walk away again.

After his confrontation with Dani's father, Michael sought the quiet of the trees while Gwen slept. After years of being in a darkened room, her sleep cycles no longer bore any resemblance to a typical day. He needed time to put things together in his own mind. If Walter was right, then the family couldn't just disappear and set up somewhere else. Dalhard would track them down again. He had to be stopped, which meant he would have to accept being part of an illegal break-in and kidnapping. People would get hurt—not faceless guards from a movie but real people who had accepted a job to pay their bills and had nothing to do with what their bosses decided. It horrified him.

197

But he couldn't make himself believe that what they were doing was wrong. Perhaps not right, but it wasn't wrong. The law didn't offer a way to restore Bernie to her mother quickly enough to stop Dalhard from disappearing across a border. Not with forged allegations of abuse and neglect in her file. Leaving Bernie with her tormentors while the slow wheels of justice ground to a conclusion simply wasn't an option.

And what about Dani? He scrubbed his hand through his hair. He loved her and wanted to be with her, a partner to her. But he didn't want to give up his entire life or his beliefs. Walter's threat gnawed at his confidence that they could find a new path.

The buzz of his phone offered welcome relief from brooding. He didn't recognize the number, but even a telemarketer would be a much-needed break.

"Do you ever answer your godsdamn phone?" The gravelly voice assaulted him as soon as he tapped the screen to answer.

"Who is this?" Michael demanded, afraid Dalhard had tracked him down. "Vapor."

"Is Dani okay?" The words popped out, driven by his rapidly pulsing heartbeat and sudden dry mouth.

"Depends on the definition. She ain't hurt. Yet."

Vapor's words did not fill Michael with confidence. She'd left so abruptly this morning. "What happened?"

"You trust me?"

Michael closed his eyes as if it would erase the loaded question. Did he trust Vapor? A criminal hacker, but a criminal hacker helping them to find Bernie. "I trust you," he said.

"She's got a way in to Dalhard's building tomorrow night. No witnesses. It's a trap."

There was oxygen in the air, but somehow none of it was getting into Michael's lungs.

"She's gonna try to deal with it on her own. Don't let her," Vapor said.

"How?" Michael managed to shape the syllable with great effort, his mind still whirling around one word: *trap*. He wasn't surprised Dani would try to take on Dalhard by herself. She wanted to protect those she cared about at any cost, even her own life.

198

"Figure it out, genius." The connection clicked.

Dani sat in her car on the lawn outside her parent's home, unable to force herself to take the final steps. This was the moment she'd been dreading for decades. She would tell them that she'd decided to do the ritual.

The cop's words kept echoing in her head: *If he gets hurt going toe-to-toe with these people, he's going to get himself dead.* And Vapor's words: *You gotta take someone's help.* Michael was determined to play hero, but he didn't have the kind of strength she and her brothers took for granted. He couldn't snap a fence pole in half with his bare hands or heal a broken bone in less than a week. *If he gets hurt going toe-to-toe with these people, he's going to get himself dead.*

He might think he could survive the Huntress, that he didn't have any secrets, but she didn't trust the coiling creature, even if it had been strangely quiet since she stood up to it in the club. Less than twelve hours ago, it was demanding a Hunt, stirring up emotions. But she hadn't Hunted and it still slumbered. Dani frowned, trying to remember the details. She'd mentally wrestled with it and then been thrown into a panic attack full of flashbacks. Could she have Hunted herself? Cracking plastic reminded her to loosen her grip on the steering wheel. *Third one ruined this year.*

"Dani?" Michael's voice interrupted her thoughts. The scent of apples and vanilla caressed her as he came out of the trees, smiling as he saw her. She forced the cracks of her armor back together, praying it would hold a little longer. The mental image of his eyes glazing over with numb fear as the Huntress devoured him... her chest physically ached at the thought. He might recover physically, but his unique blend of earnestness and optimism would be gone. She would kill him as surely as any bullet.

If only she didn't want him so badly. Michael was different from any man she'd ever even considered dating, let alone those she Hunted. Despite the nice-guy exterior, he was filled with passion and interest. He believed strongly enough to make her cynical heart ache with emptiness. She didn't want to show him the world as it was; she wanted to make the world live up to what he believed it should be.

And he was gorgeous. Her body flared in renewed appreciation, flooding heat and moisture to her groin and plumping her breasts and lips in anticipation. If he'd been slightly less interesting, she could still have happily spent hours worshipping his body with hands and tongue. But he had to have a brain and personality to go with his marble-statue-worthy good looks. It was more temptation than any woman should ever have to face.

"I heard you pull up. Where did you run off to?" he asked, his smile fading.

"I had a meeting with your buddy, Joe, who told me I should leave you alone if I cared about you. And then I picked up the blueprints from Vapor." Dani gestured at the papers on the passenger seat.

"I had a talk with your dad. Dalhard is the one who hurt him," Michael's earnest eyes stared into hers, searching.

"It can't be. He's too young," Dani blurted.

"What do you mean?" Michael's brows knotted.

"He showed up at the police station when Joe took me in. We talked. He's my age, maybe a little older. Dad was hurt twenty years ago." Dani smelled Michael's hurt as she revealed her lie of omission, but her mind was reeling with the implication.

"You met with Dalhard. Is that what Vapor meant when he called? Was that the trap?" Michael demanded.

"For an illegal hacker who works for a secret society, Vapor has a damn big mouth." Dani exhaled sharply, tilting her head back to stare at the brilliant noon sky.

"Dani, you can't leave me out of this. We're partners." Michael's quiet declaration ripped at her armor, shredding it to pieces.

"I'm doing this for you. Joe was right. You could get hurt. They shot my brother. They'll shoot you too." Dani suddenly couldn't bear to be cooped up, even in the minimal walls of the car. She jumped out of it, walking toward the forest, eager to lose herself in the shadows.

"Dani, I'm not letting you walk away." Michael chased after her, leaves and twigs cracking as he followed.

She stopped, cursing under her breath. He wouldn't let her be. She could feel him like an extension of herself only a few steps behind.

"Talk to me," he whispered, and she couldn't help looking back. He leaned against a tree, his long hair pushed back from his face. He fit with the forest, like an ancient druid. And she knew she couldn't run from him or her decision any longer.

"I'm going to do the ritual," she said quietly.

"No!" he shouted, his face pale and his fists tight.

"I have to. We both know it. It's the only way to get Bernie and my brothers back safely." *Why can't he just understand and leave it alone?* His protests hurt too much to bear.

"There's another way. We'll find it."

Deliberately, she summoned up the Huntress, setting her eyes aflame. Michael stepped forward, closing the gap between them, but she held up her hand. "I'm a monster, Michael. The hero is supposed to kill the monster to save the good guys, not try and save me and risk getting them killed."

"Bullshit!" Michael spat out the word. It sounded so strange coming from him. "I see the darkness in people every day. I know all about monsters. You're not one of them. I'm not afraid of your bogeyman in the dark, and I refuse to accept that it gets to win." His face softened, and he smoothed her hair away from her face, tilting her chin up gently. "I want you, Dani. All of you, including your crazy family and the Huntress. There's no piece of you I would leave behind. So you're not leaving me behind either. And that's final."

"But what if—?" Her half-formed objection vanished when he bent his head to kiss her.

Chapter Thirty-One

If Dani wanted to protect Michael, she needed to walk away. But the feeling of his soft lips on hers, gently tasting her, savoring her as if she were a fine wine—it was too much temptation. Besides, there would only be a few seconds before the Huntress awoke.

She relaxed into his kiss, accepting both the moment and the tragic knowledge that it would be limited. His arms held her, the warmth from his body seeping into her skin. His scent overwhelmed every other, pushing away the outside world and creating a safe cocoon for the two of them.

Awareness flared: the Huntress wasn't rising. It was still coiled inside her, but it wasn't reacting to Michael's closeness. It wasn't waiting to strike. It curled up quietly in her mind as if it were hibernating or sated.

Michael broke off the kiss. "I told you we could find a w—"

She attacked, sealing his mouth with her own. Everything boiled up inside her, whisking away doubt and self-control to leave pure, steaming lust behind. Even the Huntress's ravenous appetite faded in contrast with her own hunger to taste, touch, and claim what should have been hers all along. *Fuck them all.* The thought dimly echoed inside her, ignored as she sucked at his delicious mouth.

His lips accepted the ferocity of her kiss and deepened it, making love to her tongue and lips with uncensored passion. If she'd thought she was on fire before, now she was truly burning and had no wish to step down from the stake. She savored the sweet coolness of his mouth, a contrast to the fever consuming her from the womb outward.

A dim thought floated outside on the few neurons not aflame. The Huntress still wasn't trying for Michael. She didn't care what might have wrought this particular miracle. The only thing she cared about was fulfilling her own pent-up desires.

She moaned aloud, knotting her fists in his shirt to pull him closer. Their legs tangled together like awkward teenagers, threatening to knock them off-balance. She pushed Michael against a nearby tree while she ravished his body with her hands and mouth. He slid his arms around her waist, letting them explore while his clever tongue coaxed and played with her mouth. Dani's whole body ached for more. Her womb quivered and pulsed as if trying to break free of her skin to touch him itself. He cupped her buttocks, softly smoothing her tight jeans. Fabric barriers became abruptly intolerable.

She snarled, ripping at his clothes. His button-front shirt parted as if made of thin paper. She tore the remnants away, giving her hungry hands access to roam over the territory of her imagination. A faint sound of protest might have come from the back of his throat but he pulled her closer, leaning back against an ancient tree to keep their balance.

He tasted as good as he smelled. A faint hint of woodsmoke lingered on her tongue as she licked down his neck. His skin was warm under her hands, soft velvet over the steel muscles beneath. It was every bit as exquisite as she'd hoped.

Her fingers traced the hot ridge of his erection under his jeans. For the first time since she was a teenager, evidence of a partner's excitement spurred her on.

She wanted to roll down his body with kisses, go onto her knees and take him in her mouth. A strong jolt of approval came from her groin, encouraging her to continue the fantasy. It played out in her mind in a heartbeat. She wanted to start with her fingers, let them slide beneath his waistband to tease the thick length of him. To use her lips and tongue to explore the masculine contours of his chest as she slid down across the rippled muscle. To shove his pants aside and then take him between her lips.

The image of him towering over her, his head and sandy hair thrown back as his body shuddered at her command intoxicated her blood and fired her senses into painful awareness. She would coax him with all the ancient and modern skill at her disposal. Let him come closer and closer to the edge without bringing him over until he was ready to burst at her signal.

Her mouth watered at the fantasy. She began her teasing slide downward, but he caught her arms, bringing her back up to reclaim her lips.

"Not yet. We have plenty of time," he whispered against her.

She growled in displeasure. She didn't want *time*. Time was the enemy. Time allowed thoughts to wriggle past the emotions of the moment. The Huntress could wake from its unusual slumber at any moment. She wanted to be caught up in her feelings, not pricked by her conscience. Who knew how long this reprieve would last? Old memories threatened to spill over and taint their pleasure.

Michael paused, his hands stilling against her.

Dani kept her eyes firmly closed and her hands busy with his jeans. Nononono*nono*NO! Her mind screamed as she tried to reignite the flames against the chilling void of loneliness and responsibility.

"Dani, you can't do this." He broke away from her, panting,

She tried to yank him toward her, but he stepped out of reach.

Half-blind with lust and frustration, Dani staggered against the tree. Raking her hair out of her eyes, she found him standing a few steps away. He watched her, his bare chest practically gleaming in the sunlight.

"You don't want…?" No word could finish her question and still maintain her dignity.

"I do. God help me, I do." His rough voice and the fiery scent of lust rising from him told her that he spoke the truth.

"Then come on. Don't leave me like this," she begged, reaching for him.

"You're trying to banish old ghosts." Michael swallowed hard, trying to regain some moisture in his dry mouth. "I can feel the old hurt and regrets getting stronger. Trying to pretend they aren't there won't make them go away." His lower half threatened a general strike if he didn't finish what he'd started. And he knew what kind of fiery lust consumed Dani. The way she stared at him, her breasts heaving with each panting breath, meant he'd taken his own life in his hands by stopping at that moment.

"You don't understand. For the first time since we met, it's quiet. We have to *now*, before it's too late." Her anger was getting stronger.

"It's got nothing to do with the Huntress." He stretched out his hand to bridge the distance between them.

Dani stepped back. "If you're going to touch me, then you better be ready to fuck me."

Those words crystallized everything for him. Now he stood on stable psychological ground. "Dani, I want to make love to you more than anything else. But I want it to be making love, not fucking. I want it to mean something between us, and I want it to be more than one night. I want you to be with me, all of you with me, because you want it and not because you're trying to prove something or hide from something. I want to be partners."

"I don't have more than tonight." Her hand wrapped around a tree branch and he heard the wood cracking. He could see the tears glinting in her eyes.

"Yes, you will. I'm a greedy bastard and won't settle for anything less." He used the profanity deliberately, hoping to make her smile.

She laughed, sliding down to the ground. A tired, post-stress laugh, but still a laugh. "It just sounds wrong when you curse."

"It's true. I am greedy. I want all of you and I'm not going to settle for anything else. We'll work through the old ghosts together, but I don't want our first time to be held hostage to some ancient Middle-Eastern legacy." He settled beside her.

"And?" Dani cocked her head at him.

He couldn't guess at what she meant.

"There's something else. I can smell it on you," she clarified.

"Oh." He took a deep breath. "I can't stand the idea of you being in pain because of me. I don't ever want to be someone who hurt you."

Dani nodded thoughtfully. "You know I don't want you hurt, either."

"And I am very much in favor of that plan. I like having all my limbs and faculties intact." He took her hand in his, stroking his fingers over her soft palms.

She shivered with pleasure at the sensation. He could feel the hurt and anger subsiding inside of her. "You really believe we can find a way to save me and everyone else?" she asked.

"I know it. Like I know my life would be completely empty without you. We'll find a way. Just give me a little more time."

"This is one hell of a situation. And there's not a damn thing I can punch to make it go away." Dani leaned her head back against the tree.

205

"Dani! Michael!" Virginia's voice cut through the day like an air raid siren.

"Damn. Busted by the 'rents." Dani might sound like her typical self, but Michael could sense how thin the healed layer was. He allowed himself to be heartened when she didn't relinquish his hand as she guided him back out of the forest.

Chapter Thirty-Two

Walter and Virginia waited on the porch. Appearing half-nude in front of his girlfriend's parents was not what Michael considered the best approach to a relationship, but Walter's surprise quickly flashed to approval before settling back into seriousness. Virginia's features stayed fixed in a scowl.

"Gwen spoke with Chuck," Walter told them as they arrived at the house. "He told her we're running out of time. They're moving Vincent, Eric, and Bernie tomorrow night. He's planning to take them somewhere in Eastern Europe."

"The final part of the trap." Dani exhaled sharply. "They're only giving us one chance at a rescue, and it's on their schedule."

"I'm working on a few people with useful talents. Nada is flying down," Virginia reported. "The Strigis family is coming to recleanse and seal Gwen's shelter. They should be here this afternoon. If necessary, they will take her and keep her safe."

"You should go with them. Take care of Gwen," Dani suggested.

"Not bloody likely," Virginia snorted. "They have my boys and I'm not going anywhere until I know they're safe."

"I'll take care of it. I promise, I'll bring Vincent and Eric back. But I need to know that you and Dad and Gwen are safe." Dani looked to her father for support. Her fingers tightened around Michael's, and he felt her worry as his own.

"Vapor called and said you were planning on charging in alone." Walter folded his hands in his lap, the very image of a priest sitting in judgment.

"Did he call everyone I know?" Dani snarled, and her weariness welled up inside.

"He's wrong," Michael said softly. "We can do this."

Dani nodded. "I won't be alone."

Eric stared through the glass wall at the man lying on a hospital bed. Even unconscious, his face twisted in pain. "Who is he?"

"Captain McBride. One of our volunteers. We've been able to use a carrier virus with your DNA to transform him: taller, stronger, faster. Nothing near your limits, of course, but still a promising result," Dalhard explained. "He's been kept in a coma to avoid the more painful side effects of the genetic splicing."

"How many of them are you planning to build?" Eric couldn't keep the disgust from his voice. Torturing someone for financial profit sickened him. If Dalhard could watch the man suffer and still be eager, Eric didn't want to imagine what kind of horrors he'd be willing to unleash once his toys were ready.

Luckily, Dalhard misinterpreted it as jealousy. "He's purely a backup plan. A businessman always knows to have plan B ready to go. But since my plan A is coming along so well, I don't see any reason to explore this beyond research principles."

"Not to be rude, man, but this science shit is boring," Vincent yawned, flicking at one of the consoles. "Isn't there something more active we could be doing?"

His brother slipped further away every time they met Dalhard. Sometimes Eric caught glimpses of the old Vincent, but they quickly disappeared once Dalhard greeted them with his hearty handshake. Eric was hanging onto himself by the skin of his teeth.

"It may be boring, but I do need your help with it. You see, gentlemen, I'm like a man exploring a city with a flashlight in the dark. I have bits and pieces, but putting them together into the big picture is a challenge." Dalhard obligingly escorted them into his nearby private lounge stocked with a full bar, catering table, and overstuffed couches.

"How can we help with that?" Eric asked, staying standing. He didn't dare indulge in any of the comforts around him. He needed to stay alert and on guard to keep Dalhard's influence from worming inside.

"You've seen the city in the light, so to speak. You can help me with layout, purpose, function. For example, your family is strongly gifted. Unusually so." Dalhard settled into a plush chair.

"Oh yeah, it all goes way back. Ancient times and all that shit." Vincent helped himself from the liquor cabinet.

"But you can't be the only family with these gifts," Dalhard said.

He wasn't letting this bastard get his hands on anyone else. Eric spoke quickly to prevent Vincent from spilling secrets. "It's not something people advertise these days."

Dalhard smiled, toying with a small letter opener. The metal blade glittered as he swung it back and forth under the light.

"You know, you said we had something weird in our DNA," Vincent said before Eric could go on. "There are old legends and shit about humans getting down with gods and demons and making superstrong humans. Like us." Vincent slouched comfortably, waving his glass in emphasis. "I always figured it was kinda bullshit or something, but maybe it's real. Maybe they were, like, aliens or something, messing with our DNA."

Dalhard pursed his lips, taking Vincent's suggestion seriously. "Legends often hold grains of truth, though there does not appear to be anything extraterrestrial in your DNA."

Eric watched Dalhard playing his role of considerate advisor and mentor. It was as empty as a shed snakeskin, but he put on a convincing performance… or was the man's empathic gift preying on his mind, making it seem more believable? He'd tried to keep from touching Dalhard any more than necessary, but it was impossible to avoid it completely without tipping his hand. Vincent seemed to be falling more and more under the man's spell, drunkenly reciting a slightly warped version of the legend of Hercules. Who knew he'd been paying attention in Classical Greek Literature?

"Still, you must know others like you. It's been a pursuit of mine. I would love to be able to help others as I've helped you," Dalhard pushed.

"A few. Here and there. Nothing as cool as us though." Vincent's grin defined roguish self-confidence.

Eric started to interrupt but Dalhard beat him to it. "What about your sister, Danielle? Doesn't she possess your same gifts?"

The too-casual question fired alarm bells in Eric's brain. In previous sessions, he'd asked about their gifts breeding true. And now he was interested in their sister. The connection chilled him faster than a midwinter blizzard.

He's searching for breeding subjects.

Eric cursed himself for not seeing it earlier. The game had shifted to much more dangerous stakes without him being aware. He'd want as many gifted females as he could kidnap or coerce, turning them into baby factories. If Dalhard found out about Gwen...

"She's okay, I guess." Vincent dismissed her with typical sibling blindness. "Who else do you got in here?"

"There was one person I wanted you to meet." Dalhard picked up a phone. "Karan, could you bring little Bernadette in here?"

Karan ushered in a little girl, about nine or ten years old. Her irregularly brushed dark-blond hair stuck out at odd angles, and her eyes kept flickering about the room. She tugged constantly on her pink sweatshirt and sweatpants.

"I know you," she announced abruptly, her brown eyes latching onto Eric and Vincent. "The pretty lady is looking for you."

Dani. She wouldn't have given up. Eric's hopes sank. She'd be walking right into a trap.

"We'll hope she finds them soon." An avaricious smile flashed over Dalhard's features.

"Chuck found a new friend. She sounds really nice," Bernie continued.

"That's interesting, dear. Why don't you have some cookies?" Dalhard dismissed her.

Bernie happily dug into a plateful of cookies. Vincent happily dug into his scotch, and Eric dug into a deep depression.

"You see, Bernadette is proof that your family is not unique. She has fascinating predictive powers. It's left her somewhat unstable, but imagine if I could have found her years ago. She might have grown up understanding herself and not been left scarred by the world's disbelief..."

Eric tuned out the rest of Dalhard's grandstanding, although Vincent was eating it up, apparently without question. A man wanting to ease the plight of misunderstood children did not try and transform ordinary men into supermen. He watched the little girl sitting next to him, eating cookies and swinging her feet. She reminded him of Gwen when she was little. She smelled like clean cotton and chocolate, all innocence. One more person he wasn't going to be able to save.

"You don't need to worry so much." Bernie's low voice jolted him out of his thoughts. A quick glance showed Dalhard still focused exclusively on Vincent.

"Thanks, kid." Eric tried to give her a friendly smile, but his heart wasn't really in it.

"I was scared for a while, but Chuck told me that Michael will come soon and rescue us. He promised. The pretty lady is helping him." The words were delivered with a grave portent only a child could manage.

"Well, who told him?" he joked.

"Gwen."

With a single word, Bernie destroyed any attempt at lightening the mood. Eric's pulse started to slam against his skin with such force that he wouldn't have been surprised to see it break free. She was a medium, not a predictive. And she was in contact with Gwen, however indirectly.

Bernie patted him lightly on the knee, oblivious to her impact.

Eric looked up at Vincent and Dalhard, still talking. He needed to tread carefully, not alerting Dalhard to Bernie's true potential as a line of communication, or as a potential threat.

Chapter Thirty-Three

A rattling camper van pulled up to the farmhouse as the afternoon shadows slunk across the lawn. Dani tensed, testing the air for hints of oiled metal, gunpowder, anything that could suggest hidden weapons. Michael took his cue from her, stepping forward to stand between whoever was in the camper and the door to the house. Dani approved. Her parents would be guarding Gwen's door. She could be fairly certain this was the Strigis family coming to help Gwen, but their family had not survived the ages without learning to test their assumptions.

After Michael borrowed a T-shirt from one of her brothers' closets, they'd spent the afternoon combing through Virginia's family notebooks, searching for some way to contain the Huntress. But they were clutching at straws. Dani had done a similar search as a teenager with similar results. Texts had been lost, some were in dialects no one understood, and the two of them could only read the ones in relatively modern English. Her faint hope was dying with every hour that passed.

The driver's door popped open, and a plump, middle-aged woman extricated herself in a flurry of clicking beads and floating scarves. She took a moment to orient herself, shaking her head to settle her bushy gray-brown hair and layers of filmy material. She peered at the darkened porch, blinking. "Danielle? It is you!" she chirped happily before waving back to the camper. "Come on out, kids."

The side door opened, and a small herd of children tumbled out followed by a rotund man attempting unsuccessfully to keep them in one general area. Michael smiled and went to help.

Dani couldn't help but smile, too. She remembered her own long years on the road as a child, cooped up in a van for hour after eternal hour. The kids were probably desperate to stretch their legs. Eventually the whirlwind of activity slowed enough for her to identify four children, ranging in age from three to ten.

"Mama, I gotta go," the three-year-old crossed her legs with alarming determination.

"Inside, to the left," Dani instructed, stepping aside.

"Quickly, Mari. Jackie, help her." The mother hustled her pair of offspring up onto the porch but stopped before going inside. Instead, she stared at Dani, blinking slowly.

Her eyes were disproportionately large in her face as if she were staring through thick lenses, only there were no glasses. Dani caught a brief whiff of surprise from Michael as he joined them on the porch.

The Strigis matron tilted her head from one side to another, studying Dani from all angles. She whistled, the note so low it was barely audible. "Oh my. Oh dear."

"Laura, it's not our business," her husband took her arm, his own owlish, oversized eyes blinking slowly.

"Oh. Oh, yes, I suppose it isn't. It was rather rude." She couldn't quite look away. "I've never quite seen anything like this."

Dani stifled her impatience and frustration. She didn't need any more lectures.

"Seen what?" Michael asked.

Laura and her husband flicked their massive eyes in his direction, focusing on him. "She hasn't completed the bonding," Laura answered.

Dani's fingers and shoulders tightened. Michael's hand stroked her back, reassuring her that she wasn't facing this alone.

"I'm sorry, dearest. I'm not judging… but he asked. Oh dear, I've hurt your feelings. I'm so sorry." Laura's hands fluttered as she apologized.

"It's all right," Dani answered, willing the words to be true.

"I can understand. It's always sounded so frightening to me," the woman continued.

"Laura, perhaps we should stop talking about it," her husband suggested.

"Oh. Of course, Donald. I'll step inside and have a word with Virginia. If you'd—"

"Watch the children," he finished, shooing her into the house. "I will." He sprinted back onto the lawn to extract his offspring from a tree that was much easier climbed up than down. Mari emerged from the house to join them, her sister in tow.

Michael moved closer to Dani. "I've never seen eyes like that."

213

Dani leaned on the rail to watch the children scramble around. "They're Cassandrites, descendants of Athena from ancient Greece, or so the legend goes. They can see at great distances or focus down onto a molecular level. They can also see energy fields."

"What do they call your family lineage?" he asked.

"On my father's side, I'm a feral. Strong and fast, with enhanced senses. On my mother's, we're lillitu," she answered. "You'd know us by another name—succubus. Women who kill men through sex, or corrupt their Christian souls, depending on which book you read. An actual monster from the textbooks." She glanced over to see his reaction.

Michael wisely chose to stay silent. His scent remained steady, politely interested, with no spikes of alarm.

"I don't know how we went from divine priestesses to monsters. Were there rituals to appease the Huntress? When I was a teenager, I tried to become an archeologist to find out. I took a few courses in college."

"What happened?" he asked quietly. His concern and love wrapped around her like an aromatic blanket.

"I had to drop out." Dani looked away. She'd never told anyone what had happened. Once he knew, he'd realize she would never be the hero he wanted.

Michael held out his hand to her. "Trust me, there's nothing I haven't seen."

"I doubt you've ever seen anything like this." The memory of being held down, of unexpected weakness, swelled and cut off her air. "I can't talk about it," she rasped.

"When I was in Gwen's mind, I saw flashes from your past. I saw your senior prom and the fights. I know you felt responsible." His voice remained casual and calm, as if they were discussing a film. "I saw you flirting with Chomp to help your brothers. I saw you Hunting Josh the night I first met you."

The wooden railing creaked under her tightening grip.

"There was something else. Something you couldn't face. If you can't tell me, show me. Let me help you fight these ghosts from your past. What happened in college?" Michael slipped his hand around hers.

The simple contact soothed the chill of remembered fear and

214

shame. This could be her last day. And if it was, she didn't want this memory eating her up inside any more. He deserved to know what she truly was.

"Let's go inside," she suggested. She took him into the library, safely away from any prying ears. It was actually just a tiny nook, made even smaller by walls full of shelves for ancient books and scrolls, but it had always been her sanctuary. The familiar scent of musty paper and oiled leather soothed her enough to begin. "After hiding with some very strict relatives in Europe all summer, I wanted a normal life. I wanted it so bad, I actually ran away to go to college back here in the United States. Got myself a fake ID and a dorm room at a state school out west. I wanted to get far away from anyone who had ever heard about the Huntress. I thought I could keep myself safe with some careful feeding and be the same as any other girl." For once she didn't try to suppress the wistful yearning she felt for her earlier naïve self. Wanting normality hadn't been a crime or a bad idea.

Knowing Michael would experience everything she felt, she continued. "I went to a lot of frat parties. If one of them spent some time crouched on the floor in a daze, everyone assumed a hangover or bad drugs. No one ever connected me to them. I always went on a lot of dates, courtesy of the Huntress. I wouldn't Hunt them all, just a few, here and there. I liked being popular."

His hand tightened over hers as guilt soured the memories. She forced herself to keep speaking. "There was a party one weekend. I'd been dancing with a half dozen guys when one of them took me upstairs. We were kissing and—" Words failed her.

Hot mouth on hers, sour with beer but still showing promise. Maybe I'll let this one go. *She wasn't due to feed yet. A husky male voice interrupted.*

"Hey, we weren't all done yet." One of the guys from the dance floor stood in the doorway.

"I'll be back down in a minute." She winked.

Beer Breath began to fondle her breasts from behind. His lips were heavy on her neck.

"Maybe I'll stay and watch." Husky grinned.

For a moment, she was tempted. The thrill of exhibitionism was intoxicating.

215

To have a man standing and watching her, seeing his eyes glaze and the bulge rise inside his jeans. Maybe he'd reach down and wrap his fist around his heavy cock, unable to help himself. She'd look at him and know she was the cause. That he wanted her.

The fantasy brought on a buzz of anticipation, but practical reality interfered. This wasn't a spur-of-the-moment kind of decision. She started to make a witty comment, but her mouth only moved in slack mumbles.

Frowning, she reached up to touch her lips. They were numb, as if she'd been injected with novocaine.

"Looks like we timed it perfectly." Husky shut the door, leaving the tiny dorm room feeling too full, the air stale and spent.

"She'll be out soon," Beer Breath agreed, unfastening his pants.

Dani backed away. These two had brought her drinks all evening. She'd tossed them back, her attention focused on the party. They'd drugged her without her noticing. Her vision began to blur and her arms and legs grew heavy.

"This… thisish a bad idea," she managed to warn them, preparing to swing. Instead she fell heavily onto the bed as her legs started to give way.

"Bitch used up a week's supply," Beer Breath complained. "I'd say she owes us both *a little something. She won't remember it, anyway. Besides, she said she wanted to have some fun."*

He yanked on her skimpy shorts. Dani tried to fight, but her body wouldn't obey her instructions. This wasn't supposed to happen! She was strong enough to fight off any rapist. She didn't have to worry about it. This couldn't really be happening.

Husky ripped open her shirt and began to rub himself against her breasts. Her legs were forced open, and she felt a shocking pain.

It was happening. Inside her unresponsive body, she screamed, throwing all of her strength against the chemical barrier trapping her inside. The hurt blurred together, but she could hear them panting around her as they held her down.

The Huntress answered her scream for vengeance, and for once, she welcomed its reptilian surge and strike. As Beer Breath grunted his way to orgasm, the Huntress took him. No screams, no pleas for mercy. He froze in place then fell to the floor, silent. She smelled Husky's panic as his partner collapsed, but it was too late. The Huntress claimed him as he came.

She experienced their awakening second-hand. The echoes of all the pain they'd caused, the torment they'd inflicted or watched without comment. Self-entitled bullies

216

and sycophants, their minds were being raped as thoroughly as they'd planned for her body. She tried to scream that she hadn't meant it, but she was still trapped inside the smothering prison of her body.

Dani lay on the bed, aware of the cooling wetness of blood soaking the blanket beneath her. She still couldn't move, could barely blink her eyes or turn her head. Both boys lay on the floor, staring blankly into space. The stench of their terror mingled with fresh urine.

"Eventually, whatever they gave me wore off and I could get up. I stole a shirt and pants to make my way back to my own dorm." Dani found the words again, but she couldn't look at him.

Michael's anger smoldered around her, a banked flame waiting for a target.

"I never wanted to see my clothes from that night ever again. I wish I'd taken them and burned them. Then maybe the cops wouldn't have found me the next day."

"You say they drugged you?" The cop tapped his pencil against the desk in a clear rat-a-tat of irritation. Surrounded by cheap metal and concrete, the interrogation room chilled her physically and mentally.

"Yes," Dani kept her answers short. She'd already gone over it more times than she could count since they'd picked her up almost twelve hours ago.

"Why didn't you report the assault?" His implied accusation came through clearly.

"I was afraid. Upset. I wanted it all to go away." The Huntress coiled and seethed inside, feeding on her anger and fear.

"It went away all right. Nothing in your blood, no sign of bruises or trauma."

Of course not. She'd always healed quickly. But she couldn't explain that to this man with his petty authority and coffee-tainted breath. No one believed her. The families of the boys who'd attacked her were screaming for her head, insisting she must have drugged them. A horde of high-priced lawyers were already circling, sniffing after her blood, bringing up her reputation as a party girl. It was only a matter of time before someone found out her identity wasn't really hers.

Finally, her public defender lawyer arrived and convinced them to let her go home. On the way out, he suggested she take a plea, something minor and drug-related to avoid more serious charges. "Tell them it was a mistake, that you bought it from

217

"I left town as soon as they let me out. Took money and my go-bag and hopped a train headed east. There's probably still an arrest warrant for me out there."

Michael still stroked her fingers, and Danielle drew strength from the warm contact.

"I never told them what happened. When I came home, Mom was full of I-told-you-so crap, and even Dad said he hoped I understood now why I couldn't expect a normal life. They were both focused on Gwen, trying to stop her from hurting herself to stop the voices."

"They attacked you. You defended yourself." Michael's voice stayed remarkably calm but she could smell his building fury.

She still couldn't look at him. Not until she finished. "Neither of them ever recovered."

His fingers stilled against her hand, and she knew she'd finally managed to reveal an unforgivable secret. "Both of them are in some high-priced care facility, wearing diapers and drool bibs. I went to see them once. I had a stupid idea that maybe the Huntress could help fix them. As soon as I stepped in the room, they started screaming. One hit his head against the wall over and over, like he was trying to knock himself out. I left and never went back."

She couldn't decipher his scent. It was intense, but so mixed up and chaotic that she couldn't pick apart the pieces. She pressed on. "I didn't know it could be like that. Before that night, I'd sleep with a guy and he'd get this strange expression when he came, but they never said anything. They'd just hurry me out the door as quick as they could. Sometimes one would spend a couple of hours in a daze. That's all that was supposed to happen. But that night, I wanted them hurt. I wanted them to know what it felt like to be fucking violated."

Even now, she couldn't quite make herself feel entirely sorry. They'd deserved punishment, maybe not permanently, but something. She'd racked up more than enough sins to blacken her soul since then, though. "Since that night, the Huntress is darker than any of the stories say it should be. If I don't feed it, it makes people around me go crazy. They get horny and violent and forget about everything else."

"So you Hunt predators and force them to face their truth so the Huntress doesn't hurt anyone else," Michael finished. He still wanted to believe the best about her.

"It wakes them up. Some of them gave up addictions and shit like that. Some of them clamped down harder, trying to pretend nothing had changed. I used to try and keep track of them, but after a while, I couldn't." Dani straightened. "I don't pretend I'm some kind of one-fuck-you're-cured therapist. If I could stop, I would. And now you can go."

He blinked, confused. "Why exactly would I go?"

"You wanted me to be a hero. I'm not and I never will be. I'm just like they were." She turned to hurry out of the house, not wanting to see or smell the disgust she knew would be coming.

Chapter Thirty-Four

"Hold it right there!" Michael wrapped his hand around Dani's wrist. She could have broken free easily but she stopped, face averted. Her self-loathing seeped through the contact. He couldn't let it continue. Taking a deep breath, he steadied himself and prepared to engage. "You're not running from this like a coward."

It worked. Sort of.

"What?" Dani hissed, surprised into jerking her head up to meet his eyes.

"You heard me. You've run away from everything that frightened you. Those guys in college, the Huntress, our relationship, Dalhard." He saw red glints beginning to appear around the edges of her irises and kept going. Either this would work or he was about to be pummeled in what might be the most stupid circumstances possible. "It's time to stand up and face *something*."

Her arm tensed and he felt her preparing to strike.

"Attacking me won't change anything. It's just another way to run from what you know is true." He felt her resolve hardening along with her jaw and switched tactics, softening his voice and grip. "You have the power to fight. There's no reason you can't be a hero."

"I'm not like you, Michael. You're one of the good guys." The red faded from her eyes and he sent a silent prayer of thanks that his gamble had paid off.

"Bullshit. You're fighting like hell for your family, for Bernie, for those people in the kitchen. You care about all of them; I can feel it inside you. You care so damn much that you're terrified of letting them down. You're willing to sacrifice everything for them." He cradled her face in his hands, pressing his forehead against hers. Her skin burned against his, feverish proof of the stress she was under. He wanted to kiss her, but neither of them could afford to be distracted right now.

"Not everything. I won't risk you. I watched what the Huntress did to my father. It sucked out his life force and he never walked again. My

220

mother couldn't stop it. And that was before it made me into a monster."
Dani's fist tightened painfully in his hair as she pressed against him. A wail of misery swelled inside her, threatening to break free.

Michael wished to every deity ever worshipped that he knew an answer.

"That's not what happened."

Dani and Michael broke apart when Walter spoke. His chair sat inside the open doorway to the library, a pistol resting in his lap. He noticed the two of them staring at it. "There was shouting."

Michael shoved aside his embarrassment to focus on what Walter had said. "What do you mean, that's not what happened?"

"The Huntress didn't attack me," Walter answered.

Dani narrowed her eyes. "I was fucking there. I saw it. You never wanted to talk about it. Mom wouldn't talk about it but I saw it all." Michael felt terror rising in Dani, locking every muscle into rigidity, and knew she was remembering the horrible alien presence hovering over her father's bloody body.

Walter's eyes flashed wide in surprise before softening in comprehension. "I didn't know you were there, sweetheart."

"Vincent and I were worried. We sneaked downstairs to see what was happening. So you don't have to lie to protect Mom. I know what happened."

"Dani, I'd been hit by gunfire. I'd escaped, but I was dying. I called your mom for help, but it took too long to get to the safehouse where you were hiding. I knew she could tap into her connection to save me, but at a cost. I begged her to do it. I was ready to give up anything to get more time with her and with my children. It didn't attack me, it saved me," Walter explained gently.

"But you were screaming..." Dani's fingers tightened on Michael's. "It was awful. I used to lie awake at night and remember it. I'd want to scream, myself. Vincent ran away when he heard you. But I stayed, I needed to know if it killed you."

Michael heard the sound echoing through their linked hands. It didn't sound like a man. An unearthly howling, as if some living creature were being ripped apart. He shuddered. If she'd heard that, he didn't blame her for believing her father had been attacked.

221

Dani continued. "It sensed me there and part of it came toward me. I was ready to fight it with my bare hands to keep you safe. It laughed in my head while Mom was in a trance, and it said I would be next. But I knew I didn't want any part of it. Not then, not ever. It said I didn't have a choice, that it was already a part of me."

Walter took her free hand, gripping it tightly. "I'm so sorry you saw that, Dani. No wonder you resisted so strongly. Why didn't you tell us?"

"Who would I tell?" Dani shouted. "It took you months to be able to crawl out of bed, and Mom shut down so completely that it was like she was gone. She never even came out of the trailer. Eric and I tried our best to keep things together, especially when Gwen arrived. Vincent refused to sleep in the trailer. Did you know that? He spent six months sleeping in the truck before we could get him back inside. By the time Mom started getting up, all she ever told me was that it was my duty to become the High Priestess." The barrage of words ran out, and she looked at her father again. "Are you telling me it didn't attack you?"

"No. Without it, I'd be dead. It even gave me minimal sensation in my legs. Not enough to walk, but enough to know if I damage something. It's not a monster, sweetheart. And neither are you. It's high time you stopped calling yourself that," Walter said. "No one insults my little girl."

Dani studied the two men, each holding one of her hands. Her worldview was undergoing a major reshuffling. Michael could practically feel pieces sliding into their new places. He wondered if this single revelation would be enough to overcome years of fear.

"I don't know what to say." Dani looked at Michael. "Is it true?"

Michael extended his hand toward Walter, asking for permission. The man put his free hand in Michael's, making skin-to-skin contact. After a brief pause, Michael nodded slowly. He could sense her father's sincerity, guilt, and pride, but no gloating over a successful deceit.

"We should have talked about it. I kept quiet because your mom was so hurt by what happened that any mention of the Goddess was like rubbing salt on her wounds. I thought she must have explained things to you, and I didn't want to hurt her more by bringing it up. I should have asked you. We could have saved everyone a world of heartbreak." Walter didn't seem offended by his daughter's disbelief.

222

"I couldn't. Neither of you wanted to talk about what happened. You were both terrified, I could smell it. Then Gwen came and you focused on her and what she needed. Eric, Vincent, and me, we tried to stay out of the way." Dani looked up. "How did the Huntress work when you were with Mom?"

Michael stiffened in surprise. In hindsight, it was obvious. Virginia had been High Priestess when her children were conceived, after all.

"It wasn't really an issue, since she'd already transitioned from the Huntress to High Priestess. The Hunt is only temporary. When the ritual is completed, then the conduit opens between the priestess and the Goddess." Walter pursed his lips as he thought. "If your mother chose, she could use the Huntress to give her lover a cosmic reality check. She did it to me a few times when she was mad at me."

"I never got a choice." Dani had said the words so many times.

This time, he believed her. "That isn't how it's supposed to work. It's a partnership." Walter's gaze turned inward. "The Goddess used your mother's clairvoyant powers to send visions and warnings we could pass on."

"I'm a feral, not a psychic." Dani bit her lip.

"Maybe that's why the Huntress has been so physical with you, so different from what happened with your mom or the other priestesses." Walter glanced down at the gun in his lap. "I heard what you said about what happened in college. I didn't realize it was like that. I'm sorry, sweetheart. That's more than you should have had to deal with."

"It's why I stayed away as much as I could, except for helping with Gwen. You and Mom smelled so relieved when I came home, but I never knew if it was because I was back or because you were afraid of losing a potential High Priestess," Dani whispered.

Michael sensed the pent-up old hurts easing inside her as the conversation went on. From Walter's grip, he sensed her father taking on the pain and burden of guilt for his mistakes. His therapeutic instincts wanted to sit them down for some in-depth counseling, but his training warned him this wasn't the moment to interfere.

Dani lifted her head, her gaze sharp. "When she was seven, Gwen told me I had to go. That the Huntress would destroy us if I tried to do the ritual. But yesterday, she said I had to do it or Dalhard would win.

I've fought it so long. I know it's going to take me over if it gets a chance."

"I hope you're wrong about that." Walter frowned.

"I don't think we have a choice any more. Not if we want to stop Dalhard." Dani replied.

"I don't think it's a coincidence that he struck when he did or that he targeted your brothers. He must suspect they're my children."

Walter's grip came perilously close to crushing Michael's hand. The brief cry escaping his lips bought Michael an immediate loosening. Walter and Dani dropped hands, but Michael was selfishly pleased to note that she kept her fingers interlaced with his.

"We're going to have a planning session in the kitchen," Walter announced, wheeling his chair back. "Join us when you've finished."

He left the two of them alone in the library, his parting invitation reminding Michael of all they stood to lose: Bernie, Vincent, and Eric, even Gwen. But none of it hurt as much as the thought of Dani's brilliant stubbornness vanishing into an alien consciousness.

"I've been afraid of it for so long," Dani whispered to herself. "It seems hard to imagine it could have been any other way."

"Our minds always build up our fears to be bigger than they are. I wonder if the Huntress reacted to your fear. It's a psychic connection, it has to be influenced by the person it's connected to," Michael said, thinking out loud. "Maybe there's a way to use that to keep it from taking you—"

Dani set her fingers over his lips, her eyes dark with tears. "I know you want to save me. But we're out of time. I have to take the chance." Her other hand still clung tightly to him.

Michael wanted to argue. In a story, someone would miraculously know some forgotten rituals to control the Huntress. But no convenient third party popped up to offer salvation.

She kissed him lightly and he tasted the saltiness of her tears on her lips. "You were right. I can't run away from this. If I do, we'll lose everything that matters to us."

"I don't want to lose you." It couldn't end like this.

"I'll finally be what you see when you look at me," she smiled, smoothing back the hair from his forehead. "I'll be the hero you deserve

224

and you'll get to save the girl."

"Dani…" His protest trailed off. He knew there wasn't time. His body screamed for her, rock-hard inside his jeans. It wasn't distracted by the bigger picture. It only knew how much he loved and wanted her.

"I love you," she whispered, pulling her hand free to wrap her arms around him. "I always will."

"I love you, too." He held her, wishing the moment could last forever, but it couldn't.

Chapter Thirty-Five

Eric sneaked through Dalhard's stark halls with more care than he'd ever taken sneaking out of his parents' house. Vincent was off with Dalhard for another experiment and Eric intended to take advantage of the opportunity. The laboratory was off limits with armed guards protecting it, ditto the lower levels. He hoped he might find a phone or computer somewhere, a way to communicate with his family or Vapor. They needed to know about Dalhard's ability to cloud other people's minds through touch since the evidence suggested they weren't taking his advice to run.

The sound of sniffling caught his attention. He tilted his head, closing his eyes to track the sound. It came from one of the rooms nearby, and Eric feared he knew who it was.

The unlocked door opened easily. Clearly Dalhard wasn't worried about his acquisitions moving around on this floor. Bernie huddled on the simple mass-produced bed, a bright rag doll and a tiny bear clutched under her chin. Her breath hissed in, obviously preparing to scream.

"Hey, it's me, Eric. We met this morning." Eric immediately dropped to one knee, all too aware of her fear and despair filling the air. He made himself as small as possible, trying not to intimidate her further. He scanned the room, spotting the camera mounted on the wall. No toys littered the tiny room, and there was none of the luxury of his and Vincent's suite. It both sickened and soothed him to see her so ignored. On the one hand, no child should be treated this way. On the other, it meant Dalhard still didn't understand her true potential.

"I re-remember," Bernie sniffed, wiping her nose on her sleeve.

"I heard you crying. What's wrong?" Eric asked. If he could get her to cooperate, this would be an even better link than a phone or computer. It would be absolutely untraceable.

"Chuck says he can't talk to Gwen anymore," Bernie wailed, breaking into fresh tears. "He says the bad men are going to hurt us and

226

the pretty lady is going to die and Michael will be too sad to help me."

Eric's hopes sank so rapidly that he could feel them leaving exit wounds on the bottoms of his feet. "He told you all that, huh?"

Bernie nodded, still curled miserably on the bed.

Ghosts did make the best reconnaissance scouts, provided someone could hear what they had to report. They went everywhere and listened to everything. Eric glanced at the camera, conscious that it likely recorded every word.

"You know, we have a TV in our room. Do you want to come with me and watch? We could keep each other company." More importantly, he hadn't found any cameras in there. Eric hoped her parents hadn't drilled her on stranger danger as thoroughly as his own had.

Bernie nodded and crawled awkwardly off the bed, her toys still clutched in her hands. Eric offered his hand and to his surprise, she curled her sticky little fingers around his. It made her seem so much younger than she must be.

"Chuck said I could talk to you. But not the other one. He's been following the bad guys around to see what they do. They're getting ready to take us away tomorrow," Bernie said as they walked down the hall.

"Tomorrow!" Eric stopped in his tracks. There wasn't time to search for an opportunity anymore. He'd have to make one. He hoped there wasn't an audio along with the visual in the hall cameras. Dalhard couldn't be allowed to suspect Eric still operated outside of the man's influence.

He settled Bernie in the lounge, finding something colorful, loud, and kid-friendly to play on TV while he brought her some cookies. Then he settled himself in a nearby chair. "Bernie, is Chuck here?"

Bernie nodded, her eyes flicking to an apparently empty chair.

"Can he tell you why he can't talk to Gwen anymore?" Eric asked, keeping his voice low.

Bernie frowned, answering slowly as if she didn't quite understand. "They sealed her up with salt to keep her safe."

"So he can't get in to see her, but he can still talk to her," Eric pressed, trying to keep his body language as casual as possible. His tensed arms and hands still betrayed his urgency.

"He says they're all shouting to try and get her to hear them. Like

227

they do with me, sometimes." Bernie shuddered.

Her gift must be lesser than Gwen's. The stronger the medium, the more they attracted ghosts. In Gwen's case, strongly enough to draw in spirits who weren't even searching for a medium. "I need to get a message to Gwen. Will Chuck try to pass it on?"

Bernie looked at the empty chair and nodded.

"Tell them that Dalhard is gifted. If he touches you, he can get inside your head, make you do things you don't want to do." Eric heard the distant tapping of approaching footsteps. He hated pushing the little girl but his only opportunity was about to vanish.

"He's gone. He'll do it. He's trying hard to be good." Fresh tears threatened to spill from Bernie's eyes. "I miss my mommy. I want to go home."

"I know. I'll figure something out. I promise." Eric cursed himself for a complete fraud. He couldn't even figure out how to get Vincent and himself free, but he couldn't stand to see the little girl so upset.

"That means I have two heroes helping me. You and Michael. And the pretty lady, I guess. If she doesn't die," Bernie said as the door to the lounge opened.

"Who's going to die, Bernadette?" Dalhard swept into the room, his face narrowing in disapproval. Vincent rolled in behind, heading straight for the bar.

Bernie shrank into herself, and Eric smelled the acrid fear tainting her cotton and chocolate scent. "No one. We were just watching cartoons on TV," he answered quickly.

Dalhard immediately dismissed the matter, waving his hand to brush it aside. "Your brother and I have had quite the afternoon."

"Should have seen it, bro," Vincent crowed, beer in hand. "One hit and, bam, the heavy bag splits open, spraying sand everywhere. It was awesome. New guy was impressed."

Eric stared at the brown bottle in Vincent's hand. His brother had been drinking heavily since their disastrous "job interview" yesterday. He hoped it was a sign that some part of Vincent recognized how screwed up things were. Suddenly he realized what Vincent had said. "What new guy?"

"Corporal Ronald McBride. You saw him earlier." Dalhard's granite eyes locked onto Eric, studying him.

"He woke up, then?" Eric forced himself to shrug as if he didn't really care about the answer.

"He did, with an extra two inches and seventy-five pounds of muscle. His physical strength has increased almost eight hundred percent after the treatment. But he is nothing compared to the two of you." A proprietary smile smugly broadened Dalhard's features.

"Guess I don't have to worry about losing the job, then. When's dinner?" Eric caught himself squirming under Dalhard's study and forced himself to stay still. If the man touched him again, this time he might end up like Vincent. He had no idea why he'd been able to resist and Vincent hadn't, but he wasn't going to count on it with less than a day to escape.

"I'll have something sent up. And someone will escort Bernadette back to her room." Dalhard finally lifted his gaze.

Bernie shot a panicked glance at Eric.

"She can stay. I don't mind," Eric said quickly.

Dalhard left them, eager to focus on other matters. Eric waited until Vincent got up to get another beer. Then he whispered to Bernie. "I'm going to get us out of here. Tonight." If he had to, he'd leave Vincent behind.

"I don't want to get shot." Bernie's wide eyes stared at him. "Tomorrow the men with guns will be gone."

"Chuck told you that?" Eric hesitated. If the ghost knew something...

Bernie nodded. "It's part of a trap tomorrow. The bad man will send them all away."

If Dalhard was distracted by someone springing his trap and the guards would be gone, it might be his best chance to get himself, Vincent, and Bernie out of there. He could knock Vincent out and carry him. *Mom and Dad must know someone who can fix whatever was done to his mind.* It wasn't much of a plan, but it beat grabbing Bernie now and hoping he could outrun the guards and their bullets. If only he didn't have the sickening certainty that they were all playing into Dalhard's plans.

This was not how he'd planned for things to go, André fumed as he stalked toward his isolated office. McBride's test results were disappointing. Yes, he was stronger than even the strongest human, but he still performed far behind the ferals. It was like settling for a cheap knock-off instead of the proper designer. But he couldn't hope to build a fortune on the few ferals that Nature stingily provided.

Perhaps I'm thinking of this the wrong way. Enhanced humans like McBride would certainly satisfy any number of his clients—military juntas struggling for control, insurrectionists and terrorist groups, and even the major world militaries would be eager to acquire a few samples for covert operations. He began to pace, his heels leaving dents in the thick hand-woven carpet.

If he kept the ferals for himself, he could eliminate the major challenge in selling powerful weapons—that his clients would choose to use those weapons against him and his interests. Keeping the true power for his personal use appealed to him. All sorts of ambitions became possible with enough power.

But he needed to make certain they were actually under his control. He wasn't worried about Vincent, but Eric showed alarming flashes of independence. Of course, Eric had killed Roberts, or was it Rogers? André frowned, trying to remember the name before dismissing it as unimportant. Willingness to commit murder was always a significant proof of loyalty.

But both brothers refused to give them any further information about their family or other families like them. He didn't have their highest loyalty; their family obviously did. But if he pushed their minds much further, he risked destroying their ability to think independently, making them useless as bodyguards or assassins. At its full level, his gift would leave an empty shell that needed to be directed in every single step. He would have to keep coaxing, searching for a crack to get what he needed.

"I need a drink," André muttered, swiveling on his heel to head for the gleaming steel liquor cabinet.

"Sir?" Karan prompted discreetly from the corner.

André frowned. He hadn't noticed when the man had come in. Discretion was a good tool in an aide, but no one should have an advantage over him. "What is it?"

"I came to speak to you about McBride's test results—" Karan began.

"I've seen them. We will proceed with mass production when we get back to Europe." André noted the faint smile of satisfaction on Karan's face. He poured himself a generous glass of amber-colored scotch.

"I will let the lab know. However, there was something else." Karan paused, his fingers tightening around his tablet. "I've been monitoring various sites and information sources on the Internet, and I think we may have a problem."

"You think or you know?" André recognized Karan's nerves about delivering bad news. His aide's fingers kept caressing the smooth edge of his tablet and his left foot kept creeping askew to point at the door. Dalhard had no desire to cushion his blows or reassure Karan's fears. Instead he drained the glass, welcoming the harsh bite of alcohol down his throat.

"If I've interpreted the data correctly, I'm seeing signs of a mass exodus. Hundreds of people worldwide are beginning to vanish from their ordinary patterns. More significantly, in some cases, their information is also vanishing. Their entire digital backgrounds, erased as if they had never been. Someone, most likely an organized group, is actively trying to hide from us. I suspect they must be supernaturals," Karan finished.

His aide looked far too impressed by what he'd found. Could the little weasel be preparing to jump ship to someone more powerful? He'd quickly discover his mistake if he did. When André buried his competition, it wasn't a metaphor. "Find out who it is."

"Perhaps we should move the assets tonight instead of tomorrow," Karan suggested. "Make certain they're safe."

"I need them here to lure the sister in. We'll go tomorrow, once we've acquired her." André wasn't interested in his aide's fears, but he wasn't stupid either. "Keep a car ready to get to the airport quickly. We can put McBride and Bernadette into another car and send them on ahead."

"And what if the sister brings company?"

Do I have to think of everything? Inspiration struck in the memory of his

231

father's failure. When the original test subject escaped from his father's lab, the explosion had set them back decades, but it had also destroyed any potential leads for an investigation. "Wire the building to explode. Make sure all the evidence is destroyed, physical and digital. The test results have already been uploaded to our home server in Berlin, so it's safe to sacrifice anything that might link to trace it back to us. As the Harris family are relying on forged papers, they have helpfully covered their own trail should anyone come looking for them."

"Yes, sir." Karan withdrew. André frowned, feeling eyes on him, but the room was empty. He shrugged the sensation off. It was irrelevant now. No one and nothing could hope to stop him. He took a moment to smooth his rumpled hair and suit. Losing one's temper never enhanced one's standing. His mother had taught him that before she died, and the importance of maintaining control, or at least the illusion of control, at all times. If only his father could have learned the lesson so thoroughly.

He picked up the much-handled photo. So beautiful and strong. A perfect mate. Her brothers were useful, but she was the true jewel to be sought and won. The perfect vessel to create his own loyal army of ferals, raised from the crib to obey him. No matter what it took, he would find her.

Chapter Thirty-Six

"Nada will be here in a few hours. She can help us with the ritual." Virginia beamed at Dani from across the kitchen table. "You remember Nada, don't you?" She continued, but Michael stopped paying attention. His despair clung to him so closely that he half expected it to form a visible cloud around him.

Dani nodded at her mother's words, her fingers twitching at her clothes. The figurine resting on the table held her attention like a snake rattling a warning. It didn't seem like much, the clay pale and brittle with age. An ancient statue, less than a foot tall, of a woman with her arms outstretched to either side holding a slender scepter carved with symbols. She was naked, her unnaturally round breasts contrasting sharply with scaling on her legs. Her feet were bird claws. Heavy wings flowed from her shoulders to the ground, providing a tripod of stability. Her hair was piled in chunky layers with a strange mass on top. It could be a crown or a turban, depending on how he looked at it.

The Queen of the Night, the patron goddess of the lillitu and the *lalassu* as a whole. When the conduit was restored, the statue would be restored along with it.

Michael wanted to knock the stupid thing onto the floor and watch it shatter. He wanted to stagger outside and rage against the night sky, roaring with fury.

But instead he sat at the kitchen table, listening to tactical discussions about the best way to rescue Dani's brothers and Bernie. They were laying out multiple plans, hoping Dani would be able to tell them which plan was best once the conduit was established. Dani already seemed to be gone, leaving only a haunted shell behind as a witness.

He couldn't stomach listening to any more cheerful optimism. Scrapings from Gwen's room provided the perfect excuse for escape. Dani didn't even seem to notice when he got up from the table. Certainly no one else commented. Pushing open the door to her dank, artificial cave, he saw Gwen curled up in the corner, sketching on her pad by the light of a half dozen flickering candles.

She smiled at him as he came in, calmer and more relaxed than he'd ever seen her. Of course, given how he'd first seen her in a fetal position, moaning in terror, it wasn't that much of a stretch. He tried to shake off his building anger. This wasn't Gwen's fault, and she didn't deserve to be a target.

"Checkmate to the black queen," Gwen murmured, her charcoal pencil flying over the page. "Pieces are scattered. Have to find them before the next game."

"Hi, Gwen," Michael squatted next to her, deliberately out of grabbing range. He didn't want to repeat his visit to her mind, particularly without anyone there to help both of them out.

"Only one ride per customer." Gwen shook her head. "But I didn't think you'd both be this dense. She found all the pieces but doesn't want to play. And now it's getting closer. Close enough for hot breath to whisper on my neck."

"What's closer?" Michael asked, his training overcoming his weariness.

"The knot. Big knot. Too many choices. The station is closed, last trains are gone. Time to tidy the toys." She ripped the drawing off the pad, tossing it to the floor.

Michael picked it up. A tall man standing under an endless expanse of stars and darkness, his back to the audience. A vague hint of a flag undulated in the sky over him. "Who is this?"

"That's not for you." Gwen snatched it back, sounding as exasperated as any younger sister. "Can't explain in words. Think I'm crazy because I can't find the words. Want all the words to line up in neat rows like bars in a prison. You're being an idiot."

Michael hadn't expected such a straightforward insult from Gwen. Or was she talking to one of the dead? He glanced over his shoulder.

"I mean you, Michael," Gwen snorted. "You were supposed to love her."

He didn't have to ask who Gwen meant. "I do love her. But I can't ask her to let everyone else suffer. This is what she wants."

"She hurts herself over and over for old mistakes, and I'm the one who's crazy?" Gwen's angry laughter did not provide much evidence of

234

sanity. "Throw herself into a pit, and you watch when you could make it all right."

"How can I possibly make it right?" Michael asked wearily, tired of doing the socially acceptable thing. Ever since he'd picked up Dani's lipstick at the police station, it had brought him nothing but trouble. Dear God, could it really be only three days ago? It felt like a lifetime.

"Have to show her what she's losing. What she needs to hold on to. I tried to tell her but she doesn't listen. Hears the words but not what I say." Her outburst drained Gwen, leaving her limp against her bed. "No more happy ending as the words in a folder pin us all down like bugs in a drawer. I'm tired."

"I'll let you sleep." Michael couldn't wait for this horrible day to end. He couldn't imagine going back to work on Monday and pretending nothing had changed.

"Wait," Gwen whispered as he stood up. She fumbled through the scattered papers before holding one out to him. "This is what you need."

It was a sketch of him and Dani kissing in the forest. A lump rose in Michael's throat. Their bodies curved together lovingly, a partnership. No raw, ripping hunger ready to devour. Instead, it looked like a foundation they could build on to create a relationship that would withstand the pressures of the future.

"I finally got to see something pleasant. No blood or guts or screams. Just love," Gwen murmured, already half asleep.

Michael got up and saw Dani standing in the doorway, her teeth gnawing on her lower lip. "You left," she whispered. "I... I had to follow."

He wished he knew what to say or how they could get from this moment to the loving partnership in Gwen's drawing. They'd run out of time. He wanted to beg her not to do it, but he couldn't. But watching her sacrifice herself threatened to rip his heart and soul to pieces. It wasn't fair.

"Michael, I can't go through this on my own." Tears flowed down her cheeks. "I'm not strong enough. I hate it. I hate that I've finally found you and now it's all going to be gone."

He pulled her into his arms and experienced what she meant more completely than words could ever hope to describe. All the mixed emotions of fear, hope, worry, longing, love, and despair, slapped together into a terrifying collage. The paper scraped against itself as the drawing in his hand crumpled, and he couldn't help remembering the sweetness of their kiss.

"Let's go somewhere private," he suggested.

Dani led him up upstairs to her tiny bedroom on the upper floor. There was barely enough room to stand beside the queen-size bed with its thick dove-gray comforter. Dani let her fingers slide down the faded wallpaper. "I've never brought anyone else up here. This is the one place that was always just for me. It was safe."

"You needed a sanctuary." Michael's heart lifted at the evidence of caring, the hand-stitched quilts and well-loved books. "I'm glad you had one."

Dani took the drawing from his hand, her eyes widening as she studied it. "Gwen gave you this?"

"Ah, yeah," he admitted, embarrassed, as if he'd been caught with a dirty magazine.

"Not sure how I feel about my little sister using ghosts to spy on me." A hint of a smile twitched at the edges of Dani's mouth.

"Audiences were never my thing, either. But I'm glad I have it." He caught up her free hand in his and lifted it to press a soft kiss against her knuckles. "No matter what happens, I wouldn't change the last few days. I'm always going to treasure what we had together." Not knowing Dani would have meant continuing to live half a life, lost in hero tales and dreams.

"I wish I could change so many things. But not meeting you." The drawing fluttered to the ground as she dropped it to caress his cheek with her hand, just as she had in the alley the first time they talked.

To heck with doing the right thing. Michael threw everything aside in a mad fit of impulsive selfishness. "Be with me tonight, before the ritual."

Dani's hands went cold against his skin. "But the Huntress—"

"I told you I'm not afraid of the Huntress or what it can show me. Nothing scares me as much as the thought of not making love to you."

Chapter Thirty-Seven

Dani's breath exploded out of her as Michael turned her hand over to indulge in an exploratory kiss on her palm. His tongue softly caressed her skin, playing over the sensitive curve in the middle. Knowing he could sense what she felt, she reveled in her desire for him, the strength of her feelings for him. The Huntress lay quiet, appeased either from feeding or the impending ritual—she didn't know which and she frankly didn't care. She wasn't about to waste a moment of this chance.

He caressed the soft skin at the back of her neck, brushing aside the long strands of hair. "Let me do this the way I've imagined since we first met."

She closed her eyes and leaned her head back into his touch. Their lips met as if drawn together magnetically, exploring each other with exquisite thoroughness. She tasted the sweetness of apples and vanilla, his own unique flavor. His hair wrapped around her fingers as she slid her hands around his neck. Even as her passions flared, she held a tight grasp on her internal controls. Her last act would not be to hurt someone else.

She opened her mouth to tease his lips with her tongue, eager for more. He pulled her tighter against him, the movement threatening to overbalance them onto the bed. The thought of simply pulling him down on top of her and letting him ride her into ecstasy set her lust blazing. Michael moaned against her lips, and she smelled the spike in his arousal as his gift let him share in her excitement.

"Patience. I want to make this last," he whispered against her mouth, interspersing the words with tiny nibbles.

Fuck patience. Dani could practically feel the flames consuming her as his kisses skimmed down her neck. But she held herself back. This wasn't some sordid encounter in a back alleyway. As much as her body throbbed and yearned for completion, she wanted this too badly to rush the preliminaries. There would only be one first time for them—maybe the only time. *I might have fucked plenty of others, but Michael will be the only one I make love with.* She held tight to the barriers between her and Huntress, keeping her mental doors shoved closed with all her strength, the habit

237

of years of caution.

Michael teased her lips with his tongue. "Come back to me."

"I'm here," she murmured back, forcing her fears to the back of her mind.

"Don't worry. I know what I'm doing." He grinned. "It's not my first time."

"It's not your first time making love to a descendent of ancient priestesses with a legendary predator in her?" she growled with a grin, letting her hands enjoy the play of his muscles beneath the soft T-shirt. "Damn. Guess it means I don't have to be gentle."

"Trust me. Let me take the lead." His scent mixed amusement and lust in a way she'd never experienced before. She found the effect oddly comforting and arousing.

"Don't make me wait, Professor. I'm about two seconds away from ravishing you my way." She started to yank at his shirt, but he grasped her fingers and pulled them away.

"My turn now." His smile chased away any remnant of fear as he slowly, tortuously slid his hands along the sides of her body, lifting the edges of her T-shirt. She moaned in erotic appreciation of his warm touch on her bare skin. He gently peeled the shirt away as if unwrapping a beautiful and fragile present, easing it over her head. His clever fingers made quick work of her bra before dancing over her bare breasts like silk butterflies, learning the shape of her flesh. Dani tilted her head back, letting her hair wash over his embrace in soft waves. He accepted the invitation, pressing his lips against her vulnerable throat.

She ripped at the fastening of her jeans, eager to let her entire body enjoy his touch. The torn denim dropped to the ground, leaving her bare except for the iridescent thong clinging to her lower curves. Michael glanced down and his eyes darkened, the scent of lust growing even stronger.

It no longer felt strange to scent his reactions to her feelings. It felt right to know that he experienced the flaring spikes of desire and the raging coals radiating warmth. It was love—more than love. Love and lust and affection and respect woven into an inseparable mix. And he knew. She didn't have to struggle with clumsy, ill-equipped words.

He just knew and used the knowledge to play her as if she were a fine instrument in the hands of a master. With simple, undemanding kisses and teasing touches, her core already throbbed on the edge. She hovered on the brink of losing control, but Michael's strong grip kept her back from the precipice. Each touch of mouth and hand brought her higher, drawing out the tension.

Pushed past any level of endurance, she clenched her fists in his shirt. A growl rumbled in her belly and throat as she ripped the irritating barrier away.

"Ouch," Michael chuckled, picking at the remnants hanging at his sides. "You are impatient with shirts."

Dani contented herself with a satisfied smile and quirked eyebrow.

"Not complaining," he added. "But I believe that makes it my turn again."

He slid his hands along her breasts, his fingers brushing against the tight buds of her nipples. Each touch tightened her further, making patience difficult. At least now she could explore his chest with greedy eyes and fingers. His clothes disguised the lithe muscles underneath, hiding his beautiful physique from the rest of the world. Dani couldn't help being torn by equally selfish desires to keep him to herself and to show him off to the world so other women could eat their own tongues with envy.

He lowered her onto the bed, leaning over her to run his lips along her belly, inching tortuously lower toward the shimmering, sole scrap of fabric she wore. Dani clenched her fists in the quilt, squirming under and savoring every touch. He tongued the top of the sequined thong briefly before glancing back up at her. "Is this your idea of casual, everyday wear?"

"A girl has to have some standards," she purred. "Think of it as the toy surprise inside the box."

"Only one?"

"I'm sure we can find more." She reached for his belt, but he stepped back.

"It's still my turn. Remember?" His hands trembled against her skin, betraying his own inner conflict.

Dani grinned, delighted he wasn't as immune to her charms as he pretended.

239

"Don't doubt that I want you. You're not the only one skating on the edge." His voice was ragged as he climbed up the bed, pressing his forehead to hers to align their bodies along every point of possible contact. The thick seams of his jeans bit roughly into her bare legs.

"Then stop hanging on the edge and take the plunge." She pressed her hips against him, loving the thick length of his erection pressed against the fiery magma burning at her core. Even shielded by his jeans, his touch drove her wild. She captured his hand and pressed his fingers against the liquid heat between her legs.

His fingers slipped over the bare skin beneath her thong, and she caught a faint hint of surprise before it vanished back into masculine enjoyment. She kept herself meticulously waxed for performing. From his smile and aroused scent, he appreciated her efforts.

Every warrior knew a good offence was the best defense, and Dani hastened to press her advantage. She lured him with hungry kisses and knew she'd succeeded when his hands tightened against her shoulders and his hips ground against hers.

No more banter. No more teasing. She exulted in the passionate fury she'd ignited in her lover.

His mouth clamped over her breast, no longer lightly teasing but demanding. Deep, pulling suction flung any lingering awareness of caution out the window as they sped toward mutual satisfaction. The hot, hard length of him pressed against her and she eagerly rubbed against him. She wanted to feel him inside her so badly that she'd scream if it didn't happen soon.

"Patience," he whispered.

"I don't wait well." She ripped away the soaked thong and locked her fingers onto his jeans. *So close…*

"Then we'll have to take care of that." He pulled away, and she could have killed him if frustrated desire hadn't left her locked and shivering. He shoved his jeans down and pushed them aside.

Dani drank in the sight of him with eager eyes. Long and lithe, her professor was all sculpted muscle and sinew. His heavy erection defied gravity, straining toward her in undeniable evidence of his desire. He spread her legs wide and spent a long moment looking at her slick, swollen folds.

Her inner walls pulsed in anticipation. "Please," she whispered, lifting her hips in invitation.

He ran a single finger across her cleft, tugging it lightly over her clit. Ecstasy bloomed and she screamed her release.

Hand gripping her bucking hips, he used gentle pressure and flicking caresses to transform her orgasm into a world-shattering cascade. Exultant pressure burned through her quivering muscles again and again. She lost touch with anything resembling reality, shattering and rebuilding only to shatter anew on peaks of pleasure.

She held tight to the walls containing the Huntress despite being out of her mind with ecstasy. But the predator within might as well have been dead. Only a faint hint of awareness buzzed on the outskirts of her consciousness as she bucked and thrashed in a continuous orgasm.

But she needed more. She needed to feel the length of him inside while her body clamped and quaked. She reached for him.

Her newly awakened greed must have slipped through to him since he immediately lifted his head and met her eyes. Her pulsing flesh demanded more. "Inside. Now," she gasped.

To his credit, he didn't wait for a more coherent explanation. He bent, grabbing something off the floor. Dani couldn't help but grin as she saw the condom. Of course her Professor came prepared. Then thought took a definite back seat to feeling.

Wet and eager, there was no need to take things slow. She moaned as he slid inside her, sheathing himself in her. The stretching of her hot core taking him deeper and deeper had to be the most delicious sensation she'd ever experienced.

Until he started to move. She felt his control shatter as surely as if she'd possessed his psychometric gift. His hips began to pump, thrusting deeper and deeper into her. He curved his spine, stroking and coaxing her swollen flesh with the skill of a master violinist coaxing throbbing notes from his instrument. She clutched his firm buttocks as he rode her, matching him stroke for stroke, panting and gasping. He took her open mouth with his own, mimicking each pelvic thrust with his tongue. She abandoned any sense of self-control right along with him, letting her wild instincts rise to the fore. Primal, animalistic, she surrendered to the ancient satisfaction of feeling her man ride her hard and wet, wringing fresh orgasms from her spasming body.

She clamped down hard on him, milking and sucking on his buried shaft. He shuddered and cried out as she tipped over into *le petit mort*.

And released her hold on the Huntress.

Chapter Thirty-Eight

Michael sensed the loss of containment immediately. Even as his mind and body exploded in an earth-shattering orgasm, the alien Huntress opened like a great maw beneath him. Fangs caught at his psyche, scraping along the outer edges for purchase. He felt Dani's soundless wail of denial and fury as her hands tightened hard enough to leave bruises on his waist.

Beneath the burning rings, Dani's dark eyes softened in dismay, then hardened in determination. She began to pull away from him, wrestling with the Huntress to keep it from him. But he clung to her, shielding her from the primal whirlwind clawing at them. He refused to let the Huntress have her. He mentally pushed at the mystic predator. *You've hurt her enough! You're not welcome here anymore.* He could sense it struggling to come closer, but Dani joined her mental support to his and together they held it at bay.

He could see it overlaid on top of reality, a coiling snake with black, glittering scales with gleaming red eyes. It snarled at them, coiling around them, searching for a point to attack. Michael started to feel a sense of triumph. They could do this.

Until it swallowed them whole. Crushing pressure slammed into them from all sides, trying to force them apart. He held tight to Dani, her fear and determination matching his own. But no regret—never regret.

Let her go. Let her go, and this will all be over. The words echoed sibilantly in his head. It was the Huntress. He recognized it immediately and clung even tighter to Dani.

He became painfully aware of the cosmos stretching out in every direction. Stars roared silently in the void, massive furnaces of primal energy consuming themselves in their fury. Planets hung in darkness, unwitting prisoners of gravity. Galaxies spun in place, plowing through the emptiness with massive inertial power. For the first time, he truly understood how mind-bogglingly huge the universe truly was and how infinitesimally small he truly was.

His mind rebelled. He might be small on a cosmic scale, but he refused to accept insignificance. Size alone did not determine importance. Dani, Bernie, Gwen, Walter, Virginia, Celina, George, Kaitlin, Brianna, the Stirgises, all of them were specks compared to the cosmos, but they mattered. Every last person mattered.

The Huntress hissed; a slithering vibration wrapped around him. He sensed he had somehow passed a challenge. Dani lay rigidly in his arms, but no trace of her emotions filtered through to him. If he hadn't been in the middle of a bizarre mystical experience, he might have worried something had happened to her. But he held firm to his faith in the two of them and continued to hold her tightly.

Love conquers all? Is that it? The Huntress slammed into his mind, showing him all the horrors committed in the name of love. All the dark secrets he'd been a reluctant witness to over the years. Predators who stalked the objects of their obsession, minds full of deluded fantasies. When the recipients of their imaginary relationships refused to play along, disappointment became violence. He experienced their terror with unfiltered keenness, like a sharp blade slicing into his mind.

He saw men and women worn down by the relentless demands of mates more interested in perfection than companionship. He staggered under invisible wounds to heart and soul, fought against accumulated scar tissue burying him in a callous shell.

He fell to his knees under blows of brutality, powered by the impotent fury of those who saw others as possessions. He wept for the powerless, betrayed by those who promised to love and cherish them above all others. He bent his head over the unmarked graves of possessions who became too inconvenient to their tormentors. The Huntress chuckled, pleased to have broken him.

"This is not love," Michael insisted, irritated and offended. Did it think to hurt him with old memories? "It is possession, jealousy, and obsession. It isn't love."

The Huntress snarled at his defiance, but he wasn't interested in the predator's response. He spoke to Dani, hoping she would hear his words. "I've seen the world for what it is since I was a child. I already know all the dark secrets you're trying to shock me with. But I've seen the other side, too. Real love, filled with laughter and joy. Love that elevates and delights in their beloved's flight as much as their own." He shouted the words.

And do you think you are worthy of such love? You, whose own father cringed from your touch? His memories fell under brutal fangs, ripping them apart to pick out the most painful morsels. All the shameful and painful events from his past, brought front and center in surround sound and Technicolor.

The first time he innocently told his parents how another adult didn't like him, only to be told he was lying. His innocent bewilderment changed to crushing fear and shame.

His mother teaching him how to pretend he didn't feel emotions or receive impressions through touch. They would practice suppressing their expressions in a mirror for hours on end. She warned him that no one would ever believe him or want to be around him if they knew. The weight of secrets pressed down on him, choking away his breath.

When his girlfriend, Reagan, told him that his ability to read her mind only "creeped her out" instead of bringing them closer, her lips curled in disgust and her fingers recoiling from touching him. He could still see her walking away from him without a backward glance. Isolation froze his heart and soul, doubt beat down his self-confidence.

Being forced to see everyone's most horrible and shameful secrets. Knowing the cashier at the coffee bar was having an affair. Seeing how the man beside him on the bus imagined luring young women home. Learning the random stranger brushing past on the street beat her children. Every nasty and sordid detail came flinging out of his memory.

Enough. "Is that all you've got?" Michael demanded, tired of being the one attacked. "Come on, where's the mind-altering revelation that will make me into a vegetable?"

He saw all the times he'd been selfish, turning away from people in need because he was too tired and worn out to deal with their problems. He saw all the times he'd been wrong, from accidentally short-changing a waitress to not realizing Bernie was a medium. He saw all the bad results of carelessness, indifference, and ignorance.

And he still stood firm, unbowed by the Huntress's best efforts. He still held Dani in his arms. Still refused to allow this alien parasite to drive him away from her even as it tightened around him.

245

"You claim to show the truth! This isn't the truth. This is fear! All you can see are shadows!" he shouted. "I'm not afraid of you!"

The constricting pressure vanished. They tumbled into disorienting darkness. There was no up, no down, nothing but their mutual death grip on each other.

Well done, Michael. A woman's voice greeted them. Strange and hollow, it echoed slightly, though there was nothing for the sound to bounce off.

Light began to glow diffusely as they floated in the strange darkness, enough for him to see Dani struggling to talk to him. He ran his thumb over her cheek, brushing away the tears. They were still naked and clasped in each other's arms.

"I saw it all. Everything you went through." Dani's fingers skimmed over his cheeks and forehead, searching for injury, and he felt her desperate anxiety, the remnants of her blind terror. "I thought I would lose you."

"It wanted me to let go," Michael said slowly, piecing it together. "I wouldn't."

"It hurt you because of me." Dani bit her lip and looked away. He sensed her fear that he would reject her.

"Hey, look at me." He tilted her head back. "I just went through a mystical personality test and I held on to you every step of the way because I am never letting you go. I waited my whole life to find you, and I am not going anywhere." He claimed her sweet lips, and his body roared in enthusiastic response. "You're beautiful and strong and anyone who tries to tell you different is a damn idiot."

Her laugh, though weak, still managed to ring in the void. "It's still wrong when you curse. Where are we?"

Large blocks of tightly fitted black granite materialized under their feet. Honey-colored sandstone pillars stood at rampant attention along the edges. Exotic, colorful flowers perfumed the air, twining around the pillars as living adornment. Smoky torches blinded him to the world beyond the pillars. He couldn't help but think it looked like something out of an Indiana Jones movie. "Is this real?" he asked.

Of course it's real, the same woman's voice answered him. There were hints of movement beyond the pillars, but no matter how he strained, he

246

couldn't see them clearly, only wispy and ghost-like flashes of paleness. Michael's fingers tightened around Dani, moving to stand between her and it.

There is nothing to see. And nothing to fear. Gauzy smoke congealed, creating a translucent figure of a woman. Long dark hair, intricately curled and braided, surrounded a beautiful face with kohl-lined eyes. Linen drapes barely concealed her long legs and heavy breasts. She walked toward them, taking on strength and color with each step. Her skin was olive-dark and her hair even darker. *Welcome.*

Soft cloth fell over their shoulders, wrapping them in thick linen robes. Michael was relieved not to be naked, but disturbed at more evidence of not being in the real world anymore.

It is most pleasant to finally meet you. The woman came closer, her feet drifting through the granite floor.

"Who are you?" Dani demanded, her voice cracking with fear as she moved to put herself between Michael and the woman. He stayed by her side.

Names are tedious and limiting. I've had so many. I've always preferred something descriptive: Queen of the Night.

247

Chapter Thirty-Nine

Dani blanched as belated awareness finally twigged. "You're the Goddess." Behind her, she smelled a sudden burst of curiosity from Michael. No fear, only interest. Of course he wasn't afraid of being in some mystical alternate reality. *Every story should have one.*

It's been a long time since my Chosen Priestess raged with such defiance. The Goddess smiled in amusement.

"I'm not the first, then." Dani was surprised at her disappointment.

It was the Middle Ages, then. She grew up believing sex to be a sin, poor thing. It took ages to set her straight. But you are a different bowl of fruit. Afraid for so long. The Goddess toyed with Dani's hair, leaving a spine-tingling trail of electric energy behind.

This wasn't at all how Dani pictured meeting with a deity. *Shouldn't there be more flaming swords and booming voices from the sky?*

"She had reason to be afraid," Michael's politeness kept his words from being an accusation, but only barely. "Your Huntress violated her."

The Huntress is a representation of the conduit between you and I. It is shaped by you as much as by me. A divine frown rippled across her features like a wave on water. *You were angry and frightened, transforming the Huntress into the very monster you feared.*

"So it's my fault? Blame the victim? How evolved." Dani tensed further, waiting to get blasted by a lightning bolt. Her family wasn't big on church but mouthing off to a god was probably one of those instant-death-worthy prohibitions.

Your anger is great. You hold onto it like a shield even though it drags you down into the depths where you cannot breathe. If you continue to clench it to you, it will cost you everything. The Goddess glanced at Michael, her slanted eyes making her meaning clear.

"Leave him out of it," Dani growled.

Your love for him opened my connection to you, letting us move beyond monsters in the dark. I am not your enemy, Danielle. I want to help you. Ask me what you want to know.

"How can we rescue Bernie and my brothers?" she asked. Everyone had been so sure the Goddess would help them; this was her chance to find out.

There are many possibilities. But the strongest chance of success lies after the next sunset. But if you go alone, you will be the first to fall to the darkness. Those you love will follow you.

"That's the best you can do? You're a god!" She'd hoped for a more detailed plan that would let them evade all the dangers.

I see, but cannot interfere directly on the mortal plain. All gods need to work through mortals. You are all blessed, or cursed, with free will. Even if we know what is to come, we cannot do more than provide suggestions and the occasional nudge. The Goddess reclined on a low couch that appeared under her as she leaned back.

"There are more of you?" Michael asked eagerly.

The Goddess smiled fondly at him, raising Dani's jealous hackles. *A large number of us take an interest in your world. But that is a topic for another time. I have done my best to guide you both to this exact circumstance and moment, the best chance of survival for my people.*

"Both of us? Michael, too?" He'd been dragged into all of this because of her. His strong fingers squeezed her hand, reminding her not to underestimate him.

The Goddess focused on Michael. *I do regret the pain. There was only a thin sliver of opportunity to reach you. I needed to be forceful to ensure the messages came through.*

"My flashes," Michael nodded slowly. "The developmental therapy classes, meeting Joe, following Dani. It was all you."

Now that you've been here, it should be easier on you. Her elongated eyes focused on Dani. *You were much more difficult. I began with your parents, guiding them to each other. A time of great darkness is coming. I needed a different kind of High Priestess, one who could be a warrior. I found a line of ferals with great power to blend with your mother's bloodline.*

"So my parents' marriage is all a manipulation by you?" Dani felt sickeningly responsible.

Not at all. I merely provided an opportunity for them to fall in love. I told you, Danielle. I do not directly interfere. Harsh irritation marred the Goddess's serenity. *If I could have, I would have prevented your father's injury. Your mother begged me for his life and I granted it, knowing you would need both parents to face what was coming. The conduit was severed that night by the energy I sent through it. I crossed a line and lost the connection because of it. Left without a way to communicate to soothe your fears, I watched, helpless, as the Huntress became a vicious and cruel monster instead of a connection between us. As the time for the ritual binding approached, I knew it had become too dangerous.*

I sent a message to your sister through the dead to prevent you from doing the ritual. I hoped it would not take much persuasion for you to flee. You needed to find a way past the fear, find a connection with another person as an equal. The Goddess paused to examine Dani carefully. *You haven't quite achieved it. Fear and anger run too deep in you to trust easily. I can only hope you find your trust in time to fight the darkness.*

"Did you tell Gwen I needed to do the ritual now?" Dani demanded. She felt like a pawn on a chessboard, and she didn't like it one bit.

I did. I didn't think you would open yourself any other way. Your love and trust for Michael has done much to soothe the Huntress. Your willingness to face your fears has done even more.

"That's why the Huntress was quiet in the forest when we kissed," Michael guessed.

The Goddess nodded, still focused on Dani. *It is not the traditional route, but you have found your way to me. Are you willing to accept your role?*

"Do I still have to do the ritual?" Dani asked.

The ritual is designed to open your mind to me, to establish the connection properly. You are already here. All that remains is the testing. The Goddess flickered, vanishing from the couch to reappear standing in front of Dani. Her cheeks tingled as the Goddess cupped them with ephemeral hands. *Are you ready to wake up?*

Dani wanted to refuse. She'd spent her life trying to ignore the parts of herself she didn't like.

Michael moved to stand behind her, his hands resting warmly on her shoulder and waist. "You can do this. You're stronger than you've ever believed."

His faith warmed her as much as his touch. "Bring it on."

The Goddess smiled, revealing sharp fangs behind her parted lips. Her eyes flashed bright red and her echoing voice took on a harsh scraping hiss. *You are familiar and comfortable with the darkness. But how do you fare in the light?*

Molten sunlight burst out of Dani's skin, blinding her to everything around her. She screamed, jerking away from Michael, terrified he would be burned. The liquid light charred her skin into blistering agony. She would have screamed if there had been any unsinged air left in her lungs. All the pain she'd ever caused in her lifetime came home to scrape along her nerve endings.

She saw a parade of men's faces: all the men she'd Hunted beginning with Husky and Beer Breath and ending with Josh. She experienced their terror as the Huntress devoured them. She couldn't turn away from the sadness and worry of their families: parents, brothers, sisters, children, the same pattern over and over again. The blazing pain increased, branding the images deep into her scarred soul. She'd hurt them far worse than their crimes deserved. Every protective layer had been burned away, leaving her raw and open.

This is what your fear created. This is what you cannot be allowed to forget, the Goddess's hollow voice hissed in her mind. Her face replaced the victims' faces. *Can you live with your true self, Danielle?*

The words carried an implicit invitation. Dani could escape from the searing light, go back to the darkness and its promised oblivion. She could vanish into the void, never having to face what she'd done ever again. It would be the suicide she'd often thought she'd deserved.

If she did that, her brothers and Bernie would die. And Michael would be alone. It would be the ultimate running away. She drew strength from Michael's words. She couldn't change the past, but she could choose better in the future. She could be the protector he believed she could be. Gritting her teeth, Dani found strength she wouldn't have guessed she possessed a week ago and hissed back to her tormentor. "You think I've ever forgotten it for one damn minute of one damn day!"

You would defy me? Glowing red eyes and fangs promised eternal torment.

"I have already. Every step of the way," Dani snarled. "I'm not close to being finished."

The pain and light vanished. Dani dropped to her knees and

Michael dropped beside her, running his hands over her unblistered flesh. He looked up at the Goddess. "An illusion?"

Illusion and reality are not far apart in this place. I regret your testing needed to be so harsh. It's far more than any of my Chosen Priestesses have ever endured, though I fear it will seem mild compared to what is to come. But I needed to be certain you were not broken. You will have to be strong, not relying on anyone else, even me. But strength without love and compassion is tyranny.

Dani reached out to entwine her fingers with Michael's. The clean scent of his relief and pride swelled in the air between them. She knew he would feel her own determination and love through the contact.

The corrupted Huntress has been cleansed, though it will always be vulnerable to further twisting. Be wary of it. The Goddess seemed tired, her form flickering between translucency and solidity. The temple around them began to fade into nothingness.

It's time. Go back and draw strength from each other. Let them all know the rules have changed. Her form began to dissolve, but her eyes hung gleaming red in the darkness like a demonic version of the Cheshire Cat. *No one hunts my people with impunity. Wake them all.*

252

SUNDAY

Chapter Forty

"I'm hungry, Chuck," Bernie whined. "I want lunch."

Chuck knew he should be more patient with her. She was his only friend, the only one who could see him now that he couldn't get close to Gwen anymore. "You gotta find Eric now. He has to go see the soldier."

Soldiers were good. They got stuff done. Not like that mook, Michael. If he'd really wanted to get Bernie out, he'd have done it by now. But no, he was busy romancing a dame instead of keeping his promises. Chuck had wanted to be a soldier when he grew up, before he died.

Bernie left her room to find Eric, Chuck trailing invisibly behind. As usual, Eric sat brooding in his suite. Another mook more interested in thinking about stuff than doing it.

"Eric? Chuck says we have to go talk to the soldier," Bernie explained. "He still can't talk to Gwen."

"Is it safe?" Eric asked.

Chuck stepped through the suite walls to check the hallway, popping back in to report. "Hall's clear."

Bernie repeated what he said and Eric got to his feet. "We have to be back before Vincent wakes up."

"Chuck says the soldier will help us." Bernie slid her hand into Eric's, making Chuck unsteady with anger and jealousy. It wasn't fair that she still got to touch people and have them talk to her. It wasn't fair that she had people trying to save her and everyone forgot about him when he needed help.

The world fuzzed and popped around him until he got his feelings back under control. It took a lot of concentration to stay in the mortal world, and if he got too mad, he started to get pulled out of it.

Eric found the soldier's door without any help from Chuck. The man inside was huge, big muscles and shoulders. Chuck had wanted to look like that. But he moved weird, as though he didn't know what to do with his body.

"McBride?" Eric asked.

"Who are you?" The soldier frowned suspiciously.

Eric quickly explained, introducing himself and Bernie. McBride listened, brows pulling together in confusion. Bernie sat quietly in the corner and played with her doll. Chuck thought about telling her to do something else instead of moping like a girl, but McBride seemed to like her anyway.

"Dalhard explained everything," McBride said slowly. "He's going to give me a chance to help people."

"He's done something to you, to all of us—twisted our minds around so we can't think of shi—" Eric sent a worried glance toward Bernie. "I mean, stuff he doesn't want us to think about. He does it when he touches us. He's not planning to help anyone but himself." Eric told McBride about Dalhard's "job interview" where he'd been forced to kill another man.

"Rogers? I knew him," McBride paled. "We were in a group together."

"He's dead now. As part of a test," Eric said grimly. "We have to get out of here."

"How?" McBride asked, and Chuck nearly sank out of existence with despair. Soldiers were supposed to know what to do. McBride was supposed to know how to save Bernie.

"We have a chance tonight. Dalhard's going to be distracted," Eric explained. "With your help, we can get my brother and Bernie out while he's not paying attention."

"Will your brother help?" McBride asked.

"Dalhard's got him hard under… whatever he does. I'll have to knock him out and carry him," Eric said. Chuck glared at him. How was this mook supposed to help Bernie if he was carrying his darn brother around? *Good thing I stepped in or no one would be there to help her.*

He followed Bernie back to Eric's room to watch TV. He'd have to keep a close eye on her until it came time to leave tonight. At least Eric seemed to realize they needed to stick together, too. He better not ask Chuck to go anywhere else today if he knew what was good for him.

Karan replayed the surveillance tape, watching Eric and Bernie sneak into McBride's room. Dalhard might have given up too easily on Eric with the Silver protocols. Dalhard still didn't have his complete loyalty, no matter what the man thought.

He would have to be careful not to let any of his smugness show. Dalhard would be annoyed enough at being told he was wrong. Any insult added to that injury might be enough to provoke a lethal response. Karan took a moment to compose himself before dialing. "Sir, we have a potential complication with our test subjects."

He explained what he had seen to Dalhard. "It is not the first time I've seen signs of Eric sneaking around."

A sharp exhalation swished harshly through the receiver. "Very well. But I don't want to tip our hand to Mr. Harris quite yet. We need to know what his plans are without letting him know we suspect him of breaking ranks." Karan could hear Dalhard's fingers drumming against the glass desk. Then the thumping stopped and his boss laughed mirthlessly. "He's made a fatal mistake. He might be resistant, but his companions are not. Bring me McBride."

Rough hands grabbed at him and Dani, shaking them. After their encounter with the Goddess, both of them had collapsed into a heavy, dreamless sleep, and now Michael struggled to shake off the remnants to face their attackers.

"What did you do?" a shrill female voice demanded. *Virginia*.

"Let them wake up," Walter called up the stairs.

"Virginia, I don't think—oh my!" Laura Sturgis's exclamation was interrupted abruptly with a solid crack of fist against flesh.

Michael's sleep-drugged mind finally caught up enough to start processing information from around him. Laura stood in the doorway, hand outstretched. Virginia struggled with Dani, who had leapt up naked from the covers, intent on doing battle.

"Dani, it's okay! We're safe." Grabbing a quilt for strategic cover, Michael reached between Dani and her mother, separating the two of them as they clawed at one another.

Dani's pupils slowly began to contract and her face softened out of its warlike mask. "Michael?"

He pressed his forehead against hers, drinking in the intoxicating blend of love and affection from her. She wrapped her arms around him, breathing deeply, no doubt doing the same with his scent. He could have stayed in her embrace all day.

Except for the audience. Michael reluctantly broke apart from Dani to ask. "Virginia? Are you okay?"

"She'll be fine," Laura replied quietly, staring at Dani's mother. "She should know better than to surprise a feral at her age."

"How? How did you do it?" Virginia demanded, her knuckles whitened in her clenched hands. "What did you do?"

"What are you talking about?" Dani growled, her hands starting to curl into fists.

"The statue! The ritual!" Virginia snapped, as if those four words explained everything.

"I think we should all take a moment," Michael said, drawing on years of experience to keep calm. He could feel a blush creeping along his neck and shoulders, and he hastened to add, "Dani and I will get dressed and join you in the kitchen. Then maybe you can explain what has you all so worried."

"An excellent idea." Laura said.

Virginia looked as if she wanted to object, but Laura led her out before she could do more than pause long enough to give Michael a furious maternal glare. Her clouded eyes made it even more unsettling, but he could honestly say that being glared at by a blind mother after being found naked with her daughter was starting to feel like the most normal part of his life.

"That all really happened last night, didn't it?" Dani sank onto the bed, staring at her hands as if expecting to see claws burst out. "Everything feels different. The Huntress... I can still feel her, but it's changed. She's not hungry, not sleeping, just there, in the back of my mind. Kind of shimmering, like a rainbow."

"It really happened," Michael agreed, tugging on his pants. "And I wouldn't change it for anything. I was so afraid I was going to lose you. And now, I feel like I'm being handed everything I could ever have dreamed of."

"There's still the rescue tonight," Dani cautioned.

"We'll get through it." He leaned down to kiss her, sliding his tongue between her lips. He loved the moment when her anxiety combusted into shimmering lust. He loved even more that he was the one who provoked it.

Unfortunately, they didn't have time to indulge unless they wanted another audience and rough awakening.

A discreet interval later, they were adequately dressed and standing in front of the kitchen table, staring at the cause of all the fuss. The Queen of the Night statue had changed from ancient and crumbling pale clay into a sleek, rich terra cotta figurine that could have emerged from the kiln that morning. Michael practically had to push against the tension in the atmosphere to get to the table. The friendly celebration of the night before vanished as if it never existed.

Virginia stabbed an accusing finger at the statue, her milky eyes bright with rage. "The idol only renews with the initiation of the High Priestess. You didn't do the ritual. What did you do?"

"I didn't have to do the ritual." Dani explained a rough outline of what the Goddess had said, the irritation clear in her rough voice and narrowed eyes.

Virginia's disbelief met it gesture for gesture, arms crossed over her chest and pursed lips. "Every generation has done the ritual properly and somehow you get to skip it?"

Michael could feel the fear pushing at Virginia's mask of anger. He guessed that being surprised would unsettle her as both a clairvoyant and as someone who liked to be in control. But her misplaced fury couldn't be allowed to derail their focus. He opened his mouth to say so, but Walter beat him to it.

"We've never had the ritual go so late," Walter said, countering his wife's suspicions. "We've also never had a priestess use the Huntress as an offensive weapon. We've also never had a gap with no conduit. If Dani's initiation was beyond the norm, it makes sense." Michael could have applauded.

"The connection is there and strong," Laura confirmed, her oversized eyes blinking in slow motion as she studied Dani.

"But—" Virginia wasn't quite finished objecting.

"It's done. However it happened." Dani cut off further debate. "We need to focus on the rescue tonight. She said to go after sunset and not to go alone. But that's not much of a plan."

Michael felt the increase in clarity and precision in Dani's mind as she began to lay out plans. He felt a surge of approval from Walter and guessed that this was the result of the conduit. Dani was definitely displaying more tactical thinking than she'd ever done before. She called Vapor on speakerphone to ask about the blueprints.

"I've got what you need," the hacker's gravelly voice reported. "But the real information is all behind some impressive firewalls. It'll take me too long to crack them. I need codes."

Dani's attention flicked to Michael like the snap of a bowstring. "If you touch Dalhard, do you think you can get the codes?"

Michael nodded. "It's all secrets. But I'll need more than a quick brush to get past his surface mind. I haven't probed anyone deeply in years." Queasiness surged at the thought of opening himself up, but he reminded himself that it was for Bernie.

"We'll make sure you get it," Dani promised. "Can you get in to the security system, Vapor? Monitor the cameras and help us track down our people?"

A snort of amusement. "Child's play. They have remote monitoring."

"Good. Nada will make sure we don't show up onscreen. She's got a real gift for manipulating electromagnetic signals," Dani explained to Michael.

"I remember. Keep her away from my stuff," Vapor added.

"Before we go in, Vapor will tell us where Bernie, Vincent, and Eric are. Michael, you and Nada will go after them while I distract Dalhard," Dani finished.

"Won't we need more help than Vapor and Nada?" Michael frowned. The Goddess's warning not to go alone had been clear.

"More people means more risk of collateral damage. We know the building will be abandoned. We know Dalhard is luring us into a trap. He doesn't expect anyone else to be with me." Dani was certain. "Once you've got everyone out safely, I grab Dalhard and drag him out to you. You read his deepest secrets, and we all disappear into the night."

Michael still felt uneasy. This had to be more than only pulling out the people they cared about. Dalhard would continue to pursue them. He had resources they couldn't even dream of. They needed something to stop him. An idea occurred to him, one that might work. But he doubted Dani and her family would approve.

Hopefully they would forgive him when he did it anyway.

Chapter Forty-One

Even hidden in the trees, Dalhard's facility squatted over them like a giant in a fairy tale, ready to swallow them whole. A solid block of concrete and narrow windows, it resembled a prison more than a lab. They'd stashed the car out of sight at the beginning of the access road and hiked through the underbrush to avoid being seen. Vapor reported that Bernie, Vincent, and Eric were all on the upper floor, making it easier for Michael and Nada to get them out together. Dani dismissed the memory of Dalhard's claim that her brothers were working for him voluntarily. It wasn't possible.

The sun bled out on the horizon, crimson and purple light blazing in a final dying display as their precious last minutes of freedom ticked away before the jaws of the trap closed around them. Dani studied Michael's determined face painted with light. They'd spent the day together, stealing away from the planning every moment possible to make love. At the time, she'd reveled in it, but now it seemed more like a prisoner's last meal, a final reprieve before execution.

She tried to shake off the gloomy thoughts, but they persisted in clouding around her. *Michael isn't like you. If he gets hurt going toe-to-toe with these people, he's going to get himself dead.* Joe's words still echoed in her head. She knew she couldn't keep Michael from participating, that she shouldn't keep him from helping. But despite the Goddess's warning, part of her still believed this would be safer if she did it alone. With him there, she would be distracted, her mind always wondering if he was safe.

"Sunset," Nada reported, picking up her backpack. She tossed her long iron-gray braid over her shoulder as she hoisted the pack into place. Although she'd been a feature of Dani's life since before she could remember, there was nothing grandmotherly about Nada. Built of muscle and sinew, her skin tanned and craggy, she was as tough as the leather she crafted.

"Wait. One more minute." Michael put his hand on her arm before Dani could rise.

Frustration battled with concern. Did he see something she didn't? Waiting longer would only shatter her calm further.

"I invited someone else to this adventure," he said, answering her unspoken question.

"You did what, now?" Of all the things he could have said, that hadn't been in her top five guesses. Dani knelt in the undergrowth, trying to put together enough coherent thought to decide whether or not she was furious or hurt.

"Joe." The way Michael said the name told her he anticipated an unpleasant reaction.

"You invited a cop to our illegal break-in?" Dani couldn't quite muster the proper outrage— shock and disbelief kept interfering. *He must have a good reason.* Except she couldn't think of one.

Nada looked at them both as if they were state-custody-ready crazy. She shook her head, setting her thick braid swaying.

"Listen to me. Joe is a good guy and a good cop. He's been working to help Bernie and her mom. He can help us." Michael didn't seem concerned by the emotional turmoil his words unlocked in her.

"He's not one of us." Dani needed to make him see how bad this idea could get. Good cops didn't do illegal and keep their mouths shut. "He needs warrants, probable cause. He can't do what we need to do."

"He can do the one thing we need most. He can help us to take Dalhard down properly. Legally. We can't leave this guy and all his resources sitting here to come after us. Your father was right—we can't escape from a multinational corporation. We have to hamstring it, and to do that, we need to do it in the open. Joe's a good guy. He's worked out ways to make the information from my gift usable in the past. We need him here now. He'll see what we don't know to look for and come back with proper warrants."

His sincerity was unmistakable. His reasoning seemed sound, and that kept her from exploding at him. Trusting a cop went against every programmed instinct, but she couldn't deny that Joe Cabrera had moved beyond being a traditional cop. He'd let her go and asked her to protect his friend. He'd seen glimpses of the strangeness moving behind the scenes of normal lives, and although he hadn't embraced it, he hadn't pretended it didn't exist, either.

263

"Trust me." Two simple words. So easy to say, so hard to do. Old instincts screamed warnings at her, but she wasn't going to be that person any more. She still intended to have a very spirited discussion with Michael about why tactics and surprises didn't mix, but it could wait until they'd survived the night.

The faint crunch of gravel and the potent stench of oil and gasoline announced the arrival of a car, even though the driver kept the headlights off and coasted into position. Dani shifted slightly, standing between the car and Michael, her senses flaring into painful sensitivity. She could pick out every scent in a twenty-yard radius and hear the faint crackle of sap flowing through the trees.

The faint traces of gun oil and sweat told her the identity of their intruder before he could step out of the car. Joe took a long look at his friend before shifting his gaze to her. He noticed her guardian stance and the harsh edges of his protectiveness lowered.

"Detective," she said.

"Should I call you Danielle?" he asked.

"Dani is fine. For my friends." Her skin tingled as Michael squeezed her hand in approval.

"Hell of a thing you're asking me here, Michael." Joe looked over at the building and its array of lighted windows. "Breaking and entering is not a great way to collect evidence."

"We're not breaking. We have an entry code," Michael returned.

"Let me get a warrant. You said you had a witness, someone who can place Bernadette here—"

"Our witness is the ghost of a twelve-year-old boy who has been dead at least eighty years, delivered through a medium who is certifiably crazy." Dani couldn't help but grin at the dismayed expression on the cop's face. "Still think a judge would give you that warrant?"

"This is way more than I ever wanted to know." Joe held up his hands.

"Joe, I wouldn't ask if it wasn't important. This man is using his power to hurt others," Michael interjected. "We need your help to take him down."

"I didn't say I wasn't in. Help me find something I can reasonably bring before a judge and I'll do it. Just spare me the freaky details, okay?"

264

He held out his hand to Nada. "I'm Joe."

"Nada. I'm one of the freaky details," she replied without lifting her hands, her husky voice full of amusement.

Joe's hand dropped back to his side.

"Nada's going to make sure we don't show up on any security cameras. She'll be able to freeze them into repeating a split-second loop from before we appear," Michael explained.

"You can do that?" Joe's mouth opened in a gape before he snapped it shut. "Okay, let's get this show on the road."

They crept out of the forest, approaching the building. Dani stopped to pull Joe aside for a moment. "Watch his back."

She didn't have to explain who she meant. Joe nodded, and she exhaled in relief. She didn't doubt that Michael could handle himself, but this wasn't a movie where the heroes would catch all the breaks. The possibility of losing him stole her breath and heartbeat, leaving her drained and shaken. She couldn't stay with him once inside, but now someone else with combat training would watch over him.

She left the others out of sight to approach the massive doors alone. Standing in front of them she felt even more like she was about to walk into the gaping maw of a leviathan. "Fee, Fie, Foe, Fum, Fucker." She punched in the code on Dalhard's card.

The green light obligingly winked on. She opened the door, holding it wide with her head down as if reconsidering her choice. At least, that was what they would think when they saw it on the monitor, she hoped.

Shrouded by Nada's electronic invisibility, Michael, Nada, and Joe rushed past her to head to the stairs. All Dani needed to do was hold perfectly still so she wouldn't switch suddenly to a different position when the camera activated again. Then she needed to make sure whoever was watching stayed focused on her.

"Momma always told me to play to my strengths," she whispered as she stepped inside the lobby. An ugly guard station wrapped in thick glass and mesh dominated the space. A few plastic chairs huddled together on the tile floor near a heavy, mass-produced abstract sculpture of intertwined metal strands. She stared up at the unblinking red eye of the night-vision camera keeping an endless vigil. Dalhard would never believe it if she came meekly. Spreading her arms wide, she issued her challenge. "You wanted me. Now come and get me."

Her words fell flat, swallowed whole by oppressive silence. Dani might have scored a new personal best in emotional growth over the last few days, but she still hated being ignored.

"Fine. You want to play games? Bring it." She considered using one of the chairs but decided to play with the sculpture instead. Although it was set into the floor, she easily bent the thick rebar, ripping it out of the tile. Now she needed something that would make a satisfying crash.

Like the glass around the security station. Raising the art piece, she prepared to launch.

Like an outstretched hand or a panicked shout of protest, a low tone announced the activation of the elevator. The motor whirred as the car slid down from the upper levels of the building. Her fingers tightened on the sculpture, ready to throw it or use it as a club, every nerve in her body screaming for her to act while her mind struggled to hold on to control.

The doors slid open, revealing Dalhard. He straightened his jacket, drawing attention to his thick hands and powerful shoulders, before stepping out. With his dark hair greased back, he was practically the perfect image of a Mafia kingpin. "I assumed you would accept my invitation." He studied the sculpture. "You're not a patient woman, are you?"

"Never saw it as much of a virtue." Dani tossed aside the piece, letting it clang onto the floor and chip the expensive tiling. "Especially not with kidnappers."

"Yet you came alone." Dalhard's gaze skimming along her body left her feeling more naked than any performance she'd ever given. Lust she could handle, but not this cool acquisitiveness as if he were deciding whether or not to click an invisible "buy" button.

"I want my brothers back. Now."

"I don't believe they want to return. But I assume you still won't accept my word on it. They're waiting upstairs in my office." He held out his arm toward the open elevator. The office was on the second floor, Dani remembered from the blueprints, near the stairs. The last time Vapor had reported, her brothers were on the third floor. She wondered what waited for her in Dalhard's office. *Guns? Drugs?*

266

"Did you know that human beings are the only species stupid enough to get into a sealed box with no visible exits along with a known predator?" Dani circled past Dalhard slowly, keeping her eyes locked with his. "No other creature on the entire planet will do it."

"An interesting fact." He smiled as she stepped into the car. "Presumably, our instincts have atrophied after millennia of not being hunted."

Dani ran her hand down the smooth metal walls as Dalhard joined her. His harsh chemical scent stung her nose like a swarm of bees, but she kept her expression under control. "We hunt each other. Predators and prey all look alike. Knowing which is which   now that's the trick."

"I couldn't agree with you more." He kept his distance in the elevator as if he expected her to rush at him like an aggressive dog. He never once took his eyes off her, and there was no sour tang of fear under his expensive cologne.

It felt strange not to have the Huntress coiling and crashing against her mental barriers, struggling for release. Instead, she could sense the powerful divine connection lurking beneath the deceptively still waters of her unconscious. It might not be visible, but she felt the edges of ripples in her soul. She took comfort knowing it was still there if she needed it.

Dalhard escorted her down the hall, using a keycard to open the door at the far northern end. Inside the plush office was a sleek glass desk, thick carpets, original art, and Vincent and Eric. *The first flaw in our simple plan.* Dalhard must have moved them since her last contact with Vapor. Dani inhaled, deep and quick, not only for relief but to be certain neither was hurt. Their scents came through strong and clear: Vincent's distinctive mix of beer and salt, and Eric's earthier scent of oil and leather. No coppery tang of blood or chemical distortion from drugs. Maybe they could still pull this off.

"I'm a man of my word." Dalhard's smug smile made her want to slap his face.

"Fine. Let them go."

"Go? Sis, you've got to be kidding." Vincent shook his head. "We've got a sweet deal here. He's giving us tons of money, and you would not believe the shit he's got in the basement. It's like a lab out of a movie."

Listening to Vincent was like hearing a different audio track, one that didn't match the original footage. She glanced at Eric, wondering if he shared her disbelief. Eric bit his lip, looking aside. He couldn't be agreeing with Vincent's nonsense.

"I believe I warned you." Dalhard smirked, his lip curling in intolerable smugness.

The man had no idea how close he was coming to a fist in the face. Her arm ached from restraining herself. Neither his body language nor his scent showed any sign of fear or self-doubt.

He smoothed his oiled hair, his thousand-watt politician's smile beaming at full power. "Persuasion is always more powerful than force. My mother taught me that."

He'd done something to her at the police station—tried to cloud her mind. But she'd shrugged it off. Vincent and Eric should have been able to do the same. They must be playing along to protect Gwen. But the three of them together could surely take out one posturing sack of bullshit and beat him to the ground. She kept silent, trying to read her brothers' signals. Eric slumped and hung his head in defeat and Vincent seemed oblivious.

"She worked a similar job as you, back in the day. She took pride in it, said it gave her access to some of the most powerful men in the country." Dalhard took a healthy swig of the drink he'd poured from the bar. "It was only a matter of time before she persuaded one to marry her. Quite the romance story: stripper with a heart of gold marries wealthy businessman."

"Touching, yet boring," Dani sauntered through the office as if looking around. It brought her closer to Eric.

Dalhard continued. "I'm telling you this so you won't worry about me looking down on you because of your former profession."

Former? Look down? His brazen arrogance reminded her of dozens of preening alpha males, all believing they were entitled to whatever they wanted, regardless of who it hurt. The young lords of the football field from college, the drunken tourists who thought a girl showing a little skin entitled them to a free grope. Dalhard was no different from any of them. He just had more money to back up his desires.

Dalhard continued his monologue. "With my mother's help, my

father turned his profitable shipping enterprise into a multinational corporation with a dozen different businesses under our umbrella. She always told me it would be mine—that my father wouldn't stand in my way. He was quite the fool. Searching for supernatural powers everywhere and never recognizing the ones in his own home."

Eric kept shaking his head as she got closer. Keeping her body angled so Dalhard couldn't see, she tried to signal him to join her attack. Behind him, she could see Vincent watching the conversation as if it were a slightly dull movie on TV. Michael and the others must have Bernie by now, and she didn't want to listen to one more second of Dalhard's narcissistic droning. "I've heard about your dad. I'd like to have a word with him."

"Sadly, he died in a convenient yet tragic car accident once I was ready to take over." Dalhard poured another drink and held it out to her.

"That's a pretty big chunk of information to toss out there. Mom was a stripper and you killed dear old Dad." Dani breathed in carefully. Still no fear. "You're not worried about me knowing. Why?"

"Because you will be my partner, and a husband should never have secrets from his wife. Bad for the relationship."

His wife? This guy was further down the road to Crazytown than she'd thought. The possibility was laughable. If only she didn't smell a sharp spike of fear from Eric, as if this loon actually had the power to enforce his delusion. Time to end this. "Sorry, already taken. And speaking of taken, I'll be taking my brothers home with me now."

"What makes you think I'll let them go?" Dalhard smiled as if her words were terribly amusing.

"What makes you think I'm giving you a choice? This isn't audience participation, and you have no chance of stopping me," Dani retorted.

"Perhaps not. But I do believe he does." Dalhard pointed behind her.

She turned just in time to see Vincent's fist flying toward her face.

Chapter Forty-Two

Michael wanted to stop and make sure Dani was all right, but Joe and Nada both hustled him along, pulling him out of sight of the lobby cameras. He didn't like her playing the part of bait. Maybe it was his inner caveman, but letting her go into danger without him felt wrong. The fact that she was entirely capable of dealing with a physical threat didn't matter.

Watching her engulfed in flame still haunted him, even if it had been in a mystical dream-space. The only thought that floated to coherence during his mental agony had been that he encouraged her. If she died, it would be his fault. After their rude awakening, he couldn't stop himself from touching her, reassuring himself on every primal level. It had often moved past simple reassurance—a memory that quirked his lips and brought a stirring to his groin. Joe shot him a warning look, tapping his eye to indicate Michael needed to focus.

He nodded, repeating to himself that he had a job to do and a vital role to play. Now that he was here, it seemed much less James Bond glamorous than before. He faced the reality of being in Dalhard's stronghold and trying to take away people the man had worked very hard to procure. They all knew Dalhard was dangerous. If he found them, he wouldn't launch into a monologue or create an improbably complex villainous scheme. He wouldn't hesitate to kill them all, including Joe. He'd take away Dani and Bernie and make them vanish into European shadows.

Michael couldn't deny a certain high of geeky enthusiasm in spite of his worries. This was the situation he had always dreamed of. Being the hero. Saving the girl. All the girls: Bernie, Gwen, and Dani.

It was the right decision to bring Joe in, he repeated to himself. Dalhard needed to be taken down publicly, in a court of law. It was the only way to keep everyone safe. But if Joe were caught, this could be a career-ending moment or worse—a life-ending moment. Michael could only hope that breaking open a massive kidnapping operation would be enough for Joe's superiors to overlook any questions about the chain of evidence.

"You know where this girl is?" Joe asked quietly as they climbed the stairs. His gun gleamed softly in the dim lighting.

"Third floor. Room 3-52," Michael answered.

"Too much talking. I can only do cameras, not voices," Nada said, hushing them.

The door to the third floor had an electronic keypad. Nada stared at it for a moment, and it popped open without a sound. Joe made a faint sound of dismay but recovered quickly. Michael hid a smile at his friend's discomfort. It was nice not to be the only one facing world-changing information.

The third floor was empty, built for industry instead of intimidation: linoleum flooring and dull gray doors lining the hall stretching the length of the building. Cameras stared down at regular intervals, red lights gleaming in the artificial dusk. He trusted Nada would do her part and crept along as silently as he could.

To his surprise, Bernie's door was unlocked. But even if it hadn't been, the latch for the deadbolt was on the exterior, making it easy to open and telling Michael far too much about the intentions of those who designed this place. Once inside, he saw she was curled up under the thin blanket, whitened knuckles clutching the teddy bear he'd given her. She looked exhausted, dark bruises under her eyes. Michael knelt down beside her, stroking her hair. Immediately he sensed Bernie's despair and fear. A deep sense of abandonment sucked at her energy. She didn't even bother opening her eyes to see who had come.

"Bernie always likes this song," he whispered. "But Michael always sings it wrong."

The child's eyes fluttered open in surprise, and she smiled, whispering. "Are you really here? Or is this a dream?"

"I'm really here. I'm going to take you home to your mommy. She misses you." Michael sensed Bernie's bone-deep exhaustion pulling at her efforts to stay awake. He wondered if she'd been drugged to keep her quiet during Dalhard's trap.

"She'll need some warmer clothes for outside," Nada instructed. Joe stepped inside and grabbed the sweatpants and top from the chair beside

Bernie's bed.

"Chuck said something big happened. He wasn't sure you would come," Bernie said quietly, clinging tightly to Michael.

"I promised I would. And I'm sorry I didn't understand Chuck was real before. He helped me to find you. He's a real hero." Michael picked Bernie up, grateful for the pressure of her thin arms around his neck. Triumph left his worries far below as his spirit soared. "Let's get out of here, Bernie-pie."

"What do they have her on?" Joe asked.

"No idea. Hopefully it'll wear off with time." Michael couldn't help wondering if Dani was okay. He'd heard her ask Joe to watch his back. It still made him smile. She might want to portray the consummate devil-may-care badass, but he knew how much she cared about her family, about him, about doing what was right, no matter the cost. Neither of them had many illusions about the world—she'd asked Joe to keep him safe because they both knew the danger.

"Where are the others?" Joe closed the door carefully behind them.

"3-20—"

Michael's reply was cut off by a ragged shout from another room. "Hey!"

A man popped out from another room further down the hall. He should have looked ridiculous in old sweatpants and a T-shirt, but something about him demanded respect. "What are you doing with her!"

"Hi, Ron," Bernie breathed softly. "These are my friends."

Ron did not seem to be convinced.

"It's true," Michael added hastily. "We've come to get her out. Take her home."

The man's expression softened immediately. "You're the friends she told me about. I'm Corporal Ron McBride, army."

"Michael Brooks." Michael hastily introduced everyone. "You can come with us, but we have to get Dani's brothers out, too."

"But they're not here," Bernie murmured sleepily. "Chuck says they went downstairs."

Downstairs. Their simple rescue plan suddenly got a lot harder. Michael took a deep breath. "Did Chuck say anything else?"

"Mmm-hmmm. He said I had to be careful because the bad guys

used plastic to make the building go boom," Bernie yawned. "And Mr. Dalhard is mean. He makes your mind go funny when he touches you."

"They've wired the building with plastic explosive." Ron paled. "Did they know you were coming?" Nada and Joe's breath hissed out in identical exhalations.

"Yes. No. Sort of. It's a long story. Is there anyone else here?" Michael demanded.

"No one on this level. But they were holding me in a cell in the basement before."

Horrible, guilt-ridden inspiration struck Michael. "Bernie, is Chuck here?"

Bernie nodded against his shoulder.

"Can you ask him to go to the basement and see if there's anyone down there. And then can he find Dani? The lady I was with? Can he find her and her brothers and come back and tell us where they are and what's happened?" He hated questioning her like this, hated using a child for her gifts the same way her captors had. But he needed to know, and his available resources were limited.

"He'll do it," Bernie whispered.

"We should get out of the building as quickly as possible." McBride spoke the last words so quietly that Michael barely heard them.

"It's a plan." Michael shifted Bernie in his arms. How long did it take for a ghost to search a building? Could Chuck find them again if they started down the stairs? Michael wished he'd taken the time to ask before sending him away.

"We need to get moving. Get the corporal and Bernie to the car." Joe's fingers were flexing against the handle of his gun.

"Chuck says there isn't anyone else in the basement and the lady is with her brothers," Bernie announced suddenly. "He says we should go."

"Smartest plan I've heard all week," Nada muttered.

They ran for the stairs, not bothering to worry about silence. Michael huffed under Bernie's weight. "Nada, you take them to the car, get them safe."

"They'll see you," she warned.

"I have to warn Dani about the explosives." The original plan called for her to lure Dalhard outside, but if he suspected they were about to leave, he might blow the building for a pyrrhic victory.

"No! I want to stay with you!" Bernie clung to him.

"Bernie, I have to go and save the other people here, too." He held her tight, trying to reassure her.

"From the mean man?" she whimpered.

"Yes. He's a very bad man and he's trying to hurt a lot of people."

"Then you have to stop him." He could feel the moment she accepted it. For her, this was as clear as any story. Michael was a hero, and heroes saved people.

"Let me take her," Ron offered.

Michael reluctantly handed her over. "Bernie, can you ask Chuck what the lady and her brothers are doing?"

Bernie glanced up a few steps. "He says they're fighting."

"Who's fighting?" Michael asked.

"The lady and her brothers," she yawned.

"Who are they fighting? Guards?" he demanded.

Bernie looked again at the empty patch of air before shaking her head. "No. Each other."

"Vincent, what the hell!" Dani ducked his punch. Barely. His knuckles grazed the side of her cheek.

"I'm not going back to hiding and running!" Vincent roared, swinging at her again, his dark eyes flaring in a definite disconnect with reality.

Eric jumped at Vincent, trying to pin him down. But Vincent twisted out of Eric's grasp, dropping to the floor. "Vincent, you're not thinking straight. He's done something to you—"

"Figured it out, did you?" Dalhard interrupted Eric's plea, wrapping his hands around Eric's head. "I thought you might have succumbed a little too easily."

Dani charged at the two of them, planning on knocking Dalhard aside.

Vincent apparently objected to her plan. He leapt off the floor and tackled her.

"Don't hurt her, Vincent," Dalhard cautioned, his fingers biting deeply into Eric's skin. Eric hung limply from the grasp, his face blank. Dani's horror stiffened her muscles.

"You got it, boss." Vincent used his weight to pin her to the floor.

Dani struggled but couldn't get the leverage to get free. "Let him go!" she screamed.

"He's quite stubborn and needs persuading. Doing it this way will temporarily scramble his memory and make him incapable of doing anything without my permission. I prefer not to use this level of persuasion but it is occasionally necessary." Dalhard released Eric, who dropped to the ground as if tranquilized.

Dani remembered the horrible sensation when he'd touched her in the police station. He was a *lalassu* who hunted and abused his own kind. The thought of him crawling inside her brain, turning her into some kind of remote control toy gave Dani renewed determination.

"It needn't be permanent. But I can't allow him to disrupt our plans together." The condescending bastard smiled, like he thought he was being soothing. "Eventually his mind will wear itself out and submit to my control. I'll renew the persuasion as often as necessary until it happens."

He'd do it to her, too. Make her into a plaything. Trap her worse than the Huntress could ever have done. She wouldn't even have the freedom of her own mind.

"I see you understand." Dalhard stepped over Eric's body to tap on a side door.

"You'll see, Dani. It's everything we wanted," Vincent said, his weight shifting slightly off her.

Dani took advantage, twisting her fingers to reach Vincent's inner thigh, right above the knee. And pinched. Hard.

Vincent yelped and jumped in an involuntary reaction. Dani rolled and used her elbow to smash his face on the way out. Coming up, she saw the red drip of blood slashing across her brother's mouth. He glared at her, rubbing his leg and nose ineffectually.

"Very impressive," Dalhard smirked. "Vincent, hold her."

Her brother launched himself at her. Dani steadied herself and timed her reaction. There would only be one shot at this.

Vincent's weight was forward, well ahead of his feet. Fully

committed to his attack, he had no option to dodge or change plans.

When Dani's fist shot out and made contact with his temple, the blow contained all her strength and all his forward momentum, echoing like a thump to a hollow melon. Enough to drop him in his tracks. But it also left her open to the enemy behind her.

Dalhard's thick fingers pressed into her face. Immediately his will began forcing its way into her, slamming into the cracks in her defenses. He spoke as if making casual conversation. "I've often found that a distasteful act serves as a sort of shock to the system, making it easier for my gifts to gain hold. You love your brother very much and didn't want to hurt him."

His voice echoed as if coming down a long tunnel. Dani struggled, but her body refused to obey and her mind had fought all her life to keep something inside her. She'd never needed to keep something out.

No external evidence betrayed their battle. The two of them stood quietly, Dalhard's hands pressed against the sides of her head. Sweat glistened on Dani's skin as she tried to force him back.

"Dani!" Eric struggled to push himself up onto his knees. His skin was a ghastly shade of gray.

"He's quite resistant, isn't he?" Dalhard commented. "Should I make an example of him?"

No! Dani wanted to scream. She wanted to smash his face, but her muscles remained limp, caught in the hypnotic spell stealing through her veins.

Another man came into view, holding a gun. He had skin the color of pottery and dark hair. He had almost no scent and stared at her as if she were a bug caught in a trap. "We have intruders, sir. Two men."

"Thank you, Karan." Dalhard released Dani, letting her drop. "Go and get McBride and the girl. Vincent, pick up your brother and bring him with us. Dani, walk with me."

To her horror, her body immediately staggered to its feet and began to walk with Dalhard toward the exit.

"McBride and the girl are gone," Karan reported, helping Vincent with Eric, who could barely stand.

"They won't get far." Dalhard laughed.

Footsteps pounded down the hall. It must be Michael and Joe. She

276

tried to open her clenched jaw to shout a warning. The mental image of Michael charging in like an avenging hero only to be shot down by a scentless weasel twisted her gut with leaden pincers. *Help me!* She fumbled along the divine connection, but it was gray and cold rather than scintillating. Even the Goddess had abandoned her.

Vincent broke away from Eric, moving to stand to one side of the door, where those entering wouldn't see him right away. Dalhard stopped to watch, forcing her to watch along with him. His meaty hand clamped tightly around her arm and his influence poured over her mind, eroding her defenses.

The door popped open and Michael and Joe charged into the room. Joe turned, automatically checking the blind spot, but Vincent was too fast. He slammed his fist into Joe's head, knocking him down. Then into Michael's.

Silent screams ripped through Dani, but her body kept smiling vacantly at the repulsive creature holding her hostage. Michael fell to the ground, clutching his head. Karan let Eric drop again, holding his gun steady on the intruders. Joe's weapon bounced away on the carpet and Vincent picked it up.

"Do I have your attention?" Dalhard inquired. "Excellent. Now, we all have a plane to catch, so I suggest we hurry."

Chapter Forty-Three

Michael could barely focus on the twin guns aimed in his direction. Dani filled his vision, but he didn't need to be psychic to know something was wrong. She stood oddly, stiff and awkward like a robot on a shelf. There was no hint of a leashed and lethal predator, no jaded amusement, no dominating presence. She simply faded into the background, muted like a pastel Van Gogh.

He and Joe were being forced to carry Eric downstairs and outside. He recognized both of Dani's brothers from photos at the farmhouse. He might not have been sure which was which, but as soon as he touched Eric, he knew… which meant Vincent was the brother holding a gun on him. *He makes your mind go funny when he touches you.* Too late, he understood Bernie's warning. Dalhard had done something to Dani and Vincent. Michael wanted to rip the man apart with his bare hands. *At least Nada and Ron got Bernie out.* The knowledge was his only source of comfort.

He could sense Joe's equal frustration at being helpless and his fury at being disarmed. They emerged out of the building near two vehicles— a limousine and a heavy van. Michael recognized it as a converted police van, the sort with a thick barrier between passengers and drivers and minimal chances for escape.

"Put Eric in the van. You and I will ride up front, my dear," Dalhard ordered. With two guns on them, Michael and Joe reluctantly obeyed. They swung open the back panels.

"Michael!" Bernie wailed from inside.

Michael froze in place, Eric awkwardly balanced only halfway into the van. Nada glared fury around heavy silver duct tape fastened around her mouth, wrists, and legs. McBride sat on one of the benches, his shoulders slumped and his head cradled in his hands. Bernie sobbed, rocking back and forth and clutching her doll.

278

"Persuasion is a powerful force," Dalhard taunted, appearing with Dani on the other side of the van. "Don't be too hard on the corporal. I didn't leave him much choice."

Eric started to slip and Joe hefted him into the van before he could hit the ground. Michael struggled to breathe around his anger.

"I know you wanted to help, but Dalhard is the only one who can take care of her," McBride recited dully. "I can't let you take her away from him."

"You… you…" Michael wished he had Dani's ready supply of curse words. He'd trusted McBride. Some hero he turned out to be. Despair started to drown him. Dani stared at him with vacant doll's eyes, not even a flicker of emotion or reaction to show she lived. Just empty glass.

Dalhard using his gifts to violate her mind, painting over the brilliant colors to suit himself, repulsed Michael like the image of a toddler finger-painting over the Mona Lisa. It was a crime against more than just her. Dalhard's greed stole an irreplaceable and unique beauty and overwrote it with his own interpretation. If Michael could have shot the man, he would have.

Bernie's whimper reminded him there were other lives at stake. Karan held out a roll of duct tape. "If you resist, Vincent will shoot you."

When Karan hauled Michael's hands back to secure him, the information pouring into him only deepened his depression. They'd only glimpsed the edges of Dalhard's shadowy empire. Karan managed it all for him: drugs, human trafficking, gun running—all the horrible ways people could make a profit out of misery. As Karan patted Michael down, he sensed something dark and ugly lurking under the crisp and practical surface. He tried to home in, but the other man pulled away.

"Next time, leave me out of your rescue plan," Joe muttered as Karan wrapped the silvery tape around his wrists before patting him down.

Karan pulled Joe's identification and badge out of his pocket, holding it up for Dalhard to see.

"An investigation?" Dalhard growled.

"We can't take him with us." Karan raised his gun.

"Leave him." Dalhard's gaze flicked to Michael. "And the other one. He has nothing of use to us."

279

Bernie started screaming. Karan shut the van doors and the sound cut off abruptly. Michael staggered forward, working on a vague plan of charging his opponents, but having his arms secured behind his back left him off-balance. Still, he wasn't going to let Dani and Bernie go.

Karan hit him across the back of the head with the pistol and blackness swallowed him whole.

"Secure them in the lobby. I don't want them getting away when they wake up," Dalhard ordered Karan before tugging gently on Dani's arm. "Come away, my dear."

She wanted to ignore Dalhard's instructions, but her traitorous body refused to listen. She lost sight of Michael's body sprawling in the dirt, but the image continued to burn into her memory.

They're not dead. They have a chance. Dalhard didn't know about Vapor. He knew where they were. Someone would rescue Joe and Michael before they died of starvation, trapped in the building.

"Vincent, drive us to the airport," Dalhard ordered as he opened the limo door.

"Sure thing, boss. Don't worry so much, sis. Dalhard will take care of everything." Vincent must have thought he was reassuring her. "He's got it all worked out. He'll take care of Eric, too. Make it all better."

Is my brother still trapped inside there? Does he even care about Eric lying unconscious in the other van? Dani bit her lip, wondering... and then realized the significance of the tiny motion: she'd moved independently of the outer doll. A tiny expression but still something. Dalhard didn't have complete control.

Dalhard tucked her inside the car, following close behind. A few moments after they pulled away, she heard the van engine start behind them. No gun shot. It was a minor relief.

Just you wait, you son of a bitch. One crack was all she needed to make him pay.

"You'll love the new compound. It's an old citadel in the Ukrainian mountains. Blue skies, a mountainside covered in pines. It cost me a fortune, but the view is worth it. And, of course, a limo to take you into town whenever you wish." Dalhard's preening grated against her like sandpaper on a sunburn. "I've arranged for suitable attire to be waiting for us at the airport. In less than half an hour, we'll be on our way overseas."

A heavy rumbling pounded through the air, like the dying roar of an enormous monster. Dalhard smirked. "Good thing we got away from the old building when we did. It's been scheduled for demolition for months. Nothing to do with me or my operation. Electronic records are so satisfyingly malleable, don't you think? And explosions have a rather admirable habit of shredding bodies beyond identification."

Demolition. Bodies. *No*. Dani's head whipped around to stare at the blacked-out back window as if she could somehow penetrate the opaque screen. Disbelief emptied her heart and body, hollowing her out.

"Still thinking independently, I see. I can fix that." Dalhard took her hand in his, and the mental tentacles wrapping around her brain grew firmer. Even her lungs and heart started to falter in the absence of direct instruction to continue. Her vision dimmed, and she welcomed the darkness, trying to dive into it. If Michael were dead... she couldn't finish the thought.

Unfortunately, Dalhard let her go before she could find oblivion. Her sight cleared to show him leaning back against the seat, a sheen of sweat marring his skin. His gift was taking a toll on him.

She hated him more than she'd ever hated anyone. He'd taken everything from her family, starting with his father abducting her father and ending with Michael. A familiar answering hiss of rage echoed from deep inside her psyche. If Michael was dead, she didn't care if the corrupted Huntress devoured the whole world as long as she got her chance to take down Dalhard. She would make sure he spent the rest of his existence drooling into a bib if it was the last thing she did.

Reaching deep down, she tried to pull up the predator. It eluded her grasp like a snake slithering through swampy water. Grief threatened to choke off the anger she so desperately needed. Anger was strength. Anger would help her to fight. Michael wouldn't have wanted her to turn back to the Huntress. He'd wanted her to be a hero. She'd failed him so badly, and now he was gone forever because of her.

Hot tears began to drip from her open eyes, leaving a damp splash

281

on her jeans. One night together. A little taste before the plate was snatched away from her. If she'd ever wanted proof the gods couldn't interfere, this was it. Not even for their Chosen Priestesses.

Dani turned her mental energy back to summoning up the Huntress. Dalhard's intent was clear. Whether he proceeded with a farce of a marriage or rape, she would have her chance at him. She would join the Huntress to rip out his soul and shred his mind to pieces. And then she would end this horrible cycle, finding a way to take both herself and the Huntress down once and for all.

Chapter Forty-Four

TIME TO WAKE UP, MICHAEL! The scream echoed through his head, jolting him to alertness. Michael's head and arms were sore and the pain pulled him past the foggy confusion of waking. He instantly remembered: Dalhard, Dani, Bernie, and a building full of explosives. The building he was in now, he realized with a rapidly drying mouth as he looked around the familiar lobby. Joe lay beside him, completely out. Dull roars and rattling announced car engines starting outside.

There was no time to waste. He needed his hands to get Joe and himself out of here and rescue the others. Without pausing to think about how much it would hurt, Michael curved his back to lower his wrists as much as possible, pulling his legs together and forward at the same time. It still wasn't enough.

Gritting his teeth, he forced his arms even lower, shoving the tape beneath his butt. It scraped and clung to his wrists, burning like fire. His joints screamed as if they were being pulled apart. But despite a sickening pop from one of his wrists as it gave out, he managed to maneuver his legs through the circle of his arms.

He immediately grabbed Joe, despite the fresh agony awakening in his arms. He dragged his friend's limp body the excruciating twenty feet to the door.

The locked door. Michael's brain started to go into shock from pain. Adrenaline made his hands shake as he fumbled with the bolt, praying for time.

The door opened without warning, spilling him and Joe onto the dirt path outside. Michael stumbled, dragging Joe along with him. Bright-red taillights vanished around the corner.

No time. No time! Summoning every last reserve of strength, Michael began to haul Joe toward the treeline. Thirty feet away. Twenty-five. Twenty—

A wave of concussive debris slammed into them from behind, swallowing them in dust and powdered concrete. It blew both of them off their feet, knocked the wind out of them, and coated them in a fine film of pulverized rock.

Michael spat the clinging grit out of his mouth. A thundering, buzz-like ringing drowned out all sound around him. He opened his eyes and immediately wished he hadn't. His point of focus swam in and out without any attempt to correspond with anything he wanted to look at. Objects blurred and then came into painfully sharp focus as he struggled to orient himself. The shrill buzzing blared a continuous barrage, drowning out any sounds around him.

Exhaustion sapped at his urgency and concern. A few minutes to rest sounded like a good idea, and his eyes started to slide closed.

A painful, twisting pinch on his scraped and bruised wrist snatched him back to alertness. He jerked away, certain it was an attack, but his abused body couldn't do more than twitch along the ground.

Joe's face fuzzed in and out of his vision, and Michael offered a silent prayer of thanks. His friend's lips were moving but he couldn't make out any words over the clanging in his brain. The meaning became obvious when Joe swiveled to present his taped hands to Michael.

He managed to unwind the tape from Joe's wrists. His own was twisted and mangled enough to need cutting, the silver darkened with oozing blood. He dazedly tried to find something sharp. If he could get his hands free then he could go after Dani—

Another pinch awakened fresh agony, bringing him back. Brilliant light sliced into his eyes without warning as Joe waved a tiny flashlight back and forth across his face. Michael felt his own cry of protest more than he heard it as he tried to look away.

Joe hauled him to his feet as Michael tried to blink away purple and yellow afterimages. As they walked, his brain sluggishly engaged again. A concussion, that's what Joe was checking for. Basic first aid: don't let someone with a head injury fall asleep.

He looked back at the heaping pile of crushed concrete gravel and chunks that had been the building. He tried to make his eyes focus, but they kept slipping in and out. It seemed impossible that they'd survived.

Unless they'd had divine assistance. He remembered the shout that woke him: hollow and surreal, like the Goddess. He lifted his gaze to the star-speckled sky and offered thanks. Without her, he wouldn't have a chance to rescue Dani and Bernie, or Joe.

His mind felt a little clearer. He winced at the sight of his friend covered in dust mixed with thin patches of gleaming red blood from superficial scratches. Joe caught Michael staring at him and gave him a stiff thumbs-up with his free hand along with a sarcastic eye roll. Michael smiled, relieved Joe had the energy for sarcasm.

They reached Joe's car and leaned heavily against it. Joe opened the door and pulled out a utility knife. It sawed quickly through the blood-spattered tape on Michael's wrists, letting circulation return to his numb fingers. Tossing the knife aside, Joe grabbed his notebook and held it up. WHAT DO WE DO NOW?

Michael closed his eyes, sorting rapidly through the psychic information bundle he'd lifted from Karan. The aide expected to be leaving with hostages and had a destination picked out, somewhere with loose extradition and looser legal supervision.

THEY'RE FLYING OUT OF THE COUNTRY TO EASTERN EUROPE, he scribbled, not trusting his voice.

JFK? Joe asked.

PRIVATE AIRFIELD. Michael crawled into the car and started working on the GPS. He found the site quickly and pointed it out to Joe. Then he awkwardly pulled back out of the driver's seat and ran to the passenger side.

Joe took off as soon as Michael's feet cleared the dirt, causing him to fumble the car door closed in the wind. He gratefully clicked the seat belt in place as Joe took off at a speed that made Dani's driving look like a senior citizen's. As they drove, the buzzing in his ears started to subside, letting him tune in to Joe's ongoing diatribe.

"...told her you were going to get hurt. And what the hell was she doing walking away with him!"

"She couldn't help it," Michael replied, hoping his vision would heal as quickly as his hearing.

"She looked drugged but what kind of drug—"

"He's psychic. He can make you do whatever he wants if he touches you," Michael explained, too weary to be diplomatic about Joe's beliefs.

"But that's not real," Joe protested, his voice becoming fainter at the end, making it more of a question than a statement.

"It's real. It's all real." Michael closed his eyes to stave off dizziness. Joe didn't speak for a long time. "You really mean that?"

"Yeah. I do. I've seen it all."

"Then we don't have any time to lose." The vibrations increased along with their speed.

They arrived at the airport far too quickly for Dani. Karan unloaded the captives from the van. McBride carried Eric's limp body. Nada still glared from her bonds but Bernie seemed to have completely forgotten everything that happened. She bounced around, full of smiles and babbling constantly to Chuck. Dani hated her for her childish innocence, whether from ignorance or Dalhard's mental mind-wipes. Under Dalhard's direction, they climbed up a narrow flight of stairs into a slim private jet.

Eight rows of comfortably placed two-by-two seating suggested this plane frequently carried more than a single executive and staff. The cream-and-gold paint and leather didn't quite suit Dalhard. He must have borrowed it or hired it. He escorted her to a forward-facing window seat and placed her there, like a tidied-up toy. The pilots were speaking quietly to each other, completing checklists as the others filed in. Karan took a seat in the group across the aisle from Dani, watching her suspiciously. Clearly he didn't put much faith in Dalhard's persuasive gifts. His gun pointed at her even now, and he kept glancing out the window.

"Don't be sad. It's all going to be okay," Bernie said happily, sitting down beside Dani, bouncing a little in the plush leather seat. "We're going home soon."

Without Dalhard's permission, Dani couldn't bend her head or reply or even smile back. She hoped someone would take care of Bernie after she took out Dalhard.

"Gwen's nice. She said we could have a picnic together after the strange bird people are gone," Bernie piped cheerfully, tucking her little hand into Dani's. Her heart began to race at Bernie's words.

"And who is Gwen, Bernadette?" Dalhard asked dismissively.

"Dani's sister. She's like me," Bernie answered with a ten-year-old's pride at being able to answer an adult's question.

Dani's eyes slid shut as if closed lids could rewind time. She couldn't blame Bernie. The little girl had no idea what she was setting in motion.

Dalhard released her to kneel in front of Bernie. "Tell me about Gwen."

"Oh yeah, Gwen. She's crazy. Talks to dead people," Vincent chimed in, leaning up over the seat backs.

Dalhard chuckled. "I'm sure she's quite lovely, Bernadette, but I can't imagine speaking to the dead would be terribly useful."

Yes! She's useless! Ignore her! Dani silently cheered his misunderstanding.

"I dunno. I mean, the dead go everywhere, see everything. And they gossip like old women," Vincent mused. "Gwen's learned all sorts of stuff. Ambushes, coups… Hell, I wouldn't be surprised if she knew what really happened to Kennedy or what's in Area 51—"

"I'm surprised you never mentioned her." A hint of steel hardened Dalhard's genteel tones.

"You know how it is. Never talk about the family. First rule. Like Fight Club," Vincent shrugged. His eyes flicked back to Eric. "Shouldn't he be waking up?"

Dalhard grabbed Vincent's arm. "Tell me about your family."

If Dani could have moved, she would have kicked Vincent right through the fuselage to shut him up.

"Mom's like the original High Priestess. She's clairvoyant or some shit like that, sees bits of the present and sometimes little glimpses of the future. It's funny, she works for this 1-900 psychic hotline, but she says most people don't really want to know their futures. They want to hear something comforting and interesting. And sometimes they have the stupidest questions…"

"We'll have to meet them. It seems rude otherwise." Dalhard looked over at Karan, eagerness banishing his former irritation. Dani wondered if the aide had been brainwashed like her and Vincent. Was there a screaming kernel inside him or was it smothered by years of obedience?

"Sir, I would not recommend diverting now to collect anyone further," Karan suggested calmly, as if planning a kidnapping was only a matter of logistical maneuvering, like organizing a company dinner.

"Although I am confident in our preparations, we don't want to risk further loss."

Dalhard returned his attention back to Dani with acquisitive pride. "Indeed. I'm sure we can persuade your family to join us in the Ukraine." He patted her as if she were a loyal dog. If she could have bitten his patronizing fleshy digits, she would have.

"That reminds me. I have a gift for you." Dalhard reached up into the overhead bin to pull out a box from a high-end designer. At his touch, her body obediently opened it, moving like a puppet on strings.

A conservative suit jacket and skirt in dull blue pastel with matching stilettos. Dani wondered if throwing up counted as an involuntary response. If he tried to put that on her, she'd find out. A picture-perfect, anonymous, political-wife outfit for someone who smiled on cue and stood on the sidelines. He would take away everything she was and remake her in his own sad image of a perfect wife. Her determination to pull up the Huntress gained new urgency.

The seat belt light chimed on and Dalhard shrugged. "We'll try it on once we're airborne."

Seat buckles clicked as Dani closed her eyes, trying to summon her rage. She needed the Huntress back to have any hope of avenging Michael. *Come on!* She screamed inside, clawing mentally at her internal barriers. They finally collapsed as the plane began to move. The familiar reptilian slithering of the Huntress rasped against her skull.

Now you want the darkness? It hissed inside her mind.

Yes! Dani agreed.

The Huntress moved to the forefront of her mind. *We cannot move.*

He did this to us. Dani flicked her gaze toward Dalhard. *He is prey.*

Assent resonated through her psyche. The Huntress coiled in her mind, ready to strike as soon as their prey came in range. The plane's engines roared to full power, preparing for take-off.

Then they spluttered to a ragged stop as alarms blared in the cockpit.

"What the—?" Dalhard snapped, glaring at Karan. The plane bounced and shook, rattling its passengers like candies in a shaken jar before abruptly coming to a stop.

Smothered laughter came from the back seats. Everyone turned to where Nada rested in her seat, her mouth still sealed with duct tape. Karan stalked back and ripped off the tape, pointing the gun at her.

"I'm too old for you to threaten, boy." Nada chuckled despite the fury in her dark eyes. "Interesting thing about airplanes—lots of electronics in them. Can't fly without them."

"Turn them back on!" Dalhard ordered, specks of spittle flying from his lips.

Nada shrugged. "Can't. They're fried like butter on a hot skillet. This plane won't be going anywhere ever again."

Dalhard drew himself up A fresh wave of panic swept through Dani as the scent of his anger vanished into cold wrath. She struggled to get up, to stop him before he said the words. "And neither will you."

Karan fired his gun.

Chapter Forty-Five

"We're too late!" Joe shouted as the small cream-colored private jet began to taxi down the runway. Michael couldn't believe it. After everything he'd done, everything he'd gone through, this couldn't be how it all ended.

"Try to get close to them!" Michael shouted back.

"Their engines will flip us over before we get there." Joe accelerated anyway. Michael stared at the speeding plane as if he could somehow will it to stop pulling away from them.

To his surprise, it worked. The engines suddenly stopped and the plane coasted to a rough halt, the wheels grinding into the grass strip beside the runway.

Joe screeched to a stop beside the plane. Michael ripped open his seat belt and flung himself out of the door, ignoring Joe's shouts. Dani and Bernie were in that plane.

A bright flash lit up the inside of the fuselage and a dull crack split the air.

"Gunshot! Get down!" Joe shouted.

Michael sprinted toward the plane, his heart smothering his brain's attempts at conscious thought. He didn't care about risk. Every instinct he possessed insisted on rushing after the woman he loved. They didn't understand about booby traps or helping the injured. All they knew was that some would-be alpha prick took his woman and they were demanding some immediate, chest-thumping retaliation.

The door opened and Michael could hear Bernie wailing. He dashed to the unfolding steps and found himself facing a gun. The barrel looked large enough to swallow him whole.

"Stay where you are," Karan ordered him. He glanced over at Joe. "You there, throw your gun on the ground."

Joe reluctantly complied, his weapon clattering against the concrete a few feet away.

Dalhard emerged, a gun of his own held in his fist. "Your dead friend owes me a new plane."

Michael ignored him.

"I am rather disappointed to find you survived. But intrigued you managed to follow us. How did you manage it?" Dalhard's jovial mask began to show cracks of irritation.

McBride appeared in the doorway, specks of blood splashed across his face. He held a crying Bernie in his arms. McBride looked up at Michael without recognition. "They shot her. The old lady. They shot her. I couldn't stop it."

Vincent emerged, escorting Dani down the stairs. Once he let go of her arm, she stood limply in place. But there was something different about her, more menacing. Faint glowing dots of red outlined the edges of her irises. Michael sucked in his breath, horrified to realize the Huntress had control once again.

Her eyes widened when she saw him and the tips of her fingers twitched toward him. But otherwise she remained a statue.

"Dani, you have to fight it!" Michael called out, reaching toward her.

"Michael!" Joe shouted his warning only to fall back as Karan moved to protect his boss.

Dalhard stepped between Dani and Michael, brandishing his gun. "However you survived the explosion, I doubt you will survive a bullet."

"Dani, please. Please come back to me," Michael pleaded, ignoring Dalhard.

A swell of fury exploded, filling the air and dragging Michael's attention back to their original quarry. Dalhard's hands shook with the intensity of his rage. He hissed. "She doesn't belong to you."

She doesn't belong to anyone. Not the Goddess, not Michael, and certainly not Dalhard. Michael tuned out the possessive jealousy coming from the other man to focus once more on Dani. The red rings in her eyes were growing brighter and stronger.

Dalhard grabbed Dani by the arm and hauled her forward. "Tell him! Tell him you're mine!"

Her mouth opened but no sound came out. A faint groaning rumbled in her throat, as if she were simultaneously trying to say something and not say it.

"Tell him!" Dalhard's fingers tightened on her bare skin.

"She's not yours," Michael said quietly.

"Very well. There's an easier solution." Dalhard raised his gun and fired it at Michael.

The blast of the gun echoed across the airfield, and a cloud of dust and grit swelled up where the bullet plowed into the runway.

Dani stood beside Dalhard, her doll's face impassive despite the reddened flesh on her fingers where she still gripped the hot gun barrel, forcing it down toward the tarmac.

Karan wheeled as Dalhard tried to yank the gun out of Dani's grasp. Joe took advantage of his captor's distraction to jump on Karan from behind. McBride took off for the dubious cover of the nearby car, Bernie still clutched in his arms. Vincent stood in the middle of the runway, terrible confusion written across his face.

Dani simply stood there, gripping the weapon, her posture as inflexible and fixed as a store mannequin. Dalhard screamed at her to let it go, but she ignored him. Only a faint tension in her neck and arm suggested how hard she had clamped on, despite the burns. She hadn't moved or blinked since seizing the gun.

Set her loose! The coercive flash ripped through Michael's brain, the sort that used to bring debilitating headaches along with compulsion. But now, any discomfort vanished under clarity. He lunged forward, ripping her arm out of Dalhard's grasp.

"Get away from her!" Dalhard released the gun to swing at Michael.

The businessman screamed in pain a second later, cradling a broken wrist as the gun thudded to the ground. Dani's strike had been practically invisible. Only the snap of bone confirmed the hit.

It was eerie. Like watching a statue come briefly to life and then freeze back into stone. Michael took Dani's hands in his own. No visible response came from his touch, but he could dimly sense her presence. It was muffled by layers of Dalhard's influence as well as the coils of the raging, alien Huntress.

Open. Michael let go of himself immediately under the compulsive direction. As the outside world began to vanish, he saw Karan throwing Joe to the ground and Dalhard reaching for the gun. The practical side of him wanted to pull back, protect himself and the others. But the intuitive side warned him this was his only chance to reach Dani. He poured his consciousness into the connection between them, just as he'd inadvertently done with Gwen.

The chaos around him vanished into darkness. He heard the slither of the Huntress, scales grinding against stone.

She summoned me, mortal. You will not interfere. Gleaming red eyes hung in the darkness.

"Dani!" Michael shouted. His questing fingers found a thin, opaque layer of darkness, like a balloon skin. His fingers sank in but when he pulled back, it snapped back into its original position. His hand didn't seem harmed, no cuts or bruises, no numbness or tingling. He pushed deeper, and this time he brushed against something on the other side. He shouted again. "Dani!"

No answer came, but the darkness began to flex toward him. It curved out in the outline of a hand, reaching out to grasp his wrist.

It was her. Certainty crushed him with relief. The shadow balloon must be a manifestation of Dalhard's influence. He could dimly sense her emotions behind the barrier. Fear of Dalhard, fear for him, an overwhelming grief, burning anger. And at the bottom, something truly dangerous: bone-deep exhaustion. She had burned her considerable strength fighting Dalhard.

Scaly skin brushed across his leg and back, reminding him the Huntress was still there as well. He stroked Dani's hand through the barrier, wishing she could sense him more directly. "Trust me, I'll find a way out of this."

Nothing could stretch forever without breaking. That was a basic law of nature. Michael pushed as hard as he could at a single point, locking his arms together and throwing his weight into it.

The barrier slowly yielded, first enveloping his arms and then his head in slick, chilly darkness. He ignored the atavistic impulse to breathe and kept on pressing at his single chosen point. It was working! The membrane was thinning. *Just a little more.*

He popped through the barrier, landing hard on his outstretched arms.

"Michael!" Dani's hands patted and stroked, checking for injury.

"Quickly, before it—" He stared at the unbroken black layer

293

surrounding him. "Closes."

"Are you hurt?" she demanded.

"Come on, we'll push our way back through." He took Dani's hand.

"I've already tried. It doesn't work."

"O-kay. This rescue is not exactly going according to plan." He shook his head. Trapped inside the bubble, everything else might as well not exist. Belatedly, he wondered what kind of effect such total separation of mind and body would have.

"I guess not since we're both trapped in my brain now." She wrapped herself around him, breathing deeply. "I thought you were dead. I thought he'd killed you."

Comprehension dawned. "That's why the Huntress is back."

Dani nodded against his shoulder. "I was going to make sure Dalhard ended up a vegetable, and then make sure neither of us could ever hurt anyone else again."

His hands and arms tightened around her. Annihilating herself struck him as horrific, even if it were to avenge him. Dani continued. "Now we're both trapped in here, and I'll be a living, breathing doll for Mr. Asshat Bigshot."

"We're going to find a way out," Michael promised. "We conquered the Huntress before and we'll conquer Mr. Asshat together."

She pulled back to stare at him, lips gaping in surprise.

"What? I can swear if I want to."

He could feel the laughter bubbling up inside her, banishing the fear. It spilled out in uncontrollable bursts, pushing the darkness back... literally—it stretched the dark bubble outward.

"It hasn't done that before." Dani studied the skin, keeping her fingers interlaced with Michael's.

"Dalhard's using your own anger and fear to keep you trapped," Michael guessed. "Without it, his grip is weaker."

"The Goddess said I needed to let go of my anger." Dani took a deep breath, cupping Michael's face. "I don't want to be angry anymore. I don't want vengeance. Not if the cost is losing you."

She leaned in to kiss him. The soft caress of her lips banished every other concern. Michael held her tenderly, letting his fingers tease the sensitive skin at the nape of her neck as his lips tasted the sweetness of hers. There was no battle, no desperation. Only love and mutual exploration.

He felt the scintillating flash of the divine connection reestablishing as she opened herself fully to him. No holding back.

The dream-like world around them shifted and the bubble of shadow around them began to swell outward, stretching thinner and thinner. But holding. Something still kept it intact. Years of therapy training gave Michael insight into what. Outwardly expressed anger wasn't the only kind. "Forgive yourself, Dani," he whispered against her lips.

"What I did… it isn't forgivable." Dani rubbed her soft cheek against his as she shook her head.

"You were young. You were afraid. You didn't mean to hurt them that badly." He'd been there, inside her mind when she remembered her college attack.

"But I did want to hurt them," she exhaled softly, resting her head against his shoulder.

"Let it go. You've spent years punishing yourself for it. You've suffered enough." They were close. The bubble hovered on the edge of popping. Michael wondered if she could truly let go of the past.

"I've hurt so many people. How can I be your hero if I've hurt people?" The words were barely audible. Michael wasn't even sure she'd actually spoken them. She was so afraid of disappointing him, he could almost see it weighing her down.

"Every hero has an origin story. What defines a hero are the choices they make now, not the ones from their past," he insisted, pulling back so he could look her in the eye. "I believe in you, Dani. Together, we can make a difference. We can make things better than they are. But only if we find a way out of this darn brain of yours."

Her smile could have stopped his heart, if he had one in his mental projection. "Together, then. I can't do it without you."

The bubble burst, revealing the Huntress looming over them, her blazing red eyes lighting the darkness. Long translucent fangs dripped shimmering venom.

To his surprise, Michael wasn't afraid of the predator. And from the emotions flowing between their clasped hands, neither was Dani.

"You have no place here," she said, sounding like one of her priestess ancestors.

You summoned me. The gleaming eyes and dripping fangs crouched lower.

"And now I'm getting rid of you." Dani closed her eyes to concentrate.

Michael could see the edges of black scales catching the light against the darkness.

What light? There shouldn't have been any light here, but when he looked at Dani, she was glowing. A soft, pearlescent gleam in reds and golds danced along her skin, bright enough to illuminate the Huntress. A translucent image of the Goddess stood behind her priestess.

"You fed on anger and fear, on lies and delusion. There is nothing left here for you," Dani pronounced, her voice echoing like the Goddess's.

The Huntress hissed, opening its maw wide. But it cringed back from Dani's words. Michael grinned, certain it was finally finished.

Dani's eyes opened and brilliant starlight poured out of them, too bright to look at. When the light touched the Huntress, the scaly flesh sizzled and dissolved into nothingness. It tried to surge forward, but its entire body simply vanished into the darkness.

"Like every monster in the closet, the light reveals there is nothing to fear." Dani's eyes closed as she finished speaking and the light faded from her skin.

Well done, my Priestess. Well done. The Goddess smiled at the two of them. *Now return to your bodies before it is too late to save them.*

Chapter Forty-Six

Dani kept herself perfectly still as she returned to awareness. Dalhard's influence slipped off like a heavy blanket, letting her breathe freely again. Their fight in her mind seemed to have only taken a fraction of a second. Dalhard was still yelling, reaching for Michael. Karan still grappled with Joe for control of the other gun. McBride crouched behind the car with a wailing Bernie. And Vincent's eyes were tightly squeezed shut, his hands digging into his dark curls. She scanned the tarmac, only moving her eyes, but didn't see Eric. *He must still be on the plane.*

She released Michael's hands as Dalhard pushed him back. Michael fell and rolled back over his shoulder to come up in a crouched position. Dalhard stepped in front of her to face Michael, his hands curled into fists.

Dani slowly shuffled her feet, keeping her upper body as rigid as possible. To those focused on the confrontation between Dalhard and Michael, the lack of change would keep them from noticing her slow movements. *Thanks, George.* She sent a mental note to the kid from Michael's workplace for demonstrating the technique.

They didn't have much of a window of opportunity. Dalhard might be half-blind with rage, but Karan's sharp eyes would catch her soon enough. Michael's eyes never even flickered in her direction. He trusted her to do her part, even though they hadn't exactly set up a plan. He couldn't have demonstrated his faith in her any more clearly. The realization lightened her heart and would have brought a smile to her face in a less life-and-death situation.

"You might be able to temporarily hold on to people by frying their brains, but you can't persuade someone to join you through coercion," Michael said to Dalhard.

"I don't need her mind willing. Just her body," Dalhard snapped back. The scent rolling off his body began to take on the taint of disease. He was beginning to go past the point of sanity. Dani only needed to move a few more inches and she'd be in the perfect position.

"They'll always break free from your control. They have morals. They're not like you." Michael slowly stood up.

"Enough talk!" Dalhard roared. "It won't save you!"

"Actually, I'm distracting you," Michael pointed out with a weary smile.

Dani slammed her fist into Dalhard's temple, knocking his unresisting body to the ground. She could smell the utter shock pouring off him as she stood over him, mind and body once again alert and in control. "We need to talk," she growled, lifting her foot to smash her heel into his ribs.

Dalhard rolled with surprising agility, wincing as he hit his broken wrist. But he got back up onto his feet. "How?" he sputtered.

"Like the man said, I'm not like you. And I won't be controlled." She bent to pick up the discarded gun on the runway.

"Leave it!" Karan snapped, shoving Joe away and pointing his weapon in Dani's direction. Joe went sprawling and everyone else froze in place.

Dani remained in place, hunkered into predatorial waiting. She'd forgotten about him in the heat of vengeance. The lack of scent kept dropping him out of her awareness. "The odds aren't in your favor."

"My employer and I will be leaving now. And while you might outnumber us, none of you are armed." Karan held the gun steady, his calm demeanor restored. Either he had nerves of steel or extensive military training.

"Wanna bet I'm slower than a bullet?" Dani tensed her muscles, preparing to move. She wasn't about to let them get away. She noticed Joe slowly moving into a crouch, preparing to tackle Karan again.

"Perhaps you could reach me before I could fire a second shot," Karan mused as if considering a possible experiment. "Perhaps you are even quick enough to dodge a bullet in midair. But he is not." With unbelievable speed and precision, Karan shifted his aim to Michael. "Stay where you are, or I will shoot him in the head."

Fear drained her potential speed and her heart. Joe went motionless, and Dani sent up a grateful prayer. She didn't doubt Karan was capable of shooting Michael even in the face of his own death. He'd do it without a second thought, because it was necessary.

"Shoot them all!" Dalhard ordered, moving to stand beside his aide. A vindictive smile lit his face. "Start with him!"

"Shoot him and you shoot the only thing keeping you both alive," Dani warned.

"We are at an impasse. One I have no desire to prolong. Sir, if you will go to the limo, I believe it is time for us to depart."

"I'm not leaving without—" Dalhard began, spittle flying from his lips.

"We have lost this round, sir. Any further investment would be simply throwing good money after bad," Karan told his boss. "Unless you truly wish to die here, in which case I shall bid you good luck and leave you here to negotiate."

Dalhard jerked his torn and dusty jacket into place before stiffly walking to the limo. Karan remained absolutely still. His aim at Michael never wavered.

It wasn't fair. Dani longed to rip into her enemy. If she'd been capable of growing fangs and claws, she would be doing it. Her fury demanded the right to rend and destroy. But she would not endanger Michael.

He glanced over at her, a hint of worry in his eyes and his scent. The intensity of her thirst for vengeance must be coming through to him. He would be afraid of her doing something stupid and violent. She pulled up the memory of his disappointment in her after she'd attacked Redneck. The possibility of seeing the same disappointment again in his eyes cooled her rage.

She would let them go for today. They couldn't disappear. She'd hunt them down and make them pay.

Dalhard got in the car. As soon as the door clicked closed, Karan began to back toward the limo. He kept the gun trained on Michael, not even glancing back to see where he was. He went straight to the driver's door as if a string connected him to it.

Once he was inside, the limo screeched away in a haze of burnt rubber. Michael's surprise swept through Dani's lungs like fresh mountain air, stinging a little in its clarity. Was he disappointed she hadn't charged after them?

His relief as he pulled her tight into his arms answered her question.

299

"They left me," Vincent whimpered, collapsing onto the tarmac. His outburst reminded Dani that there were more casualties to deal with than her and Michael.

"You got cuffs?" she asked Joe, nodding toward Vincent.

Joe pulled the silver restraints out and slipped them around Vincent's wrists. Her brother didn't resist, staring after the limo as if his heart were broken.

"Michael!" Bernie broke free from McBride and came charging up to Michael, wrapping her arms around him. "You saved me, just like you promised!"

"I had some help." Michael knelt down to accept the hug. Dani smiled, a soft ache building beneath her heart. Bernie might think it was all over, but her life would change forever. She and her mother would have to go into hiding.

"Bernie, I'd like you to meet someone. This is Dani. She helped me to save you." Michael pointed at Dani.

"Hi," Dani said awkwardly.

She needn't have worried. Bernie launched herself at Dani with terminal enthusiasm. Her little arms wrapped around Dani's waist. "Thank you, pretty lady."

Dani brushed her fingers through Bernie's hair, smiling at Michael.

"Eric is still unconscious in the plane. Along with… Nada." McBride's shoulders hunched as if under a heavy weight. He avoided looking at them. "She saved us all."

"I told her," Bernie told them proudly. "Chuck said you were safe and coming after us. Nada said she would make sure the plane would stay here. She said she couldn't stop the cars because she couldn't be sure to get both at once. She says not to worry about her. Just bring her home to her family."

McBride stiffened, glancing at Dani, Joe, and Michael.

"She can speak to the dead. If she says that's what Nada wants, it's true," Michael explained, moving closer to Dani and Bernie.

"She's not mad at you. Honest," Bernie said, trying to reassure McBride.

It wasn't successful. McBride shuffled into the plane. Michael rubbed Bernie's shoulder. "What do you say, kiddo? Let's go home and

300

see your mom."

With a whoop, Bernie ran to where Joe was loading Vincent into the back seat. She claimed the front and bounced on the seat, fiddling with the radio.

Michael pulled Dani against him and she inhaled his unique scent, letting it saturate every fiber of her skin and hair. She couldn't imagine even trying to live a life without him. Those terrifying minutes when she'd believed he was dead still haunted her. "You're stuck with me now," she whispered, playfully nipping at the strong line of his jaw.

"I would never have it any other way," he whispered back, seizing her lips with his.

Her fingers tightened in his hair as his hands cupped her tight against his body. He deepened the kiss, making it both a promise and a demand.

His hips ground against hers, and she moaned, feeling the hot length of him pushing against her. Her inner core blazed with aching, moist heat. The scent of their combined lust drowned out everything else. She was surprised it wasn't visible, like an aura of orange and apple blossoms.

Her fingers hooked into his shirt, preparing to rend the fragile fabric.

"Not to interrupt, but what the hell? You know they're going to fly out of the country with some damn fake ID. They got away." Joe's frustrated explosion broke them apart.

"I didn't get everything. Some hints, a couple of account numbers. There wasn't enough time." Michael frowned.

"Even if you did, I can't put you on the stand. I can't put any of you on the stand. Which means I can't even charge them with kidnapping," Joe snarled, frustrated. "I might be able to get a murder indictment, but they'll be long gone."

"It's a start. We'll use what we have to track him down," Dani corrected him, strangely content with her circumstances.

"We'll get you information you can use. Or at least, that Interpol and the SEC can use. Or some other agency." Michael shrugged.

"So you're telling me there's a plan?" Joe asked.

"What plan?" Michael smiled.

301

"Please tell me there's an actual plan." Joe looked ill.

Michael pressed a soft kiss against Dani's cheek as she answered. "No plan. Just faith."

TWO MONTHS LATER

Epilogue

FBI MANHUNT FOR ESCAPED MILLIONAIRE CONTINUES. The title scrolling across Michael's phone was practically longer than the story. Even in the distracting bustle of patrons at the Blue Curtain, it didn't take long to read. A corrupt businessman was no match for the news of a local New York celebrity spotted buying shoes at two a.m. Dalhard easily escaped the authorities, but plenty of law enforcement agencies were eager to introduce themselves. Despite Joe's worries, raids on Expanding Horizons, Right-Hand Man, and a dozen other companies provided enough evidence for the courts. Dalhard's domestic accounts were frozen. But Michael knew the man possessed any number of hidden foreign assets and accounts.

He sipped at his beer, moistening his dry mouth. Dalhard wouldn't accept defeat. Michael could predict it with the same certainty as tomorrow's sunrise. Having seen Karan's eyes as they escaped, Michael was certain the other man would come after them as well. Of the two, he wasn't sure which was more dangerous, but together, they were still a formidable threat.

He reminded himself of the victories as the audience clapped for Opal's new solo act. Bernie was back with her mother, whose record had been courteously expunged of all false data. Virginia arranged for them to join a community of *lalassu* under new identification. There was also a new live-in nanny who happened to have extensive experience with mediums and psychic visions. Chuck now spent most of his days running messages between Gwen and Bernie, both of whom were delighted to have a new friend. He missed her, but she was safer hidden.

Eric was recovering slowly. He'd been unconscious for almost two days after Dalhard's psychic attack. His mind had been ransacked and overwritten, and it needed time and specialized care to heal. Michael suspected one of the frequent visitors to the farmhouse might have been a healer, but Virginia still held her secrets close.

The only real casualty was Vincent. His carefree outlook had shattered, possibly beyond repair. He spent his days lurking at the farmhouse, avoiding the rest of the family as much as possible. He obsessed about Dalhard's control, afraid the man still had hooks deep in his mind.

Despite doing intensive psychic work, Michael couldn't promise him mental freedom. Dalhard's poisonous insinuations were incredibly difficult to distinguish from ordinary thoughts. Dani's brainwashing might have been obvious, but Vincent's had developed over time, becoming a part of him. There was no way to guarantee it had all been removed.

And McBride vanished shortly after Nada's funeral. None of them knew where he had disappeared to, but the urn containing Nada's ashes had vanished as well.

"Ladies and gentlemen…" The announcement interrupted the chill of trepidation before it could send more than a frisson of fear along his nerves. He tucked away his phone, eager for the grand finale.

The curtain rose to reveal Dani in all her glory as Onyx. Her dark hair was pinned into a thick bun on top of her head, with tiny wisps framing her face. She wore a gorgeous black silk robe that glittered with invisible sequins.

"It's time for the night to end and for us all to say good-bye." Onyx paused to smooth her robe. "Usually that wouldn't mean so much to me. I'd be ready for the next adventure to start, always looking to a new horizon. But over the last little while, I've come to realize how important the people in my life are. It's made me feel a little sentimental."

She smiled at the audience, finding Michael easily. He grinned at her as she winked at him, timed perfectly for him alone. He couldn't keep a certain smugness from his smile, able to see through her careful façade.

"Earlier in the show, I said dreams vanish at the end of the night. But it's not entirely true. Some dreams are still around when you wake up. So I wish you all a little piece of the dreams you've found here." She lifted the microphone and began to croon *Dream a Little Dream of Me*, soft and sultry.

Michael whistled along with the rest of the audience as she tugged at the tie of her robe, letting it slide to the floor in a silken puddle. Beneath, she wore a sheer, black, fitted nightgown, tied at the front with white ribbons.

She slid the first ribbon open, then the next. Each line loosened the nightgown a little more, revealing the skimpy bra and thong beneath. When it fell to the stage, she reached up and pulled the pin from her bun, letting her hair fall around her shoulders.

The audience applauded, and soft hoots burst from a few. But Onyx seemed to hold them all spellbound. Michael couldn't help but compare the emotional atmosphere to the first time he'd come to this club. Then, the Huntress had whipped everyone into a dark sexual frenzy. Now it was still intensely sexual and sensual, but the darkness had vanished. It was teasing between lovers, intimate and powerful. People smiled, hands clasped under the table, eyes shining as they swayed softly to the music. It didn't bother him any more to have other men watching her, wanting her. *Enjoy it all you want. All you get is Onyx.*

The song wound to a close and Onyx curled up on a small daybed on the back of the stage. Their eyes met again and she smiled, the roguish grin flashing briefly though the dimming house lights. The rest of the room faded into insignificance and they were the only two that mattered. Michael raised his beer bottle to her in a silent salute.

I'm the only one who sees Dani.

TO BE CONTINUED IN *METAMORPHOSIS*…

Snow's ethereal silvery beauty was best appreciated by someone who wasn't having to slog through it, Ron McBride decided, pushing his way through clinging white drifts. Halloween might be a few weeks away but this far north, winter already had a solid grip.

Without the strength of his enhanced muscles, this cross-country detour would have dropped him hours ago. As it was, he was beginning to wonder if he'd made a fatal mistake. Hell of a thing if his paranoia ended up killing him.

Four months of running. Four months of carrying the burden which weighed down his jacket pocket. Never staying in any one place for more than a few days. Always making his way further north and west, searching for the tiny community Virginia had told him about. He'd already learned the fine art of scrounging for cash-only day labor but now he had to be extra careful. It was too easy to accidentally lift more than he should have been able to or move faster than human reflexes allowed. People noticed and then he had to leave quickly.

Yesterday, he'd hitched a ride with a trucker who'd promised to take him to one of the remote supply towns in northern Canada, near the Alaska border. Ron couldn't even remember the name through the fatigue fog drowning his brain. But he did remember the man at the rest stop. The one dressed in plaid and jeans, with a baseball cap pulled low over his features. There had been a jarring addition to the traditional trucker uniform. Expensive leather boots.

He didn't know if who the man was or what he was doing there, but he wasn't about to take the chance. He ducked back out the door and began to walk. The snow fell lightly on him, promising to cover his tracks in fluffy obfuscation. His dark clothes would help him to disappear into the dense woods.

Nearly twenty hours later, his choice didn't seem so brilliant anymore. There was a lot of wilderness up here. He could wander for weeks and never come across another human being. He only had a few basic survival rations in his backpack. Without warmth and shelter, he wasn't going to have to worry about Dalhard finding him. His corpse

311

would vanish without a trace.

The picturesque puffs of snow floating down from the sky might make a lovely postcard but they clung to his hat, hair and clothes, melting and refreezing into dense chunks of ice, weighing him down. His fingers shook with cold despite being pressed into his armpits as he walked. He was going to have to stop soon and take a chance of pursuit catching up to him. Just a little further.

The light was fading into gray-blue twilight. Ron knew he had to stop and build a shelter but his body seemed to have acquired a terrible inertia, plodding endlessly. It took more effort than he wanted to believe to force himself to stop and actually look at his surroundings.

Black silhouettes of pine trees jutted into the sky all around him. The steadily falling snow piled into waist high drifts. He needed some bare ground and a fire. Numbly, he remembered a lesson in survival training. Birch bark burned, even when wet. Staggering through the snow, he peered into the forest, searching for tell-tale white trunks.

His frozen fingers bled as he pried strips of bark from a birch and broke branches to burn from a nearby pine. He found a small gap in the snow, blocked by three large trees growing close together. He used a branch to sweep away the sparse accumulation of snow and laid out the supplies for his fire. It took him three tries to get a match to light and another three before he got a piece of birch bark alight. Luckily the branches he'd broken were relatively dry and pitchy, catching easily and flaming brightly.

The warmth hit him like a truck, sparking an irrational temptation to crawl directly into the tiny fire to thaw his frozen body. He clenched his jaw against the pain of blood returning to numb extremities. He'd just give himself a little time to warm up and then he'd go collect more wood and see about a shelter. Just a little time.

His weariness seduced him into dangerous unconsciousness. Ron felt as if he'd only closed his eyes for a moment when a snuffling sound popped them back open. His fire had burned out and the cold ground had leached the remaining warmth from his legs. It was dark, far too dark.

His body wanted to collapse back into sleep. A tiny piece of his brain shrieked warning that if he did, he would never wake again. He had to get up, get moving again.

As he rocked back, preparing to rise, the darkness in front of him moved.

Adrenaline cleared away the twin clinging cobwebs of exhaustion and cold. The image in front of him suddenly resolved into perfect clarity.

Less than five feet away from him was a bear.

It was monstrous, the shaggy head easily the size of his torso. Even on all fours, the shoulders would reach his waist and the massive hump over them would be halfway up his chest. If it stood, he guessed it would measure ten feet. Dark brown shaggy fur blended into the darkness, except for a short slash of golden brown over its shoulder, almost like a crescent moon.

The bear huffed at him, clacking its jaws together. Ron slowly moved up, using the tree trunks for balance. His legs were numb and sore, ensuring he would have no chance of outrunning the creature.

Except it didn't seem aggressive.

It kept looking at him as if trying to figure out what he was. Perhaps it hadn't seen a human before. If ignorance kept it from trying to eat him, Ron was happy to keep it that way. He thought bears were supposed to hibernate in winter, though. He vaguely remembered reading that a bear who was awake in winter was considered especially dangerous.

"Good bear. Nice bear," he croaked.

The bear's ears went flat against its skull, exactly like an annoyed cat. It snorted and shook its head.

"You don't want to eat me, Mr. Bear," Ron continued. "Just go on and find a pik-i-nik basket somewhere." He stopped as the creature let out a low growl.

Okay, so much for the human-voice-calms-wild-animals theory. The bear reached out with a massive paw and raked through what was left of his fire. A few glowing coals shone amid the ashy remains. Then it poked at the remaining flakes of birch bark, growling again.

When it turned and began to amble away across the clearing, Ron saw his chance. He eased himself around the trees and started walking slowly out of the bear's sight. A good plan and one which might have worked if his legs had cooperated.

His stiff limbs collapsed under him, dropping him to the ground with a massive thud. The bear's attention immediately swung back to him and primitive instinct took over. It didn't matter how many times he'd been told to never run from a wild animal, his feet were pumping before his brain could consciously give instruction.

Running wildly through the woods, he heard the bear crashing behind him. *This is it*, he told himself. *I'm going to die now.* He tried to summon his enhanced strength for a leap into a tree but his abused muscles had already had enough. He slammed into the trunk and then rolled down the hill on the far side, his backpack flying off and scattering his belongings across the snow.

A tree graciously halted his downward tumble, but did so by catching his head and shoulders with a tooth-rattling abrupt stop. Stunned, he could only stare at the top of the ridge as the bear looked down on him. The life of Ron McBride, ended by Canadian wildlife. Embarrassing, but at least no one would ever know. He braced himself for the inevitable crunch of jaws.

The bear stared at him, outlined against the inky sky. Then it turned and walked away.

He couldn't believe his luck. Instead of being a bear's before-bedtime snack, he was going to get to die of a combination of exposure and a concussion. He patted his jacket, feeling for the hard lump he carried. Still intact. He tried to force himself to his feet but he was too weak. Wearily, he stared at the green and blue lights floating in the sky above. Maybe this was for the best. All the things he'd done and seen. Maybe they should go to his grave with him.

Resignation pulled him down into the darkness.

To be continued ...

Acknowledgements:

First of all I want to thank my very best girlfriends, Sarah and Chris. You believed in me before anyone else did and gave me the courage to believe in myself. No one could ask for better friends in life.

Next I'd like to thank the ladies of ORWA: Malena for her gentle support and tutoring; Shirley, for listening to me moan and still always encouraging me; Teresa, who shared her experience with self-publishing and told me to go for it; Lucy, who pulled apart my point of view problems and showed me how to make them better; and Susan, who has been my social media and promotion guide, sitting me down and helping me to understand just what I was getting myself into. All of you helped me to take this idea floating in my head and make it into something worthy of sharing with others.

Thank you to the folk at Emerging Minds for helping me to understand how therapy works and thank you to the ladies of Capital Burlesque for their eager assistance. Any mistakes I made are my own.

Thank you to the ladies at Red Adept Publishing. Lynn, for taking the time out of her busy day to explain the editing process to a rank amateur. Alyssa, thank you for ripping my precious story apart and helping me to build it better. I'm indebted to you for your insight and humor. Joann, you kept warning me I would hate you but you only made me work harder to make it all right. And to Carmen for the final polish. Thank you for all your support.

Thank you to Glendon from Streetlight Graphics for his amazing cover. Looking at it for the first time made me feel like a real author. And thank you, Samianne, for your beautiful snake interstitials.

Thank you to Ryan Parent for his beautiful photography. It's not often that I like pictures of myself.

And thank you to my friends and family. I'm sure you've all gotten tired of hearing about my dreams to write over the years but you all kept encouraging me. It meant a lot.

And finally, thank you to you for reading this book. The difference between a writer and an author is that someone is willing to pay for the stories an author writes. By buying this book, you're making one of my dreams come true and I will always be grateful.

A final shout out to Marvel for the X-men, Avengers, Agents of SHIELD and Guardians of the Galaxy and the dozens of other storylines they've pulled me into over the years. Without you, I'd have had a lot more time to write. But been a lot more bored and uninspired. You taught me that format doesn't matter. Just tell a good story and it will stand up to almost anything.

About the Author

Jennifer Carole Lewis is a full-time mom, a full-time administrator and a full-time writer, which means she is very much interested in speaking to anyone who comes up with any form of functional time-travel devices or practical cloning methods. Meanwhile, she spends her most of her time alternating between organizing and typing.

She is a devoted comic book geek and Marvel movie enthusiast. She spends far too much of her precious free time watching TV, especially police procedural dramas. Her enthusiasm outstrips her talent in karaoke, cross-stitch and jigsaw puzzles. She is a voracious reader of a wide variety of fiction and non-fiction and always enjoys seeking out new suggestions.

She has been making up stories since before she could read and write. This is what she's always wanted to do. Thank you for making her dream come true.

For more information about *Revelations* (including behind-the-scenes commentary), more books on the *lalassu* and updates, you can go to www.pastthemirror.com or find Jennifer on Facebook or Goodreads. You can also follow her on Twitter at @jclewisupdate.

61412274R00175

Made in the USA
Charleston, SC
21 September 2016